### Staying Dead
"An entertaining, fast-paced thriller set in a world where cell phones and computers exist uneasily with magic and a couple of engaging and highly talented rogues solve crimes while trying not to commit too many of their own"
—*Locus*

### Curse the Dark
"With an atmosphere reminiscent of Dan Brown's *The Da Vinci Code* and Umberto Eco's *The Name of the Rose* by way of Sam Spade, Gilman's second Wren Valere adventure…features fast-paced action, wisecracking dialogue, and a pair of strong, appealing heroes."
—*Library Journal*

### Bring It On
"Ripping good urban fantasy, fast-paced and filled with an exciting blend of mystery and magic…this is a paranormal romance for those who normally avoid romance, and the entire series is worth checking out"
—*SF Site*

### Burning Bridges
"This fourth book in Gilman's engaging series delivers… Wren and Sergei's relationship, as usual, is wonderfully written. As their relationship moves in an unexpected direction, it makes perfect sense—and leaves the reader on the edge of her seat for the next book."
—*RT Book Reviews*, 4 stars

### Free Fall
"An intelligent and utterly gripping fantasy thriller, by far the best of the Retrievers series to date"
—*Publishers Weekly*, starred review

### Blood from Stone
"Extreme fun, nicely balanced with dark stuff…and a scene in a museum that had me whimpering with joy"
—*Green Man Review*

**Laura Anne Gilman** took the plunge into murky writing waters in 1994 when she sold her first short story. Four media tie-in novels and a respectable number of short story sales later, she made the move to full-time writer in 2003. She is the author of the Cosa Nostradamus books for LUNA Books (the "Retrievers" and "Paranormal Scene Investigations" urban fantasy series), a young adult fantasy series for Pocket, and more than thirty shorter works of science fiction, fantasy and horror. She also writes paranormal romance as Anne Leonard. Laura Anne lives in New York City. You can contact her at LAG@lauraanne gilman.net, or find her online at suricattus.livejournal.com and www.lauraannegilman.net.

# laura anne gilman

# HARD MAGIC

MIRA

First published in Great Britain 2011
MIRA Books, Eton House, 18-24 Paradise Road,
Richmond, Surrey, TW9 1SR

© Laura Anne Gilman 2010

ISBN 978 0 7783 0496 8

54-0811

MIRA's policy is to use papers that are natural, renewable and recyclable products and made from wood grown in sustainable forests. The logging and manufacturing processes conform to the legal environmental regulations of the country of origin.

Printed in the UK
by CPI Mackays, Chatham, ME5 8TD

Dear Reader,

Sometimes the most colourful characters are the ones you don't plan for. When Bonnie Torres first appeared in the Retrievers series, she was a walk-on character, a bit player.

Bonnie, though, wasn't having any of it. She insisted on playing a larger part, becoming part of the ongoing story. And then, when I paused for breath, she insisted on getting her own story, "Illumination" in the anthology *Unusual Suspects*. And then she demanded the chance to tell her own adventure—and that of her fellow PUPIs, the Private, Unaffiliated Paranormal Investigators of the Cosa Nostradamus.

New York City's a tough place for a twentysomething Talent to make her mark. But I suspect Bonnie's up to it....

*Laura Anne Gilman*

For Sioux. Who else?

# HARD MAGIC

*You might say that it all started with a phone call, that morning in my hotel room. Only it didn't, not really. The wheels of my life were in motion long before then. Before the first murders, before the first job. Before I had ever heard of PUPI: before there was a PUPI for anyone to hear of. Before all hell broke loose, and the* Cosa Nostradamus *was almost destroyed…*

*For me it started years earlier, when I was still in college, and my dad had gone missing for the last time, with just a cryptic letter left behind, and with a stranger listening in on my thoughts. That was when my life changed, when everything that was to come, began.*

*But I didn't make the connection, not then, and not for a while later.*

*I'm better at putting the pieces together, now. I have to be.*

*It's what I'm trained to do.*

*The world changes.*
*If you're lucky, you know it's happening.*
*If you're really lucky, you know you're part of it.*
*This is my part.*

# prologue

The second body wasn't quite dead yet. The eyes stared up; not asking questions, just staring. The killer was tempted to finish the job, but instead focused on adding the final touches to the scene. It was almost perfect…and yet, something remained undone. Something felt off.

Outside, a car passed down the street, its engine clearly needing a tune-up. The noise made the killer scowl; why didn't people take better care of their tools? That idiot was going to find himself by the side of the road, his car overheated at best, at worst.…

Contrary to what they show on television and movies, cars don't catch fire easily. They're designed better than that, even the older vehicles. It takes serious effort to blow one up: pouring on accelerant, or explosives…

Or magic.

The killer paused, fingers curled around the car's door-latch, and thought about that, humming over the possibilities. The idea of the car going up in flames was pleasing. It would burn hot, blue and white. The flames would rise up from the upholstery, lick at the roof, fill the entire garage and, if the firefighters didn't arrive soon enough, take the entire house with it. Easy enough to accomplish: just a controlled match of current, and a single directed thought.

Pleasing, and satisfying, that thought. Artistic, even. A fitting end to the entire matter.

But it would also draw too much attention. This wasn't about headlines, or media coverage. The fewer people who noticed, in fact, the better. And fire might spread, injure others. That wasn't the plan, either.

So, regretfully, the car was left intact and unscorched, the two bodies arranged in the front seat as though they'd just come home from an evening away, and simply forgotten to get out of the car.

The killer did not wear a watch, but there was a sense of valuable time passing, seconds ticking away and the window of opportunity closing. Setting everything up had taken exactly the time allotted in the plan, but the woman had fought harder than expected, losing a shoe in the process, and disposal had made more of a mess than expected. That was unacceptable.

Using a plastic garbage bag taken from the workbench, the debris was quickly packed away, and the last traces of struggle tidied up. Pack it in, pack it out, the killer thought without any sense of irony. Sorting through what was normal trash and what might carry identifiable trace was too difficult to judge: everything visible had to be considered potentially incriminating, even if nobody ever investigated. That was the hallmark of success.

Within minutes the garage was clean and peaceful again, a proper abode for the gleaming chrome beast stalled within. The attached mini mansion had never been disturbed; there would be no evidence found there.

There were no last looks, no photographs taken for posterity.

It was done. Lights were turned out, the door closed, and silence claimed the space.

Inside the garage, the second body stirred, death held at bay a few seconds more. Vision gone, the fingers spread as though searching for something beside it on the car seat, stilling inches away from its goal—the already cooling hand of the other figure slumped in the passenger seat.

**one**

The dream was back. It always came back when I was stressed.

*The site was deserted; I sneaked through the fence and into the house. Lucky for me the alarms hadn't been turned on yet.*

As usual, my brain was telling me that it was only a memory; that I already knew what I would find, that it was okay for my heart to stop pounding so fast, but the dream was in control.

*The door called to me. I could feel it, practically singing in the rain-filled dusk. My flashlight skittered across the floor, allowing me to pick my way around piles of trash and debris. No tools left out; the carpenter's daughter approved.*

*"Hello, beauty," I said to the door. Or maybe to the woman in the door: in the darkness, in the beam of light, she was nakedly apparent now, a sweet-eyed woman who gazed out into the bare bones of the room with approval and fondness.*

Even now, the beauty of Zaki's work astounded me, and I mourned again for that loss.

*"Who are you, then? That's the key to all this. Who are you?"*

*The door, not too surprisingly, didn't answer. But I knew how to make it talk.*

*Or I thought I did, anyway.*

*It was all instinct, but J had always told me that instinct was the way most new things were discovered—instinct and panic.*

*I held my hand over the door the way I had with the tools, carefully not making physical contact with it, and touched just the lightest levels of current, like alto bells sounding in the distance.*

*The woman's hair stirred in a breeze, and her face seemed softer, rounder, then she disappeared behind the leaves again.*

I hated her, this woman I'd never known, never met. Hated her for being the reason my father was dead.

*Zaki really had been an artist, the bastard. I could feel him in the work. But I didn't know, yet, what he had been feeling.*

*evidence doesn't lie*

Shut up, *I told the voice.* I'm working.

*I touched a deeper level of current, bringing it out with a firm hand and splaying it gently across the door so that it landed easily, smoothly.*

Oh, how I love her, such a bad woman, such a wrong woman, and I cannot have her, but I will show her my love....

*Zaki, melancholy and impassioned, his hand steady on the chisel, his eyes on the wood, sensing even through his distraction how to chip here, cut there, to make the most of the grain. He was concentrating, thinking of his object of affection, the muse who inspired him. So focused, the way all Talent learned to be, that he never saw the man coming up behind him, the man who had already seen the work in progress, and recognized, the way a man might, the face growing out of the wood.*

I knew what was about to happen, in my dream-mind, and tensed against the memory.

*The blow was sudden and sharp, and the vision faded.*

No, *I told my current.* More.

*It surged, searched, and found...nothing. No emotions from the killer. No residue of his actions. It had been too long, or he had been too good, too quick. Or I needed to be better, sharper.*

You were a kid, I wanted to tell my then-self. You did what you could, and you did as well as you could. But you can't talk back to memories, only relive them.

*"Damn it." My flashlight's beam dropped off the door; I was unwilling to look at the face of the woman who had cost my father his life.*

★there is always evidence★

*The voice was back. And probably right. I let the beam play on the floor, unsure what I was looking for. Scan, step, scan. I repeated the process all the way up to the door, then turned around and looked the way I had come.*

*"There."*

*On the floor, about two feet away. A spot where the hardwood floor shone differently. That meant that it had been refinished more recently than the rest of the floor, or been treated somehow.... Zaki would have known. All I knew was that it was a clue.*

*I touched it with current, as lightly as I could. Something warned me that a gentle touch would reveal more than demanding ever would.*

*"The killer's actions, I beg you wood, reveal."*

*J's influence: treat current the way you would a horse; control it through its natural instincts. Current, like electricity, illuminated.*

*A dent in the floor, sanded down and covered up. The point of a chisel stained with blood? No. The harder end, sticking out of a body as it landed, falling backward...*

Oh, Zaki, you idiot *was all I could find inside myself, following the arc of the body.* For a woman? For another man's woman when you had Claire at home?

*And then I saw it, the shadow figure of the killer, indistinct even in his own mind—shading himself. That meant the killer was a Talent, if of even less skill than Zaki. Had that been a factor? The man—the foreman, I knew now—jealous not only of the carpenter's attraction to his wife, but of his skill to display it, driven to murder?*

*The chisel was removed, wiped down, and…*

I still flinched, even years and dreams later.

*The blood alone flared bright in the pictorial, a shine of wet rubies in the shadows as the foreman dipped the chisel into a cloth still damp with the blood, laying the trace for me to find, a week later.*

*Find, and be unable to do anything about, save live with the knowledge that my father had been murdered, and the murderer still walked, unpunished….*

I woke up, and the still-powerful sadness of dream faded, although it never really went away. Zaki had been dead for three years, though, and I'd learned to live with it. My depressing reality was more immediate: three months out of college, and I still didn't have a job.

I thought about putting the feather pillow over my face until I turned a proper shade of blue and suffocated. Even knowing that it was the overblown act of a spoiled five-year-old didn't stop me from contemplating it, running through scenarios of who would find me and what they might say or think or do. Eventually, though, I shoved the pillow to the side and stared glumly up at the ceiling.

No, I wasn't quite that desperate. But it was close.

Nobody wanted to hire me. It wasn't that I didn't have brains. Or enthusiasm. Or dedication, for that matter. I just…didn't know what to do with any of what I had. I guess that was showing up in my interviews, because nobody was saying "welcome aboard."

Something had to break soon, or I was looking at a short-term career goal of flipping burgers or, if I was lucky, pulling beers at a semidecent pickup bar.

"Oh, the hell with that." I got out of bed and stripped down my sweat-soaked T-shirt and panties, replacing them with my sweat-dried gym clothes, fresh socks, and my sneakers, and headed down to the hotel's gym. The only way to interrupt a self-pity party was with a good hard run.

I got back to my room, feeling only a little bit better, just in time to take possession of my breakfast order. I let the room-service guy in and tipped him, the door barely closing behind his back when the phone rang. I dropped the receipt on the table and picked up the phone, telling myself not to make any assumptions or unfounded leaps of hope. This early, though, it might be good news. Did people really call at 9:00 a.m. with bad news? Didn't they put that off as long as possible?

"Bonita Torres."

"Ms. Torres? This is Sally Marin, at Homefront Services."

I could tell by the sound of her voice that the news wasn't going to be good. Damn. Deep breathing is supposed to be good for panic, wasn't it? I took a breath, held it, and then let it out. Nope, didn't help.

I shifted the phone to the other ear, and tried to relax my shoulders, kicking off my sneakers and peeling off my socks. There was no reason to panic. My checkbook was still decently in the black, I wasn't in debt, if you could ignore a credit card or three coming due at the end of the month, and I had a degree from a top school packed with all my belongings in storage while I lounged around in a swank little suite on the Upper East side of Manhattan on a lovely, not-too-hot summer day.

Life could be worse, right?

Life could be a hell of a lot worse. I knew that firsthand. I took another deep breath and stared at my feet—I'd painted the toenails dark blue, to keep myself from thinking about the demure pale pink that was on my fingernails—and wiggled them. Yeah, things could be worse. But they could be shitloads better, too.

The brutal truth of the matter was that I needed a job, and not a minimum-wage one, either. Joseph kept telling me to relax, that I'd find something, but much as I love J, and he loves me, I couldn't mooch off him for the rest of my life, letting him pay for this hotel, my food, and my clothing. Sure, he had money but that wasn't the point. Comes a time, you've got to do for yourself, or self-esteem, what's that?

The problem was, J's been doing for me for so long, I think we've both forgotten how for him *not* to. Not that he spoiled me or anything, just… He's always taken care of me. Ever since I was eight years old, and an instinctive cry for help had literally pulled him off the street and into my life.

The dream came back to me, and I shoved it away. My dad, rest his soul, always meant well, and I'd never had a moment's doubt that he loved me, but Zaki Torres had been a crap parental figure, and his decisions weren't always the best even for himself, much less me. J had taken one look that day, and arranged to become mentor to that mouthy, opinionated eight-year-old. He taught me everything I needed to know and a bunch of stuff he figured I'd want to know, and then, ten years later, had the grace and wisdom to let me go.

Not that I went far—just off to college for four years. But even then, J was there, the comforting shadow and sounding board at my elbow, not to mention the tuition check in the mail. Now that phase was over, and it was time to be an adult.

Somehow.

And that was why I was starting to panic.

"I'm sorry, Ms. Torres," the woman on the other end of the phone line was saying. "Your résumé was quite good, of course, but…"

I kinda tuned her out at that point. It was the same thing everyone had been saying for the past three months. I'm smart,

I'm well educated—the aforementioned four years at Amherst will do that—and I'm a hard worker. All my references were heavy on that point. I've never shied away from a challenge.

Only these days, nobody wanted to hire someone with a liberal-arts degree and minimal tech skills, no matter how dedicated they might be.

It wasn't my fault, not really. I know how to use computers and all that. It's just that I can't. Or, I can, but it doesn't always end well.

I'm a Talent, which is the politically correct way of saying magic user. Magician. Witch. Whatever. Using current—the magical energy that floats around the world—is as natural to me as hailing a cab is to New Yorkers. Only problem is, current runs in the same time-space whatever as electricity, and like two cats in the same household, they don't always get along. They're pretty evenly balanced in terms of power and availability, but current's got the added kick of people dipping in and out, which makes it less predictable, more volatile. Which means a Talent…well, let's just say that most of us don't carry cell phones or PDAs on our person, or work with any delicate or highly calibrated technology.

I'm actually better than most—for some reason my current tends to run cool, not hot, meaning I don't have as many spikes in my—hypothetical—graph. Nobody's been able to explain it, except to say I'm just naturally laid-back. I guess it's because of that I've never killed a landline, or any of the basic household appliances just by proximity the way most Talent do, but there's always the risk.

Especially when we're under stress. You learn to work around it, and I wouldn't give up what I am, not for anything, but sometimes current is less a gift and more a righteous pain in the patoot. Especially when you're trying to find a job in the Null world.

Ms. Marin had finished making apologies, finally.

"Yes, thank you. I do appreciate your taking the time to speak with me." J taught me manners, too. I hung up the phone, and stared at my toes again. The sweat of my treadmill workout seemed far away, and the dream-sweat closer to my skin, somehow.

Damn it. I had really hoped something would come out of that interview. Something good, I meant.

Lacking any other idea or direction, I wandered over to the desk, where a pile of résumés, a notepad, and my breakfast—a three-egg omelet with hash browns and ketchup—waited for me to get my act together. There were still half a dozen places I needed to call, to follow up on applications and first interviews. I sat in the chair and stared at the notepad, with its neatly printed list—the result of ten weeks of intensive job-hunting—and felt a headache starting to creep up on me. At this rate, I really was going to be begging for temp jobs or—god help me—going back to retail. My life's ambition, not really. I might not know what I wanted to do, but I knew what I *didn't* want.

I forked up a bit of the omelet and took a bite, less because I was hungry and more because it was there. Other Talent found their niche, why couldn't I? All right, so a lot of them became artists, or lawyers, or ran their own companies, where their weirdness wasn't noticed, or was overlooked. None of that really interested me, even if I'd had an inch of artistic or entrepreneurial talent, which I didn't. Academia maybe, but the truth was that while I loved learning, school mostly bored me.

Me bored was a bad idea. When I was bored I did things like create a spell that would burn out selected letters in neon signs all over town, until it looked as though there was a conspiracy against the letters *Y* and *N*. Listening to people's

crackpot theories about what had really happened for the rest of the week had been fun, but…

But I needed something to *do.*

They say you should follow your interests, go for what you're passionate about. To do something that mattered would be nice. I needed to be able to get my teeth into something, to feel that it was worthwhile. Other than that…I didn't know. I guess that works if you've got some kind of artistic talent, or want to make the world a better place, or have an isotope named for you. Me, not so much.

There had been a while, after Zaki's murder, when I'd thought about going into law enforcement, but it was tougher these days for Talent to make it—less shoe leather and more high-tech toys. I might make it through the Academy, but spending the rest of my life pounding the pavement, unable to advance, didn't thrill me. And J was even less happy with the idea. He wanted me in a nice, safe office. Preferably a corner office, with an assistant to handle the heavy lifting and typing.

I scowled at the list again. Three advertising agencies, two trade magazines, and a legal aid firm. That was all I had left.

"Screw it. Shower first." Whatever the cause, I was sticky and sweaty, and my hair was kind of gross. Maybe washing it would get my brain going.

The bathroom was reasonably luxe, with scented shampoos and conditioners and soaps, and I took my time. I thought I heard the phone ring, but since I was soaking wet and had just lathered up, I ignored it. This place wasn't quite pretentious enough to rate a telephone in the bathroom. I'm not sure J would have let me stay here if there had been one—he's sort of old-fashioned and genteel, and things like taking a phone call while you're on the crapper would give him frothing fits.

The thought, I admit, made me giggle, even in my depression. J is such a gentleman in a lot of ways, old school, and yet he kept up with me pretty well. I wonder sometimes what crimes he committed as a young'un, that he was the one to be landed with me.

Far as I could tell, his only mistake had involved being in the wrong place at the right time. Zaki had enough sense to know he wasn't a strong enough Talent, and didn't have enough patience to mentor me, but his first choice was a disaster waiting to happen, and even as a kid I knew that the moment he introduced us. The guy was…well, he wouldn't have sold me to pay off his gambling debts, but I wouldn't have learned a whole lot, either.

The moment was still crystal-sharp in my memory: Zaki's worried presence, hovering; Billy's pleasure at being asked to mentor someone for the first time in his life; the smell of a freshly washed carpet that didn't hide the years of wear and tear…

With an amazing lack of tact that still dogs me, I'd used my untrained, just-developing current to yelp for help. That had attracted the attention of a passerby on the street below, who— despite having already done his time as a mentor, and being way out of our league—came up the stairs, took one look, and took on the job.

Zaki had been lonejack, part of the officially unofficial, intentionally unorganized population of Talent. J was Council— the epitome of structural organization. Despite that, they both got along pretty well, I guess because of me. I wasn't the only lonejack kid mentored by a Council member, but I was the only one we knew of who *stayed* at least nominally a lonejack.

"Maybe if you'd crossed the river, you'd have had a job offer waiting for you when you graduated," I grumbled. "Why do you insist on thinking that nepotism's a dirty word?"

Truth was, I didn't think of myself as either one group or

the other, and maybe that was part of the problem. Born to one magical community, raised in another, Latina by birth and European by training, female imprinted on a—oh god, use the word—metrosexual male… Issues? I probably should have *subscriptions* at this point.

My hair's short enough that it doesn't take long to wash, and by the time I got out of the bathroom, toweled off, and wrapped in one of the complimentary bathrobes, the strands were almost dry. I'm a natural honey-blonde, thanks to my unknown and long-gone mother, but it hasn't been that shade since I was fourteen—I was currently sporting a dark red dye job that I had thought would look more office-appropriate. So much for that thought doing me any good. Maybe I'd go back to purple, and the hell with it.

Contemplating an interviewer's reaction to that, I walked to the bedroom, and saw that the light on the phone was blinking. Right, the call I'd missed. Whoever called, they'd left me a message.

My heart did a little scatter-jump, and my inner current flared in anticipation, making me instinctively take a step away from the phone, rather than toward it. Normally, like I said, my current's cold and calm, especially compared to most of my peers, but I'd been out of sorts recently, and wasn't quite sure what might happen. Bad form to short out your only means of communicating with potential employers. Plus, the hotel would be pissed, and complain to J.

Once I felt my current settle back down, I let myself look at the blinking light again. You could call first thing in the morning with bad news. Okay. You didn't call and leave a message with bad news, did you? I didn't know. Maybe. Just because everyone seemed eager to tell me no to my face didn't mean that was the only way to do it.

All right, this was me, keeping calm. Hitting the replay button. Stepping back, out of—hopefully—accidental current-splash range…

"This message is for Bonita Torres. Two o'clock tomorrow afternoon." The speaker gave an address that I didn't recognize, not that I knew damn-all about New York City, once you get past the basic tourist spots. "Take the 1 train to 125$^{th}$. Be on time."

No name, no indication of where they got my name or number, just that message, in a deep male voice.

An interesting voice, that. Not radio-announcer smooth, but…interesting.

Someone smart would have deleted the message. Someone with actual prospects would have laughed and said no way.

I've always been a sucker for interesting.

# two

One of the first things J taught me was, before I decided on anything with repercussions, to step back and consider that decision from every possible angle. It only took a few minutes of thought, and sanity reasserted itself. The voice-mail message was weird, but intriguing. Or maybe it was intriguing because it was weird. Did that make it a good idea? No. In fact, it probably made it a very bad idea.

J said I should consider, and think sanely. He didn't say anything about *listening* to that sane voice, and very bad ideas were often a lot of fun.

The guy hadn't left a phone number for me to call back and say I'd be there, though. Oh god, and if this was from one of the résumés I'd sent out, I'd look a proper idiot calling now to follow up, if I'd already gotten an interview.

I picked up the phone and was about to dial the callback code when I realized that, idiot, the call had to have come through the hotel switchboard. So I dialed 0 for the front desk, instead.

"Hi. This is room 328? I just had a call come in, and they didn't leave a name or number to reach them at, I don't suppose…?"

No, the woman at the front desk told me regretfully, they couldn't. I didn't know if it was a technological thing or a legal thing, and I didn't bother to ask. The reason didn't make a difference. I hung up the phone, still clueless, and stared at the paper with the details written on it, on top of the list of names and places I was supposed to call back. Handwriting was supposed to tell you about a person, right? My handwriting's like J's—squared and solid, and easy to read. I'd have made a crappy doctor.

Maybe it was one of these places I'd already submitted my résumé to. Maybe it wasn't. Maybe it was through a contact of J's who had thought my mentor would tell me to expect the call. That didn't sound right—J would never forget to tell me something like that—but it was a possibility. Maybe it was a joke, a prank, or a weird cold-call solicitation. I had no idea, and no way of finding out—except for showing up.

Tomorrow afternoon. All right. That gave me the rest of the day to follow up on my other résumés, and still get out and wander around the city before dinner with J. And then tomorrow…would bring whatever tomorrow would bring. Maybe J would have some idea what all this was about. I was pretty sure he'd have an opinion, at least.

The carrot of playtime in Manhattan dangling in front of me, I made short work of the remaining names on my list. Not that it took much; two résumés were still "under consideration"; two were thanks-no-thanks; at one place the HR person was out and would get back to me at some point before the next millennium, maybe; and one place, hurrah, they wanted to see me again on Friday!

The fact that this was Monday didn't fill me with huge levels of optimism, since if I was a hot prospect they'd get me in quick, right? But it was the best offer I'd gotten so far, so I thanked the nice guy on the phone, confirmed the time and place, and hung up the phone not quite as terminally depressed as I'd been earlier. Also, I'd determined that the mysterious phone call hadn't come from any of these places, so that option was dealt with.

Was I going to show up tomorrow? I honestly didn't know.

But for now, I had the afternoon to myself. I threw on a pair of black pants and a hot-pink T-shirt and my boots, left my stress at the door, and made my escape.

Johnny, the twenty-seven-year-old engineering student from Tehran, was doorman today. He wished me a nice day and held the large glass door open, and I hit the sidewalk like a greyhound sighting a rabbit.

I grew up in Boston, went to school outside the city, had been to Rome and Paris and London and Dubai and Tokyo and a dozen other major cities with J dragging me around. All that travel gave me a reasonable sense of sophistication, but drop me in the middle of New York City and I felt like a little kid again. There's not more current running through the wiring of Manhattan than anywhere else; it's not any more vibrant or powerful…but somehow it always feels that way to me.

Not just me, either. J says there're more Talent in New York, Chicago, and Houston than anywhere else, and more of the fatae, the nonhumans of the *Cosa Nostradamus*—those with and of magic—too. I wasn't so blasé that I wouldn't be excited about the chance to see more fatae. Sure, there were some up in Amherst; my freshman composition teacher had been a dryad, and a couple of centaurs used to hang around the stables I rode at, taunting the ponies and stealing grain and treats. But the exotics, the rare breeds, they were in New York, where nobody even looked once, much less twice.

The hotel was only a ten-minute walk from my destination: the Metropolitan Museum of Art. Specifically, the Temple of Dendur, the reconstructed ruins of a building once dedicated to Isis. Anytime the museum's open, you'll find people standing there under the glass walls, staring at the installation, soaking up the ancient ambience. Some of us are soaking up more than that. The Temple by itself may or may not have been anything especially mystical or magical in its original location, beyond whatever the faith of its followers gave it, but when it was re-located to the museum, they managed to place the sandstone structure directly over a major ley line convergence, one of the sweetest in the city.

Ley lines are like a funnel for natural current, the energy of the earth itself, the basic stuff magic is formed around. I wasn't going to suck any of it up today, just say hello, make my curtsy, as J always said. It's only polite.

Someone came up next to me. I assumed another tourist, someone who didn't know not to stand so close, gawking at the Temple, same as me. Half-right, anyway.

"You're new."

Oh lord. Not that I didn't appreciate attention, when I was in the mood, but… "You're using a very old line."

"Old and tested and true. I'm none of those things."

I laughed, and turned to consider the owner of the voice. Tall, well above my own five-six, and nicely built, with deep blue eyes and raven-black hair setting off evenly tanned skin. Might be too old for me, by a smidge, but if he didn't mind I wasn't going to say anything.

Oh, the outlook for the afternoon had definitely improved.

"I'm Gerry," he said, offering one nicely formed hand, the fingertips bitten but not torn up. There were just enough calluses to make his skin firm, rather than soft, and he shook like a guy who had nothing to prove, a single solid pump. "I'm harmless in public, entertaining in private, and up-to-date on all my shots and papers. May my old lines and I buy you a cup of coffee?"

This hadn't exactly been the distraction I'd been thinking of, but when you're made such a very nicely packaged offer... I cast a look over the Temple, and be damned if I didn't feel a very distinct smirk coming off the energy rising out of it. Or maybe that was just me, projecting.

"You may, indeed."

Three hours and more than one cup of coffee later, I knew enough about Gerry to know that he would be a disaster long-term, even if I had been thinking that way. I also knew that he had a very confident appeal and a sweetly coffee-scented kiss, and if I hadn't been otherwise promised for the evening, we might have gotten better acquainted. Not *that* well acquainted, no; I'm an unabashed flirt, not a skank. But he was sweet, and he gave me his phone number and e-mail, with strict instructions to get in touch.

Maybe I would. Maybe not. Gerry was sweet, but he didn't have even a twitch of Talent, didn't seem to know anything about the *Cosa Nostradamus*—I'd been subtle but thorough on that—and I've always been shy about getting involved with Nulls. It gets...complicated. Better to stick to your own kind, who already know the deal.

I made it back to the hotel just in time to change for dinner. J's not a fuddy-duddy, even if he is Council, but there are standards for our dinners together, and I appreciate them as much as he does.

Promptly on the dot of 6:00 p.m. I was dressed in my favorite red dress, a Monroe-style haltertop, pearl drops in my ears and rings on my fingers, feet cased in strappy gold sandals and my hair combed into a semblance of tidy curls. A spritz of perfume, and I was ready to go.

At the dot of 6:02 p.m., the touch of current that *felt* like J wrapped around me, and a second later the Translocation took effect, moving me from my hotel room in Manhattan a hundred-plus miles north to J's place in Boston.

Translocation's a basic current-skill. I'm decent at it. J's prime. I landed in his living room like I'd stepped in from the hallway, not a hair out of place.

"Good evening, my dear." He was pouring wine, a deep red liquid that made my mouth water. I was more of a vodka martini girl, but my mentor had a fantabulous wine cellar, too.

He was looking good, and I told him so.

"Well, I had a hot date tonight, had to brush off the good suit."

Joseph Cetala had just pushed over seventy, and looked it, but every year had been kind. His hair was still thick, if bone-white, and his patrician cheekbones were hidden under still-firm skin. I have no objections to my looks—they do the job and pale skin and a pointy-pixie chin suit me—but man did I used to wish I were his biological daughter, just for those cheekbones.

I took a glass from him, and sat on the sofa. The shaggy white-and-brown throw rug got to its feet and shuffled over. "Hey there, good boy. How's my good boy?"

"He's getting old, same as me."

"Nah. You guys are never gonna get old. Are you, boy?"

Rupert woofed, and shoved his wet nose into my hand. I wasn't much for pets, but Rupe was less a pet than a member of the household. J said all Old English sheepdogs were smart, but I personally thought Rupe got a double helping of brains. I always got the feeling he wasn't so optimistic about me.

J took his own glass over to the leather chair and sat, crossing one leg against his knee, and looking, I swear to god, like an ad for something upscale and classy aimed at the Retirement Generation. Even in my nice dress and pearls, I still felt outclassed.

Funny, really. I leaned into the sofa and looked around. The only way to describe J's place was "warm." Rosewood furniture against cream-colored walls, and touches of dark blue and flannel gray everywhere, broken by the occasional bit of foam green from his Chinese pottery collection. You'd think I'd have grown up to be Über Society Girl, not pixie-Goth, in these surroundings. Even my bedroom—now turned back into its original use as a library—had the same feel of calm wealth to it, no matter how many pop-culture posters I put up or how dark I painted the walls. And yet, J was just as likely to wear jeans and kick back with a beer when he was in the mood, so I guess I should know by now that you can't judge a body by the decor.

J used to tell me, when I was, oh, thirteen and felt particularly floundering-ish, that I would grow up into who I always was. It sounds nice, I guess, but I'm still not quite sure who that is. She uses a lot of hair dye and has an interestingly eclectic wardrobe, and might have a lead on a job, though. So that was all right.

"What's for dinner?" I asked.

"I'm trying something new."

From some people, that news would make me nervous. J, I swear to god, was born in the kitchen. I don't think he owned a single cookbook or has any of his recipes written down, but he's never fed me anything that was less than really good, and it frequently goes into orgasmic culinary experience range. I learned how to cook by the time I was ten, just by osmosis, and had my first set of proper knives when I was fourteen.

Haven't done much cooking lately, though. Nobody around to feed since graduation, I guess.

"You are looking particularly glowy tonight, dearest. Either the job hunt has resulted in a hit, or you have met a new admirer."

I think J gets a kick out of my social life, although he tsk-tsks periodically over my inability—lack of desire, really—to settle into one steady relationship. So long as I'm happy, he's happy. I mean, he didn't blink the first time I showed up with a new girlfriend, and never asked when she went away and a new boyfriend showed up.

I'm not particularly into labels. I just like *people,* is all. Doesn't matter what body parts they've got, so long as there's a brain and a sense of humor and a healthy idea of companionship.

"Both, maybe," I told him. "But it's the job thing that's interesting. I was in the shower when the call came in…."

J listened the way he always did, with his entire body leaning forward, his hands cupped around his glass, his gaze not unblinking but steady on my face. When I finished, he leaned back, took a sip from his glass, and didn't say anything.

"What?"

"You intend to follow through on these instructions?"

"I'd planned to, yeah. You think it's a bad idea? Are you getting a vibe?" I had what J called the *kenning,* not quite precog but a sort of magical sense about things. But he'd been honing his current for a lifetime before I came along, and that meant he picked up more than I did on a regular basis.

"Nothing so strong as a premonition, no. I will admit, however, to a sense that something is slightly… What is that horrible word you used to use? Hinky. Something feels hinky about it."

That made me laugh. "Well, yes. That probably goes without saying. Anyone calls out of the blue, doesn't give basic details, all mysterious and like?" I didn't roll my eyes, but my voice conveyed the "well, duh" more than J deserved. "That's half the fun!"

My mentor shook his head and mock-sighed. I love J more than life, but he and I diverge pretty seriously on our ideas of fun.

"If you wanted me to, I could get you a job...." He let the offer trail off, the same way he did every time he made it. J had, once upon a time, worked for the State, and then did some work for a high-powered law firm that still listed him on the masthead, even though he hadn't, as far as I knew, taken on a case in over a decade. If I couldn't be a cop, I guess his reasoning went, why not be a lawyer?

Just the idea made me want to tear my fingernails off and use them to dig an escape route. I never, ever told him that, though I suspected he knew.

"There's just something about that message," I said, doing my usual not-a-response to his offer. "Something that makes my ears prick up, and no, I don't know why. I figured I might do a scrying, see what comes forward."

"You and your crystals." The disgust in his voice this time was real.

"Just because we've gone all modern and scientific with current doesn't mean some of the old ways aren't valid." It was an old argument, older even than the split between Council and the scruffy freelancer lonejacks. When Founder Ben— Benjamin Franklin to Nulls—nailed the connection between electricity and current with his kite-and-key trick, most Talent changed, too, working the scientific angle to figure out more and more efficient ways to do things—and how to work this increasingly electric world to our benefit. A lot of the theories and practices of Old Magic got tossed, and good riddance, but

I'd discovered that I could scry better with a focus object than with current alone, and the smoother and rounder the shape, the better.

So yeah, I have a crystal ball. Deal.

"I just…" It was difficult to vocalize what I wasn't really sure of. J was patient, waiting. I might have mentioned the dream, but I didn't. Talking about Zaki always made J feel guilty, as if there was some way he could have prevented it, or stopped me from finding the killer, or done *something*.

"There's something familiar about the voice. No, it's not someone I've ever met. I'm not even sure I've ever heard the voice before, either, so it's not a radio announcer or anything. But it's still familiar, like I've got memories associated with it, except I can't access those memories, either." I'm usually pretty good at that, too, so J didn't press further.

"Hinky," my mentor instead diagnosed with confidence, putting his glass down and heading into the kitchen as something chimed a warning. Rupert abandoned my petting and trudged after his master. I could have followed, but we'd survived this long by not crowding each other in the kitchen. Tonight he was showing off.

J was probably right. Whatever that mysterious call was about, it was not going to be for an entry-level office management job with decent pay and benefits. But it wasn't as though I had anything else urgent or particularly interesting to do, except maybe give Gerry a call.

This mysterious meeting sounded like it might have more potential.

"Dinner's ready," J came back to announce. "Bring your wine. And you've made up your mind already, haven't you?"

J long ago taught me not to shrug—he said that it was an indelicate movement that indicated helplessness—so instead I lifted my free hand palm up in supplication for his understanding. "It's not like anything else is panning out. And if it is hinky…I may not be as high-res as some, but I can take care of myself. You taught me well, Obi-Wan. Worst case scenario and it's for a sleazy, low-paying call-girl job, I Translocate out and have a good story about it later." I wasn't quite as breezy as that sounded, but I did a pretty good job of selling it, because J's shoulders relaxed just a bit.

I knew what he was worried about, even if he didn't say so. J was twice-over retired now, but once upon a time he'd been a serious dealmaker in the Eastern Council, maybe even a seated member although if so he never admitted it, and even now if he said jump a lot of people made like frogs, both here and in the Midwest. There were also a lot of people he'd pissed off along the way, some of whom might want to take a late hit, if not directly on him, then through his family. And to the *Cosa Nostradamus,* the mentor-mentee relationship was as tight as it got, even more than blood.

He'd had another mentee, years ago, but Bobby was not going to be the target for anyone, anyhow. Not now. Full Council honors out in San Francisco, and you'd better have a topped-up core to take a whack at him or he'd eat you alive. So it was just me J got to worry about.

"And you'll ping me as soon as you're out?"

He had to be worried to ask me to ping. It was a good way to send a quick message, but not much on the formal manners, and most of the older Talent seemed to think the way we used it now was a sign of the coming Apocalypse or something.

"Yes, Joseph." The use of his full name was my sign that the discussion was over, and since he knew better than anyone how like unto a pit bull I could be in the stubbornness category, he let it go and fed me, instead.

★ ★ ★

Later that night, back in my hotel room, I got out my crystals. The plain wooden box, about the size of a shoe box, was lined in thick, nubby linen—silk was so clichéd—and held three scrying pieces: a rose quartz ball about the size of my palm, a clear quartz shard the size of a pencil, and my traditional, kerchief-and-skirts scrying globe, also clear quartz. The third piece wasn't entirely clear all the way through, with an imperfection about midway, but that really didn't matter for my purposes.

The rose quartz stayed in the box; I wasn't going to need that one tonight. Sitting cross-legged on the hotel-room bed, the lights out and the television off, I put the ball down in front of me and kept the shard in my hand.

It was warm, as if it had been waiting for me to pick it up. J taught me that everything had current, even inanimate objects, but I wasn't sensitive enough—what the old-timers called Pure—to pick it up.

Pure or low-res, all Talent use current, and we all use it about the same way, but I've never heard anyone describe it exactly the same way. It's like sex, or religion, I guess; you gravitate toward whatever works for you. Me, I like things tangible. As in life, so in my head; as in my head, so created in current.

The smaller crystal helped me ground and center. I had an even smaller black quartz one that I wore on a chain when I thought I'd need a boost on the go, but J thought that was sloppy, and reflected badly on his training, so I didn't use it too often.

"Breathe in, breathe out. 10. 9. 8. 7. 6…"

By five, as usual, I was deep in my own core, the current I carried with me all the time. You could source current from outside, either tame—man-made wiring, power plants, stuff like that—or wild. Wild was ley lines, electrical storms, that sort of thing. Nature's own energy. There were pluses and minuses to both, which was why you always wanted to maintain your own power, filtered, tamed, and tuned to your own quirks. Core-current was safer to use, faster to call up, and no surprises lurking in the power stream.

I put the fragment down, and placed my hand on the globe, palm curved over the top. The stone was cool at first, and then my fingers began to prickle. I opened my eyes and looked down. Sparks were flicking inside the globe, running from my fingertip down to the imperfection, where they fractured and bounced back to the surface. They were mostly red, which wasn't what I wanted. I focused, turning one strand this way, another that, and the hues faded to a more useful blue. Like cooking, you could do a lot with basic ingredients and a few pots, but it was easier when you had everything properly prepped.

"All right, baby, show me what you got. What's waiting at tomorrow's interview for me?"

That was about the level of specifics I hung at. There might be a way to get actual details out of the future, but I'd never known anyone who could do it consistently—and then there was the problem of interpreting those details. What seems perfectly obvious in a precog has a tendency to go another way entirely when it's all happening.

But vague? Vague I could do.

The crystal was filled with blue sparks now, and I lifted my hand slowly, not wanting to startle anything. "Whatcha got for me? What's waiting for me?"

The sparks began to settle, and I opened myself up to whatever visual might come.

Letters. Black against pale blue, hard and spiky letters, like someone writing fast and angry.

*No Cheating.*

And then the crystal—my damned expensive quartz globe—cracked like overheated safety glass, shards and chunks scattering all over the bed.

I stared down at the mess, feeling the sting on my skin where tiny fragments must have nicked me.

"Sheeesh." I pulled a shard out of my hair, and dropped it into the largest pile of debris. "All right, fine. I can take a damned hint."

At least I knew one thing for certain. Whoever had called, whoever was setting this up? Way stronger Talent than me. And there was something else to seriously consider: that blast could have hurt me. Any of those shards might easily have done damage—but didn't.

I got up, yanked the cover off the bed and wrapped up the useless corpse of my crystal in it, and dropped it to the side of the room, where Housekeeping could deal with it later, then put a Do Not Disturb sign on the door.

Big day tomorrow. I needed my sleep.

## three

My interview—or whatever that mysterious summons actually ended up being—wasn't until 2:00 p.m. So, of course, I slept through the wake-up call, and the usual breakfast knock, and even the construction work being done on the street outside, courtesy of ConEd, finally waking up a little before noon. This wasn't as unusual as it should be; I was born a night owl, and J never really trained it out of me. The one single 8:00-a.m. class I had in college, I dealt with by staying up all night and going to sleep afterward.

The sight of the crumpled-up bedspread in the corner was a sobering thing to wake up to, though. Last night I was tired and well fed and probably more than a little inebriated—we had knocked off that bottle of wine, and then another during dinner—and the real hit hadn't settled into my brain. This morning, it was all cold hard facts. I was going into an unknown situation that was clearly run—or at least guarded by—someone with way more mojo than I had. Someone alert to, and unhappy about, anyone scrying what they had planned. Suddenly, J's concerns weren't quite so dismissible.

I was still going—pit-bull stubborn, that's me—but with caution, damn it. And, I decided suddenly, without pretending to be anyone I wasn't. Screw that—it hadn't gotten me anywhere so far, and whoever this was, they were the ones who came calling, not the other way around. Let them get what I got.

Out went the demure, if very nice, navy blue interview suit, and the sleeked-down, styled hair. My own, comfortable clothing, and my own comfortable look, thank you much. When I got out of the shower I applied my makeup and then ran my fingers through my hair and ruffled it madly. The image that stared at me from the full-length mirror was a hell of a lot more familiar now: my hair, still dark red but the short strands now fluffed around my face like a bloody dandelion puff, my eyes lined with a discreet amount of black kohl and mascara, and three basic gold studs in my left ear, while my right ear displayed a single sapphire stud, a fourteenth-birthday present from J.

I'd been tempted to finish it off with buckled cargo pants and a mesh T-shirt, all in black, but common sense won out. I was going for me-hireable, not Goth club-kid. So a bright red silk shirt; sleeveless, like a fitted vest, went over my favorite skirt, a long black linen circle with enough pockets and loops to carry everything you might need in a daily routine, up to and including a carpenter's hammer. J might be hoity-toity lawyer-man, but Zaki'd been a craftsman, and I learned early on about always having room for your tools.

I didn't like the way using the pockets interfered with the swing of the skirt, though, so everything—date book, newspaper, wallet, sunglasses—got tossed into my carryall. It was a graduation present from J—soft black leather, and probably the most expensive thing I owned—so I didn't think I'd lose presentation points for using it instead of a briefcase.

There was a moment's hesitation at the shoes, but I squashed J's voice in my head and went for my stompy boots instead of the more interview-acceptable, sensible heels. Shoving my feet into them felt like coming home, and when I stood up again, I felt ready to take on the whole damn world.

Never underestimate the power of a pair of good, stompy engineer boots.

Leaving the hotel, the daytime doorman—an older Asian guy named Walter—wished me good luck, making him third after the two chambermaids in the hallway on my floor. I thanked him, too, not sure if I should feel good that they bothered, or depressed that everyone in the hotel seemed to know I was job-hunting. Still, the entire staff had been really nice to me, and it wasn't like I was in a position to turn down good wishes.

The smart thing probably would have been to take a cab once I got cross-town, but the racket-clack of the subway was like a siren's lure. They're noisy, and usually overcrowded, but I could get a pretty current-buzz off the third rail without trying, and you see way more interesting people on mass transit. I'm all about the people-watching. Unfortunately, Tuesday at 1:30 p.m., heading uptown, seemed to be the dead time on the 1 train, and it was just me and an old guy reading a day-old newspaper, and two teenage girls in Catholic-school uniforms, whispering and giggling to themselves.

It took about twenty minutes to get uptown, with me obsessively checking the subway route map on the wall behind my seat at every station. Damn, I was going to be late…. I got off at what I hoped was the right stop, and left the guy to his paper, and the girls to their giggles. Places to go, people to impress!

The office—or whatever it was—didn't exactly inspire confidence. The address was a mostly kept-up building off Amsterdam Avenue, seven stories high and nine windows across. Brick and gray stone: that looked like the norm in this neighborhood. We weren't running with a high-income crowd, here. Still, I had seen and smelled worse, and the neighborhood looked pretty friendly—lots of bodegas and coffee shops, and the kids hanging around looked as if they'd stopped there to hang on the way home from school, not been there all day waiting for their parole officer to roll by.

And only one of them, a short kid with Day-Glo green hair, shouted out a comment to me, and yeah it was rude, but it wasn't insulting, so I gave him a grin and told him to call me as soon as he could grow some facial hair, too. His friends hooted and shoved him hard enough to knock him off the stoop. Normal stuff.

I could work around here, yeah. Assuming this wasn't just some recruiter's office, or… Nerves surfaced again, and got shoved down. Come on, I chided myself, hoisting my bag more firmly over my shoulder, you faced off against a cave dragon when you were nineteen…how much more difficult could this be?

I wasn't sure I wanted an answer to that, actually.

Pushing the appropriate intercom button in the foyer got me buzzed in through the lobby doors. There was no camera lens visible, so either they were really trusting, or they were using current to watch the door. I couldn't sense anything, but that could just mean that it was subtle—meaning well-done. The office was on the top floor, just to the right as I came out of the elevator. From the hallway, it looked as though there were two office suites on each side. I went to the correct door, marked by a brass 7-C, and turned the handle.

Walking into the office itself was reassuring; the space was clean, well lit, and surprisingly large. It was also filled with people.

All right, four other people. Three guys and another woman, seated on what looked like almost-comfortable upholstered chairs. None of the usual waiting-room coffee tables filled with out-of-date magazines, thank god. In fact, no coffee table at all, although there was a coffee machine and a bunch of mugs on a counter against the far wall, along with what looked like a working sink and a mini fridge. Nobody else was drinking coffee, although one of the guys had an oversize travel mug with him.

I let a flutter of current rise, and it got one, two, three, four equally polite touches back in response. Everyone here was a Talent, nobody was masking, and nobody was going to make a fuss about it. The fact that there were other people there was both worrying—competition for the job—and comforting— it probably wasn't a setup or sideways attack on J after all. But that left the question: what the hell *was* it? I had no idea what the percentage of Talent was to the entire human population, but even in New York it had to be single digits. This was either deliberate selection, or a massive coincidence.

Based on the backlash last night, I wasn't counting on co-incidence.

I lifted my hand in greeting. "Hi."

"Hello." The woman responded first, giving me a once-over that reminded me eerily of my old junior-high math teacher. Not that this woman was old or stern or anything, just…*assessing,* that was the word. Tall, blond, and cool, with curves that could probably stop a truck. I let my eyes linger, I admit it. "I'm Sharon. That's Nick." She pointed to the one with the travel mug, a dark-skinned moose of a guy who barely fit into his armchair. He nodded, his expression not changing from one of resigned boredom. If he hadn't played football at some point, maybe even college level, I'd tear up my people-watching skills and eat them without sauce. So, was he muscle, or was there something in the brainpan, too?

"That's Pietr." She pointed that finger at the second guy in line, a slender guy in khakis and pale blue button-down shirt matched to a screamingly expensive tie, and with a profile that would make a classical sculpture cry in envy. He was almost pretty, with skin as pale as mine, but something about the way he held himself kept the impression in check; like a serpent— shiny, but not cuddly. He met my gaze evenly, his pale gray eyes possibly the sweetest things I'd seen in weeks, and a smile flickered and was gone. Oh, he was trouble, you could tell it right away. And not all good trouble, either.

"And that's Nick, too."

No problem telling them apart—if NickOne was a jock, then NickTwo was a nerd. Short and scrawny, brown hair and brown eyes, and totally unimpressive in the same kind of khakis Pietr was wearing, but a less expensive-looking shirt and tie. NickTwo was the kind of guy you'd either ignore…or pick first for your team. I didn't know which yet, but I was suspecting the latter. That probably meant that NickOne had brains, too, because whatever this gig was, I was starting to get a feeling they weren't hiring for sheer meat-power.

They were all dressed more formally than I was, but only Sharon looked like she actually belonged in an office, with her tailored blue skirt and suit jacket, and stylish, low-heeled pumps. She wasn't wearing much makeup, or it was applied so well you couldn't tell, and with simple gold jewelry on her fingers and in her ears, she could have just come from a meeting where she wasn't serving the coffee. She was also, I guessed, older than the rest of us, by anywhere from five to ten years, so make her maybe thirty.

"I'm Bonnie. You guys all summoned by a nameless message on your answering machine?"

Four nods; obviously they'd exchanged more than names before I got there.

"Anyone know what this is all about?"

Four headshakes.

"Great." Talkative bunch. "Anyone want some coffee?"

Nobody did. "All they have is skim milk," NickTwo warned me, and I nodded. Fine by me, so long as it wasn't powdered nondairy crap. I went to the counter and pulled out a mug, pouring a dose of black tarry stuff I wouldn't feed a rat, and adding as much sugar and milk to it as I could, to try to make it palatable. Didn't really help, but it was something to do.

Sharon went back to her newspaper, and NickOne stared into space, as if he was having some in-depth conversation with space aliens. That left NickTwo and Pietr as possible conversationalists. I sat on the only remaining chair, balanced my mug of coffee on my knee, and waited. Time passed. Finally, bored out of my skull, I turned to Pietr on my left. "So why are you here?"

"My parole officer said I needed to prove I'd gone on a job interview, to keep from going back to jail."

NickTwo blinked—I guess they hadn't gotten around to that topic of conversation yet—but Pietr looked dead serious, so he was either dead serious, or a better joker than I could ever manage. Or, possibly, both.

"Seriously?" NickTwo asked, his brown eyes going wide and kidlike in awe.

"For serious, yes." Then he cracked a smile, and shook his head. "Nah. But it was strongly suggested to me by persons of importance that I get a job to keep me out of trouble. So when this call came I figured, what the hell."

"I think they'd need a lot more than a job to keep you out of trouble," NickTwo said, leaning back in his chair with a vaguely disgruntled look. Looked as though I wasn't the only one to have pegged Pietr straightaway.

He didn't take offense—just the opposite, actually. "You're probably right. What's your excuse for being here?"

NickTwo shrugged, his skinny arms rising in a very Gallic shrug. "I graduated, got a part-time job that pays pretty well, doesn't eat my life…and it's boring the hell out of me. The message I got said I'd find this of interest. So….I'm waiting for them to interest me."

"Same here," Sharon said, raising her head from the newspaper without even pretending that she hadn't been eavesdropping. "I'm a paralegal. Good money, no future, boring as hell. My message told me that, if I wanted to stop wasting my life, to show up here, at this time." She folded the newspaper and put it on the floor next to her chair. "How 'bout you, big guy?"

NickOne blinked and came back to us. "Nifty."

"What?"

"My teammates call me Nifty."

I mentally patted myself on the back. Teammates, yep. Point to me. And ohmahgawd and holy shit. "You're Nifty Lawrence." I didn't mean for my voice to squeak, but it did anyway. I'd dated a guy in college who was totally into football, not the pros but the college games, and Nifty Lawrence was supposed to be hot enough for the first round of the draft when he graduated, which would have been last year. "Hands like a god, could catch anything on the field, including low-flying seagulls," my ex had claimed. So why the hell was he here, instead of sweating out the coaching appraisals and counting his cash?

"I am." He looked sort of embarrassed by that fact, and tugged at the sleeve of his navy jacket as though he'd just realized he was wearing it and wondered how that happened. "And before you ask, I looked around, and decided that maybe just being good enough to go pro wasn't reason to do it. I mean, I'm good but I didn't love it. Getting my MBA and finding a corner office somewhere seemed smarter than spending five or ten years getting my head knocked to the turf. Only it takes money to pay for grad school, even with loans. So, I need a job, too."

My opinion of his brains went up, considerably.

"So what about you?" he asked me. "Boredom, or desperation, or something else entirely?"

"All of the above, I think. A whim? I was curious to see what the deal was." I looked around, suddenly struck by a thought. "You guys all had messages—did they all say 2 p.m.?"

"Yeah," Nick said, and Nifty nodded. Sharon frowned, obviously thinking the same thing I was, but Pietr was the one who said it. "Who schedules five interviews all at the same time?"

"More than that," Nick said, pulling out a battered old-fashioned windup pocket watch and looking at it. "It's almost 2:20, and we're the only ones here."

Four heads swiveled as though we were pulled on a string, to look at the closed door behind us, leading into the rest—I presumed—of the office.

The door remained closed.

"Anyone know the protocol of how long you wait before you assume you've been blown off?" I asked, and like we'd rehearsed it or something, the four of us looked at Sharon, who was the only one who seemed as if she might have a clue.

"What, I'm mother hen now?"

"Cluck, cluck," Nick said, unabashed when she glared at him. Nifty laughed, and she split the glare between the two of them. Oh, Miss Blonde did not like being mocked, even gently.

I'm not much as peacemaker—I never got the hang of being soothing, and while I can dance around the truth I'm crap at lying—but it looked as if it was gonna be my job anyway, just to keep things nonviolent. "Look, I'm straight out of college, don't know a damned thing, and I know Nifty's the same, considering he's only a year older than I am. I don't know what Pietr's background is, but getting anything straightforward out of him is impossible. I know that already, after ten minutes." He made a seated, ironic bow in response. "You and Nick, on the other hand, already have jobs, so you must've gone through this successfully before, and I'd trust your opinion over Nick's on something like this."

"Hey!" Nick sounded like he wasn't sure if he was supposed to take offense or not. I did say peacemaking wasn't my thing, right? But it seemed to work, because I could practically see the hackles under Sharon's chignon subside, and she gave a grudging nod.

"By now, I would expect someone to at least check on us, see who was here, maybe call one of us in," she said. "Unless they have this room on closed-circuit camera…"

"They don't. I checked." Nick sounded quite certain of that. "And anyway, the bunch of us in one small room, nervous or anticipating, and a seeing-eye camera? Would last about ten minutes."

"Speak for yourself," I told him. "Some of us have actual control."

"I don't," Nifty admitted. "Local stations stopped interviewing me before a game, after their cameras kept fritzing."

Probably another reason why he decided against a career in pro football. He wasn't going to make it as a sportscaster, either, with that handicap. Corporate America was definitely a better bet.

"So by now," I said, "someone should have come out to count noses?"

Sharon nodded. That's what I had thought. My nerves were starting to hum again. Was anyone even back there, behind the closed door I'd been assuming was the main office? If not, then who had let us in? "And nobody's had the slightest urge to get up and walk out, despite the fact that we don't know crap-all, and this mysterious voice has kept us waiting almost half an hour already without any explanation?"

"I thought about it," Sharon admitted. "I'm still thinking about it. But…"

"Yeah," I said. "But." But we were all there, anyway.

The five of us sat there in silence, uncomfortable now, for another ten minutes. The time ticked by in my head, each tick louder than the last, and finally I'd had enough.

Stubborn, I am, yes. Also curious enough to kill a dozen cats, and not really good with the patience thing. When I think about something, I have to follow it all the way through to the end.

"Hell with this." I put my mug of coffee—still undrunk, because it really was disgusting—on the floor and stood up. "I want to know what the deal is."

"What, you're just going to barge in there?" Nick looked somewhat taken aback, but Pietr had a gleam in those eyes that made me think he'd been about three seconds behind me. He liked trouble, yeah. Being in, or causing, or both, I didn't know. I had a tiny tremor of precog that I was going to find out, though.

"Yep," I said in response to Nick's question, and I marched my boots over to the door, knocked once soundly, and waited.

No answer. Not even the sound of someone shuffling around on the other side. That wasn't good.

I knocked again, and then tried the door handle, fully expecting it to be locked.

It wasn't.

My current swirled once, deep inside me, then went still. I could Translocate out of here now, if I wanted to. I could yelp for J, ask his opinion. I could...

I pushed the door open and stepped inside, hearing at least one person get up and move behind me. Nice to know someone had my back. I was betting on it being Pietr.

The door opened up into a larger room, done up like your basic office—beige carpeting and walls painted to match—and furnished with a large wooden desk with a leather chair behind it, two upholstered visitors' chairs, a bunch of framed inspirational-looking prints on the walls, and basic white blinds on the windows, two of them, on the far wall. There was one sickly looking plant I immediately wanted to rescue, and a couple of photos on the desk, facing away from us, but not much personality otherwise.

The body sprawled facedown on the floor next to the desk didn't contribute much to the room's decor, either.

## four

"Holy shit." The words came from my throat the moment they hit my brain. Maybe not the most articulate of reactions, and I don't have much of a filter, sometimes, but...hello? Dead body. A little freaked-out. I think I could be forgiven.

Sharon looked over my shoulder to see what I was reacting to, and then slid past me while I was still standing there, trying to take it all in. She knelt by the guy with careful precision and lifted his wrist, I guess to try for a pulse. I almost snorted. Not much point; even from the doorway I could tell he was dead. You didn't lie facedown that way if you were just sleeping, not even if you'd passed out. Trust me, I've seen a lot of people passed out.

"Holy shit," I said again.

There was a dead body in the office. We'd been sitting there, just talking, drinking coffee, and there had been a dead body in there all that time.

"I guess the interviews are canceled?" a voice said in my ear, and I dug an elbow into Nick's side. Not that it wasn't funny, in a sick way, but it didn't really seem...respectful. Or something, I don't know.

Did I mention the freaked-out part? Dead body. There. My current was very still, deep inside me, and I stirred it just to reassure myself that it hadn't suddenly disappeared. I didn't carry a lot of mojo around with me—why would I?—but touching it was like having a blankie or a stuffed bear; the need for comfort was a natural human instinct. I'd place even odds everyone else in the room was doing exactly the same thing. Like checking for your wallet after someone else's been robbed: maybe stupid, but almost impossible to stop yourself.

Nifty moved past us, too, nowhere near as smoothly or gently as Sharon, and that made me think maybe we should get out of the way—or at least stop standing in the doorway before someone decided to go *through* us, one way or the other. I didn't really want to get closer to the body, but the only other alternative was to go back into the waiting room, and I didn't think that would look good.

Why I cared what looked good in front of people I'd just met and wasn't sure I liked and was probably going to be competing for a job against was left unanswered.

"There's no blood," Pietr said, and I jumped. Despite thinking he was the first one behind me, I hadn't seen him until he spoke. He'd somehow faded into the blah-colored walls of the office like some kind of two-legged chameleon. How a good-looking guy can disappear from my awareness... I guess it showed how freaked-out I was.

"Wha?" My voice came back with a croak, and I cleared my throat and tried again. "What?"

"On the carpet. There's no blood."

I forced myself to ignore the fact that the body was a body, and looked again, starting with the torso—I didn't want to look at the face, not yet—and moving over the probable track he'd taken to land there. Pietr was right. No blood, no signs of violence, spilled drink or food on the desk—no sign what-soever of what had happened.

By now, all of us had moved through the doorway and into the room, although Nick and I were still hanging back. I felt I should be doing something, but I didn't know what, so I just stood there and watched.

Sharon and Nifty were turning the body over, gently, like it was going to matter to the guy now. I kept cataloging details, focusing on that so I didn't have to really see what they were doing, in case blood suddenly spurted or something. Clothing. The guy had on a nice suit, gray pinstripe, that looked more expensive than the office would suggest. He was also missing his shoes, gray dress socks visible as they turned him. That was weird. A head of dark hair, thick and curly, and I couldn't tell in this light if he was going gray or not. I looked, finally, but couldn't see much of his face, because Nifty was blocking the view. I was kind of relieved, actually. A face would make it—him—real. A real dead body.

"Should we be moving the body?" I asked. "Aren't the cops going to want it to be left alone, for investigation?"

"You going to call the cops?" Pietr sounded horrified by the idea. I stopped. Wasn't I? Weren't we? Wasn't that what you were supposed to do if you found a guy dead? I had no idea what the protocol was for this kind of thing. J would know. I reached out, instinctively, to ping him and then stopped. He'd hear "dead body" and freak, and yank me home, and that wouldn't solve anything.

"I…"

"Not me," Pietr said firmly. "Natural-born non involver, that's me. I say we back out and pretend we never saw anything." He talked scared, but he didn't move, and his gaze was sweeping the room to make sure he didn't miss something. He might not like cops, but he wasn't scared. Far from it.

"I guess we should call someone," Sharon said, but she sounded weirdly reluctant. Not scared or even unnerved, but reluctant, like a dog that didn't want to give up a bone. "The guy's definitely dead. No visible wounds, no spilled blood, but there's no pulse, no lung movement." She sounded as if she'd memorized a medical handbook on how to tell someone was dead. For all I knew, she had.

Nifty had a small mirror in his hand, holding it over the DB's face. He flipped it shut, like a compact, and put it back in his jacket pocket. Wow. I hadn't known anyone actually did that anymore, checking for breath. Did it really work? The thought distracted me for a moment, then I came slamming back. How had the guy died? How long had he been dead? Had it been while we were sitting there, and if so, oh shit, could we have done anything to save him?

That thought made me feel vaguely ill.

"I think he had a heart attack," Sharon said, although her voice was, for the first time, lacking what I'd already assumed was a customary take-charge sharpness. "Totally natural, probably instantaneous. No sign of any kind of external violence."

My throat closed up at her words, and I had to force myself to breathe normally, shards of my dream coming back like an acid flashback. External violence. Murder? I hadn't even thought...

Nifty looked as confused as I felt. "We just found him here like this. Natural reaction would be to call the paramedics first, even if he is dead, and let them deal with the cops. Right? So why not call the cops, too? What if they have questions for us?"

Sharon looked at him as though he'd just suggested she take up pole dancing. "You think the five of us, here in an unmarked office, with no reason to be here except a mysterious phone message, and a dead body just happens to be in the other office, aren't going to become the immediate persons of interest to the cops, no matter how he died? You think they're going to believe how we all ended up here on the basis of some strange phone message from god knows who, for an unspecified interview for an unnamed, unknown company none of us sent a résumé to? I don't know about you, but I don't need that shit in my life."

Nifty blinked, processed, and nodded reluctantly. Nick let out a sigh, and even Pietr seemed to agree with her logic. I obviously had a different take on the police than my companions. Then again, I'd never actually ever had any dealings with the police. So what if they asked me a few questions? I didn't have anything to hide. Then it hit me. "You guys…all lonejacks?"

They nodded.

"You're not?" Pietr moved away from me, as though I'd just admitted to having cooties. I shrugged. "Dad was lonejack. My mentor's Council. I never really thought about it." Wasn't quite true, but explaining would take too much time and energy.

The *Cosa Nostradamus* wasn't exactly one big happy family. Or we were, but there were two distinct branches of the family tree. Council was organized, focused, and monied, mostly. Not more or less law-abiding than any given lonejack, but less likely to take heat for it, I suppose. Council policed themselves: that was the point of Council. Lonejacks were on their own, and liked it that way. If my dad had been any indication, they really didn't appreciate official-type people asking questions about their private lives, even if they hadn't done anything wrong.

J and I, we ran in our own little world, I guess. He'd never pushed me to go Council, or kept me from having lonejack friends, but mostly I sort of floated between the two worlds, and never felt I belonged particularly in either one. I'd always thought of myself as child-of-a-lonejack, but would probably identify as Council if pushed. I'm not sure they'd acknowledge me, though. It hadn't ever been an issue before, but now I felt it like an ache: where would I go, if they had to take me in?

"Don't let your guard down just yet, if you were smart enough to raise it in the first place," Pietr said, breaking into my thoughts. "It wasn't a heart attack, not the way you meant, anyway." He'd somehow gone from standing against the wall to standing next to the body, and the way the others reacted I don't think they saw him move, either.

"You can tell, just by looking at him?" Sharon's voice got real cold. "You have a doctoral degree you forgot to mention?"

"Idiots." He sounded totally disgusted with the lot of us. "Can't you feel it?"

The moment he mentioned it, I understood. There was a hum in the room, something faint but unmistakable. The sound of current, simmering in the wires, normal in any modern building, yeah—except the humming was in the body, too.

Everyone carries electrical current in them: it's how our bodies work. Muscles moving, heart pumping, neurons firing, etc. Once the body dies, the electricity does, too. If you're Talent, you've got current in there, too, not just in your core-supply, but everywhere, filling your entire body. But it flits even faster than electricity when the person dies and control's released. Everyone knows that.

If current was still in the body, and the body was dead, then it meant that the current we were sensing was from an external source—and still keeping a grip on the body.

That…probably wasn't good.

"You think current killed him?" Nifty sounded less surprised or horrified than fascinated.

It happened sometimes, when a Talent overloaded, took too much current on, either by accident or ego, and it shorted out their system. Mostly it just made you nuts, frying the brain cells, but it could kill, too. Sometimes it killed everyone in the area, too, just for the sin of being too close. I was suddenly really glad I hadn't gotten close, and from the look on Nifty's face, he was wishing he were another ten feet or more away. Sharon didn't seem to be bothered at all, still kneeling by the body, her skirt folded neatly under her knees.

"But overrush shouldn't still be lingering," she said. "It should fade once the final flare-out happens, not hold on to him."

A damned good point. I didn't think I wanted to hear Pietr's response.

"I think someone used current to kill him," he said anyway, and that stopped everything cold. Even Sharon blanched.

I *knew* I didn't want to hear it.

"You think one of us did it?" Nifty asked, his deep voice a little tight and rising. "But we were all there, together—hell, Sharon and I arrived at the same time, first, and the rest of you…"

Nick started to babble. "We don't know anything about each other. This could be a setup—"

"Stop it!" Sharon's voice cut through Nick's stream of denial like forged steel, cold and hard. "None of us did anything."

"And you know that how?"

"I know."

"How?" Pietr was like a damn terrier with a bit of meat; he wasn't going to let go, even standing over a dead body.

"I just do, all right?" Our cool blonde was pissed, and not in the mood for being questioned. I got the feeling she was like that a lot. "I could tell if any of you were lying, or trying to keep something from us. It's what I do. So just shut up with the paranoia. None of us killed this guy."

"Venec."

"What?" That distracted her from her pissiness, at least a little.

Nifty had gotten up and gone around to the desk. "His name's Venec, Ben Venec. Or at least, he's reading a newspaper that was mailed to a Mister Benjamin Venec at this address." Nifty pointed a finger down at the *New York Times* folded on the desk, but didn't touch it. "There's nothing else here. This guy wasn't using the desk." He took a piece of tissue out of his pocket and used it to pull open the drawer. "Nothing in here, either. Definitely not using the desk. That's weird. People usually dump stuff into the desk drawers first off, even before they bring in plants or photos."

By now, Sharon had gotten up and moved away from the body, smoothing her skirt and looking like she was about to start issuing orders again. Something got me walking across the carpet the three feet it took to take her place.

"What are you doing?" Nick asked, watching me.

I put my palm over the guy's chest, still not looking at his face—this was easier if I didn't think about him as a person.

"Asking the current," I said, already sinking into my core and not really aware of anything else, other than the idea that this wasn't a very good idea. I'd done this sort of scrying before, but only with people I knew, or things that belonged to them. The last time I'd done it, in fact, had been with tools that belonged to my dad, just after he'd been killed, which was why I'd thought of it. Death just seemed to call out for a final scrying.

*Tell me something,* I whispered to the hum of current wrapped around this guy's chest. *Tell me something about why you're there. Tell me why I dreamed of death, again.*

That last bit slipped in, but I let it go rather than worrying. Sometimes I'd get something, maybe detailed, maybe vague. More often I wouldn't get anything. In light of the past twenty-four hours, what I got this time really shouldn't have surprised me.

I got tossed on my ass, back into the side of the desk.

"Motherf— Ow!" I don't swear much, but it felt warranted. That *hurt*.

"You all right?"

"What happened?

"Holy hell, girl, what did you do?"

The voices broke out over my head, surprised and concerned, in varying registers. "I didn't do a damn thing," I said, as soon as the birds stopped tweeting in circles around my head. It took a second, and then something slammed into my head, like the tail end of an aftershock. "Damn. Whatever's wrapped itself around that guy, I've felt it before."

"What? When?"

I had to think for a second, then the memory connected with something else, and I had it. "Last night. I tried to scry, get some detail on this interview, and got kicked back, hard."

Nifty knelt beside me, not touching me. "Is it the same signature?"

I had to think about that, too. Signature's the specific feel/taste/sound of current. Wild current's like springwater— fresh and pretty much signatureless. Canned current, the stuff that comes out of electrical wiring, has a specific and easily recognizable signature. Core-current? J's I could recognize a mile and a millimeter away. Some unknown guy? Tougher. Maybe impossible. But if it was the same, it meant that the killer had been in my brain before I even got here. It meant the killer *knew* me.

I went cold, locking down everything except the question at hand.

"Nothing I could recognize," I said, finally. "It was sharp, like a lightning bolt, but if it was wild, it was a while ago." There was a flavor to it, or more like a lack of flavor, like flavor had been stripped out of it. But I didn't know how to say that without sounding like a crackpot, or that the hit to my head had been worse than it looked.

Nifty was working his jaw like he had a hard thought between his molars, and my gaze, untethered from anything my brain was doing, watched it in fascination.

"Someone…one of us did this?" Sharon sounded as though it was something unthinkable, something…obscene. As though somehow being Talent made you immune from the urge to kill.

I wished that were true. I knew all too well that it wasn't.

"It came from through here," Nick said. He was looking up at the ventilation system, holding a hand up like he was trying to coax something out of it. Which he was, actually. The arm moved, tracing a path down through the wall. "There's wiring here that's not normal. You'd expect to see it in a modern high-rise, not this place. Too jazzed, too much power. Like laying in a midnight snack of current." He saw us all staring at him, and shrugged those skinny shoulders with a sort of rueful embarrassment. "I spent a summer working as a runner at a construction copyshop. I stared at a lot of blueprints, got a feel for wiring."

"So whoever it was, they had to have planned this." My brain was totally focused now, no hesitations or freaked-out gibbering. For the first time in months, I felt that I had, if not a direction, then at least a path underfoot. "Or at least knew that the wiring was there. Question is, was this guy the actual target? Or was someone just trying out the available power, and he was in the wrong place at the right time?"

"No." Pietr's voice was coming from the door, this time. How the hell did he do that? "The question is—why the hell are we still here, poking around trying to figure out who and why? What the hell does it have to do with us, other than we've now put our fingerprints all over the room for the cops to find?"

That was a damn good question.

"I'm not in the system," Nick said, shrugging.

"I am," Sharon said. "Standard security profile for some of the clients my firm works with. And having my profile flagged for a suspicious death would not be good for my career, since it looks like this job's not going to pan out to anything."

"So why are you still here?" Nifty asked, not quite getting up in her face, but close to it: he was challenging her to leave, to abandon us. And when the hell, I wondered, did we become "us"?

"Because…" Sharon let the sentence trail off, obviously trying to put her thoughts into some kind of order before speaking them.

"Because we're curious," I said, jumping in. "We don't give a damn about this guy, particularly. We don't know who he is, and we've got every reason to be pissed off and scared. But we want to know *why*, more."

"That's insane." Nifty sounded like I'd just insulted his mother.

"Sure, but you got another reason for standing there with a dead guy's day planner in your hand?"

Nifty looked down, and put the book back on the desk as though it was about to bite him. I'd made my point, though, and I could practically see his hackles go down.

"So what now, genius," Sharon asked, but not pissed-sounding, more like she really did wonder what I was going to suggest.

So did I.

"Now you congratulate yourselves on a successful job interview."

Sharon shrieked. So did Nifty, in a deeper but no less shrieky voice. Nick jumped back a full foot, and sparks of current appeared in his hands, deep blue and arcing all over his fingers. And Pietr, I swear to god, I was looking right at him and I *saw* him fade out of sight this time.

They all seemed like reasonable things to do, when a dead body sits up and starts talking to you.

"Stand down, people." A door none of us noticed before slid open and another guy walked in. He was tall, taller even than Nifty, if half his mass, with orange-red hair tied back in a ponytail. The color looked natural, and a guy wearing four-hundred-dollar boots probably isn't the sort to do Day-Glo dye jobs anyway. Flame-head walked past where Pietr had just been and offered a hand to our dead body. The DB took it, hauling himself to his feet.

They didn't look a thing alike: flame-head was tall and skinny, and DB was squared-off and dark, but they stood together like bookends, totally unconscious of how they mirrored each other. My fifth-grade dance teacher used to try to hammer that kind of unconscious grace into us, mostly with abject failure.

I also noted now that DB was seriously hot. Not good-looking, the way Pietr was, or even Nifty's dark, corn-fed handsome, but *hot*.

"How did you create the illusion you were dead?" Sharon demanded. "You had no pulse, no breath, no nothing!"

Flame turned to DB and smirked. "I told you I could do it."

"And you were right," DB said easily. "Get over it. Gloating's bad for your digestion."

That voice. That was the same voice I had heard on the answering machine.

"What the hell is going on here?" Nifty demanded, his body pulling up so he looked the way he must've to the guys who'd faced him across the scrimmage line: big, bad, and needing to hit something, hard. "Who the hell are you people?"

"You're the guy who called," Pietr said, looking at DB. "I recognize your voice."

I wanted to say *me, too,* but I think the shock had seized up my vocal cords, because I couldn't say a thing. Probably just as well; standing up and breathing, DB was the yummy, intense sort I really like, and I'd probably have embarrassed myself if I had been able to say anything. Flame wasn't quite as yummy, but when you looked at him magically, oh wow. He had an inner core that seriously radiated, like…

The current that had knocked me sideways. It felt familiar because it was—it *was* the same signature as the current that shattered my scrying crystal last night.

Son of a spavined bitch. They had damn well better hire me. These bastards *owed* me.

"You wanted people who didn't freak when faced with freakiness," Nick said, as if he'd just figured out the last missing piece of a puzzle. "Whose first thought wasn't to run, but to look."

"And you all passed, with flying colors," Flame said. He seemed to be the spokesperson of the two, stepping forward, literally, and taking the floor. "Even in the face of…unfortunate circumstances, all of you stepped forward and used your respective skills to observe and gather details, integrating information as it was brought forward rather than choosing a conclusion and then sticking to it no matter what." Flame smiled at us, a wide, approving smile that looked false but somehow felt real. "You all worked together, as a team, despite having no reason to do so. Not a prima donna among the bunch."

"Which means what?" Sharon asked, her hands fisted on her hips, like she was going to walk out if she didn't get answers, stat. Hah. Flame's definition of a prima donna was clearly different from mine.

"It means you're hired," DB said, his expression almost— not quite, but almost—looking pleased about the prospect. "All of you."

There was a slight popping noise, and four more chairs appeared in the office, distributed neatly around the desk. Someone was showing off. From the look DB shot his... partner? I was guessing it was Flame.

"Please," he was saying, gesturing to the chairs. "Sit. I will explain."

"That would be nice," Nick said, sitting in one of the chairs and leaning back in it as though he had all the time in the world. "Starting with who the hell you are."

Pietr stuck to his position against the wall, but the rest of us took the offered chairs, mainly because, at least for me, my knees were still wobbly. DB righted the overturned leather desk chair and sat in it, effectively reclaiming the desk as his territory, while Flame rested his right hip against the edge of the desk and gazed at us as though he was about to start a lecture.

"Ah. Where to start. At the beginning, yes, Ben, I know," he said before DB could say anything. I was right, they were partners—not sexual, not unless I was reading them all wrong, and I didn't do that very often. But business partners, in whatever this was, yes.

"My name is Ian Stosser." He waited, like we were supposed to have heard of him. "Ah. My partner here, whom you have already met under…awkward circumstances, is Benjamin Venec."

Venec nodded once at us, his gaze sweeping restlessly from face to face. It wasn't boredom but evaluation; I knew, having used the same sweep myself more than once. The look of a people-watcher. Stosser was the talker, Venec the looker. One prodded, the other collated responses. Good teamwork. Good cop/bad cop. Or whatever they were.

"Several years ago, there was an incident in Seattle. The Madeline case." Stosser paused, probably for dramatic effect. "Do any of you remember it?"

I did. Nifty shook his head, and so did Pietr and Sharon. Nick was the only one who spoke up.

"The girl who was raped and murdered. They never found the killer. She was *Cosa*," he said to the others. "Sixteen, still in mentorship."

That meant that she was still a kid, supposed to be protected, taken care of, not just by her mentor but by every adult Talent. That's the theory, anyway.

"She was killed by strangulation, but the coroner was never able to say exactly how, because there wasn't any of the usual marks or indications in the autopsy. There were rumblings, maybe she'd been killed by someone within the *Cosa*. That someone had used current to subdue and kill her. Madeline's mentor offered a huge reward, but nobody ever came forward."

I knew about the case because Madeline and her mentor had been Council. J had been part of the investigating team flown out to look into the alibis of a couple of the guys they suspected. Nothing had ever been proven, nothing had ever been done. He'd come home and hugged me really tight, and never said a word about it after that.

"That's right. A dead end, totally untraceable, unprovable... Then." Stosser started pacing, forcing us to follow his movements. "But it got us, Ben and me, to thinking. Why was it untraceable? We all know how to detect current—it's one of the first things we're taught in mentorship. We gather it, manipulate it, direct it, imprint it... A current-signature is like a fingerprint, and therefore, like a fingerprint, it should lead you back to the owner, if you only know how. They had suspects, and my contacts tell me that the signature connected to one of them. So why couldn't they do that, why couldn't they make that connection for Madeline?"

"Because nobody could agree on the validity of the identification, because there were too many personal conflicts...and not everyone agreed on the validity of the identification, leaving enough doubt that they couldn't do anything about it." I hadn't learned about that from J—I'd done some digging myself, after. All this had been just after Zaki had been killed, and murder was a lot on my mind.

"Right." Stosser gave me a look of approval, professor to bright student. "But what if...a large what-if, but work with me here, what if there was someone who could and would do the work, tracking down the evidence and building a case based only on the evidence...totally unbiased by any other allegiance than a dedication to the facts...to an insatiable desire to know What Happened?"

I could hear the capitalization in his voice, even before he made quote signs with his hands around those last two words.

"What if there was a place that people could turn to, for crimes committed outside the abilities of the Null police force and court system—crimes by Talent against Talent?"

His comment cut so close to my own pain that I was literally breathless for an endless second.

"There isn't," Sharon said, her I-know-everything voice back. That tone was already starting to irk me, even though I knew she was right. "Council won't trust anything not Council, and lonejacks…"

"Lonejacks won't trust anyone," Nifty said.

"That has been true, traditionally," DB said, and I really needed to stop thinking of him like that, since he wasn't actually dead anymore. "But traditionally, Talent did not attack Talent, either. The Madeline case was high profile, but even that didn't get much chatter. So what you don't know is that there have been others…and the numbers are growing."

I felt a chill in my spine. Zaki had been one of those numbers, killed by another Talent. I hadn't realized… I had always thought he was an aberration, a tragic fluke. Talent killing Talent…there weren't that many of us to begin with; the lines of community had always kept us safe from each other. What had changed?

"The world is changing. We're changing…" Stosser did that dramatic pause thing again, while I reminded myself that there was no way he could have been reading my mind, that not even the purest Talent could do that without permission. "And we need to change other things in order to keep up. Including how we react to those changes."

"And you want to be part of that change," Pietr said, sounding intrigued despite himself. "How?"

"Puppy."

"What?" I couldn't have been the only one hearing that wrong.

"P-U-P-I." DB—Venec—spelled it out. "Private, Unaffiliated, Paranormal Investigations. The name was Ian's idea—" he shot his partner a rueful glance "—but it has the benefit of being easily remembered. A team of trained forensic Talents, shorn of their normal affiliations of lonejack or Council, answerable only to the evidence, the truth. A handpicked group of investigators who don't care why, only how, and who. A group who can deliver evidence to be used to prosecute and punish Talent who think they can escape detection by ordinary methods."

"And you want to hire...us." Pietr's voice was carefully noncommittal.

"Any of you can get up and walk out at any time," Stosser said, coming to rest by his partner's side, hands clasped behind his back as though to keep them from waving about while he talked. "There's nothing keeping you here against your will. We chose your names not by random chance, but because each and every one of you met our criteria for intelligence, independence, determination, curiosity, and a certain...dogged stubbornness."

Nifty coughed deep in his throat, like a strangled laugh, and I had to grin in self-recognition. All the traits J occasionally despaired of, suddenly touted as employable virtues. That was funny.

"You're free to walk," Venec said. "But none of you will. The fact that you made it this far, through all of our tests, means that you are perfect for this challenge...and the job is perfect for you."

He smiled then, an arrogant, challenging smile, and a shiver ran through me that had nothing whatsoever to do with the ghoulishness of what we'd been discussing. He was yummy, yeah, and intense...and offering me what just might be the job of a lifetime.

This was either going to be a clusterfuck of monumental proportions...or a whole lot of fun.

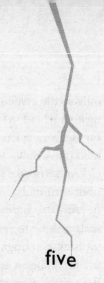

five

My mentor took the news about as well as I'd expected.

"Absolutely not! Impossible! You need a real job, not this...irresponsible pipe dream! Stosser—bah, Ian Stosser has always been a troublemaker, and this partner of his, this Ben Venec...I've never heard of him. Who is he? What are his credentials? Where is their funding coming from?"

J had been ranting for almost an hour now, ever since I Translocated into his Beacon Hill apartment and told him the results of the afternoon's meeting. Periodically I used a strand of current to check his blood pressure, an intimacy he allowed me only because he was too distracted to slap the tendril away, and then went back to my own thoughts. Eventually he would run down, and we could have a reasonable discussion.

Not that it mattered. I had already made up my mind.

It took another ten minutes, but finally my mentor dropped into his chair and stared gloomily across the room at me. I lifted my head up from the paperwork I'd been flipping through, and met his gaze evenly.

"And you didn't hear a word I said, did you?" he asked.

"I heard every syllable," I said in the same measured, reasonable tone he was using now. "I even agreed with some of them."

"But you disagree with the overall conclusion."

I scratched the tip of my nose and tossed the folder of papers onto the end table. The salary they were offering was passing-decent, the benefits not worth mentioning, and none of it mattered, really. None of it had since The Guys, as I'd started thinking of them, had given us the pitch.

"Joseph. You know they're right. About the need for this—for unbiased investigators for the *Cosa*—and about how very good I'd be at it."

J knew what I was talking about, and I knew that he really didn't want to think about that. His expression didn't change, but he shifted in his chair, just enough to let me know he was uncomfortable.

"That was different," he said, not meeting my gaze.

"Of course it was," I agreed. "I was just a kid looking to see what had happened to her dad, after he left me a mysterious letter and then disappeared. All I did was poke around into a few dark holes—" including one that belonged to a loan-sharking cave dragon "—and ask a few questions, and use current to trace down the clue that led to the guy who killed my father…"

I played dirty then. "And then I couldn't do anything." I paused, letting that statement drill down a little. "There was no one to go to with what I knew, then. Not even you could do anything. I had no evidence, nothing that could be used in an ordinary court of law, and no way to give Zaki justice. He wasn't Council, so Council wouldn't get involved. There was no way to get closure, unless I was willing to do the deed myself."

Zaki hadn't been much of a dad, but he'd been a good

person. He didn't deserve to get killed over a woman he hadn't even touched. And he would have hated me having blood on my hands, especially in his name. That, not legalities, not any sense of civilized behavior, had been all that had stayed me. But J never needed to know that, if he hadn't twigged already.

"Child, you are a dirty pool player."

"Equal parts nature and nurture," I said in reply, and it was true. I might be the child of drifters and grifters, but J hadn't gotten to where he had in his career by always playing by the strict interpretation of the rules. Always legit, sure, but maybe not always kosher. There was no way I was going to grow up a delicate, idealistic flower, under those conditions.

J had a crease between his eyebrows, meaning that a headache was creeping down from his scalp. I didn't want to cause the old man any worry—I never wanted him to worry about me ever—but I couldn't back down. Not about this.

Meanwhile, I had my own forehead-crease forming. There was something niggling at the back of my brain, about this job. Not a bad thing, just a thing I needed to remember, or a connection I needed to make. If I left it alone, it would come crawling out on its own.

"Dirty pool," J said again, then leaned back in the chair, letting his legs sprawl in front of him. Rupe appeared from wherever he'd been hiding during the rant and settled his shaggy body on the carpet next to J's chair. "You really think that this…wannabe investigational unit can accomplish anything? Do you think they will make a difference?"

"We won't know unless we try." And then I played even dirtier. "Would you have been able to use us, something like this, out in Seattle?"

I didn't have to say anything more; part of loving someone is knowing what still bothers them. He sighed, and all the argument went out of him, just like that. He reached down to pet Rupe's head. "I hate to say it, and when I say hate I do mean hatred, but…yes. We could have, and by god, we *would* have, if I had anything to say about the matter."

J was a stickler for honesty, even when it hurt.

"You are correct, Bonita. This may be exactly what the *Cosa* needs…and, more to my regret, it may be exactly what *you* need."

It wasn't a paternal blessing, exactly, but it would do.

The question of my employment settled for the moment, J gathered all the paperwork from me and spent about an hour explaining it all, in excruciating detail. His grudging approval of their having health insurance and a 401(k) set up would have been funny if it wasn't all so surreal, and I signed in the places he marked without really paying much attention. The paycheck had suddenly—and probably stupidly—become secondary to me. I was never going to make a good mercenary.

The initial argument, followed by what seemed like endless paperwork, took so much out of us that I vetoed his cooking, and we ended up doing take-away Thai and beer instead. J sometimes forgets he isn't fifty anymore.

We had a few more rounds of "do you think this is a good idea" over the last of the six-pack, and I went back to New York under his current, a little before midnight. All this Trans-locating back and forth between Boston and New York was starting to make my neck ache. Next time, I thought as I crawled into bed, I was going to take the Chinatown bus. Or, considering I now had a paying job, maybe I'd go crazy and take Greyhound. Or hey, Amtrak! Or maybe, once I got an apartment, I could drag J down here for dinner, for a change. I hadn't cooked for anyone in a long time….

That thought consoled me as I put my head on the pillow

and was out almost before my eyes were closed. I slept well, no dreams intruding, so the wake-up call at 6:00 a.m. was a rude shock. I rolled over, snagged the receiver, grunted something into the phone. and then dropped it back into the cradle. "Oh god," I moaned, and then rolled out of bed for what I supposed would be my first day at work.

Supposed, because at the end of the interview yesterday, they'd just handed us the papers, and told us to think it over, and they'd either see us today, or not.

I got out of the shower and stood in front of the closet, hesitating over what to wear. For some reason, a perfectly office-appropriate slim blue skirt and white blouse didn't feel right. I dithered for a while, then finally opted for a V-neck sweater the same shade of red as my hair, and black pants with subdued buckles and loops over a pair of heeled black half boots. Not quite my stompy boots, but they'd do for confidence. You couldn't be wimpy, wearing boots.

The subway was packed with people going off to their jobs, some of them slow-eyed and grumpy, others bopping along to their music, or nose-deep in newspapers or magazines. I didn't even bother to try to get a seat, just grabbed a handrail and concentrated on not focusing on the hum of current running through the subway, for fear of accidentally damaging someone's electronics. I was used to ignoring the hum of electronics in the dorm, but that was familiar ground…hopefully in a few weeks, this would be, too.

I got out at my stop, along with a dozen other people, and wasn't all that surprised to see Nick loitering outside the building when I walked up. I'd figured he'd take the offer, too. He was wearing dark blue jeans and a cotton sweater over it, brown like his eyes, and he looked less scrawny than he had on Tuesday. Weird.

"I did some looky-loo on our bosses," he said, without even a good morning. "Ian Stosser's Council, like you. Major hotshot. Sat on the Council itself, out in Chicago."

I'd known that already, thanks to J's ranting. See, there's Council, and then there's *Council*. They're split into regions and each Council Board—also less formally known as Mage Council, from waybackwhen days—handles the stuff that comes up in their region. Each one's independent, and while a couple of Councils can get together to do something specific, nobody's got more say than the other, and you don't get say over anything that happens outside your region. It's all pretty strict, and goes on the philosophy that if there's trouble, Talent will find it, fling it, and generally make it worse, if left to their own devices. J hadn't been very complimentary on Stosser's attitude or his ideas during his rant last night, but he'd been forced to admit that the man got things done, mainly by a combination of hard-nosed arrogance and sheer slippery charm.

"He got kicked out of Chicago for something nobody's talking about," Nick went on. "Which means it was probably seriously embarrassing to someone, else the gossip would be everywhere."

"Several someones, is what I heard," I agreed. "My mentor knows people who know people, and even they don't know what happened. But Stosser wasn't kicked out. He left under his own power. That means he won, whatever it was." If he had lost, he'd have been buried. Powerwise, not literally, far as I knew, although there was that risk, too. That was how it worked, at those levels.

"Huh. Means he's got smarts as well as power, probably. Reason enough to throw in with him," Nick said. "Even if he is Council."

"Venec isn't," I said, trying to ignore the slam on the Council. Wasn't anything to me, was it?

"Nope, he's pure lonejack. Quiet, though. Wherever he's been, it was behind the scenes. Don't know how those two hooked up. Every source I checked knew Venec's name, but nobody had anything to say, good or bad."

"He's the dangerous one," Pietr said, making us both jump.

"How the hell do you *do* that?" I demanded, more than a little irritable. "Damned Retriever, that's what you are."

"Not really," Pietr said. "Don't you want to know why he's dangerous?"

"No." I did, of course I did. But be damned if I'd give him the satisfaction, after he made me jump like that. His gray gaze lingered on me, solemn as a judge, and I couldn't read a damn thing that might be going on inside.

Unlike Nick, seeing Nifty come around the corner was a surprise. He'd said he needed a job, yeah, but I just hadn't gotten a joining-up kind of vibe from the former athlete.

"Are you people going in, or are you waiting for the bagel fairy to come by and drop off a pump and a schmear?"

Nick and Pietr looked blankly at Nifty, like he'd just spoken Swahili or something. I just shook my head, amused.

"You totally stole that line from someone else," I accused him, following the boys into the foyer, where the same invisible someone buzzed us in the moment we approached the door. I listened, but still couldn't pick up any hint of current in use, which just made me more determined to track it down as soon as I had a spare moment.

"My coach," he admitted, holding the door for me. "I don't even know what a pump is. I just hope it's not rude."

"Pumpernickel. A kind of bread. Or bagel, in that case. You haven't been in New York long, have you?" If he was a native East Coaster, I'd eat J's favorite hat.

"Nope. I was in Detroit, talking to someone about another

job, when I got the message. I guess I'm going to have to find a place to live…you know of anywhere?"

"Soon as I find something, I'll let you know." The hotel was nice for a short term, but I needed to find an apartment. Something I paid for, not J, and that was going to be another argument. Or maybe not. We'd see. Part of the directed, non-mercenary vibe I was grooving on right now included less of a need to be totally independent. NYC was *expensive*.

The office door now had a small, nicely discreet copper-plate sign on it: PUPI Inc.

"Woof," Nick said, half joking.

"Woof-woof," Nifty echoed, an octave deeper, as though he had to prove he was the bigger dog. Like there was any doubt of that, physically at least. Save me from boys and their egos….

"That makes me the bitch, and don't you forget it." I really hoped Sharon was going to take up the job offer, too. Much as being surrounded by males could be fun, it also got boring after a while, and being the only female in the pack was not going to be a laugh riot on bad days. The vibe I'd gotten off Sharon yesterday was that she might be a control freak know-it-all, but she wasn't going to be a tight-ass about it. We'd be fine.

I hoped. I really, really hoped. I liked having female friends, but my college buds were scattered to the winds of employment now, and without e-mail or a cell phone, it was going to be tough to keep up with them. Knowing that it was inevitable didn't make the knowledge any less painful, so I tried not to linger on it, instead looking forward. New job. New friends. New—

"Wow."

Nifty had gone in through the office door first, and stopped so suddenly I almost broke my nose against his back. "Hello? What? Brick wall, do you mind moving?"

"Oh, sorry." He went all the way into the office, and I heard Nick behind me say something rude when he ran into my back as I stopped dead, too.

"Sorry," I muttered in turn, and moved aside. Nick, still pissed, didn't even look, just walked in…and then stopped dead.

"Ah, glad you're here." Stosser was sitting on a new, damned comfy-looking chocolate-brown sofa, looking up at us over a clipboard on his lap. His orange-red hair was tied back in a braid, and he was dressed in black jeans and a black pullover, making him look even more like some kind of satanic candle. "Try to be prompt in the future. We have a lot to hammer into your heads and not a lot of time to do it in."

"Good morning to you, too," Nick muttered, sounding offended, and not just because we'd done a three-body pileup in front of the boss.

"Right. Good morning. Sorry." Stosser's reportedly famous charm made a brief appearance, and then he turned it off. "You all dressed appropriately, good. Come with me."

He stood up and walked through the now totally redecorated space that had blown our minds for a moment, clearly expecting us to follow. The half-assed kitchenette of yesterday was now a full beverage station, with a brand-new coffeemaker, a hot-water dispenser, a wet-sink, and an open cabinet filled with plain white mugs and boxes of really nice teas and coffees. There was also a larger refrigerator that, I was guessing, had real cream in it now. The old rental-style waiting room furniture had been replaced with the brown sofa and a matching loveseat over a dark cream carpet where there'd been linoleum before. A bookcase took up the entire length of the wall, next to the door into the inner office, and was filled with what looked like textbooks. The room seemed larger now, somehow, although I knew that it had to be an optical illusion. Right?

Obviously, the office design fairies had been through overnight. J's concerns about them not having enough money to back up their paycheck promises seemed less likely now. Unless, of course, they were putting all the money into set-dressing…

"Are you four coming, or not?" Stosser asked over his shoulder, and walked through the inner door.

We were.

It was easier to accept the transformation of the inside office, but only because we were all a little numb at this point. Instead of the cheap mock-executive layout, the room was now dominated by a dark wood table, oval shaped, with nine conference chairs placed around it. The walls were covered with more bookcases, filled with more textbooks, and I had a sudden thought that I'd walked right back into college. It wasn't a good thought. I knew we were going to need training, but I could do without the reading assignments.

There wasn't anyone else in the room, and Stosser didn't stop, either, walking across the room and reaching for a sliding door I was embarrassed to realize I hadn't noticed before.

Or maybe it hadn't been there before to notice. Current can't bend time or space, but if you've got enough money, enough mojo, or enough people working hard, you can do a lot of internal renovations. Evidence to date was pointing to Stosser and Venec having major mojo and money, both.

A hallway, painted a flat white with a neutral pale green carpet, led to three doors on the left-hand side, and a blank wall on the right. I figured at this point they had put at least two of the offices on this floor under lease, a long enough term lease to allow them to connect doors. No wonder they hadn't taken space farther downtown; even if the Guys were made of money, this still had to be taking a major crunch out of their funds.

We turned at the first anonymous door and went in.

"About time you got here."

The room was likewise flat white, with one window, the shade drawn, and more of the green carpet. Sharon was sitting at a small conference table, about large enough to sit five comfortably, and all seven of us if we squeezed. DB—all right, Venec—was there with her, still looking as sleepy-bored as he had yesterday. I guess we were all on board, then. Even dressed down in black slacks and a plain white shirt, Sharon still looked classier than anyone else in the room. Some people had it; some didn't. She did. At least I could enjoy looking, since I didn't get any vibes she'd be interested in me, even if I hadn't gotten the lecture last night from J, over his second beer, about not dating in the workplace.

As if I didn't know that already. Sometimes he really did forget I wasn't fourteen anymore.

"I wish we had time to ease you into things, allow for a gradual learning curve. But we don't. You all have a lot to learn, and fast. We either sink or swim from the word go, and we are determined to swim." Venec was up and moving this time, while Stosser took one of the empty chairs around the table, and we followed suit. My boots kicked the table with a solid thunk, and I flinched, but nobody else seemed to notice. I made sure my soles were planted firmly on the green carpet, where they couldn't make any more noise.

"I'm glad that you all decided to join us—not surprised, but pleased. Knowing you as well as we do, I'm sure you all did your due diligence the moment you left yesterday, and have determined that the majority of those who know us are convinced that we're lunatics. How dangerous a lunatic seems to still be open for debate."

It was funny, but nobody laughed. Stosser seemed to have gotten all the showboat comic timing of the pair.

"Make no mistake," Venec went on, fixing that dark gaze on each of us in turn. "We are not lunatics. But we have the potential to be quite dangerous. Not to each other, and not to the *Cosa* as a whole, but to individuals within the community. To those who have had a stake in upholding the status quo, in remaining out of the light, beyond any official notice or censure. And there will be some who do not want that to happen."

Venec talked like J did, not so much with the big words and flourishes Stosser used, but a quiet deliberation, knowing exactly what each word meant and how best to use it. Stosser was the showboat, the ringmaster. Venec… I didn't know what Venec was, yet. But I thought, with the part of me that thought like my mentor, that it might be smart to watch Venec's hands whenever Stosser was talking.

"What he's trying to say," Stosser interjected, "is that the *Cosa* as a whole is not on board with what we're trying to do— particularly the lonejack community. Although getting them all to agree that they disagree with us is…a slow process."

There were several snorts at that. What made lonejacks lonejacks was an inability to play well with each other. It made sense that they'd resist anyone policing them.

"What they don't understand is that we're not here to police them."

I started guiltily, then decided it was sheer coincidence, not Stosser somehow reading my mind or, god forbid, me using my thinking-out-loud voice.

"We are not here to enforce laws, or interpret them, or pass judgment in any way, shape or form." Venec picked up the narrative again. "We will investigate, and report our findings to all concerned, evenly and without bias. If you have an agenda, dump it on the table now. If you can't…get out."

There was a short silence, and both of the Guys watched us carefully. Convinced that nobody was leaving, Venec went on. "The lonejacks will, as always, make up their minds on an individual basis—"

Nick snorted, and Sharon almost smiled, and I sensed an inside joke I wasn't privy to. Venec ignored them, and kept talking.

"While not actively opposing us, the Council has formally renounced our organization. This is what we are up against: They will not demand that their members comply with any requests we make, nor will they be held by anything we discover. We have, in fact, been told that the Eastern and South Councils have refused to allow us access to…pretty much anything they can control, up to and including their members. The Midwest Council hasn't ruled in or out yet, nor has California."

Midwest—which meant Chicago for all intents and purposes—was the closest to lonejacks Council ever got: they were pretty rough and ready, and seriously cranky about their independence. California? The San Diego Council never said anything before they had to. I bet a lot of them remembered the Madeline case, too.

Stosser's turn. "We've been dubbed CSI wannabes." His pale skin flushed a little, but his voice remained steady. "It's a fair, if unkindly meant, assessment—*Cosa* crimes, as committed by *Cosa* members, investigated by *Cosa* members."

Nick raised his hand then, as though we were back in grade school, and I swear his nose twitched. "Does that include the fatae, too?"

Oh, good question. Nicky was a couple of steps ahead of me, damn it. I should have been on that already. Not that it was a competition…but it felt like it. First day on the job, got to prove you're the brightest and the bestest.

"For now…we're focusing on the human component. The fatae have long dealt with their own problems, without asking us for help."

Stosser's dry response was an understatement. The East Coast had probably the largest population of *Cosa*-cousins, the nonhuman magicals, but only a few of the more human-shaped breeds spent much time mixing. Manhattan was different in that regard but there was probably still the same "you to yours, we to ours" mentality that the *Cosa* specialized in.

"If the fatae come to us, we will offer our services equally, without prejudice or bias. Again, if you have a problem with that…"

Sharon shifted slightly, and Nick had a vaguely constipated look on his face, but nobody moved.

"Shune. You have a problem?"

Nick shook his head. "No sir."

Venec narrowed his eyes, and tilted his head just slightly to the left. "You sure about that?"

"I just… I've never met a fatae." Nick sounded like a scolded six-year-old. "That I know, anyway."

Venec laughed, maybe the first unscripted thing he'd done since we walked into the office yesterday, and my reaction was totally, overwhelmingly visceral. I could resist a hot bod, or a nice smile, or even a good line, but damn, I was a sucker for a real, rich laugh, and Benjamin Venec had one that should have been illegal. Damn.

"Don't worry about it. You'll be just as jaded as everyone else in a few weeks."

Then he was back to hard-ass drill instructor, and I could breathe again.

"Now you know the deal. Expect resistance, not acceptance. People won't want to talk to you, they're not going to help you out, and no matter how much the client says they want the truth, nobody's going to thank you for anything, especially if you tell them something they don't want to hear.

"But you will be telling them the facts as discerned from the available evidence, nothing more or less, and that is your sole concern."

He paused, then sat on the last unused stool and set his hands flat on the white tabletop. "And now we will begin to teach you *how*."

I didn't know it then, but even as we were getting rolling, so were others.

"Ian Stosser is a sick man."

A scoffing noise from one of her companions made the speaker shake her head, shoulder-length auburn curls trembling with the movement. "I know what I am talking about, Michael. Brilliant, perhaps, I would not deny that claim, or that he probably, somewhere in his head, means well. But Ian is mentally unstable, and totally incapable of considering the cost of this mad plan of his. The cost to others individually, and the *Cosa* as a whole. He has never shown any regard for the lives of those around him, lives he would risk destroying for his Cause.

"He cannot be allowed to continue. It is not safe to allow him to continue."

"Oh come on, now," the scoffer chided her gently. "Don't you think that's just a bit…overly dramatic?"

The woman leaned toward him, her entire body conveying a sort of desperate conviction, her gaze including the others so that they too leaned in, making sure not to miss what she had to say.

"Dramatic only to make my point. I would not be here, none of us would, if it wasn't urgent. You know that. That's why you're here, isn't it, all of you? Not just to humor me—but because you know it's not right."

There were five people seated around the table, three men and two women somewhere between thirty and fifty; to all outward appearances a group of friends meeting for drinks at a fashionable hot spot after work. The buzz of the crowd around them, sliding up to the bar, or waiting for their table, was the perfect mask for their conversation.

None of them denied her claim. None agreed with it, either, although the other woman nodded her head thoughtfully. They all knew Ian.

The first woman went on, selling her position. "I've kept my mouth shut until now. I've not interfered with Council decisions even when I thought they were dangerously misguided. But this… Ian's gone too far now. All indications are that he's gathering his tools even as we speak, and despite what he may say—despite what he may even believe!—nothing good will come of this. Nothing."

She might have been desperate, but her words carried a sound conviction to them, the undertone of authority almost impossible to deny.

"What would you have us do?" a second man asked, raising his now empty glass over his shoulder to signal for a waitress to bring a refill.

Her own glass was still half-full: she had been too busy talking to do more than taste the contents. "Help me stop him. However and with whatever it takes. For our safety—and his own."

## six

"Focus. Stay focused...."

"I *am* focused!" Or I would be if Nifty would stop hovering over me like a huge, dark-winged moth on steroids. "Back off, big guy. You're supposed to be helping, not pestering."

Trying to ignore my partner's looming presence—no easy thing considering the sheer bulk of him—I returned my attention to the pattern on the paper in front of me.

I could do this. I knew I could. It was easy, once you knew the steps, and the steps had been hammered into us for two weeks now. I could do it.

When Stosser had told us, that first day, that we were going to learn, I'm not sure what we were expecting. Handouts, maybe, or lectures, based on how many books there were in the office? What we got was hands-deep in the guts of magic theory. Most of what you learn in mentorship, past the basics, involves memorizing spells handed down, tested and true, that have a distinct result to a specific invocation. What we were doing here, now, was none of that. It was stripped-to-basics logic and intent-to-cause current-use. If anyone had ever thought that magic was a game, that current was a soft skill, they knew better now. This was pure New Ways—current as hard science.

The past two weeks we'd been under a strict no-use rule in the office—no current allowed for *anything*. Instead, the time was filled with lectures, and readings, and theoretical exercises designed to break down what we thought we knew, and rebuild it in the service of whatever Benjamin Venec and Ian Stosser told us to do; reading up about blood splatter and bullet trajectories, fingerprinting and footprint identification as it was done in the Null world—and then talking, endless talking, about how it *might* be done with current—and, more important, how it might be *hidden* by current. Because that was the thing; using current to bring down current. Theoretically. We were, as Nick said more than once, making this up out of hope and whole current. And that meant we had to *understand* it.

I'd never been on the cutting edge of anything before. I wasn't sure I was enjoying it.

It wasn't helping that in the past week, anything that could go wrong seemed to be doing so with a gleeful glint in its eye. First the coffeemaker had died in a splutter of sparks that had us all looking accusingly at each other. Then Sharon had gotten stuck in the elevator with Nifty when both of them were coming back from lunch—not together—and I don't know what they said to each other but body language when we finally got them out said it probably wasn't polite. And, just yesterday, Stosser had hit the table with his fist, trying to get some point or another into our heads, and the entire table—a solid wood table—collapsed as though termites had taken up residence in the legs.

"Gremlins," Nick had diagnosed. "We definitely have gremlins."

"There aren't any such thing," Sharon said. "It's just a myth Nulls made up to explain a series of noncatastrophic events."

"Uh-huh."

Normally, I'd side with Sharon on this one. Sometimes crap happening was just crap happening, and we were under enough stress that any mechanical failure in the building could easily be explained by someone's current getting a little frisky, even without them realizing it. But I couldn't see the Guys not noticing—especially since they were the ones driving us so hard. And I didn't know of any current-flare that would take out the legs of a wooden table….

So, gremlins? I didn't know. But I was looking around carefully whenever I entered a room, and taking the stairs whenever possible, rather than the elevator. Just to be cautious.

Somehow, we managed to survive without anyone getting killed, or saying anything too regrettable, and finally, reluctantly— as much to shut us up as because they thought we were ready— the Guys were letting us try actual physical tests of what we'd been discussing. I was so very tired of theory at this point, being able to actually use current rather than just talking about it was a relief. Except for the part where translating theory into practice was damned difficult.

"You going to stand there and stare at it all day, or what?" Nifty wasn't quite as annoying as Sharon, but he had the needling thing down to a damn art.

"Shut up." Dipping a mental finger into my core, I drew out a slender cord of current, waiting while it soothed from a deep blue to dark green, responding to my will. I saw it as a malleable cord, just so long and just so wide, and it became that cord. Behind me, I could feel Nifty grounding himself, creating a pocket of current that would, ideally, support and balance me while also protecting anyone passing by. Ideally.

He was doing his job. I needed to do mine. The trick was to do it delicately, with just the right touch, and not overdo it, not overstress the powder.... You just touch the tip of the current to the paper, and—

The next thing I knew, I was flat on my ass about six feet away, and there was a large lump of ex-football player lying on top of me.

"Normally I don't mind being on the bottom," I managed to get out, "but damn it, Nifty, off!"

He stirred, but didn't get off me, and his elbows were pointy as hell.

"I mean it, Lawrence, you're crushing my damn ribs. Move!"

"I'm trying," he muttered, digging his elbows in even more, just as the door crashed open and the workroom was filled with people.

Or three people, anyway. When you're flat on the floor, even one body's too much of an audience.

"Everyone all right?" Venec asked.

"Don't know yet," I said, still trying to get air back into my lungs.

"Man, Torres, you really blew that one," a voice said from somewhere to the left of Venec.

I was in no mood for puns, and just turned my head and glared at Nick from under Nifty's tree-trunk arm. I'd done some hand-to-hand with the guy—that was part of our training, too—but somehow he seemed heavier now.

I was just about to use current to shove him off me when someone beat me to the push. His body lifted smoothly—more smoothly and way more gently than I would have done it—until he was standing on his feet again. Sharon went over to check him out, but he waved her off. They weren't exactly buddy-buddy with each other, and there was no way he was going to let her see any weakness. "I'm okay. Just gotta get the ringing out of my ears."

He wasn't talking about a possible concussion; we had—all right, I had—managed to set off the office's internal alarms. Again.

"Torres? Are you all right?" Venec asked again.

"Yeah." Everything felt okay, anyway. I was sore, and pissed off, and probably bruised seven ways from Sunday, but nothing was broken.

Thankfully, the alarm shut off then, and I felt a little better.

"Maybe you should just give up on the delicate jobs," Sharon suggested, managing to sound both concerned and bitchy in the same tone. I glared at her. Snooty bitch, just because she got it right the first time…

Venec interrupted then. "All right, everyone, back to work. Lawrence, take ten. Outside. Let Mendelssohn fuss at you. It will make her feel better. Torres, let's do it again. Without the explosions this time, if you please."

He didn't offer me a hand—or current—up. I didn't expect it. The one thing I'd learned over the past few weeks of training was that if you screwed up, you had to get yourself out. The Guys were all about building teamwork—that's why we worked in pairs or groups, not alone—but they'd hammered into us that you also had to be ready to deal on your own in an emergency, too. There just weren't enough of us to go around, and not all of us, apparently, worked well with each other. Nifty and I were fair enough, and Sharon and Nick were a charm. Me and Nick complemented each other surprisingly well, but put Pietr and Nifty together and all you got was ugly, et cetera. Pietr and I got along so well they'd stopped pairing us together, which was disappointing. And Nifty and Sharon?

Not even Stosser was optimistic enough to pair them together without supervision. Not until they got their respective egos under control, anyway.

Sharon, also, we'd discovered, had paramedic training, and that made her the de facto medic for the group. Venec was right. Being able to boss us around like that always put her in a better mood, especially when she could do it to Nifty.

I really hoped to hell that Venec and Stosser knew what they were doing, pairing us all up and down like this.

"Torres? Today, please."

I crawled to my feet and limped back to the table. The paper with the gunshot residue was ash now, naturally, but I was pretty sure…yep. Venec slid another sheet onto the table, and stood there, his arms crossed, watching me.

"Again."

"Yeah, yeah, I know."

Some of the others were…not scared of Venec, exactly, but cautious around him. You got the sense that he had a nasty edge, if pushed, and god knows that he didn't hesitate in telling you when you hadn't met his standards. Nifty seemed to soak it up; I guess it was a lot like training camp.

Okay, it *was* training camp. Only without the Gatorade.

Me? I don't know. I guess I'm just not easily intimidated. Venec was trying to change that. If he could shake me, he'd know where my weakness was, and then he could hammer on that until it wasn't a weakness anymore. The Guys had been up-front about what they would be doing, and why.

So far, I felt relatively unhammered. By them, anyway: this gunpowder trace was kicking my ass. Literally.

Unlike Nifty, Venec didn't crowd me, physically or currentwise. He stood nearby, close enough that I could smell whatever cologne it was that he used, something with lime and spice and something stale, like tobacco. It didn't sound nice, but it made me want to put my nose to his skin and just inhale.

Uh-oh. I pulled my libido in for a scolding. Bad form, that. If you don't fish off the company pier, you sure as hell don't cast your line off the corporate yacht, either. The image was amusing enough that the moment of heat faded away. Not gone—once you're aware that someone's hot it never quite goes away—but under the surface, where it wouldn't embarrass me.

Magically, it was easier to relax into him. Reaching out with those other senses, I could feel him next to me, solid and grounded like he was made of flexible concrete, ready to catch whatever needed catching, without breaking.

Reassured that he had that side of things handled, I brought my attention back to the assignment.

Current, check. Pull and extend, steady hand, strong but gentle control, like petting a skittish kitten….

Some Talent used spoken spells, or waved their hands, or some other way to focus their will. We weren't allowed to do any of that. "Senseless showmanship," Stosser called it, ignoring the fact that he was the showiest showman I'd ever met. Venec practiced what his partner preached, though; when he showed us something, it was stripped down and sparse. That was what we were supposed to be. Efficient and understated.

"I've never been understated in my entire life," I muttered, even as the slender cord of current touched the residue.

No explosion this time. Current glimmered, then sank into the gunpowder dust, filling it the way water filled a sponge.

Now, the next step. Remembering to breathe slowly, evenly, I called the current back to me.

"Steady," Venec said, as if I needed the reminder. My ass and back still ached, and I had no desire to take another flyer across the room. Calm, calm. The rumble of disturbed current subsided back into my normal cool swirl; my control held; and the grains of gunpowder, plumped with current, rose off the paper they had been caught against and reassembled in the air. The next step was to draw out from their scattered display something more compact and readable.

Venec's voice was soft in my ear: there, but not interrupting my concentration. "Let them show you. Don't force your will on them."

I nodded, feeling a trickle of sweat drop down the side of my face. Using current burned calories; the more you called down—or the more focused your control—the more you burned. Right now I was dying for a chocolate milkshake, a thick hamburger, and a plate of pommes frites.

Hunger aside, my current behaved itself, drawing the gunpowder off the page and then allowing it, as directed, to retrace its original trajectory, back to the point of explosion.

"There. The shooter was standing at a…forty-degree angle. Approximately." I studied the hovering display, and tried to translate it into a horizontal display, rather than a vertical one. "To the left. About two feet away?"

"To the right, and closer to three feet," Venec said, totally ruining my sense of accomplishment. I drooped, and the powder fell back onto the table, scattering in a totally useless pattern.

"Damn."

"Oh for— Torres." His hand came down on my shoulder and turned me around to face him. The interesting thing about Venec was that, yeah, he was good-looking, but his dark eyes overpowered the rest of his face, pure damned charisma pulling you hip-deep and close to drowning. Egomaniacs and geniuses had eyes like those. "You just manipulated gunpowder remnant with current. Without blowing anything up. That alone should have you feeling pretty damn cocky. So you didn't get every detail right—you managed to perform the test properly. That's all this is about, right now. We don't expect perfection." He dropped his hand away from my shoulder as though he'd just realized he had touched me. "Yet."

"I bet Sharon nailed it," I muttered, aware I was sulking and not really caring if the boss saw it or not.

Venec's gaze stayed on me, but it wasn't quite so piercing, letting me breathe a little. "Sharon is older than you are—" all of five years, yeah "—and you each have different strengths." I was going to argue, but he overrode me. "What was Ian wearing this morning?"

I had barely seen Stosser before we were sent off to practice, and it took me a minute to remember. "Ah, jeans, blue, acid-washed, so he probably got them in some thrift store some-where, but they didn't have any holes so they might have been really expensive jeans made to look like they came from a thrift shop. On top, a red dress shirt, three-quarters buttoned over a blue rib tank. Hiking boots, brown. Don't know about socks or underwear. Hair was pulled back with a leather clasp. He really can't work the crunchy granola look, you know."

"He was born with a silver spoon in his mouth and a bad fairy in his closet," Venec said, like it slipped out without his brain's knowledge. He shut down right after that, his entire body language denying he'd ever said any such thing about his partner.

Too late. I managed not to laugh, but felt better. Even the bastard taskmaster had a snarky side. Good to know.

Venec recovered fast. "But there, you just made my point for me. A recall like yours—the ability to not only observe quickly but to retain accurate impressions hours later—is as useful a skill as any Sharon, or any of the others, bring to the table. If you all repeated the same skills, you would be a horribly one-dimensional team, and that's useless to us."

I lifted the paper and used a breath of current to wipe the debris back onto the sheet. "You think we're ever going to actually get to use any of this stuff? I mean, for real?"

Since we'd signed on, the Guys had been running our asses ragged learning how to sift physical debris without compromising it, raise fingerprints off a dozen different surfaces, and extrapolate blood splatter and gunpowder residue, along with a few classes in lock picking and identifying basic current manipulations. It was all interesting, and every day we figured out new ways to use current, but that was all that had happened. The *Cosa* was keeping their distance. Nobody—as far as we knew, anyway—had come calling for our services.

Sure, we got paid, and learned stuff, and the Guys seemed unconcerned about how long it was taking for us to start earning our keep, but I wasn't about to sign a lease on any of the apartments I'd seen, just yet. Not that any of them had been blowing my socks off. Two weeks of searching the ads and calling after leads, and I had my choice of either crap apartments in neighborhoods that would give J nightmares but were within my price range, or getting a roommate in a better area. I really didn't want a roommate. Did that for three years of college, and that was three years too many. Waking up in the morning with a roommate giving me the hairy eyeball because there was someone sharing my bed, or trying to lecture me on self-respect was not my idea of good living conditions. I had no self-esteem issues, thanks muchly, and my personal life was nobody's business but my own.

"What's the matter, Torres?" Venec goaded me, instead of answering. "Worried that you're going to be running scenarios for the rest of your life?"

"Or at least until the money runs out."

There was a flash of something on Venec's face; I'd hit a nerve, I guess. I went back to staring at the gunpowder residue, coaxing it into cleaning itself onto the sheet of paper. Stosser had money, and from the way Venec looked and talked I'd guess he had access to some, too, but I was betting they'd mortgaged everything they had on this, and it had to pay out, probably sooner rather than later.

Not even cave dragons wait forever for repayment. The Guys needed PUPI to work, and fast.

The rest of the week was more of the same, with the added joy of the ventilation system breaking down on the warmest day of the summer yet. Dog days, yeah. That could totally have been coincidence, or bad building management...but it *felt* like gremlins mocking us, especially after the coffee machine died for the third and final time when Pietr tried to prep a spell in the break room, and Sharon and Nifty got into it over the finer points of historical magic, which I don't think either of them knew a damn about, causing the lights to flicker badly enough to give us all headaches.

Of course, the latter wasn't gremlin-provoked, just the two of them butting heads—and current—as usual. But all told, it was a tough five days, and when Friday afternoon rolled around, Stosser kicked us out with firm directions to take the weekend off and do nothing even remotely current related. "You guys have been stretching, and while that's good, we don't want you to stretch until you break," he said. "So take a few days to recover, and we'll see you back in here on Monday."

He didn't have to tell me twice. I made some arrangements to look at a couple of apartments on Sunday and, when I woke up—reluctantly, groggily—to a Saturday filled with glorious sunshine, declared it a total R & R day. I sorted through the pile of clean laundry, found appropriate day-off clothing—a long black linen skirt with deep pockets and a T-shirt with a green-haired punk troll giving the world the finger printed on it—and got dressed before I could let myself fall back asleep. Grabbing a book off my to-be-read pile without even caring what it was, I shoved it into my backpack with my notepad and a couple of pens, stopped by the local overpriced deli to buy a sandwich and a bottle of water, and headed out to the Park with the rest of the known city-dwelling universe.

Fortunately, most people seemed interested in either sprawling on the Great Lawn, or strolling, and I found a pretty granite fountain in the middle of a circular walkway that wasn't overcrowded, and claimed a spot on the rim. It was surprisingly comfortable, with the sun on my legs and arms but not in my eyes. I dropped my backpack, pulled out my book, and started to read.

I'd made it about three chapters in when I was interrupted by a familiar voice.

"Hey."

I looked up, and sighed in resignation at the familiar form trying to loom over me. "You know, this city's too big for this to happen."

"Welcome to New York, girl. Biggest small town in the world."

Nick sat down without asking, and, incidentally, blocked my ray of sunlight.

"Move over," I told him, pushing at his rib cage with one finger to show I was serious. He slid over, stretched his legs out in front of him, and leaned back.

"That line about the biggest small town in the world? I thought that was Paris."

"Nah." Nick sounded certain of that, so I let him have it.

A minute passed without him saying anything more, so I tried to go back to my book.

"You been to Paris?"

"Yes." I turned a page, maybe a little more ostentatiously than was really needed.

"A lot?"

Clearly, the hint was lost on my coworker. "A few times." It wasn't really any big deal.

"Wow."

The tone of his voice made me pause. All right, maybe it was. I forgot, sometimes, that J and I didn't exactly lead the normal Americana life.

I lifted my head from my book and frowned at Nick. "Did you follow me?"

"Nope." He crossed his heart like a five-year-old telling a lie. "Was on my way home from work when I saw you, figured I'd be cohort-ly and stop. If you want to be alone…"

He made as though to get up, and I stopped him. "Home from work? Were we supposed to…?" A flutter of panic hit my rib cage. Had I missed something? We were all still on probation; I couldn't afford to miss anything….

"Relax, Torres. Home from my other job. All right? I want to pay off my student loans before I'm thirty, and I can't rely on this job to cover me. Not all of us have a comfy background to fall back on."

"Bite yourself, Shune." I hadn't mentioned J's background, or J much at all, but it didn't surprise me the others had done some digging. I'd done the same on them. Nifty I already knew about. Sharon Mendelssohn was exactly what she seemed: well-educated daughter of a middle-class family who blended really well with the Null world. Nick was the eldest son of gypsies—lonejacks who chose not to settle within any one region—

who'd really only appeared on the radar when he went to college. Pietr Cholis, like Sharon, was mainstream all the way, except for a stint in the juvie facilities when he was thirteen. Me, they'd get the whole story: lonejack daughter turned Council mentee, Phi Beta Kappa goth-girl, one arrest for trespassing with intent to protest, no convictions. I doubted my investigation into my father's death was on any record; to the rest of the world, Zaki Torres just disappeared one day, same as my mother did, three months after I was born. No foul play on her part—she just decided she didn't want to be a mom, handed me over to Zaki, and split. All I'd ever gotten from her was fair hair and paler skin that—thank god—didn't burn or freckle.

Nick had gone quiet, his head tilted back to let the sunshine wash over him, but I was totally distracted from my book now. "Hey."

"What?"

"You wanted to see a fatae, right?"

His eyes opened, and his head came into an alert position so fast I swear I heard it crack. "What? Where?"

"Over there." I pointed with my chin, trying not to be obvious. Some fatae didn't mind, but some got really pissy about being outed. "In the leather jacket." It was too nice a day for that jacket, which was why I'd noticed him in the first place.

"He's not…" Nick started to say in disgust, and then stopped. It wasn't obvious—the obvious ones didn't stroll around Central Park on a sunny Saturday afternoon—but once you actually looked, the evidence was there to be noticed.

"What is it?"

"He, and I have no idea." I'd met a few over the years, obviously, and J had trained me on the basics: the different kinds of breeds and where they came from, and how to not be an idiot when confronted with one, but without a checklist I couldn't do more than land-based, air-breathing, bipedal. "That jacket on a day like today, he's probably from one of the warmer countries, not Nordic or northern. Land-based, obviously. No gills visible."

There were some fatae breeds with horn or antlers, but this guy's head was bare, except for a crop of dark curls. It was what was under the hair that gave him away. His ears were not only elongated, they were tasseled with tufts of fur at the tip and lobe, and the skin at the back of his neck, where it showed above the coat's collar, was dappled with close-cropped, fawn-colored fur.

His hands were in his pocket, and his feet were covered by boots, but I would have laid down money that his nails were more like a horse's hooves than a human's. His face was humanlike, too, close enough to pass if you didn't stare, but the lower half moved oddly, as if the bone structure of his mouth wasn't quite the same as ours. I had the sudden thought that a lot of FX guys in Hollywood might be fatae, or know some pretty well.

We watched as he walked past us. I got the feeling he knew we were watching, but there was no way to tell, not without being either obvious or rude, or both.

A tune sounded from his pocket, and he took out a cell phone and answered it. His hands were shaped like human hands, but with three thick fingers instead of five more slender ones, and each curved down, ending with what looked like a soft miniature hoof. He managed the phone like a pro, though.

He turned, as he passed, and looked directly at us. It was then that I realized the reason his mouth looked strange was because of his double rows of teeth.

*Sharp* teeth.

The urge to pull current wiggled in my belly, but I held steady. Carnivore did not mean threat, automatically. Not anymore, anyway. Probably. But the fact was that he saw us— more, he *saw* us—not just as human but Talent…. I forced myself to relax. Some fatae could sense current, even though they didn't use it the way we did. That was all, no need to be jumpy. Gremlins or no, we weren't in anyone's crosshairs.

And then the fatae was walking past us, talking urgently into his cell, and I heard Nick let out a little sigh.

"You're disappointed?" I asked.

"No. Okay, maybe a little. I guess I thought he'd be more… impressive."

He'd missed the teeth, obviously. "Some of them are scary as hell," I said. "Someday, if you're a good boy, I'll take you to meet a cave dragon."

"You do not know a cave dragon." He sounded indignant, and I laughed at him.

"I do, actually." I even really did have an invitation to return. And I was pretty sure it was meant in a "stop by and say hello" manner, not "stop by to be lunch."

Nick started to get excited about the thought. "How about a dryad? I heard there are a lot of them in the Park."

"Probably are," I said. "It's an old park. But they're tough to meet, and not always good to meet, either."

"What do you mean?"

I put down my book, resigned to the fact that Nick wasn't going to shut up anytime soon. "You *ever* read any fairy tales when you were a kid, Nick? The real ones—the Grimm versions, not the Disneyfied ones."

"Sure. Um. No, not really." He shrugged. "I mean, I got my basic history during mentorship, so…"

"Well, you should. Read them, I mean. Because a lot of

them aren't so much stories as lessons. About how to behave—and not get sunk in a swamp, or cooked and eaten, or run out of your home or any of the other things that happen to idiots who disrespect the fey folk."

I wasn't sure how much of it I believed, really. But the breeds had been around forever, since before the Old Magic days, when we were still trying to figure out why some people could start fire by staring at a stick, and other people burned those people with those same sticks. The fatae didn't use magic, but they were *Cosa Nostradamus*, same as us. *Cosa*-cousins. It paid to keep up-to-date with what your relatives were up to, and what family feuds were dead and which ones still simmered.

I didn't say any of this to Nick, though. I didn't know how to verbalize it without sounding preachy and uncool, and I was discovering, much to my surprise, that I really wanted to fit in. It wasn't just about being good at the job, although I wanted that, too. Sharon's elegance, Nifty's charisma and pull, Pietr's total cool and calm, even Nick's fumbling geeky charm, it all made me want to be part of the group. Where did I fit in? I had no idea. But Venec and Stosser thought we could be a team.

Why had that fatae looked at us? Was it just a case of *Cosa* acknowledgment? Was that creeping sense of menace and uncertainty real, or just a remnant of the crap from the previous week? I couldn't tell, so I let it go.

"So, what's your other job, anyway?" Maybe he could get me part-time work there, if I needed it. If this all went south on us and we got kicked to the curb.

"You promise you won't tell anyone?"

I sketched an X against where I figured my heart was, more or less, hopefully with more élan than Nick had managed. "Promise." How bad could it be?

"I'mamassagetherapist."

Once my brain untangled his hurried mumble, I sat up and looked at him with, I'm afraid, a gleam in my eye.

He saw it. "See? People only love me for my hands."

"Awwwww. We'd like you even if you didn't have hands at all. Can you massage with your toes, too?"

"Hmmph." He didn't quite stick his tongue out at me, but I swear I could hear him thinking about it. "All right. I need to go home and collapse for a while. See you Monday, if we're still employed." He hauled himself upright, and waggled his fingers at me, a sort of dorky goodbye wave. I waggled my fingers back, and he walked off, heading toward the east side of the park. I wondered suddenly where he lived, and if there were any apartments for rent in his building. Why hadn't I asked him that?

Well, there was always Monday, if I didn't see anything tomorrow.

And, as he said, if we were still employed.

I picked up my book, but the fascination of reading about the life and times of an eighteenth-century courtesan had dimmed, somehow. The flash of that fatae's teeth, and talking about fairy tales, however briefly, had stirred some depth of unease in me that I couldn't blame entirely on stress or overwork. Or gremlins.

Was it kenning? Was I having one of my rare moments of precog? No. It didn't feel right. But something was wrong.

I closed the book and shoved it into my backpack, wrapped up what was left of my sandwich and tossed it into the nearest green trash can, deciding on my direction because I had already turned that way to find the trash. J used to say that he could think better while he was walking; maybe it would work for me, too. If nothing else, I'd been spending way too much time the past week sitting on my ass. Exercise was a good idea.

The path I was on seemed to circle endlessly on itself since I never seemed to get closer to the buildings in the distance, but rather kept diverging past seemingly endless fields, rocky outcrops, and tiny scenic ponds. It was hard to believe the entire thing was man-made, but if you looked again, more closely, there was a perfection under the natural surface that could only be crafted. Nobody out enjoying the day seemed to care, so I let that thought drop and waited to see what else came to replace it.

My mind remained blank. All right, maybe Stosser had been right, and we did need the break, and all this was just stress-related. I rolled with the blankness, and let my body go on automatic—until something hit the back of my head and bounced off.

"Hey!" All the paranoia came slamming back, and some instinct made me look, not behind me, but up.

The branches shook, but I couldn't see anything moving.

Not that it mattered. I had a pretty good idea, once my heart rate calmed, what was up there.

A good idea, though, wasn't a fact. I looked up at the branches, judging from the movement which ones had been disturbed. There was a cantrip we had been testing that, if it worked, would show us the way a suspect had run, based on the displacement of air. So far it had failed pretty miserably, but if I applied the basics to the pattern of the leaves rustling…

I thought hard and fast, drawing a few threads of current up out of my core and casting them into the air, toward the branches.

"Follow the trail of the passage unseen," I directed it. With established spells you didn't need to actually speak them out loud, but the words helped focus the intent, and right now that cantrip needed all the help it could get. The threads hovered midair, as though they were confused, or uncertain. Current didn't actually have emotions, or any kind of sentience, so that meant that I was uncertain. More focus was needed. All right, then.

"Follow the trail of the passage unseen. Lead me to the pranking hand."

The air shimmered as the current went to work, like the heat signature of a fire, and a handful of leaves changed from dark, healthy green to a sickly looking yellow, as if they'd aged immediately. Then the shimmer moved on, changing another set of leaves, and the first set went back to green, moving along deeper and higher into the tree, until I couldn't see it any longer.

There was a startled squawk and a loud rustle of leaves, and a branch swayed as though something had tried to escape being turned yellow. I caught a glimpse of fluttering wings, and a shock of hair a color even I wouldn't dare try.

Hah, I'd been right. A piskie. Winged pranksters of the *Cosa*. It probably thought I was a Null, and would have spent time looking for the person who threw that nut at me, rather than retaliating.

I made a mental note of the wording I'd used—specifics were clearly needed to get the proper results. I hadn't used enough current to actually catch someone, but that could be amended in later test trials. Maybe even use current to tag someone, so we could find a culprit in a crowd? Odds were we'd never need something like that, if we were called in after the fact, but a Talent cop could use it....

"And how would you introduce that into the court records?" I asked myself. "Your honor, I know that it was him because he had a bright yellow splotch on his forehead?"

I wasn't too worried about the piskie being chased too far by the spell—if she or he went far enough away the spell would wear off. I thought it would, anyway.

"Not that having bright yellow fur would stop the bugger. Idiot piskie would probably think it was some strange badge of honor, almost but not quite getting caught." Piskies were pranksters, but they were pranksters who respected competent opponents far more than they enjoyed clueless ones. That was probably why they hadn't been hunted down and eaten over the years.

It hit me then—I'd not only used current offensively, I'd done that before, although not quite so easily or without planning—but I'd done it automatically, with an eye not for the immediate result, but a long-term refinement for job use.

Huh. I wasn't sure if that was good or bad, being so—call it proactive—but there was an extra lift in my step as I continued on my way through the park, and the unease and paranoia of earlier slowly faded away.

## seven

Sunday passed without me shouting eureka! at any of the apartments I was shown, and then Monday morning rolled around again, and we were back at it—studying, practicing, refining, and wondering when—if—we were ever going to get a chance to actually use any of this on a case.

A male voice shouting "What the hell?" down the hallway was the first and only warning I had that it was going to be one of Those Days. The overhead lights were the victim of the office gremlins this time, a trail of them blowing out with tiny little implosions, like the sound of someone popping their bubble gum.

"Do we have to replace those, or is it the landlord's responsibility?" Nick wanted to know. Stosser looked—as much as I could tell, in the dim emergency lighting—grim, while Venec just looked pissed. We all stayed low while they had a short, closed-door session that left them looking, respectively, more grim and more pissed. But a little mage-light got us through the morning, and when we came back from lunch, the lights had been replaced.

Nobody asked if the landlord had actually done it or not.

On the plus side, reporting my fine-tuning of the tracer cantrip during our morning meeting got me praise from Stosser, a snort from Venec that was almost like praise, and a glare from Nifty, who'd apparently been fiddling with an alternate refinement that hadn't worked so well.

"Lawrence is good on the power stuff," Pietr said, when I brought the topic up. We'd escaped Nifty's glower to hit the little Indian place on the corner, just the two of us. Nick had brought in his own lunch, and Sharon had declined, as always. I couldn't tell if she was being antisocial, or just saving money. "Full-on power, and quick planning, stuff he used on the field, probably. That's how his brain is trained. I'd want him on my side in a fight, for damn sure. But I don't think he's very good with finicky details. You, that's what you're really good at."

"Gee, thanks."

My coworker waved a piece of naan at me, scolding. "That was a compliment, Bonnie. Finicky details are what make things work. Like…like needing an engineer to make a building safe, while the construction workers are making it solid."

I thought about it, and decided to let him live after all. Especially since he'd offered to pay for lunch. And it was a pretty good lunch, too. Not haute cuisine by any stretch of the imagination, but the place was clean, the bread fresh, and the food spicy. And it was reasonably priced. Another plus to being here rather than in midtown.

But the topic at hand interested me more than food. "Venec says that they hired us because our skills complemented each other."

Pietr narrowed those gray eyes and tapped his fork against the side of his plate in a quick, almost syncopated rhythm.

"Makes sense. Only…" And he caught the same thing I had. "How did they know, that quick?"

I had my theory about that. But I'd have to check it against other people's experiences, and I wasn't quite ready to share the particulars of my history with anyone just yet, so I couldn't bring it up.

"Same way they knew to call us, I guess," was all I said for now, and the conversation moved on to the ever-popular "Nifty versus Sharon" sweepstakes. Right now, Sharon was ahead on sheer skill, but Nifty was a favorite for style.

We went back smelling of cardamom and cinnamon, and were once more under the hammer: my attention to finicky detail might be my strength, but apparently Venec thought I should be able to lift steel and tote cable, too.

"Is that all you've got? I could snap you in two and not even raise a sweat!"

Bastard. That was my new nickname for Benjamin Venec. Much more appropriate than DB, although there were times I wanted him to be that, too…. Right now the most amazing eyes and gorgeous forearms meant a lot less to me than the fact that he was a sadistic sonofabitch.

The pressure in the room was unbearable, and I didn't mean that in a metaphorical way. Venec had lowered the ceiling on us, magically, and I thought my spine was about to snap. Nick, across the room from me, was bent double, too, a look of frustrated agony on his face.

We knew Venec wasn't actually going to crush us. Probably. But that didn't mean he wasn't going for the maximum hurt, to make his point.

"All you have to do is *push,* children. Push! Shove it back at me!"

I wanted to shove it, all right. All the way down his damned throat until he choked. But the more current I pulled into forcing the downward pressure away from me, the more the pressure seemed to increase. This wasn't getting us anywhere. I just didn't have the brute force, and neither did Nick. We'd tried combining forces about ten minutes into this exercise, and all that did was double the pressure in response. I didn't see any way other than going totally flat and letting it…

Wait a minute. Just…wait…

Oh hell. If I thought about it any longer, I'd never have the nerve to try it. Without warning Nick, I dropped to my stomach on the floor, pulled all my current from the upward push, and reconfigured it in my head from a solid form to a ball of lightning that rumbled across the carpeted floor, picking up more and more static charge as it went, until, instants later, it slammed into Venec's ankles and sparked against his own current-use.

The thump as he hit the floor was, I purely and gleefully admit, seriously satisfying.

"Oh. That was sneaky," Nick said, dropping to the floor in exhaustion as the pressure suddenly disappeared. "Wish I'd thought of it."

I acknowledged the praise with a weary grin. My body hurt too much to do anything more.

"What were you doing?" Venec asked him. The bastard had already recovered and was sitting up, cross-legged on the floor like he'd planned to do that all along. I was pleased—hell, gratified—to see that the neckline of his off-white shirt was gray and damp with sweat.

"Working on a way to negate the friction and slide out of range," Nick said, rolling over on his back and speaking to the ceiling, now back up on the ceiling where it belonged. "Elementals do it, right?" Elementals were microentities, not fatae exactly, but some weird offshoot of current that lived in and off the flow of electricity itself. Jury was still out on how intelligent they were. J said they were only borderline aware and in his opinion about as smart as your average goldfish. "So I'd reverse the static charge, make it slippery instead, and force an escape route that way."

"Huh. An interesting solution, and it might have worked. Keep trying, and once you've got it, see if you can find a way to speed it up."

Nick rolled his eyes. That was Venec's response to almost anything: assume it can be done, and then find a way to make it work faster. The fact that he was right—if we needed something like that we'd need it to hand immediately—didn't make the instructions any the less annoying.

Without saying anything more, Venec got up and walked out of the room, leaving us still lying there. That was how lessons ended—we'd gotten the point, now we had to follow up on the assignment. At some point, one or the other of the Guys would find us, and give us some other impossible task.

"I bet Nifty just shoved the ceiling and it got the hell out of his way," I said, too tired to really be cranky.

"And Sharon glared at it, and it whimpered and retreated into a corner," Nick said, not disagreeing.

"And Pietr convinced it that he wasn't there to be crushed."

Nick snorted. It was funny 'cause it was probably true.

"You were pretty sneaky there yourself, too," he said. "So much for your straight-shooter persona. I'm onto you now, Torres."

Straight shooter? Me? I guess that was funny 'cause it was true, too.

And then we got up, and went back to work.

That was how the days passed, working and sniping and

working some more, and then it was Friday again, and after a month, the weeks developed a recognizable pattern: get up five days out of seven, get hammered all day by one or the other or both of the Guys, stagger out too exhausted to do anything but go back to the hotel, order room service, and fall asleep, then take a day off to recover, and spend Sunday unsuccessfully apartment-hunting.

I felt bad, not having any time to spare for J, but he told me he understood, and I'd see him as soon as things got settled. I could hear the hurt in his voice, though, and I hung up the phone feeling worse, not better.

I also took the time to strip out the last of the red dye from my hair, and was reacquainting myself with my natural hair color, a shade and texture that inspired Nick and Pietr to try and come up with appropriate nicknames for me. I responded by dubbing them, respectively, "Ferret-boy" and "Fade." Nifty was still Nifty. Sharon seemed to defy nicknaming.

Between coffee and a seemingly unending supply of junk food and pizza, we managed to survive the workload, and even learn some new things without passing out or killing each other. The gremlins kept up their work, too, but we—almost—got used to it.

By the end of the second month on the job, everyone seemed to have gotten a second wind. The work was still killing us, and I thought my brain was going to explode from the sheer volume of information we were being given to read and hear and hands-on learn, but there was more life in everyone, come quitting time, than there had been before.

Knowing the Guys, that just meant next week was going to ramp up a notch and hammer us all over again. But for now, the moment was good. It was Thursday, which was almost Friday, and I had a line on an apartment that I thought might work, overpriced and undersized, but in a good location, and an appointment to see it tomorrow morning before work. It would be nice to have that settled, at least. I was on first-name basis with all of the staff at the hotel now, and didn't want to think about what it was costing, even if J had gotten a long-term deal.

"Hey. You want to grab a drink?"

I was sitting in the break room, trying to get my eyes to refocus after Sharon flubbed—rather impressively—a basic illumination spell. Even Nifty'd been quiet after that disaster, mainly because he hadn't been able to do much better. We were trying to rework it to illuminate specific things—blood splatter, fingerprints, random body parts—on order, but so far, all it would do was act like a dimmer switch set on spastic. I'd been up half the night before, trying to break down the components of the spell to see where we were going wrong, but hadn't been able to come up with anything yet.

"What?" My train of thought broken, I looked blankly up at my coworker.

Nick clarified his offer with exaggerated patience. "Drink. Alcoholic. Bar. After work. Any of this sounding familiar? Nifty found this absolutely horrible place downtown. Gives dives a bad name, but excellent brews on tap."

"We having a team-building exercise?"

Nick smirked. "Call it whatever you want, the hangover's still the same."

Hard to argue with that kind of logic. The thought of a little social interaction sounded good. I was starting to go stir-crazy, even through my exhaustion, and the staff of the hotel, while nice, were being professionally friendly, not real friendly. My dating life was stagnant. Although Nick had indicated once or twice that he wouldn't be adverse to a little after-hours research, I liked him but not in that way. Sharon was clearly not into girls, and Nifty wasn't my type—too self-important. Pietr, while undeniably cute, and a good guy…unnerved me a little. Not in a bad way—I didn't think he was crazy-stalker type or anything, just…unnerving. I was going to have to go looking, eventually, but when did we have time? Another reason to get an apartment; maybe I'd meet someone in the building…. For now, though, just not being in the office was a good start.

"Yeah, sounds good," I decided. "Did you ask Sharon?"

An expressive roll of the eyes was answer enough. Nick worked well with her, but I don't think they were buddies outside of the office. He was right. Sharon probably wouldn't be caught dead in the kind of dives he and Nifty seemed to enjoy. Although we might be doing her a disservice, now that I thought about it. Just because someone carries off classy doesn't mean they always are. I should know that, having lived with J for more than a decade. "Ask, anyway. It's polite."

"All right. I—"

The sound of the buzzer made both of us jump, and Pietr appeared in the doorway, looking as startled as I felt.

"The door," he said. "Someone's at the door."

Christ. Two months we've been here, and I didn't even know we *had* a doorbell.

Stosser came out, the black jeans and unfortunate yellow pullover he'd been wearing earlier in the day now changed out for dress slacks and a pressed, button-down shirt just the right shade of white to make his hair seem muted. Damn it, I'd just seen him five minutes ago, when he told us to take a break! If he was hiding a changing room and closet in this place, I wanted to know about it. Especially if there was a shower in there.

"Look competent, children," was all he said, almost offhand,

and then it was like a nuclear blast went off under his red-headed scalp, the charm practically oozing like honey out of him as he opened the door and ushered the newcomer into our office.

"Ah, Ms. Reybeorn, welcome. Please, come into my office, and we can discuss your situation in more comfortable surroundings. May I fetch you coffee? Some tea?"

The honey filled the entire room, and for an instant Nick and I went from being exhausted twenty-somethings to alert, intense investigators; professionally going about our business and yet aware of the newcomer, in a nonintrusive way. I could *feel* Stosser's current gilding over me as he walked what had to be our first potential client into the back office, but be damned if I knew how he did it.

Our Ms. Reybeorn was around fifty or so and carrying it off well; short brunette hair styled carefully to play up her cheekbones and downplay her chins, minimal makeup applied well enough to look like no makeup. She was wearing black, but so did three quarters of this city, so that didn't mean anything. Her shoes were screamingly expensive pumps in a demure two-inch heel, and the glint on her fingers when Stosser took her arm in his said diamonds, plural. Real diamonds, too, not fakes. Talent could tell, don't ask me how.

Huh. Maybe I'd be able to put a security deposit down on a decent apartment, after all.

They went out of the break room and into the main office. The door closed behind them, and the glamour dropped, much to my relief. It was great that Stosser could make clients see us that way, but it was damned uncomfortable to see it yourself and know how far from the truth it was.

Nick collapsed in the nearest chair, craning his neck to look back at the door. "You think we're supposed to hang around and find out what's going on?"

I shrugged. "Probably." And even if we weren't, I sure as hell wasn't going anywhere now, not even if Venec dismissed us early for the day and personally kicked us out the door. My mind was racing too hard with possibilities to think about anything else; beer and social chitchat just couldn't compete.

Where would the boss have taken her? Probably the chat room, which was the smallest of our spaces, down at the far end of the office, and the only one that didn't look as though it was braced for impact. The other three rooms, while they had chairs and tables, also doubled as work spaces, and had suffered at least one explosion, implosion, or unfortunate incident in the past month, in the course of our on-the-job education and the occasional gremlins. Oh, please don't let anything happen while she was in there....

"The alley's probably clear by now," Nick said, swinging his body out of the chair and standing up. "Let's go find the others."

The alley was the hallway that connected the two parts of the office. A couple of weeks ago, someone had painted a dark green line down the lower third of the far wall, so it was no longer quite so sterile looking, but you'd never mistake it for anything other than a way to get from point A to point B, and nobody lingered there.

With Stosser and the mysterious maybe client safely tucked away, we stuck our noses into the nearest workroom and found Sharon, her chin in her hand, still sulking.

"I think I know where it went wrong," she said when we came in, not even looking up to see who it was.

"Yeah? Okay, no, don't distract me," Nick said impatiently. "We've got news."

We might all be different, personality-wise, and maybe we

didn't always have a lovefest going on, but the Guys had it dead-on about us being curious. Sharon dropped whatever she'd been mulling over and turned in her chair to face us, those wide blue eyes alert.

"What?"

Nick got there before I could. "Stosser's in with a maybe-client."

"Seriously?" She looked to me for confirmation—that's me, detail girl—and I imitated Nick's usual half-arm shrug, clumsily, sitting in the sole armchair in the room, the one that Stosser usually claimed.

"Female, well dressed, looking stressed and more than a little worried. Fifty-something. Money, if not filthy rich. Maybe more important, Stosser was expecting her, since he knew her name and must have buzzed her in through the lobby—" we still hadn't figured out how they did that, damn it "—and he was wearing meet-and-greet duds."

Sharon picked up on that immediately. "He wasn't before. He had on that awful shirt, so he had to have changed, and fast."

"Yeah." Nick was pacing, door to window, and then back again. As usual, the shade—an expensive double-baffled one—was drawn, so that you couldn't see out…or in. Wasn't much of a view, anyway.

"So what do you think is up?" Sharon asked. "We have a job?"

I raised my hands, palm up, to show my total ignorance. "Maybe. Hope so. Haven't a damned clue, nor where to find one. But I figure we'll get told, if anything actually happens."

Pietr appeared out of nowhere, already in the room. "Hey, did you guys hear—?"

"There's a maybe-client in-office. Yeah," Sharon said, as

though she'd known about it for hours. By now, we were used to Pietr's disappearing-reappearing act. He swore he didn't do it on purpose, but nobody except maybe Pietr believed that.

"God, I'd love to actually have something to *do*," he said, sitting on the floor next to my chair and resting his head against my knee in a way that was becoming habit with us. I petted his hair absently, the way you might a puppy's head. Silky hair. So unfair, when guys get great eyelashes and great hair, and, hell, Pietr had pretty much great everything.

"Are you crazy, or just out of your mind?"

The three of us looked at Nick like he'd just displayed wings or something over his polo-shirted shoulders.

"You don't?" Sharon asked. "Then why the hell are you here, for the fun times of getting your head handed to you by our esteemed taskmasters?"

Nick patted the air at her, telling her to back off. Usually they got along fine, because Nick was mellow enough to get along with anyone, but even he had a limit. "Sure, I want a case, want to be able to prove myself, do something with all this. But I also want to not make a total idiot out of myself. Let's face it, so far we've got a handful of useful tricks, but we're a bunch of twenty-somethings with a handful of tricks, that's all. None of us has any kind of background to be doing this, not and get listened to, not even Stosser and Ben, really. I joked about making it all up as we went along but we're not even doing that—we're *hoping* that we're making it up. The truth is all the spells and the skills might be completely useless, because we have no idea what spells or skills are going to be needed!"

You ever driven really fast, in a car, or on a bike, and then hit a brick wall? Me neither, but I knew what it felt like, now.

Nick was right, damn him. From the looks on everyone else's faces, they were having the same come-to-Jesus moment.

Okay, yeah, we'd all wondered it, when the Guys first proposed the job, and maybe since then, deep down and quiet. But facing the question out loud like that, after all the work we'd been doing, that was a whole 'nother thing. Out loud, we asked *when,* not what if it doesn't work?

Nick wasn't done with us. "And even if we do manage to figure out the whodunit of whatever whatdunit we get, who are we going to tell, anyway? It's not like we've got a police force to back us up or anything. So who enforces what we discover? Did any of you stop to think about that, while we were blowing up blood splatter and highlighting broken locks?"

That, I could answer. My words to J back at the beginning came back to me in a rush of renewed conviction. "Anyone," I said. "We tell anyone who will listen, and people who won't, and we don't hold back what we know, once we're sure. We let the truth be known."

"And that will do…what, exactly, Bonnie?" Nick didn't sound angry or scared, just tired. "I haven't let myself think that far, just going day to day and hoping it all makes sense, but what then?"

What, he thought I had all the damn answers? "Then we let someone else take over. Our job's just to get the truth out. To not let people get away with crimes, just because they're magical ones. We're investigators, not cops or prosecutors. We point 'em out, not lock 'em up."

"So who does?" Pietr asked. "Not Null cops or courts, that's been proven time and again, usually to our cost. Witch hysteria's been the least of it."

"No, not Nulls," I agreed. "Council has means to deal with people, once they have proof, and lonejacks…you guys probably have the same, only it's not formal or organized, but it's there. It has to be." Didn't it? The Guys had to have thought of all this—why hadn't anyone asked them?

"And if it's not?" Sharon was being devil's advocate, and didn't seem to care what the outcome was. Her previous job as a paralegal coming to the fore, I guessed. "We shout our proof into the wind, and nothing changes."

"Knowing the truth changes everything."

Unlike Pietr's stealth-walk, we heard Venec push open the door and come in. I still jumped when he spoke up, though—don't ask me why. Maybe I just figured he was going to lurk and listen until we ran ourselves into the ground, and then bail us out, as usual.

Unlike Stosser, he hadn't changed clothing, still in shirt and jeans, and wasn't projecting anything other than his usual intensity. He took one of the other chairs, and leaned his elbows on the table.

He looked tired. I don't know why I hadn't noticed it before. Those eyes got me, every time, and distracted from the lines of exhaustion on his face, I guess. I wondered if he counted on that, used it…

"If you had doubts about our process, why didn't you ask us?"

I looked to see if anyone else was stupid enough to respond to that. Nick looked at Venec with a wide-eyed little boy expression, like he'd never doubted Santa Claus *ever*. Pietr, I swear to god, faded into the paint like a chameleon. Venec's gaze passed over me, and I just shook my head a little, and smiled. Not me, Boss. Go chew on someone else, this time.

"Do you really have a process for that, or are you just going to play the dice however they roll?"

And there was Sharon, striding in where even fools might tiptoe. I wasn't sure if I wanted to cheer her on, or hide under the table until the fireworks were over.

To my surprise, the fireworks fizzled. "I see that you've already figured out our visitor may change things around here a bit," he said instead, not so much sidestepping her question as ignoring it with a completely straight face. "Maybe more change than you think."

Venec let us hang on to that thought just long enough to Translocate a soda out of the fridge in the break room, open it, and take a sip. It was so casual, you didn't quite realize how much current it had to take to make it look that casual. One-upmanship, the demonstration of why he was the boss and not to be questioned, or just unconscious arrogance? With Stosser, the answer would be both A and B. With Venec, who knew? Not me. Not yet, anyway.

"Ms. Reybeorn was recommended to us through a friend of a friend who had heard we might be able to help her," he went on. "Torres is correct. That's what we are here for, what we're meant to do. Not to put criminals in jail, but to determine if there is in fact a criminal act. To help people find the truth, pleasant or not."

"Mostly not," Sharon said. "I'm betting." She didn't push on the unanswered question—maybe she didn't really want to know, either.

"Speaking of betting, and being practical, does this Ms. Reybeorn have money to pay?" Pietr asked.

"Oh yeah," I said without thinking, still looking at that soda can. "She's Council. And I mean *Council* Council." The name had finally kicked something loose in my brain, once I stopped poking at it. "Or if not her, her family." Being a seated member didn't earn you a paycheck, but it did bring you connections, and those connections almost always came with business benefits.

"Yeah?" That had Venec's attention, fast. Ooo, I knew something the Guys didn't! Or one Guy, anyway. I didn't have time to treasure the moment, though, because Venec and the others were looking at me like a particularly tasty slab of informational meat. It was unnerving, a little, having your own curiosity turned on you....

"Council? Yeah...not here, though. Chicago."

"Ah." Venec leaned back and looked almost smug. I was going to take a wild guess that he and Stosser had a bet going, where the first client would come from, and he'd just won. Wasn't just Sharon and Nifty who played tug-of-war over lead position I guessed.

"Midwest Council hadn't told us where to get off, had they?" Sharon recalled.

"No. They were still fence-sitting as to whether we might be more useful than disruptive," Venec said, and the others started to discuss what that fence-sitting might mean, if anything, if a Council member—maybe even a sitting member—had hired us.

I let the conversation wash over me, still focusing on the soda can in Venec's hand as if it was a scrying crystal. My memory had always been good, but there was so much stuffed into it now I was having trouble doing a straight recall. If I could only remember why I knew the name... It had to be something J had said; that was the only connection I had to the Midwest, but what?

That thought in turn reminded me that I needed to reschedule dinner with J, soon. He wouldn't pry about a job—all right, he would, but not before working himself into a lather about it. Better to call him. As soon as I had time.

Damn it, what the hell had I heard about the Reybeorn family? It was in there, I could feel it, but every time I went digging for it, the thought disappeared. Damned frustrating. I *never* forgot stuff!

Before I could puzzle it out, a faint chime sounded in the air, the shimmer that accompanied it marking it as current-noise, not electronic. A summons, unmistakably, not so much urgent in the feel as quietly demanding our obedience. Since we were all here—except Nifty, and I didn't think Nifty would generate that kind of noise even if he was ballsy enough to try summoning anyone that way—there was only one place and one person it could have come from.

"Children, grab your kit bags and brush out your hair," Venec said, standing up and confirming my guess. "We've got a client."

## eight

I hadn't been keeping track of time, so I don't know how long that meeting actually took—not very long, certainly. There was still light outside the window, but in the summer that meant nothing in terms of time-telling. Ms. Reybeorn was nowhere in sight by the time we trooped into the chat room. Nifty joined up with us along the way, wiping still-damp hands on his trousers and looking inquiringly at us. Wherever he'd been—and I could take a guess—he'd missed the recent events.

"We may be in business," Nick told him as we walked, and Nifty's entire face brightened, like a kid being told Santa had managed to shove a pony into his sled. Did little boys dream of having a pony the way little girls did?

Just as well that Ms. Reybeorn had already left the premises; this was our smallest room, and the five chairs and a narrow table pretty much filled the space before everyone was inside. Why Stosser didn't come to us, rather than bringing us down here... From someone else—Sharon or Nifty, for example— I'd have guessed a power play. But he was already the boss; why would he need to do that?

Whatever the reason, it was seriously cramped with all seven of us jammed in there, and I only hoped that the air-conditioning was up to the job, and nobody blew the fuses again.

The chime faded away, and like a magical case of musical chairs, everyone tried to find a place to park their butts.

Sharon took the seat next to Stosser, resting her elbows on the arms of the chair so that she took up as much space as possible, as though mimicking Nifty's much-larger bulk. He had taken the chair at the other end of the table, so rather than being at Stosser's left hand, he anchored the table for him. Pietr slid in between Nifty and Venec, taking the last chair pulled up to the table. His clear gray gaze met mine, and he dropped me a wicked wink.

Joy. More maneuvering, and because I wasn't fast enough, now wherever I sat would be seen as choosing sides.

Nick and I ended up avoiding the table entirely and perching along the windowsill, close enough to contribute, but without the pesky placement implications. That was my plan, anyway. I suspect Nick just wanted an excuse to cozy up. There was enough room on the ledge for his skinny ass, but I had to sit half on, half off. Nick shifted, pulling at my arm to bring me closer. We fidgeted a bit until achieving a compromise, our hips bumping against each other.

Nick was a skinny geek, but he had manners. And he smelled good. I really did like folk who smelled good; it was even more of a turn-on than looking good. I hadn't dated anyone seriously since months before graduation—my last steady had decided to take a job in California, and I'm not about long-distance relationships, so we'd cooled it off mutually, and without too much trauma. It was clearly past time to find a new playmate—especially if daily exposure to Venec didn't lessen the hormonal impact he had on me, which didn't seem likely at this point.

Keeping coworkers off-limits raised the question of *where* and *when* I was going to find that new playmate, though. Or even finding someone long-term. I wasn't averse to long-term, just 'cause I'd never been able to manage it just yet. I—

"Are you with us, Torres?"

I blinked, hoping to hell I hadn't just said anything out loud. No, just caught not paying attention. Damn. "Yessir." The curse of a true blonde—when I blush, I blush hard. By the time everyone looked back to Ian, I probably matched my old hair dye, and wanted to sink through the floor. I tilted my head a little, letting my hair fall forward to hide me while I recovered, and caught Venec watching me. He saw me watching him watching me, and I swear to god, that gaze of his intensified until I felt like the only person in the room.

Which I wasn't. I looked away before the blush went farther than my face, and tried to pay attention to what was going on outside of my libido.

"All right," Stosser said briskly. "If you haven't figured out the what of things by now, you're fired. Here's the who.

"Two months ago, Charles and Patty Reybeorn, ages seventy-five and seventy-two, respectively, were found dead in the front seat of a brand-new Benz sedan, parked in their garage in a rather exclusive and well-to-do suburb of Chicago. The exhaust had been backed up, and the initial cause of death was listed as vehicular suicide."

"Nice car," Nifty said. I had to take his word for it—I could recognize basic logos, and knew the difference between a coupe and a sedan, but that was about it.

"Initial? There was cause to doubt it?" Sharon had pulled in a notepad from somewhere and was jotting down notes. Boss's pet, I thought uncharitably, annoyed that I hadn't thought to carry one with me, too.

"No, not initially. Both the local police and the Midwest Council, to which the deceased both belonged, were satisfied with the conclusion. However, there were a few details that raised eyebrows."

"Such as?" Sharon paused with her pencil over the pad.

"First, there was no known or probable reason for the couple to commit suicide. They were both in decent health, financially secure, and on good terms with each other, which might rule out a murder-suicide scenario."

"People off themselves for reasons that seem perfectly valid to themselves, but nobody else even noticed," I said. "Not having a clear motive doesn't seem like enough to reverse the ruling."

"True. And the local police did not. Over the daughter's objections, the case was closed."

"And the daughter is our client?" Nifty had missed seeing her come in, and had to be caught up on that detail, Nick listing the vitals, including the fact that I'd spotted her gemstones and known the name.

"I remember her now." That got everyone looking at me again, this time with various levels of startlement and anticipation. "No, I never met her, never saw her before today. But my mentor has friends out in the Midwest region, they're major players there. Or were, anyway, I guess. Oh man, the daughter, Rose Reybeorn. Damn. She doesn't just have money. She's got strings on people, and she doesn't mind pulling them."

"So our new client wants to use us to yank chains?" Sharon didn't sound really pleased about that. I wasn't, either, honestly. Made it all seem…petty. I wondered, idly, if there was insurance involved, since it was so important it *not* be suicide. Except the last thing the Reybeorns needed was money….

Okay, I was going on gossip, and gossip about money was almost always wrong. But even so, I didn't see a Reybeorn needing a death settlement to make ends meet. Even if her ex-husband had sucked up in the settlement, she'd done well for herself since then.

No, there was something else about the deaths, something that had made it so gossipworthy....

"There was one other thing that bothered our client," Stosser went on. "The police can't explain it, either. The Benz, the car they allegedly committed suicide in...didn't belong to either one of them. It wasn't a recent purchase, a rental, or a friend's loaner, so far as the police have been able to determine. In fact, nobody seemed to know *who* it belonged to."

Yeah. That was it, the detail I was trying to remember. The unclaimed death-car.

Pietr exhaled with a sharp whooshing noise. "That could raise an eyebrow, yeah. And the cops pooh-poohed a possible murder weapon of unknown ownership? Nice. Not."

"I can see why they called it a suicide," Nifty said, taking up the mantle of devil's advocate the way Sharon had, only with less 'tude and more calculation. Sharon was contrary by nature. Nifty, I was starting to understand, used it as a tool, or maybe a weapon. "No matter who the car belonged to, it was in their garage, and I'm guessing there wasn't any forced entry, no signs of a fight...."

"Yes, without any signs of foul play, which I'm assuming there weren't—" Sharon started to say, when Venec cut in.

"Never assume anything unless you have evidence in front of you." He let the rebuke sting, and then added, "However in this case, you are both correct—the medical examiner found no signs of violence committed on the bodies other than those attributable to the means of death."

They hadn't found any unexplainable marks or wounds on Madeline's body, either.

"So, what do we do? I mean, the cops have been all over the case, and probably half a dozen private investigators, before she had no choice but to turn to us." Nifty raised his hands in a "don't shoot the messenger" pose when Stosser looked at him. "Hey, man, it's the truth. We're not going to be second-string, much less first. So what does she expect us to do that nobody else could?"

And we were back to the original question, like Nifty and Stosser had planned it. I didn't think they had, of course…but Stosser took the on-a-silver-platter lead-in like a pro.

"To use magic to discover who killed her parents, and why."

Oh. Right. "Uh-huh." Sharon, of course, put all our thoughts into words. "That easy?"

Venec took ownership of the conversation then, his smile showing way more teeth than it had to for social comfort. "If it were easy, none of you would have jobs."

Game and match, Venec.

The first trick, everyone agreed, was to get our hands on the death-car itself. Exactly how we were going to do that was a mystery to us, since we were in New York, without any official standing, and the car was, presumably, still in Chicago, but the Guys seemed to have an idea. While they hammered it out, we were sent off like tardy schoolchildren to read a case study Stosser had put together on identifying the different species of midsize winged fatae based on flying patterns and wingspread, as seen from the ground.

"But…" Sharon had started to protest. Stosser didn't even hear her, already working on the next thing and dismissing us from his awareness in that way he had, so it was Venec who laid down the law.

"The car's not going to go anywhere or have anything new

done to it overnight, Mendelssohn. This is a case, yes. It's our first case, and it's important that we do good and look good. So everyone will get their hands dirty. But don't think it's your sole responsibility. Life goes on, and so does your training. Flying fatae, people. There will be a quiz."

"I'm an investigator, not a bird-watcher," Nick had grumbled to me, but quietly, and Venec pretended not to hear him. For a guy who had been all excited about the chance to see fatae, Nick didn't seem all that excited about learning to recognize them. I thought about pointing out the inconsistency, but decided it probably would just make him crabbier. Getting a green light and then seeing it turn to yellow was frustrating; I was with him on that.

Orders were orders, though. We all took our packets, loaded up on coffee and doughnuts from a platter that had appeared out on the front counter while we were in the meeting, and headed off to separate areas of the office to do the assignment. Stosser had been very clear about that: hands-on material we did in groups, but reading was a solitary occupation. I think he figured we needed the time away from each other during the day, too.

My usual favorite spot—the sofa in the entry room—was claimed almost immediately by Pietr, who settled himself with the complete and total self-consciousness of someone who knows he's being a pig. I shot him an evil glare, and went off to find somewhere else previously unclaimed.

"If you want us to do our job, you must allow us to do our job."

Oh. I stopped halfway through the door of workroom #3 as the voice hit me. Damn it, we needed to have In Use placards put up outside the offices: I had almost walked in on Venec holding a conference call with a bunch of other people. Their figures shimmered like holograms in the space, and I flattened myself against the wall instinctively to keep out of range. I had absolutely no damn idea how they were managing this, and walking into the middle of an unknown current-spell was always a bad idea.

There were three floating busts, two women and a man. The women were older, the man younger. I recognized one as Ms. R, and the others had enough of a staticky resemblance to assume they were members of the family.

Venec didn't look away from this display, but made a subtle, unmistakable hand gesture to indicate that I should come into their range of vision. I'd never seen him use it before, but I knew exactly what he wanted me to do. I wished, briefly, for Stosser's gilding-the-lily spell, squared my shoulders and tried to look professional as possible, and walked into view.

"This is Bonita Torres, who leads our initial evaluation team."

I did? Most excellent. I channeled J at his Council best, as much as I could, and inclined my head gravely first to Ms. R, as our client, and then to the others. "I regret the circumstances of our meeting," I said. "Sympathies on your loss."

"Indeed," Ms. R said. "You seem rather young to be leading a team."

"Ms. Torres led her first investigation while she was still in college," Venec said smoothly. "And to a successful conclusion, as well. You are in excellent hands here, I assure you. But in order to begin, we must be able to examine the car itself."

I kept my face professional, but inside things were chasing around each other going "what the fuck?" because how the hell had Venec known about that? Nobody knew about that, except me and J and my dad's girlfriend Claire and a nameless cave dragon up in the Adirondacks…

And the strange presence that had shadowed me the entire time I was digging into my dad's disappearance. The one that had congratulated me on a job well done, given me a vague idea about maybe going into law enforcement, and then disappeared....

I had almost forgotten about it, written the voice off as a hallucination, my understandably overstressed brain dealing with my father's murder as best it could. Even the dreams had forgotten it, for the most part.

Because it couldn't be Benjamin Venec, three years before I even knew he existed, or he had any reason to know I existed. It wasn't impossible, no, but it was damned improbable and that was as good as impossible. Right?

Or was that why he felt so familiar to me, why I knew when he was in the room, why he watched me, sometimes, like...I didn't know what it was like. But it was intense, and overwhelming, and it made me want, very badly, to crack open his brain and see what was inside.

"The car is still in police custody," the man with Ms. R was saying. "Although the case has been closed on their part, they don't know who the owner is. I expect that it will go to auction at some point. They haven't seen fit to tell us anything, naturally."

"Of course." Venec was trying to stay soothing and politic, but he really wasn't good at it, and his body language was muttering impatience. Stosser should have been handling this interview, really. Could the client see how annoyed the boss was, through the interface? Hopefully not. Venec made an effort, stilling his body and letting the lines of his face smooth back into pleasantness. "The fact remains that we need to be able to examine the car itself as part of our preliminary investigation. We simply need to determine the best way to achieve that. With your permission, I will make contact with the officer in charge of the case and arrange it as soon as possible. We will update you as soon as there is news."

He closed the fingers of his right hand into his palm, a subtle little spellcast, and the connection flickered and died. Sweet. He looked up and saw me watching his hand, I guess, because when I met his gaze there was this little, secret smile on his lips. Not the fang-baring smile he'd given Sharon—no less dangerous, but in a totally, totally different way. If a random guy in a bar had given me that smile, I'd have bought him a drink and gotten his number. I wasn't used to not going after what I wanted. Venec, on the other hand, seemed to be all about control, self—and otherwise. That just made me want to rattle his cage, just a little. But he'd be expecting the obvious approach, so I went sideways.

"That's how you handle clients? Not even a good afternoon, have a nice day?"

Venec let his annoyance show now. Point to me! "I hate dealing with people."

"So I noticed." I thought about confronting him with my suspicions about his—or Stosser's—intrusion into my earlier life, but decided that now really wasn't a good time. Either he wasn't, in which case where did he get that information, or he was, in which case...okay. It had nothing to do with the game I'd decided was happening between us now. That voice in my head had helped me when I needed it. I owed them thanks, not complaints, even if it was a little...creepy.

If he was, it also confirmed my suspicions of how and why I'd gotten that phone call. He, or maybe Stosser, had followed through on that implicit promise of employment, all those years ago...which suggested that they'd been planning this for a lot longer than any of us had estimated. In light of all that, why would I be upset about a little violation of privacy?

If he did it again, ever, I was going to kick his ass. Hard.

"So," I asked him instead, "how are we going to convince the Chicago cops to let us get our mitts on an impounded vehicle?"

"We aren't."

"Um?"

Pietr would have grinned when he heard someone say something like that. Nifty might have rubbed his huge hands in anticipation. Me? When Ben Venec looked at me with that considering expression, his eyes dark and serious and with a pull like riptide, I knew we were in deep trouble. And by "we," I totally meant "me."

## nine

We didn't, after all, have a quiz on flying fatae, although I wouldn't be at all surprised to walk in one morning and get handed a multiple-choice paper. Instead, at the close of the workday, we got assignments. Sharon and Pietr were set to compile dossiers on everyone even remotely associated with the deceased, using, in Venec's words, "whatever sources you come across, just don't tell us how you did it." Nifty was told to hone and perfect my follow-the-suspect cantrip, in case we needed it. He looked at me, startled, as though I might object. I just looked back at him, impassive. Normally, a spell belonged to the person who crafted it, as much as magic could belong to anyone. But I wasn't about to start a squall over it; if it did come in handy, I'd bring it up when raises were discussed.

Nick and me? We got to take a road trip.

The next morning I reported early, if not bright, and had my sense of doom confirmed. *Trouble* probably wasn't the word for what Venec had in mind. *Insanity,* maybe.

"You ready?"

I looked Venec straight in those deep brown eyes, and didn't blink. "Ready."

The first thing I noticed was that Chicago in mid-September was a lot cooler than New York, or even Boston. That was the damnable thing about Translocation—it never gave you any time to acclimate. I didn't think it was the lake-effect breeze that was making my skin prickle, though.

Nick appeared a few feet away from me, trying to look as though he Transloc'd every day. He looked around, saw me, and came over. "He's good."

"Yeah." There were probably a lot of things Benjamin Venec was good at. Best not to think about that, though. "Hey, Nick, isn't it a crime to impersonate a police officer?"

He shrugged, and started walking toward our goal, a long, low building at the other end of the near-empty parking lot. "Yes. But we're not."

"We're not?" I asked, catching up.

Nick looked over his shoulder at me consideringly, letting his gaze linger in a way that I'd probably have slapped a stranger for. "Are you wearing a uniform? Carrying a badge?"

I had to admit that no, I was not. I was, however, dressed in dark blue coveralls that looked an awful lot like police-issue, and carrying a fake walkie-talkie that looked an awful lot like ones the actual police employees were carrying—fake, so that we didn't have to worry about cracking one open with current—and we were walking through the corridors of an impound facility as though we had every reason to be there.

The mock-up ID cards Venec had pulled out of god-knows-where, which didn't actually say Police Department anywhere on them, weren't going to get us out of trouble if we were stopped, so the trick was not to get stopped. That meant looking as if we belonged. I slumped a little, and tried to feel as put-upon as possible. Apparently, that was what it took to pass as a civilian employee of the state, because nobody even looked twice at us as we flipped those ID cards at the single bored cop on duty, bypassed the main building, and walked out into the impound yard.

Damn, there were a lot of cars there. Most of them were junkers, crap rides I'd be ashamed to park next to, and an un-nerving number of them had what looked like bullet holes in the doors or windshields.

Yesterday afternoon, I'd been chatting via current with a Council powerhouse; now I was wandering a graveyard of broken cars. Never let it be said this job didn't take you places.

A little farther in, and the cars got nicer: no rust, gleaming chrome, and intact interiors. I figured these were the ones im-pounded during search-and-seizures, rather than being aban-doned or towed. Nick was scanning over the tops of the cars and checking numbers against the list on his clipboard.

"There. That's the lot number. And there's the car."

"Wow." I wasn't much for cars as a rule, but if you had to go out in one, that was the way to do it. Huge, sleek, and gleaming with chrome and silver paint, like a Grande Dame of an era a long, long time ago. I didn't even want to think about what kind of mileage to the gallon it probably didn't get.

Or the fact that two people had died in it.

"All right, let's get to it."

When they selected us for this job, the Guys had officially-in-front-of-everyone appointed me team leader—apparently that much of what Venec had told the client was true: whatever initial evaluation team we had, it was mine. Of course, the entire team consisted of me and Nick, so it wasn't much of an accolade.

That hadn't stopped Sharon from doing an obvious slow simmer, though. I hoped to hell Stosser knew what he was doing. The Guys were smart and savvy and all that, but I was starting to wonder about how much attention they paid to the stuff right under their noses....

"Do you think Sharon's pissed? About me being made lead, I mean."

"Yep."

"Great."

He snorted at my tone. "Shar's going to be pissed over the air entering a room before her, Bonnie. It's just the way she is. Doesn't mean she's pissed at *you*."

For some strange reason, that actually did make me feel better. I sort of liked Sharon, for all she was a prickly bitch. I wanted her to like me, too.

Nick reached the car first, and put his kit down on the pavement next to it. A flip of the latch, and a gleaming array of tools were revealed inside. To anyone watching, he was just a tech doing whatever it was techs did to cars. I put aside any thoughts of Sharon, or the rest of the team, and put my brain full on the problem at hand.

We already had, courtesy of the client, the full police report on the state of the car as it was found, as much as they could determine. A good thing, too, because I didn't know a damn thing about cars, and I suspected Nick wasn't much better. He'd let enough slip in the past few weeks to make me think that if he hadn't been Talent, he probably would have been a tech geek, not a grease monkey, but current made both hobbies problematic.

So while he was making like he knew what he was doing, I stood back and just looked at the car, getting a feel for it. Ideally, the Guys and every crime drama told us, you got to look over the crime scene itself, create a visual record of what happened—or might have happened. Getting called in late and third-hand like this, we didn't have the option. The car had been taken out of context, the crime scene manhandled, and god knew how many Council Talent had been futzing current all over the place without a clue. All we had was what was left. It had to be enough. Our future depended on it.

The Guys hadn't said that. We knew it anyway. Ms. R was too high-profile to flub.

So. Time to do what the Guys seemed to think we could do. I had taken a quick hit of fresh current off the city grid before Stosser Translocated us into the facility, and my core was still assimilating the new energy, weaving the man-made current into my own cords until they were ready to work together.

"Come on, pixie-girl, get started."

"Shut up." My white-blond fluff really seemed to bring out the nickname instinct in Nick. Pixie-girl and dandelion seemed to be his favorites. It amused me, but letting him know that would miss the whole point of the game.

And he was right; sooner started, sooner out of here. I was discovering a distressing honesty in my genetic makeup—sneaking into places made me nervous. Not just about getting caught, but because it was *wrong.*

They really should have sent Pietr; I didn't think he had a bone of morality in him. But they hadn't: this was my job to do…or screw up.

*All right,* I thought at the car while I walked toward it, trying for the same calm tone I'd use to approach a dog I wasn't sure about. *Let's see what you've got.*

The entire lot was visible to the main building through a large glass window on the second floor, but it was still early, and there didn't seem to be anyone around to wonder why a tech was standing next to the car, passing her hands over it with six inches between her hands and the metal.

If a Talent were to walk by and look out, they might be able to see the current flickering from my palms to the surface of the car, coating it like dusting powder, but they'd have to be paying attention. Nulls, the rest of humanity without a magical clue? Wouldn't see a thing.

Odds were good that the Council investigator, whoever he or she had been, did the same thing—looking over the car to see if there was any sign of current having been used on it. The difference was, that was probably all they'd been looking for, and there were damned few things in this world that didn't carry a touch of current on them, even just in passing. A car where two Talent had died, if they had actually died here, and not just been dumped?

If I were suffocating to death, I know I'd have used current to try to stop it, break a window, call for help, *something*. Can't imagine these two were any different.

So I was looking for something different, going deeper and lighter all at once. There were traces of current in the seats, yeah…and in the frame of the car itself. Some in the dashboard, too, which made me wonder if the car would even work now, or if all the high-end extras were fried. Whoever bought this car at auction might be in for an unhappy surprise.

"Go in clean." Venec's voice in my memory, giving last-minute instructions while Nick fidgeted, eager to be gone. "Don't have an agenda. Don't expect to find anything. Don't *look* for anything."

Easier said than done. Another voice from my memory, this time J: "Keeping an open mind is good. Too open, and things fall out of it."

This was my strength, Stosser had said when he picked me for this job. My ability to see, and observe, and remember details other people didn't catch. Question: How did I do it? Answer:

I didn't *do* anything. Everything was there, and it came to me, and my brain just *took* it. So how did I intentionally *use* it?

Current stirred within me, and I fashioned it into a net, the kind that fishing boats use out in the deep sea, throwing it over and dragging it behind them, to see what they can glean. Cops look for something that's wrong, or out of place, something hinky. Council probably looked for something familiar, to confirm their expectations. My net was set for everything, not only the stuff that jumped out at you but anything trying to hide, something so innocuous or ordinary that it might be overlooked, or something so wildly wrong it might not be noticed because it was so impossible.

Improbable doesn't mean impossible. Don't bring an agenda to the gathering. Don't eliminate anything. Not yet.

The net snagged, and I tugged it, carefully. The normal neon-bright blues and greens darkened to black where something physical stuck, hot red to where current sparked back against it. The urge to grab it and run swelled, and I tamped it down. Gently, gently. I needed to gather without destroying, take without leaving any trace of myself behind, or letting anything of myself infect the evidence, to muddy the scene. Damn it, those TV shows make it look so easy, just swab and bag. Venec said most of the TV shows got it wrong, anyway.

Brain on the job, brain on the job! My muscles started to cramp up, but I couldn't afford to deal with it. Gently, gently…

"I have physical trace," I said to Nick, not breaking my focus to see what he was doing.

"Show me."

*here*

Pinging was mind-to-mind contact, the closest thing we had to telepathy, but seriously limited. You had to know someone pretty well to actually get words across, much less complicated conversations, so I stuck to basics, more a sense of where things were than an actual description.

*got it* Nick's pingback was triumphant, and I felt the current-net jerk and then sag a little when he Translocated the trace back to the office. The important part of his assignment was done: he had the lightest touch of all of us, so hopefully his current wouldn't adhere to anything too badly, or distort any previous signature.

Now for the current-trace: I sent a narrow thread of yellow filtering into the net, racing along the existing strands to where the hot red still glowed, making the strands sticky in a way I couldn't really describe. It would have been nice to toss this to Nick, too, but that wasn't how it worked, not like the physical stuff. A twist of the now-sticky net and it all came back to me, stored not in my core but a separate place, hollowed out and waiting. The weight ached like brain-freeze, all this stuff-not-me in me. I didn't like it, not at all.

"Done." I was sore as hell, physical to match the magical. Nothing an hour of deep-tissue massage wouldn't take care of, hopefully. I stretched, fingers reaching for the sky, and felt something in my back crack. "So, any idea—"

"Hey. What's up? I thought they closed this case?"

I didn't need a ping to feel Nick's sudden panic and frustration at the interruption, because the same things were flooding my system. I turned to face the intruder.

Late sixties, maybe. Hispanic, stern-faced but not threatening. Wearing a suit, not coveralls. No briefcase, no walkie-talkie on his belt, no tech-growth clinging to his ear. Middle management.

"Do I look like I get to make decisions?" Nick, stepping in front of me, hefting his tool kit. "Some bright child wanted another run of the engine, make sure there wasn't anything missed that could come back and bite us on the lawsuit. Word is the vic's daughter isn't happy with the verdict, so brass wants us to CYA. So we get to come down and waste everyone's time proving what we already know, instead of dealing with the backlog that actually needs us." He put just enough disgruntled professional in his voice to back up the story, and I could see the suit start to back down, reassured.

Then: "Who placed the work-order? All ongoing investigation requests are supposed to pass by my desk."

Oh, shit. I was ready to really panic, try to Transloc out of there right in front of the guy, when Nick took a step closer, his hands in plain sight, totally nonthreatening.

"You already signed off on it," he told the guy, his disgruntlement modifying into honest puzzlement and a hint of much-put-upon underling. He was one hundred percent convincing as a loyal and long-suffering schlub.

"I did?"

"Yeah, sure." Total assurance, confidence, security in those words, and like Stosser's glamour, it soaked into the suit, making him believe it, too. Oh, I so needed to learn how to do that!

"All right, then. Make sure you lock everything up again when you're done, and damn it, don't scratch the finish! Car's supposed to go to auction next week—not surprisingly, the daughter refused to claim it, after all that."

The suit nodded once, briefly, to me, and turned away. We waited until he disappeared out of sight behind the first line of junkers, before breathing a sigh of relief.

"These are not the droids you're looking for?" I was more impressed than my comment indicated.

Nick shrugged. "It's not polite—" that was an understatement "—but he really didn't want to deal with the paperwork, and I didn't want to deal with him. A little pushing seemed the lesser of two evils, overall. You ready to go?"

He made it sound easy. I could have been choked to the gills with current, and not been able to pull that off. "Yeah, yeah. The hell with Pietr, you could have been a serious Evil Mastermind, you know that?"

"Nah. Too much work. Same with the NSA."

"The what?" I'd heard him, but I wasn't sure I'd actually heard him.

He gestured with his tool kit that I should precede him out of the bay. We were supposed to go out to the parking lot and walk about a mile away before calling for a Translocation back. "The NSA. Yeah. I got calls, starting about halfway through college. I started keeping a lower profile, after that. Like I said, too much work. They still keep calling, though. So did a few less official organizations. Venec just got in with an offer I couldn't refuse."

"Which was?"

"Excitement, puzzle-solving, and nobody shooting at me."

"Better offer than I got," I had to admit, holding the fire door open for him. Besetting honesty wasn't always my sin, but something about Nick seemed to draw it out of me. "I got offered a job, period."

He shrugged again. J was right; it did look ungraceful. "You didn't have any other options, I bet," he said, not meaning for it to sting. "I did. They had to woo me."

We walked through the parking lot, and the fresh air and sense of a job accomplished almost relaxed me. "Huh. Are you saying I'm easy, mister?"

"Torres, after almost two months working with you, I think I can say with some veracity that you're not only easy, you're cheap."

Ouch. "Ha. I—"

I didn't get a chance to say anything more, because the sound of something slamming past me way small and way fast triggered drop-and-freeze reflexes I didn't even know I had. Nick had the same ones, the way he hugged the pavement next to me.

"They said no shooting, damn it!" he yelled, even as I was pinging home.

*get us the hell out of here!*

## ten

An emergency Translocation's fast and nasty, and it's not something you want to do on a regular basis, but I was never so damn glad to feel the molecules of my body being sucked through a current-straw in my entire life, and when we popped into place back in the office, I could have wept with gratitude.

"What happened? Did you get your evidence?"

Venec was damn near shouting, and everyone was crowding around us, and my gratitude got tempered, fast, with annoyance.

"Someone shot at us, and all you can ask is if we got the evidence?"

That stopped them, for about three seconds. Then the clamor started up again. I ignored them, turning to look at my partner, who was still sprawled on the floor next to me.

"You're bleeding. Oh god, did you—"

"Nah," he reassured me, lifting his bloody hand away from his shoulder. "Took the pavement too hard, is all. I think."

Sharon shoved her way through everyone else, and for once I was actually glad for her abrasive take-chargeism, because it didn't take long at all for her to send someone off for bandages and stuff, and to get Nick out of the jumpsuit and his T-shirt underneath so she could see the damage better.

He was right; it was just a nasty-looking pavement burn, tearing his skin open in places and oozing blood, but nothing that was going to need more than a few wipes and tape. The skin around it was pale and flushed-looking, but that was pretty much his normal skin tone. He did not, unfortunately, show to any better advantage undressed than dressed, and I made a mental note to get him started on some basic weights, try to bulk him up, before I worked on any more cases with him. He might be a fast thinker, but sometimes you needed a fast hitter, too.

"You got the evidence?" Venec let Sharon deal with the medical stuff, and knelt down, leaning forward into my personal space with that pit-bull intensity. Those impossible eyes bored right into me, and if you'd asked me on my life I couldn't have told you what precise color they were, but I knew every wrinkle and sag around the edges, and the exact shade of soot-black his eyelashes were. Damn damn damn. "We got what Nick sent back, safe and secure," he said, "but was there anything else in the car?"

"Yeah." The weight of what I was carrying suddenly, now that I thought about it, felt like cold iron in my brain, and his gaze-hold on me was lessened enough so that I could look away. "I got it. I…" I hesitated, suddenly aware of a problem.

"What?" Stosser swooped in, eavesdropping, if listening to something you had the right to know could be considered eavesdropping. Could it? My head hurt, so I stopped thinking about that and focused back on the problem at hand.

"I don't know how to get rid of it, though. I mean, we spent so much time learning how to gather, I guess…I don't know how to dump it." And I had to do it soon, I knew that, otherwise it would be tainted with my own signature, and nobody would ever believe it wasn't tampered with.

"We thought of that."

Of course they had. I wish to hell they'd thought to tell us all that before—although I suppose that was my lesson, to think of this stuff myself, and ask. Like the man said, if you've got questions…

Then again, he hadn't actually answered Sharon's question, had he?

With that gaze still on me, I was relieved that it was Stosser who offered me his hand, hauling me up off the floor with more power than his skinny frame suggested. Skinny, maybe, but not frail. I wouldn't stack him up against Nifty, but he could probably take most of us in an unfair fight. I got the feeling those were the only kind boss-guy fought.

"The chat room," he said to me, dropping my hand and turning to walk away. It was almost as though he was pissed off at me, or something. I tried to think about how I might have screwed up…by getting shot at? We didn't know who, or why, or anything, so how could he assume it was my fault rather than Nick's? Because Nick got hurt? That made no sense at all.

I tabled that question, too, and followed him out of the room. First things first; to get this stuff out of my brain, and into evidence.

Stosser let me change out of the jumpsuit and back into my own gear, then had me sit in the armchair while he perched on the desk, taking up his usual lecturer pose. He was wearing another of his crunchy-granola outfits today, and I was starting to wonder which was the real Stosser, the stylish image-conscious guy, or the one who didn't seem to remember that his hair was Pippi Longstocking red?

"All right," he said, either not aware or not caring that I was dissing his style-sense. "What we're going to do is this. You open your core—"

"Whoa." All thoughts of anything else went right out of my head. "I the hell will *not*."

Stosser made a placating gesture that was obviously supposed to calm my objections. "It's all right."

I didn't feel at all placated. "The hell it is."

Your core was a private place. It was the seat of your personal current, the furnace that fed our abilities, the…well, it was *private,* was all, and here my boss was telling me blithely to open up and say ah?

"You're doing all the work," he said. "I'm not going to go in, you're going to take it out. That's all."

"Uh-huh. And you've done this how many times before?"

"Once." I liked the fact that he didn't hesitate in answering, or try to fudge the number. But reassuring did not translate to reassured.

"You experimented on Venec?"

"Ben did the experimenting, actually. As I said, I am merely the receiver. You will control the entire process."

Oh, he was a cool one, not a worry in the world. J was right: Stosser was a schmoozer of the highest order, and his calm assurance and smooth delivery worked, even when you knew he was working you. Amazing. Also damned annoying, because I dislike being manipulated. But he was paying me for the privilege, so…

"You don't seem at all curious about who was shooting at us," I said, trying to make myself comfortable in the chair.

"I let Ben handle those details," he said. "Especially since nobody was actually shot."

Oh. There. Just on the edge, just a sliver, but it was there if you were watching for it. Ian Stosser wasn't anywhere near as cool about that shooting as he wanted us to believe. He was pissed, or worried, or something seriously not-calm. I noted it, and let it go.

Stosser didn't seem to notice that I'd caught him. "Now, when you're relaxed, I want you to reach down inside and imagine your core like a Fabergé egg, hinged, and filled with fabulous treasures that are meant to be displayed...."

His voice droned on, soothing and scholarly, and I tuned it out the same way I used to tune out professors in gut courses back in college, because by the time they got to the second or third long-winded sentence, I already knew what they were talking about.

Same here. The image of the Fabergé egg worked, and I spared a moment to wonder if he'd have used the same image on Nifty, or Sharon, because J took me to see an exhibit once when I was a teenager, and although I thought at the time that they were horribly gaudy things, the *idea* of them stuck with me. It was amazingly easy to see my core, not as an egg, but in the same way: my own personal, private treasure that, if I wanted to, I could open up and display some part of it to someone else, so that they could see how fabulous the secret was....

*show me?* Stosser's mental voice, not so much pinging as wafting by. But under the polite exterior there was something harder, something less pleasant, and I shied away from it. *show me*

He was the boss. Reluctantly, I touched that thread of current with one of my own, and brought forward the evidence I had collected; the shards of broken current, remnants of power-use, impressions of emotions and actions trapped by the endless webs of current that surround us, at all times. Delicate, tricky stuff, and every touch was done with mental breath held, for fear of cracking something and rendering it useless.

Stosser opened his current up wider and took those things from my touch, never—as he promised—actually going into my core, just looking at the one small section I opened to him and taking the things that were there.

Curious, my current followed, and he allowed it access... not to his own core, but to a wide-open space that made my eyes hurt from the reflected light; all gleaming white, sanitized, and empty.

*evidence locker* he told me.

It was...amazing. Impossible. A virtual space made of current, outside anything physically existent. We might be making this shit up as we went along with baling wire and chewing gum, but my god, this was some amazing wire and gum.

I could *feel* the entrances, now that I was inside, and knew that I'd be able to access it any time I wanted to, in the future.

*anyone on team can* Ian agreed, *once they have the key*

And a small portion of that endless space darkened, shadows appearing, as he carefully, gently, placed the trace I had collected into one corner, labeled it, and locked it down. I got a sense from him of a key, glimmering pale green neon, tucked into a pocket, and the sense, likewise, that there was one in my pocket, too.

Anyone on the team could get in here, but only the two of us could open that particular spot, unless we gave them the key.

He released his hold on my current-strand, and I slid slowly backward, feeling myself leave a place that didn't exist, sliding easily, gently, back into the awareness of my body.

Stosser was still sitting there, leaning against the desk. I was still in the chair. My legs were tingling like they'd gone to sleep and were only now waking up, but otherwise...

I checked inside. Yeah, the heavy weight of the trace was gone.

"If I asked you how you made that, and you told me, would I be able to understand any of it?"

"Possibly," Stosser, said, standing up, but he didn't elaborate. All right. Every wizard gets to have his secrets. For now.

"We should rejoin the others now that the fuss will have died down, and determine who will be working on what."

"And figure out who was shooting at us?" Just because I wasn't going to let him know I knew he was hiding something didn't mean I was going to let go of the topic. I was still unnerved by that, and figured Nick would be, too. We deserved to know, if there was something happening.

"I told you." Stosser was, in direct contradiction to the myths about redheads, remarkably mellow, but every now and again some vinegar leaked into his voice. "Ben is dealing with it."

And with that, at least for now, I had to be content.

We walked back into a madhouse. The fuss hadn't quite died down, mainly because Venec had disappeared, Sharon tried to take control of the situation, and then she and Nifty got into a shouting match over who was actually in charge of the situation. Nick had sided with Sharon, and Pietr… Where the hell was Pietr, anyway?

"They've been like this since you left." His voice appeared at my elbow. "Personally, I don't think either of them's fit to lead a cat to tuna, but nobody asked me."

"Probably because they couldn't find you, Fade, m'boy."

He looked hurt, and I felt as if I'd kicked a puppy, which was exactly how he wanted me to feel. So I kicked him in the shin.

Stosser leaned with the door against his back, and watched them with what really only could be described as the sardonic eye of a jaded third-grade teacher. "You want to take odds on when they'll start pulling hair?"

"You'd know about that more than we would," Pietr said. Good point—his hair was close-cropped to his scalp, and mine was chin-length: hair pulling wasn't something we had to really worry about.

Meanwhile, our two darlings were facing off, literally.

"You're a know-everything busybody but that doesn't mean you have a clue about how the real world works."

"Oh, because spending four years knocking people down with big bad muscles makes you so smart? You've never even worked in—"

"Children!" That vinegar was back in Stosser's voice, and it splashed over them, stopping them hard. I guess class was back in session. "You can fight out your alpha pack issues later. Right now, there's work to be done. Lawrence, Mendelssohn. You two need to work together, not against each other. Go over the physical trace Shune sent back. A 3-D sketch before you touch anything, and then lift any prints you can find. Odds are they're useless, but we have to document everything, so anything we find is validated. Shune, are you up for work, or do you want to watch this one?"

Nick flexed his arm carefully around the makeshift sling Sharon had rigged for him, and managed a one-armed shrug. "I'm better as a pair of eyes at this point, boss."

"Fine. Torres, you do the same. Try to learn something useful. Cholis, come with me. I have a job for your particular skills."

Pietr's expression verged somewhere between pleased and really worried. I didn't blame him, but was more worried about having to get between Sharon and Nifty without making things worse. They exited, and the four of us were left standing, silently, in a really awkward face-off, two glaring and two trying to look anywhere but at each other.

"All right." Sharon was the one who capitulated first, surprising all of us—including, I think—Sharon. Her body language was still tense, but her shoulders relaxed a little under that linen blouse, and I didn't feel the same electric vibe off her. "It's been a really long day that we weren't expecting, and this is stupid. Nick, you're the one who handled the stuff. You direct us."

Nick looked started as hell, but rallied. "All right. Who's got a decent handle on the 3-D sketching?"

"That would be me," Nifty said. His voice—and vibe—still had a bit of challenge in it, but not anything that demanded a takedown. Anyway, it was true; I was an abysmal failure on that level, and I'm not sure the others were much better.

"All right, then you get started with that, and Sharon, you've got the best recovery skills. When he's done with the sketch, see if you can lift anything useful off anything. Bonnie, we need to get it all cataloged, before we forget what was found where."

He dispatched us with evident satisfaction, and a little arrogance, but probably he hadn't been deferred to a lot in his life—if you're skinny, geeky, and not a tech-god, you don't get a lot of respect, no matter how smart you are—and damn, Sharon had managed us Council-worthy. If she'd chosen me, Nifty might have felt it was a girl thing, and if she had pushed herself forward we all would have been annoyed, but this way Nifty was appeased, and Nick felt gratitude toward her, and me.... I didn't care one way or the other, I realized. I was still worried about who the hell had shot at us, and part of my mind was still chewing over how easily Nick had *pushed* that supervisor into letting us go, and there was another part of my mind still working on the concept of the white virtual storeroom, and wondering where the hell Venec was and what he was doing, and there just wasn't any room left in my head for dealing with intragroup politics.

I'm crap at group politics, anyway.

We broke for the second workroom, where Nick had sent the materials.

"So what happened to the trace you picked up?" Nick asked me, quietly enough that the others might not hear. Information was power. I guess he was playing, too.

I thought about how I'd not let Stosser know I knew he was upset, and figured we all were playing, one way or the other.

"It's dumped and safe," I said to him. "But we're supposed to focus on the physical first." Physical was easier to work through, Venec had lectured us. Current left a trace on the physical that was harder to blend into the original form, and could be broken down more easily for investigation.

That was the theory we were working under, anyway. Reality didn't always scan with theory.

The gleaming white worktable looked more barren than I'd expected: from the expression on Nick's face, he'd thought he'd brought back more, too. I ran over the checklist in my mind, and it seemed to match the items laid out and casting dark shadows on the table surface. I guess it just seemed like more, in the stress of the situation. Interesting.

"Bonnie?" Nick had gotten out the evidence logbook—a fancy name for a plain three-ring binder we'd never used before—and settled himself at the empty edge of the table. He was looking at me, his little ferret nose practically twitching.

Right. Recall time.

"Three crumpled wrappers, wedged deep into the backseat; a wad of dried gum from the floor mat; ash from the bottom of the otherwise-emptied ashtray; a couple of hairs taken off the upholstery, passenger-seat headrest, and one from the backseat behind the driver's seat; a scoop of mud from the front half of the undercarriage; a scratch of dried crud from the rear left fender; and what I thought was a nail clipping that got caught under the door handle of the driver's side."

"You thought?" Nick paused midscribble. "We're not supposed to think, Bonnie, just report."

"Fine. A fragment of something that looked like a fragment of nail, caught under the door handle. Better?"

"Don't snarl at me, I'm just trying to do this right."

"You want to see a snarl, ferret-boy? I'll show you a snarl."

"Ferret?" His voice rose and the tip of his nose twitched, only enhancing the resemblance

"Children," Sharon murmured, taking one of the stools at the table across from Nifty, down at the evidence-laden end. "You need a score card to tell who's squabbling with whom around here."

I laughed because it was true.


Maybe it was just me and that connection-thing we had going on, but I knew without looking the instant when Venec came into the room. He was almost as quiet as Pietr, but there was some difference in the air when he entered that distracted me from my study of the sketch of the nail clipping—and I was right, it was a nail—and made me look up to see him walking through the workroom door.

Unlike Stosser, he didn't change his clothing like a runway model; jeans and a dark blue knit sweater that made his eyes look even darker, leather shoes and a single silver strand around his wrist that I hadn't noticed before. Interesting. Silver wasn't the magical element the fairy tales claimed, but it did have certain useful properties I wondered if he knew about....

"You're back," I said, to alert the others. "Did you find out who shot at us? And why?"

He shot me a glare that could have wilted a redwood. "Yeah, you're number one on the Chicago cops most-wanted list. Relax, Torres. It was just an overeager security guard with rubber bullets, alerted by the fact that neither of you bothered to wave your passes over the exit bar when you walked out. It's been taken care of."

Oops. In our defense we were a little distracted, but the look on Venec's face suggested that he didn't want to hear even justifiable excuses.

"What do you have? Show me."

I slid away from the table, hearing everyone else do the same, so the boss could have a better look at the 3-Ds. They floated above the table and turned slowly to display all sides, black lines and white spaces tinted with just faint bits of color, like pencil and watercolors. Most of them were actual size, but Nifty had enlarged the nail at my request, so that I could determine if it was a fingernail or a toenail or something else entirely.

"And have we gotten anything out of this motley assemblage of crap?"

Fucker. We'd been busting our current for three hours on that "assemblage of crap," and he walks in and dismisses it out of hand? All the hot in the world, and I was still ready to throw something heavy and pointed at him.

His hands came down on the table next to me, and the table creaked as he leaned on it, looking at my sketch. The edge of the object was ragged and thick, and there were striations along the surface that looked weirdly familiar.

"Toenail?"

"Looks like. Except it's damned unlikely."

He looked at me, and I remembered again I wasn't supposed to have an opinion, not yet, just evaluations. I backtracked a little, and made a full report. "The clipping is in the shape of a half-moon, with a jagged edge that suggests either being bitten or torn off. A nail. It was found under the driver's-side door handle. Unless we're dealing with someone who is extremely prehensile, it seems unlikely a toenail would have gotten caught there."

"All right. A reasonable assumption within the context of the findings. But don't rule anything out just yet. Is the nail necessarily human?"

I stared at him, my mouth falling open. Bastard. I hadn't even thought of that.

"Lawrence." He moved on, leaving me scrambling furiously, trying to think of some way to compare the sketch against all the known clawed fatae breeds. We hadn't learned how to run DNA tests using current yet. I had a feeling they'd be in our near future, though.

"There are distinct tooth marks in the gum, but I don't think we'd be able to tell anything except that whoever chewed it had molars." Nifty stared at his sketch, and then looked into the air at nobody in particular. "I don't suppose anyone's got some brilliant ideas on how to get a sample of saliva off old dried-up gum?"

Nobody did.

"That's your assignment, then," Venec said. "Find a way."

Nifty's jaw dropped; I had a feeling a lot like the way mine had, and then he shut it with a snap. He put his game face on, and nodded tightly. "Yessir." He might squabble for captainship of the team, but Nifty knew who the Coach was.

I guessed that made Stosser the owner of the team?

Nick had been working on the ashes. "I compared them to

some fresh cigarette ash…." He saw Venec's expression, and hurried to add, "No, I didn't bring them in. I went outside and found some, okay? Not a total idiot to compromise evidence."

That earned him a grudging nod of approval. "Go on."

Nick shrugged. "It's cigarette ash. According to the police report, both victims smoked. So, hardly a surprise. It was high-quality tobacco, though, from the looks of it. Goes with the victims' backgrounds—they weren't the kind to be smoking cut-rate cheapies."

"Verify that."

Nick nodded.

Sharon was next. She shrugged. "There were hairs. I couldn't tell anything from just a sketch."

Venec's glare returned. "You couldn't tell how long they were, if they were straight or curly, bleached, dyed, or naturally colored? Graying? Blond or brunette? Split ends or recently trimmed?"

Oh man. I suddenly felt as though I'd gotten off easy. His words were like bullets, hitting Sharon hard, right in the chest.

"Hey." Nick slammed his hand on the table. From his wince, I guess he hadn't meant to hit that hard. "Give us a break, okay? We're making this shit up as we go along, in case you've forgotten, and you and Ian both disappeared on us."

Venec looked around then as though just realizing that his partner wasn't in the room. "Where did Ian and Cholis go?"

We all shrugged. "Stosser said he had a different job for ghost-boy, and away they went," Nifty told him, his face still closed and tight. He could pick on Sharon, but Boss-Guys couldn't? I tossed that around and decided that it felt right.

"Damn it, I warned him…" Venec muttered, then seemed to recall that we were all looking at him avidly, waiting to see what he said next. Apparently, the Guys weren't entirely in accord. That was so not reassuring.

"All right, no matter. You have your observations recorded?" We all did.

"Then it's time to take a break, get some fresh air. Unlike what you see on TV or read in books, you can't work days straight and expect to get anything other than punch-stupid. Go, get a drink, use the bathroom, walk around the block, and get yourself some lunch. Shune, have that bandage checked. It looks like you're bleeding again." Directions given, he turned and walked out before we could recover enough to ask him anything more.

We all looked at each other, and I got the distinct feeling that nobody was going to take more than a bathroom break before we returned to the table.

I got up, feeling my lower back complain. Damn but it had been a long day already, even without the time-shift from here to Chicago and then back again. What time was it, anyway? "Right. There's a decent pizza place on the corner. I should bring back a pie or two?"

"Make it three," Nifty said, to nobody's surprise. Current burned calories, yeah, but his metabolism still thought he was in training or something.

"And a Diet Coke."

"And a regular Coke. Not a Pepsi. And an iced coffee."

Good lord. Offer to do a favor, and that's what you get. "Give me cash then, people. I'm not the damn pizza fairy."

On my way out through the lobby, a wad of cash stuffed into my front pocket, I saw a guy walking in, and did a full turn-and-walk-backward to watch his progress, because damn, he was worth the obviousness. Oh-my-god tall, and the kind of golden-blond that makes me feel washed out. Total surfer-boy tan and build, and dressed in a kind of uptown casual that said money but also that he worked for it.

He caught me watching—not that I was hiding anything—and smiled at me. Not an ah-hah smile either, but a really nice, warm, hi-there-yourself kind of smile.

He wasn't a local boy, that was for sure.

And then I was out the door and he was in, and I tucked the memory into the folder titled Fine Men and focused on remembering the lunch order.

I came back twenty minutes later to shouting.

"You're taking advantage of her grief and her hopes, and I call that fraud, at best!"

The voices were coming from the chat room. Not loud, as shouting went, but audible from where I stood. I looked down the hallway at the other end of our space, where the workroom was, and hesitated.

Oh hell. I'd never make much of an investigator if I didn't investigate, right? I put the pizzas and bag with the drinks down in the hallway where anyone with a nose could find them—hoping they'd have enough sense not to eat in the workroom—and moved as quietly along the hall as I could manage. Needed to get Pietr to teach me that ghosting thing, if he could.

The chat room's door was open just a chink, as if it was inviting me to snoop.

"Your mother has engaged us—" Venec, and I could tell that his temper was about to snap. Uh-oh.

"My mother is deluded."

The snap was audible even out here in the hallway. "Your mother is in full possession of all her faculties, and possibly a few you seem to have abandoned. Or do you really believe that your grandparents sat in a car that didn't belong to them and *willed* themselves to die, when they were both in excellent health, excellent finances, and with excellent prospects?"

"There was no sign of it being anything else. The police and the local Council both investigated...."

"The police were handicapped by not knowing that your grandparents were Talent. And the Council..." Venec's voice didn't get any softer, but it went from lecturing to conversational, in the space of one word. "The Council has its own reasons for wanting the case closed. Your grandparents had both friends and enemies in high places, and none of them are interested in close examination."

"You really believe that they were murdered?"

"We are not willing to let any assumption stand without looking at every possible angle and scrap of evidence. What that evidence tells us...we don't know yet. That's what the 'unaffiliated' in our name means. We don't answer to any authority except the evidence."

"I don't like this. You said it yourself. There are reasons not to dig into this."

"No, I said that there were people who would rather we didn't dig. I never said they were reasons I accept."

Steel would have bent before Benjamin Venec would, and in that instant, I admit it, I was almost embarrassingly proud to work for him.

"Now, Ms. Torres, if you would join us?"

Bastard, I thought for the third time that afternoon, and pushed the door all the way open to see Venec and the surfergod from the lobby both looking at me.

"Hi." No excuses: he caught me, fair and square, and I already knew excuses didn't fly with the Guys. "I'm Bonita Torres. I'm one of the investigators working on your mother's case."

"Yes, we...met, if you can call it that."

For a moment I thought he meant in the lobby, but then I remembered the four-way telecurrent conversation I'd been on the edges of, and blinked. "You look better when you're less staticky," I said, without thinking, and then felt my skin flush bright red from knees to ears. So much for my suave professional veneer.

He grinned, Venec looked even more stone-faced disgusted, and I tried to extract my foot from my mouth without choking.

"We were just about to get back to work," I said to Venec, trying very hard not to look him in the eye. All I needed was to get tangled up over that, too. I swear, I hadn't been this awkward since I was a hormone-riddled thirteen-year-old. Damn it, neither of them were *that* much all that.

"Didn't I tell you to take a break?"

"Pizza and caffeine for everyone. But we all felt like we were on a roll, so…"

I hoped to hell I was saying the right things. How much did you say to the boss, in front of the disgruntled son of a client, without actually letting them know that we weren't so much on a roll as freaking out about our jobs going down in flames if we didn't produce something?

"Excellent," Venec said. "Now, if you will excuse us?"

"Jack," the surfer god said. His tone seemed to have totally mellowed, without a trace of the earlier anger. "I seem to have made an ass out of myself, and I can only assure you it's merely because I am protective of my mother, especially after what she went through with the police and insurance companies after her parents' death, and…" He shrugged. On him, it looked good. "I still don't believe that you're going to find anything new, and my mother is wasting her time and money, but it's her time and money to waste." His expression got tough again. "Just don't promise her anything you can't deliver."

"Are you making a threat...Jack?"

Oh, Venec's voice was so smooth, his face so calm, it took Jack and me both a minute to realize he was dead serious.

"A warning."

You could practically feel the thunderheads gathering between the two of them again, current simmering just under the surface, not unleashed, not yet, but posturing, getting ready to show itself. I wanted to be the hell anywhere but there, but was afraid to move toward the door for risk of setting anything off. Alpha goddamn males.

"Hey, Ben, did you—"

Oh, thank god. Stosser appeared in the doorway as though he'd been summoned.

"Oh, sorry. Am I interrupting something?" His narrow face was as guileless as ever, and he seemed genuinely taken aback at seeing someone he didn't know in the office. I believed that about as much as I believed in the Easter bunny.

"No. This gentleman was just leaving. Jack, this is my partner, Ian Stosser."

"A pleasure," Ian said, stepping forward and offering his hand. Jack took it so smoothly, you'd never know he'd been an inch away from anger a second ago. "You're the son, yes? My condolences on the loss of your grandparents. They were wonderful people."

"You knew my grandparents?"

I wasn't sure who was more surprised by that, Jack or Venec.

"Only by reputation. My father was one of their earliest investors, back...oh, two decades ago. He had the good fortune to be involved in the downtown retrofit they did, managed to pay for my college education with what he earned. But he spoke well of them personally, too."

Smooth like syrup. Council schmoozing takes the day.

"Not that your mother knows that, I am sure," Stosser went on. "We were just one of many people your grandparents worked with over the years. But I do have a fondness for the family, as I'm sure you can imagine, and finding out who murdered them will be a high priority for our firm, I assure you. You were just on your way out? Let me walk you to the door, please, and we can let Bonita and Benjamin get back to their work. Rest assured, they're among the best we have, and they're working nonstop—well, I see that they've paused long enough to cram some pizza down their throats. Bonita, you might want to go join them before they eat everything, including the cardboard."

I've never been onstage, but even I know an exit cue when I hear one.

# eleven

Thankfully, my coworkers had indeed used their brains instead of their stomachs, and moved the pizzas into the second empty workroom next door.

Unfortunately, all three boxes were now empty. "Hey!"

Everyone looked unconvincingly innocent. Nifty averted my wrath by pulling out a paper plate with two slices still on it, and presenting it to me with a flourish. They were even the ones with pepperoni on them, making my stomach rumble in anticipation. I was definitely running on empty. "I risked life and limb to save these for you," he informed me. "I will expect gratitude at some later date."

"You jocks, all the same," I said, taking the plate and grabbing a chair. My core might have been shaken by the display between Venec and Jack, but my stomach didn't give a damn about anything except food. It had been a long damn day already, and I'd used up more current than I normally did in a week.

If the job kept up at this pace, I was going to have to budget more money for groceries.

Nick came and sat next to me. He had a smear of tomato

sauce on his cheek and I handed him a napkin, indicating where to wipe.

"Oh. Thanks." He swiped at it, then wadded the napkin and tossed it overhand into the trash can. Perfect shot. I was jealous. "Where'd you go?"

"Heard shouting. Decided to snoop."

"Shouting?"

Having info that the others didn't was a definite rush, and I was just petty enough to wait a moment, relishing it. I thought about playing them out a bit longer, then decided that would be cruel—and possibly dangerous. "Client's son came to pay us a visit, accused Venec of being a fraud."

"To his face?"

"Yup."

"Wow." Nick took that in, and then asked, "Was there much blood, and do we have to clean it up?"

"And do we have to dispose of a body?" was Sharon's practical question.

"Nah. Stosser showed up in time to avert disaster, cooled things down." I didn't mention anything about Jack's hotness—Sharon and Pietr might or might not be interested, but I wasn't feeling in a sharing mood about that right now. Especially since they only saved me two slices of pizza. Lucky for them, nobody had touched my iced mocha. I had a feeling I was going to need the extra espresso shot I had the pizza guy dump in there.

"Fair warning," I said. "Venec's probably going to come by to see what we're up to, soon as he gets the steam out of his ears."

"Joy." Sharon sounded significantly unjoyous. "Why can't Ian be the one to supervise us?"

"Because Stosser's good at lecturing but not so good with

the hands-on," Nifty said, folding the pizza boxes in two between his huge hands, and shoving them into the garbage, one at a time. "You haven't figured that out? Plus, Venec's not nice enough to forgive anyone's stupid mistakes."

"You think Stosser's nice?" Pietr finished the last of his soda and added it to the trash bag.

"Nicer, anyway, yeah."

I was with Pietr—I didn't think Stosser was nice at all. Just more socially adept at being an asshole. But for once, I kept my mouth shut. Peacemaker, me. Right. I could hear J laughing, all the way up in Boston.

There was still coffee left in the cup, but it was the dregs, thick and gunky, and I decided I didn't need the sugar or the caffeine that badly. I stood up to put it in the garbage bag before Nifty tied it, and felt my knees quiver.

"What the hell?" Sharon asked, echoing my thought perfectly, just before whatever it was hit like a goddamn tsunami.

There was a flash, hard and bright like a sword coming down on my spinal cord, and my knees didn't just quiver, they buckled and collapsed. I went down, hitting the floor hard and painful with my face. Someone—either Nick or Sharon, from the sound—crashed into the table, and I could hear Pietr swearing but didn't see him anywhere, no surprise.

Sparkles danced in front of my eyes, multicolored neon twinkles, and my skin felt tingly, as if I'd spent too much time sucking up current from a thunderstorm. I grabbed for the most solid bit of Manhattan rock my senses could reach, and shoved myself into it, letting the shock flow through and out of me, not letting it find purchase in my physical body.

Even as I was doing that—and assumed everyone else was doing the same—there was another zinging blast of current. This time it was directed not at us, but away, out of the building, hissing like an angry missile and homing in on someone outside, down the street.

That second burst of current had a familiar flavor, faint but recognizable; not one but two signatures, twined together. The Guys, slamming back at whatever or whoever had taken a shot at us. And slamming hard, from the feel of it. Wow.

"What?" Nifty started to ask, his voice thin and reedy, and I could see the shadow of his body move across the floor as he started to get up.

"Stay down!" Nick shouted, his voice harsh. "Stay low and ground, you idiot!"

Grounding was all you could do, in a situation like this. Not that I knew firsthand, but it sounded as though Nick did. I scrambled in my brain, trying to remember everything I'd ever been taught. Grounding kept your current from overrushing, or flaring, either of which could be fatal. A Talent learned to ground before learning anything else—if you didn't have grounding you couldn't have control, and if you didn't have control you had nothing except a charred-up, wizzed-out husk.

Only most Talent never had to ground under anything but the most controlled, chosen conditions. This…wasn't that.

I felt sick. Not in a bad way, more the way your stomach feels in the middle of a really wild roller coaster, topsy-turvy and excited all at once. The air was thick and heavy, like soup, and I had trouble drawing a breath.

*all right?* The ping came across as a general feeling of concern, rather than specific words, as if the sender was too busy to really focus.

*yeah* I sent, even though I wasn't entirely sure about that. Probably the others all sent the same back, because what else were you going to say? We were a lot of things, not all of them good, maybe, but wusses wasn't one of them. And I was betting that nobody, but nobody, wanted to look bad in front of the Guys.

*what happened?* I started to send back, and was cut off by an impatience-scented command.

*stay still*

It felt like an hour, but was probably closer to five minutes before the heaviness in the air eased, and we felt secure enough to sit up and take stock.

The single window in the room, with the framework which had been painted over years before and resisted being unstuck, was shattered. I didn't even remember hearing the glass break. Other than that, everything looked the same. Current usually had a physical manifestation—it wasn't so much a *thing* as a means of *doing* a thing, or, in old-fashioned terms, the magic that worked the spell—but I couldn't see the result of a thing being done, if so. Unless someone went to a hell of a lot of trouble just to break a window.

"What the hell was that?" Sharon asked, her face sickly pale under her blusher. The part of my mind that didn't let up noted that it was really the wrong shade on her—she needed something pinker. Stupid details. You focus on the stupid details while your brain tries to process the bigger shit.

"Current strike," Nifty said. He wasn't pale, but his hand was shaking slightly as he picked up a shard of glass and looked at it.

"You're sure?" Pietr asked.

"Pretty damn sure."

"What's a current strike?" Sharon asked, making me glad I wasn't the only one wondering.

"Pure current," Pietr said. "Used as a weapon. Considered more civilized than hexing someone, for some reason." He was sitting cross-legged on the floor, picking glass out of his thick hair. I didn't even want to think about what might be in mine. I put my hand up to my scalp, carefully, and was relieved when it came away clean. I wasn't bleeding, nobody else was bleeding, everything was fine. I just needed to wash my face and take a nap, and everything would be fine.

"Remember what you said about being shot at?" I asked Nick. He just grunted, wincing as he moved his bandaged arm. God, was that only this morning? It felt like days ago, now.

"I think I'm going to be sick," Sharon said. Nifty managed to get the garbage bag in front of her before she put action to deed. The pizza in my stomach rumbled in sympathy, and the aroma almost made me barf, too, but I forced it down. My current was simmering on high, excited in a bizarre and not-pleasant-to-think-about way by the near hit. It wanted to come out and play.

Not a good idea. I issued control, and forced it to settle to a reasonable level, listening to my heart beat rather than the crackle of magic inside.

The door opened, and I could see everyone else tense up. I didn't. I knew who it was.

"Everyone in one piece in here?" Venec asked, his voice rough but rock-steady.

"Yeah," Nifty said, the bulk of his body shielding Sharon from view until she was finished. "Well, except the window. We're shaken, but intact."

Venec and Stosser came in. They were winded, like they'd chased the guy down the block physically, and Stosser's skin was flushed. Venec had an evil glint in his eye, and I wondered if they'd caught the guy, and if so, if they had killed him. Not if he would, but if he had. In that moment, with that look, I had no doubt at all that the men I worked for were completely capable of killing someone who attacked them, or theirs.

And we, god help us, were theirs. I wasn't sure what that twisting sensation in my chest was all about, but I didn't think it was connected with the current strike so much as it was…something way more dangerous, right in this room.

"So much for the guy this morning just being an overeager security guard," I said nonchalantly, not letting that feeling show in my voice or my face. Venec glared at me, not happy with being contradicted, but then he looked away, about as much an admission of truth as I was going to get. Sure, the two attacks might be unrelated—one a Null-style attack, the other Talented—but this close together, I didn't think so. And I'd bet good money, neither did Venec. Maybe the gremlins hadn't been gremlins, either. Something was up, and aimed at us.

The question was…what?

"Did you catch the fucker?" Nick asked.

Stosser shook his head. His ponytail was loose, and the orange-red strands fell over his shoulders, making him look, swear-ta-god, like Jesus Christ crossed with the little girl from all the Wendy's ads. "Didn't even get a good look at whoever it was. Did anyone get a chance to tap the current, get a feel for his signature?"

We all looked at him as though he'd lost his mind. One minute we're eating pizza and the next we're flat on the floor, under attack, and he wants to know if anyone sampled the guy's current?

"Next time," Nifty said, maybe a little heavy on the sarcasm. Stosser just nodded, like that was an acceptable answer.

Either he was too distracted to really hear what Nifty had said, or J was right all along, and Ian Stosser was an out-and-out nutter.

With my luck, it was both.

"Everyone go home," Venec said, his voice still hard.

"What?" Sharon was indignant. "But we have all the stuff out, and we haven't gotten the chance to look at anything yet, not in-depth!"

"Yeah, I wanted to try something with the hairs, see if I could graph an image of the head it came from," Nick said. "Maybe match it up against the victims, or not."

"Everyone go home," Venec repeated. "I'll put a lockdown on the room. It will all be there in the morning. Nick, that's a good idea, but you'll try it in the morning. People, do not argue with me."

Anyone who argued with Benjamin Venec when he used that tone of voice was not me. I picked my sore and aching body off the floor, shook my head carefully to see if any glass shards fell out, and then got myself the hell out of there. The rest of them could do whatever they wanted, but I had a date with a long hot bath, a vodka tonic, and room service.

I was fine in the elevator, listening for the comforting hum of electricity. I was fine walking across the lobby, smelling the faint aroma of curry.

Walking out into the street I had a moment of panic; if this wasn't random, if all the attacks were actually attacks and not coincidence, then weren't we easy targets, out here in the street? What if the guy, whoever he was, was still around? My heart raced, and my gut surged again, and this time my core surged with it, swirling like a multicolored windstorm looking for something to knock over.

★go home, torres. it's all right.★

The touch was so gentle, so reassuring, for an instant I didn't recognize it. With Venec's assurances cradled inside me, control reasserted itself. I walked to the subway station, slid my

Metrocard—that still worked, thank god—and leaned against the wall, waiting for a train to come and take me home.

It was all right. For now, in this instant, it was all right. The Guys had it under control.

By the time I got to the hotel, and managed to avoid the afternoon doorman's concerned queries—I guess I looked like the day I'd had—the reassurances and the shock had both worn off, and I was in the full-blown throes of my usual reaction to stress. I wanted to snog someone. I considered calling that boy from the museum; what had his name been? The fact that I didn't even remember his name decided me against it. I did have standards, even if J despaired of them sometimes, and that a person had to be memorable was up there in the top five. Who else did I know in the city? Only my coworkers, and even if I were willing to ignore J's very smart advice and go there….

I suppose I could do the tried-and-true route of hitting the bar scene, but I really didn't want to have to work at it. Like Venec had said, we'd done enough today.

Venec. Hmm. Now there was a pleasing thought…

And proof that I was more shook up than I'd thought. Bad thought. Very, very bad thought. If snogging your coworkers was bad, doing it with the boss was even worse. I could practically hear J having an aneurism right now, just over me thinking it. The list Why Not was long and convincing, even if I had reason to believe that, in other circumstances, we'd be flame and fuel and a whole lot of burn.

I bet Venec was damn good in bed, or wherever else you got him. Those eyes had seen a lot, I'd bet….

I shoved that thought down deep, almost afraid that it would develop tendrils of its own and waft uptown to where it shouldn't be heard. Impossible, but a lot of what I'd spent the day doing some folk would say was impossible so what the hell did I know?

"All right. Room service. Some food that wasn't pizza, maybe some really stupid porn or macho action flick on the pay-per-view, a good night of sleep, and you'll be ready to go in the morning and kick them all on their asses 'cause you are the *best* damn puppy in the pack."

And they'd damn well better believe it, because while I might not want to be Alpha, I'd tasted having the lead, and I'd tasted subordinate, and lead tasted much better.

The room-service menu was on the side table where the maids always left it. I had pretty much memorized the admittedly small offerings, and would be better served—literally—to go out and get something myself, but eating out alone always depressed me. Room service felt more like luxury than depression, for some reason. Probably because J never let me eat in bed.

"Eeny meeny miney moe, with which sandwich should I go?"

A sparkle of current flashed over the chicken club, and I yelped and dropped the menu.

"Idiot!"

Current responded to will. That's all a spell or cantrip really was, a vocal way of directing your will and telling current what to do. You didn't have to say it out loud—I never did—except I just had. Not meaning to, no, but I'd been using so much current today, way more than anything normal, and I guess I needed to learn how to sound a quitting bell or something because yeeep.

Was this going to be normal for me, now?

I bent to pick up the menu—I guess chicken club it was—and the phone rang. I reached over and snagged the receiver, assuming it was going to be J, because I'd just left my coworkers and who else was going to know to call me here?

"Ms. Torres?"

My heart, I swear, stuttered a beat at the sound of that voice. "Mr. aah…" He was a Reybeorne by blood, but I didn't know if he'd followed Council tradition and taken the "power" name.

"Jack, please."

"Jack." Well. That was no damn help at all. "To what do I owe the quite unexpected pleasure of this call?" J didn't raise me in a barn; I knew how to have manners when I needed 'em.

"I was wondering if it would be too very forward of me to invite you to dinner tonight. It seems the least I can do, after my bad behavior this afternoon in your office."

No, the least he could have done would be to invite the Guys out to dinner, purely in a professional capacity. This…was not professional.

I should say no. I really should say no.

I wasn't going to, of course.

"Pick me up in half an hour," I said, and hung up the phone. If he had my phone number, then he knew where I was staying, too.

In any other town I might have worried about what to wear, where we were going, how dressed up I should be. One of the best things about New York was that the only possible response to all that was "don't sweat it." I hopped into the shower and scrubbed, and then, wrapped in one of the true luxuries of this hotel, a huge Turkish towel, contemplated the contents of my regrettably limited wardrobe.

I was heading to the lobby, hair dried, makeup applied, and nerves thrumming, before the half hour was up. When in New York, go black, and you can't go wrong. Fortunately, most of my wardrobe started and ended with black, so I was already there.

I caught a glimpse of myself in the elevator lobby: blond

puff of dandelion hair for once neatly tamed around my head, eyes and lips demurely outlined, black silk sleeveless blouse showing off just a hint of cleavage over black tuxedo pants and, for the final finishing touch, a pair of black leather half boots with a four-inch stiletto heel. I could dance all night in them, but don't ask me to run.

Goth-grubby served me well a lot of the time, but after thirteen years with J, I could do Expensive Arrogant at the drop of a well-blocked hat, too.

Jack walked into the lobby just as I hit ground. Looked as though I had guessed right—his casual suit of this afternoon had been dressed up with a dark blue silk tie and spiffier shined shoes. We looked like the epitome of Nice Restaurant-Might-Go-to-a-Private-Club-Later Clientele.

"Bonita. You are well named."

Oh god. As if I hadn't heard that line twice a week since I hit puberty. I actually preferred the "oeee, baybee, you lookin' fine" howl I got this morning from one of the stoop-sitting boys uptown. But still; when dressed Up, one acted Up.

"I think we certainly class up this joint, yes," I agreed in a roundabout way, and accepted the offer of his arm, tucking my hand in the crook of his elbow.

The doorman—I thought his name was Marco—gave me a wink when he hailed us a cab; I got the feeling he wasn't expecting to see me home again that night. And I'd been such a good girl while I was here, too! Sheesh.

Jack gave an address to the cabbie, who lurched away from the curb fast enough to shove me up against Jack's side. Neither of us seemed to mind that much.

"Again, I apologize for my behavior this afternoon. I'm normally quite even-tempered, but when it comes to my mother I will admit to being slightly…protective."

I settled myself against the back of the seat, leaving a few inches between our bodies. "I'm the same way," I said. "I totally understand." I'd faced off against a cave dragon for my dad. Too late to be helpful, but I hadn't known that at the time.

Although, really, dragons get a bad rap.

Traffic wasn't bad, and we'd barely had time for the usual exchange of first-date pleasantries before the cabbie was turning off Madison Avenue and onto a side street in midtown. Jack paid the guy, and got out, offering a hand to help me exit.

The restaurant was a steak house, age practically dripping from the low ceilings and Dutch-style landscapes on the walls. The crowd was an interesting mix of young and been-there-since-the-founding, and the waitstaff moved across the crowded floor like matadors. If the food was half as good as the ambiance...

It was. I like my steak done but not overdone, and the chef understood perfectly. Unfortunately, by the time our slabs of meat arrived, I'd already decided that contrary to my doorman's opinion, I was going back to the hotel tonight, and I was going alone. Jack was charming, and thoughtful, and smart, and clearly looking for a no-promises last night in the big city. All of that normally would suit my needs to a T, but...

But he was the son of our client. Our only client, right now. And just a few hours ago he'd been angry enough to maybe take on my boss in a battle of macho current.

As I said, I have standards. I also have a suspicious mind. And as much fun as I'd probably have tonight, it just wasn't worth it, long-term. Not unless I knew exactly what it was Jack was angling for.

J would be so proud of me.

The fact that I looked into Jack's eyes and was acutely aware that they weren't an intense black-brown had nothing to do with my decision at all. Damn it.

Whatever the logic, it still meant that I ended up, at eleven o'clock, protein craving satisfied, standing alone in front of my hotel, with absolutely no desire to go to bed, alone. And yet, I'd sent away my only possible companion for the evening with a kiss on the cheek and a phone number scrawled on the back of a business card tucked in my pocket.

"Ah, hell." I nodded glumly to Marco, and took the lonely elevator up to my lonely room.

That wasn't exactly lonely.

## twelve

"Ah." The man sitting in my room lowered the newspaper he'd been reading and glanced at the clock on the nightstand. "You're home earlier than expected."

And my hotel room was cleaner than I'd left it. Somehow, I doubted the housekeepers had done a pre-midnight raid.

"Lovely to see you, too, J." No reason to ask how he got in— he was still footing the bill; the staff would be more than happy to open the door for him. Damn it, I knew I should have called him earlier. This is what happens when you procrastinate.

I walked past my mentor and unhooked my shoes, tossing them into the closet. I was tempted to strip down to panties and bra, but it wouldn't slow him down, much less shock him.

"You were planning to stay all night and surprise me with breakfast when I dragged myself in at the crack of dawn?" I asked, trying for nonchalant and pretty much failing. J still had the ability to turn me into a nervous nine-year-old, afraid if I did something wrong he'd send me back to my father. He wouldn't, not ever, and even at nine I knew that, but...

"If that was what it took," he replied calmly. Too calmly. Oh shit. I turned around and took inventory.

My mentor was sitting in the only armchair in the room, paper now folded, his legs crossed at the ankle, his hands resting quietly in his lap. He was angry, I could sense that in his stillness, and the faint crackle of current snapping just under his skin, even if his expression was calm, his eyes lidded like he was about to take a nap. I couldn't figure out why the hell he was angry, and that made me cautious. But I was tired, too, and frustrated, and more than a little stressed, and while my current always settled under stress, my temper didn't.

"Right. What's the deal, Joseph? You hie yourself down from Boston in the middle of the night, sit in my room like a disapproving parent, which, much as I love you, you're *not,* and even if you were, I am legally, technically and morally an adult, and glower at me as though I was just caught making out with the girl next door you fancied." I ran out of breath after that, and paused. "So what's up?"

J had raised me to be a straight shooter, even though he could be a politic bastard when needed, so he responded in kind and got right to the point.

"You're quitting."

"What?" I thought that I'd heard him, but it wasn't registering in my brain.

"That job. No more." The anger showed in his face, finally. "Did you really think I wouldn't hear what's been going on?"

I swear, for a moment I honestly couldn't figure out what thing going on he was referring to; it had been that long and crazy a day. Two days. Whatever.

"The entire local Council knows that someone tried to take your bosses out this afternoon!" He had obviously taken my hesitation for trying to make some sort of denial.

Oh. *That* thing.

"No," I said, "I'm not. Quitting, I mean." There was no point in denying we'd been thwanged, although thankfully right now J was focusing on the Guys being the target, which, maybe yes and maybe no, because that blast had shattered the window of the room *we* were in.

And also the room the evidence was in. Hmm.

A part of my brain sliced that observation out of the conversation and carried it off somewhere else to examine, while the rest of me tried not to argue with my mentor.

"Bonita. You are not… I will not allow…" J's face contorted as he tried to get his anger under control. Current escaped and flared in sparks around his ears, a sure sign that he was not only angry, but upset. Upset enough that his usual ability to find exactly the right words had apparently gone pffft.

"You won't allow? *Allow?*" As usual, and contrary to most Talent, the more pissed off I got, the quieter my current got. When I was a teenager someone told me that meant that I'd never be really high-res, never be able to source-up and do madly impressive things. To me, even then it also meant that I didn't have to worry about losing control. Seemed a fair trade.

Right now, my current wasn't the cold core of stillness that worried me, just quiet, as if it was waiting for me to decide what to do. But we were still in the danger zone, between his heat and my cool. When two fronts meet, you got thunderstorms. Every Talent knew that, and god knows we'd had a few nasty storms when I was a teenager. I didn't want to be that kid anymore, I *wasn't* a kid anymore, and it was time J dealt with that.

"I'm not quitting," I repeated. I wasn't shouting, exactly, but I wanted to make sure he heard me. "I'm certainly not going to quit because someone who didn't have the guts to identify himself tried to psi-bomb our building." I might have quit over actually being shot at, maybe. Not that I was going to. And I sure as hell wasn't going to tell J about that, if he didn't already know!

I couldn't remember the last time I kept something even remotely important from my mentor. It felt weird, like wearing someone else's shoes.

"Yes, you are!"

Oh shit. J was standing up now. And shouting. The little vein in the side of his forehead was pulsing, too. I should back down, placate him, get him into the chair and mellowed out, at least for now. No matter how good a shape you were in, that kind of vein-twitch couldn't be a good sign.

Those were my thoughts. What came out of my mouth was a little different.

"You may have bought me but you don't own me."

Thirteen years ago, Joseph had given my dad a huge cash loan that was never repaid. J hadn't expected it to be repaid. I wasn't supposed to know about it, except Zaki mentioned it once, drunk off his ass and feeling love for all mankind. I guess I'd been saving it, all these years.

I guess there was a part of me that still was that stormy kid. Damn.

"Bonita! How dare you think—" He gathered himself with visible effort, sensing the thunderclouds forming, too. "That's neither here nor there, and I won't let you sidetrack me with a childish taunt. You will tender your resignation in the morning."

I'd cut him, but he was still angry. My current knotted itself in my gut, still not cold but cooling rapidly. Why wouldn't he listen to me? "I'm twenty-one, legally an adult, and by most standards a pretty smart one. I can make my own decisions. Even if you think that they're stupid." I tried to gentle my voice a little, because I did know where all this was coming from, even if I thought it was a little pointless, and I'd already said hurtful stuff. "You can't keep me wrapped up and safe in a bell jar for my entire life!"

He was still current-sparking mad, but the vein-tick was slowing down. Good, I'd gotten through to him. Eventually, hopefully, his common sense would kick back in. "There's a difference between being safe and throwing yourself into the line of fire!"

We could stand here and argue all night. I really didn't want to, and I wasn't going to. "This is important to me, Joseph. I can't tell you why, or what I think it's going to do, but this— this job—is what I need to do, and it's where I need to be. And if you can't deal with that…I'm sorry, but then that's going to have to be your problem. Not mine."

Oh god, it hurt to say that.

I went to the closet and pulled out a pair of flat shoes, and slipped them on.

"Feel free to crash here if you're too pissed to Transloc. I'll sleep on the sofa when I get back."

And tomorrow, I'd do something about getting an apartment, finally. Somewhere only I had access to the keys.

Before J could react, I'd—gently—closed the hotel-room door behind me, and headed to the elevator. I needed to walk, maybe burn off some of the crap racing in my system.

The streets of Manhattan late at night in early fall are one of the most wonderful things in the world. The air is cool and charged with more than just current, and the lights seem to shine in a way they don't in other cities. People were out and about, even at eleven-thirty, walking and laughing and standing outside of bars and restaurants, smoking or talking on their cell phones or just hanging out. I felt almost invulnerable, walking among them, as though it was all one big party. Even the cops cruising the streets in their squad cars added to the feeling of festivity rather than concern. A roommate of mine in college, Debbie, had once said that the safest place to be was where the hookers were, because that's also where the johns were, and the drug dealers, and therefore all the cops, too.

Manhattan was like that: all the bad stuff and the good stuff mixed up under neon lights and rushing traffic.

Boston, even on its best days, couldn't match it. And J wanted me to give this up?

No, he didn't. The sound of my shoes on the pavement was a nice counterpoint to the trudge-trudge-trudge of my thoughts. He wasn't asking me to leave New York. Just my job.

The job I'd only had a few months, and wasn't sure was going to last a few months more. The job we'd only just kicked into gear, that was giving us the chance to prove ourselves. Quitting would be…

It would be quitting. I'd never quit anything in my entire life. Not even the piano lessons J had signed me up for when I was ten. I was never going to be a musician, but I could play well enough not to embarrass myself, or let anyone in on the fact that I had no interest in music I couldn't dance to. A PUPI was stubborn? They got that right.

A subway entrance loomed up in front of me and I descended the steps without thinking, pulling my MetroCard out and sliding it, and me, through the gate.

In the past thirty-six hours I'd been shot at, psi-bombed, I'd dumped an otherwise very hot date, and been yelled at by my mentor. It wasn't what you'd call a successful day, unless your idea of success was seriously different from mine. The fact that I was humming under my breath and feeling the urge to smile at the couple across the subway car from me made no sense at all.

Neither did the fact that I got out at the stop down the street from the office.

It was almost midnight. What the hell was I doing here? It wasn't as if I had a key to get in or anything, and once I was there what was I going to do?

Smart would have been to grab a beer at some corner bar, stew for a while, and then either find a cute companion or, more likely, go back to the hotel and have breakfast with J, who would've calmed down by now and be willing to listen, if not agree.

Instead, I walked into the office lobby and, almost without surprise, heard the door buzz me in.

This time I caught a faint whiff of current, like the smell of burned cinnamon. Venec. He'd been in my head, I could "feel" him now. There was a current-lock on the door, triggered by some sense of us that Venec had placed on the normal door mechanism. And hadn't bothered to tell us.

"Because we're supposed to figure it out. Duh." This wasn't college. We didn't get a syllabus on the first day telling us what was going to be on the final exam.

The lobby was eerily quiet, and I had a moment of unease…. Was something lurking there, just waiting to take a potshot at me? Okay, stop thinking like that, now, or you're going to be a gibbering wreck. Shoved off that track, my brain then wondered how many offices there actually were here, and how many were expanded like our own. Okay, much safer, saner tack to take, good brain. If we did well, would the Guys take another lease, and then another, until the entire floor was a warren of workrooms and meeting spaces?

I discovered that I liked that idea, the thought of an ever-expanding space entered into by one simple door. And never mind the rats in a maze thought that followed—sometimes a maze could be protection as well as annoyance.

What might be coming in the front door that we'd have to escape through the back wasn't something I wanted to consider, though. Not right now, not tonight. Instead, I dropped my jacket on the rack, and headed to the first of our workrooms. Entering the white-walled space, I closed the door behind me, and drew up a single thread of current, directing it to expand until it covered the walls, floor, and ceiling with an almost impossibly thin layer of protection.

There was no way in hell I was going to do cleanup, if something went wrong.

"What the hell are you doing?"

I kept on doing what I was doing, which in this case was adding liquid to a vial. I was pleased to see that my hands didn't even shake, not a little. "Do you ever sleep?"

Venec glowered. "I could ask the same of you. What are you doing?"

I didn't even bother asking how he got through my protections—he owned the place, or co-owned, which was the same thing anyway, and I'd have to do some serious mojo to keep him out.

His question made me look up, and I sort of understood why he was glowering. There were splotches of black all over the walls and ceiling, and my hands were covered in a slightly more red stain.

"Shit. I forgot to protect my clothing. Does blood come out of silk?"

Victory for me—I made Venec blink. He recovered fast, though.

"You're working blood splatter?"

"Yeah, sort of. I had a thought...."

It wasn't really even a thought, and I hadn't realized I'd had it until I was already in the workroom, but once I started working it seemed to make sense.

"Sympathetic magic. I know, it's old-school and not reliable and all that. But the basis is sound, the idea that like effects like. So I was thinking maybe we could use blood to pull blood-trace up, even if we didn't *see* it."

"Interesting." His voice had dropped an octave, I swear, almost like a growl. Grrr, Big Dog. "You're starting to think like a proper forensic magician. Good."

I focused on the three puddles of blood in front of me, trying to distract myself. "Is that what we are?"

"As good a term as any, and better than most. Forensics is the science of examination—the collection, identification, and analysis of physical evidence relating to a crime. A forensic photographer uses a camera, a forensic scientist uses, well, science—a forensic magician…"

"Uses magic. It's just retro-hip enough to take off." I approved. I'm sure that totally made Venec's night.

He ignored my approval. "You've already heard Ian's speech about the need for an impartial investigation, probably enough times by now to recite it in your sleep."

"Close, yeah. An investigative force without bias, without an agenda. Results that are based only on the evidence, and not conjecture, desire, or malice." I didn't try for Stosser's tone, but the word-for-word was damn near perfect.

Venec laughed, that deep sound that made every nerve ending in my body shiver, and he put his hand on my shoulder, and I would be damned if I could hear a word he was saying, because all I could think was "oh my god, am I drooling?"

Probably.

"Show me what you've got so far," he ordered.

Work. Right. "Two of those puddles of blood are mine," I said. "The third one's from a rat—and please don't ask how I got it, because I really don't want to think about it. If you dip a glass rod into one—" and I demonstrated with one of the thin straws I found in the supply closet "—and charge it with current…like this," and I gently touched a spark to the tip, letting it flare dark blue enough so that Venec could see it. J taught me that making current visible was showing off, and a waste of power, but sometimes it was faster than trying to explain. Venec nodded as though he understood, and I went on.

"The current fills the blood, like we were doing with the blood splatter. But there, we were trying to do a rewind, draw it back to a previous position. This time, I want it to find something similar. So I tell it, not to go back, but to go…" I tried to think about exactly what I was telling it. "To go sideways, sorta. I visualize a magnet, clicking to its match, and…"

And as I said it I willed it, and the glass rod dipped and swooped until it hovered over the left-most puddle.

"That's my blood."

"Dowsing. Interesting."

Those two words totally drooped me. "Oh. Right. I guess nothing new or brilliant in it, then."

"Torres, every application builds on methods used before. That's how it works. So no, maybe not groundbreaking, Nobel-prize-winning brilliant. But if it works, then it's a damn good step."

Venec was a lousy negotiator, and a piss-poor front man. But his approval made me glow.

And then I yawned, a huge, jaw-cracking yawn, and the moment was broken.

"Torres. Go home. Go to bed. I don't want to see you here

until nine. And for god's sake, do me a favor and look like crap when you show up, will you? Because I really hate people who can function on less than six hours of sleep."

The subway back to the hotel wasn't quite so entertaining at 2:00 a.m. as it was at 11:00 p.m. The people smelled worse, for one. Then again, I probably wasn't anyone's idea of a treat, either. I sniffed at my sleeve, and picked up the scent of sweat, blood, and…hmm. That would be Venec's scent, whatever it was. "Nice," I said, and glared at the old guy who looked over at me like I was too young and too female to be out alone. He dropped his gaze first, and I was glad when he got off the train at the next stop. He wasn't twigging my creep-o-meter, but I really wasn't in the mood for disapproving glares. I'd get enough of that waiting for me when I got home. I really hated disappointing J, but I wasn't going to back down.

My resolve was unbroken by the time I got back to my hotel, and it was also unneeded. The bed was still made, the room empty except for a note written on hotel stationery, in J's usual perfect handwriting.

> *Bonita,*
> *I am an overprotective ass, and have retreated to my antediluvian cave to ponder the many ways of my overprotective assness. Allow me a father's worry, and forgive me my excess, and I will try to remember that you are indeed an adult—if not always an adult with the best judgment.*

I snorted at that.

> *Call me when you are ready. I promise that I will not yell. Much.*
> *All my etc,*
> *J*

I put the sheet back onto the table, shucked my clothing and draped it over the chair, and crawled into bed, the weight of the day finally catching up to me and turning my bones to lead. I didn't think Venec had to worry about me showing up too early this morning. I wasn't even going to lay odds on getting there by noon.

## thirteen

I was off by an hour; thanks to track delays, I didn't stagger into the office until twelve-thirty. I looked better than Nifty, though.

"Man, who dragged you face-first through the cement mixer?"

He looked up from the sofa, where he was stretched out on his back, his size-ginormous feet flat on the floor. "Hah. Very funny. Where the hell were you? You missed Master Benjamin taking us through a mock search-and-destroy mission."

"And you got destroyed?" He really did look like hell; there were scrapes on his face and his eyes had a puffiness around them that wasn't, like mine, from lack of sleep.

He hauled himself up off the couch and tugged at his pullover, a nice gray shirt that had seen better days. "Laugh now, little girl. Just 'cause you missed it this time, don't think you'll get away forever. After that, we'll see if you still make jokes."

"Ms. Torres. So glad you could join us."

Benjamin Venec himself, standing in the doorway. It was like the late-night confab never happened; that bastard looked as though he'd gotten a full eight hours of downtime. I wonder if there was a spell for that. J said not, but he might have just thought I'd abuse it.

The thought made me grin, reluctantly. All right, I would have, yeah, but in a good cause.

"Ahem."

I wiped the grin off my face, fast. "Yes, sir. Sorry, sir." If he wasn't going to make any mention of my work last night, be damned if I was going to bring it up. Sharon and Nifty could fight over who got to be top dog; I just wanted to get in and do my job.

"Lawrence, you ready to get back to work?"

"Yessir."

There was no way Nifty looked ready for anything other than a stiff drink and a long nap, but I wasn't going to say word one, not with Venec standing there glowering like a very dapper Thor himself.

"Then get off your ass and get back in there. You, too, Torres. Evidence doesn't wait for your schedule."

Oh man. It sounded as though the entire team was going to get schooled today.

We followed him into the office like chastised little ducklings. I was sort of curious about what Venec had put the group through this morning, but not enough to ask questions. Not when the boss clearly had something else in mind.

Nick and Sharon were seated around the main worktable, at opposite ends, with Stosser leaning against the far wall. There was a thermos of coffee on the table, and a mostly empty box of doughnuts. Someone—probably Nifty, had made sure there was at least one butterscotch-coated crème bomb left, and I glommed it with satisfaction. One of the great joys of being a Talent was that using current burned calories, and while mostly I still had to watch what I ate, a busy day on the job burned like a thousand calories, easy. Today sounded like it was going to be one of those days.

I heard the sound of a toilet flushing off to the side, and Pietr came back into the room, wiping his hands on his jeans and sliding into the chair farthest from Sharon. Nifty and I took the remaining seats, which put me directly between Sharon and Nick, and a very distinct tang of frustration. Great. Something had soured this morning. I so didn't want to know, and I even more didn't want to get caught up in that. Venec closed the door behind us and Stosser took over, as usual.

"While you were having your morning playdate—" the looks on my teammates' faces at that confirmed Nifty's comment that it had been anything but play "—I was setting up the afternoon's assignments."

You could practically feel the tension in the room ratchet up, me included. I'd finally be able to get my fingers into the rest of the trace we brought back, see if there was anything useful there.

"Shune, Sharon? You two will be working with the current-trace Bonnie brought back."

I think my jaw fell open, and only shock kept me from yowling a protest. That was *my* trace! I found it, I brought it back, I should be able to play with it! Stosser, you bastard!

"But I thought…" I started to say, and then I saw the look in Nick's eyes, and my jaw snapped shut. The Guys were savvy enough to know that for whatever reason, Sharon and Nick didn't want to even look at each other right now, much less work together, and yet they were harnessing them to the same task. Uh-huh. Boss-guys, you bastards. This time, though, the thought had a tinge of admiration. They were going to make Sharon and Nick work through it without ever having to deal with it directly, whatever "it" was. And let everyone else be on alert: personal tiffs would not be allowed to get in the way of the work.

"Pietr, you're on records. The cops haven't been able to find the legal owner of that car. I expect you do to better."

Pietr nodded. I didn't envy him that; sitting and sifting through boxes of legal paperwork would make me nuts.

"Lawrence, Torres." Venec handed us each a small blue note card. "Name and address of individuals who were known to have come into conflict with the victims prior to their deaths."

"The cops didn't already clear them?" Nifty asked, not even looking at the card in his hand.

"They are Talents. The cops might not have known the right questions to ask," Stosser said, his voice a little tighter than usual, as though he'd been having a bad morning, too.

Nifty shifted his weight, as if he was getting ready to launch himself at an opposing player. "There've been Talented cops before, you know. Even in Chicago."

Especially in Chicago, actually. There had even been some fatae in the Blue Line, years ago, from the stories J told. Not so much anymore, though. Medical exams apparently got a little tougher. I didn't say any of that.

"There have been. We can't assume one of them was doing the interviewing, or that he or she was free to ask any particularly pointed questions." Venec took control so smoothly I wasn't even sure it was him, at first. "Go, talk to them. Lawrence, be blunt, and watch 'em like a hawk. If they think you're a dumb jock, they might get cocky. Torres, your contact's Council. Don't play the connection. Don't even mention it. If they're halfway smart, they'll smell it on you, and make their own assumptions."

The assumption being that the Council had sanctioned the questioning, and therefore they should answer fully and freely.

"Is that legal?"

Stosser looked at me as if I'd just suggested they tap-dance nude in Times Square.

"Right. Never mind." Apparently, despite the fact that we were supposed to bring truth and justice to the *Cosa*, we didn't have to worry too much about the technical details of entrapment or whatever. Was I the only person in this office who didn't have a beef with cops?

"All right, people. Load up on your caffeine, and then take a hard hit and get going."

A hard hit, in Venec-ese, was recharging current directly off a main source, ideally something large and powerful, but sometimes just the nearest configuration of electricity. Everyone had their favorite. I knew that Nifty liked skyscrapers, and Nick would rather focus in on a power plant, dipping into the maelstrom of current that rests inside each generator, while Pietr preferred to source wild. Sharon kept her preferences to herself.

For me, it had become the subways, maybe because I was riding them so much now since coming to Manhattan. The rush of energy was like a power plant, but directed, channeled into a forward motion, constantly in use, constantly turning over and regenerating. Plus, it gave me something to do, other than worrying about what I was about to do, on my way downtown. I stopped off at the hotel to change clothing for something a little more interview-worthy, and—keeping in mind my vow of the night before—asked Julie at the concierge desk to find me a couple of those apartment-hunting magazines, for later. I was hoping that her "service is everything" motto would make her dig up a few personal contacts, too. They might like having me there, but there was nothing a professional concierge liked more than a challenge, and finding a reasonably priced apartment in Manhattan, as I knew well now, was certainly that!

My target worked in the Wall Street area, in a little legal firm in a big building. The Guys had already made an appointment for me, and I arrived exactly on the dot—after walking around the block twice, to kill some time. The waiting area was modern-expensive—cream leather and chrome and glass that made me afraid to sit for fear I'd smudge the furniture. The receptionist didn't even bother to look at the little paper slip the guard in the lobby had printed out for me, but buzzed me in without hesitation when I presented myself at the front desk.

"Ms. Torres?"

The man waiting on the other side of the glass doors was tall, slope-shouldered, with hair the color of a burnished foxtail. Redheads were just showing up all over the place, weren't they? Made me glad I'd gone back to blonde.

"I'm William Arcazy." I knew that already, having actually read my dossier. "We can talk in my office."

His office was very nice; not large, but a real desk, and real leather chairs, and actual art on the walls, not framed posters or cheap photos. His suit was expensive but not obviously so, and his haircut had probably cost more than my shoes, and I don't skimp on my footwear.

"I've been hearing talk about your organization for a few weeks now. You've got the community in quite a flutter."

*Community,* in this conversation, could mean either the Council, specifically, or the entire *Cosa,* generally. I went with the former. "The community is not always so good with change."

"In other words, we're hidebound on one side of the aisle and paranoid on the other?"

Since that was exactly my opinion, I just smiled.

"I'm always willing to be of assistance, although I'm not sure what I can tell you that might be relevant to your investigation."

Truth was, I didn't know what he could tell me, either. I didn't even know what to ask, or look for.

*connections*

The ping was soft and brief, but I'd felt it before, this week, and years ago, when I was investigating my father's murder. Not a mentor's advice, but a commonsense reminder of what I already knew, a reassurance that I was doing the right thing. It was also a tacit acknowledgment that they knew, somehow, that I knew what they had done, back then.

Venec might be crap at client-handling, but he was a pretty damn good teacher, because the moment he gave me that one word, I knew what to do.

"You and the Reybeorns had business deals together. Tell me about that."

Arcazy leaned forward in his chair, his forearms resting on his desk and his expression open and forthright. He had green eyes to match his red hair, but his complexion was interestingly olive. The impression was less like a fox than a red panda; cute, yeah, but thoughtful rather than clever, careful instead of crafty.

"I had been introduced to them by a mutual friend."

"Ah. A Council friend?"

He nodded, and I saw it. Just a tiny adjustment in his body language, but it was like a shout to me; Venec was right. He had made the assumption.

I'd never agreed with the common lonejack belief that all Council members were sheep, but at the moment I had an almost overwhelming urge to utter a low "baaaaaaa." Arcazy might be careful, but he wasn't careful enough.

Or was he trying to see how careful I was? Damn the tight-wire I was walking here....

"We did a few deals together, yes. The Reybeorns, as I'm sure you've already learned, were big in real estate. Buying and selling, mainly...what's called 'flipping.' They'd buy a building that was in a downslide, make some basic refurbishments, and then sell it to someone who was into gentrification but didn't want to start at the extreme low end. It's not a high-margin business, but it did well for them, for a long time. They had the eye for what was worthwhile, and knew exactly how much time and money to put into the properties to make a profit, even in a down market."

That fit with what had been in the original briefing. They'd started with money, and used it to make more money. Not filthy lucre style, but more than enough to keep their grand-children pretty, as I knew for a personal fact.

"And you joined them in some of these deals?" My notebook was out, and I made a quick note, but was more interested in his reactions than his responses.

He nodded. "Their knowledge, my money. Our mutual friend made the suggestion. My job is sometimes twelve-hour days, five days a week, and I don't have time to hunt down deals like this myself. I liked them, and I trusted them to make good decisions."

"Until this most recent deal."

Always make your questions statements; that had been one of the first things the Guys taught us. Questions put people on guard. Statements make them want to correct you.

"Actually, not until after our last deal." Arcazy frowned in quick thought, doing time calculations in his head. "We'd made good money on the last building, but I was thinking about buying property myself—a little cottage out on the Cape, a place to get away from it all, between cases. That would suck up what I considered my 'play' money, what I used to invest in the properties. The Reybeorns were upset, of course, but not about the money. They had other people lined up anxious to work with them, so they wouldn't lose anything even if I backed out. No, it was…it was more about my buying property without consulting them, if you can believe it. They accused me of not respecting them. We had words."

"That seems a small thing, to make you lose your temper in public."

Arcazy looked embarrassed. He didn't blush, but I bet when he did it looked better on him than me. "You'd think, after ten years of arguing before judges, I'd have learned to keep a better rein on things. And I can, when I'm working for other people, solving their problems. But that…" He stopped, and shook his head. "Yes, I lost my temper, and I said some things I shouldn't have. I told them I wanted out of all our deals. That they needed to buy me out of the buildings we still co-owned, because I wouldn't work with someone who tried to control what I did in my off-hours."

Oh, I could so relate to that.

"But you had no reason to believe that they were trying to cheat you?"

He went from embarrassed to surprised in an instant. "Cheat me? No, never." He sounded confident about that, at least. "They weren't the type. I know, everyone hears 'developers' and they immediately assume sleazy, but they weren't like that, not at all. Yes, it was about the profit, but they also liked making things better. When a family bought one of their houses, and moved in and made it a home, that was as much a reward as the money.

"It was kind of quaint, but sweet. One of the reasons I liked investing with them. Other than the fact that they always made a profit, of course."

"Of course," I echoed.

He looked me directly in the eyes. "Rumor has it this isn't just a formality, that you really think they didn't commit suicide."

"We were hired to determine exactly what did happen. We

do not go in with any predetermined idea of the result. That would only hamper our investigations." Another quote-perfect line from Stosser.

He sighed, his shoulders slumping in a move that felt both practiced and sincere. "Horrible as it might sound…I almost hope they didn't. Commit suicide, that is. The thought that someone would kill them is terrible, but…suicide's worse. They enjoyed life so much."

A faint buzz went off, and he looked at his desk. I prepared to make my farewells, assuming that he was being reminded of another appointment.

Instead, he invited me out for a drink.

"My doctor's orders," he explained as we were walking down the hallway, and he waved good-night to the reception-ist. "Too many twelve-hour days, like I mentioned before, and my stress levels were climbing too high. That was why the place on the Cape, too. So twice a week, if I don't have to be in court, I'm supposed to kick out an hour early and go do some-thing relaxing, and totally non-work-related."

He took me to a nice little Irish pub a few blocks away, and a drink turned into drinks-and-light supper, the way I'd halfway expected it to. We ate at the bar, very casual…and he followed up with an invitation to have coffee in his apartment, since it was early yet, and he lived right around the corner.

Oh, he was about as subtle as a bear coming out of hiber-nation. I admit it, I'm a born snoop in addition to having an eye for an attractive playmate. I said yes.

His condo was like his office: quietly classy, expensive without advertising the fact, and totally a bachelor pad, right down to the black towels in the bathroom and black sheets on the bed. Yes, I looked. At least they were plain cotton, not satin. I'm not sure I could have taken him seriously, if he had black satin sheets.

I told him that when I came back from using the bathroom.

"Oh, please tell me you're single." He was futzing around in his top-of-the-line but Spartan kitchen with a chrome-and-black coffee machine that had to have cost more than I made in a month.

"Now is a really bad time to ask," I scolded him. "A lawyer should know that plausible deniability is no excuse in the face of the law."

"Nitpicker. Are you married?"

"No."

"Engaged?"

"Nope."

"Looking for a wealthy lawyer to snag?"

"God, no."

"Thank god."

I choked back a bad case of the giggles. This wasn't going to go anywhere right now, despite whatever he might be plotting, but I definitely wanted to see Mister Arcazy again, to see where it might lead. Sex is always fun, but sex with another Talent has that extra edge to it, no matter what their experience levels—and I was betting that Will had some significant experience.

In the back of my mind there was a thought that I probably should have said no to the drinks, to the dinner, and not even be thinking about sex. But the urge of the previous night hadn't ever been settled, and I was still too damned twitchy and feeling the need. I didn't like being that unsettled.

To my credit, I did extract myself from Will's apartment before six, despite an unspoken invitation to stay longer, and headed back uptown to report in. It wasn't as though we worked nine to five, and better a little late than never, right?

When I hit the office, Sharon and Nick were still there,

staring intently at some spot in the middle of the table. So that's what it looked like when you were in the magic-evidence room. Interesting.

"Torres." Stosser was in the hallway talking to Pietr, who looked like he'd swallowed an entire nest of canaries. "You're late."

"I stopped for dinner. I'm here now." I realized after the words left my mouth that being flippant probably was not the smart choice when being reprimanded.

"I realize that you're still young and inexperienced, Bonita, but we would appreciate it if you would remember that your obligations to the office and the investigation come before your personal life when we are on a job?"

Stosser had gone totally Council on me, and I responded exactly the way I was supposed to: I stood up a little straighter, took the blow square, and apologized.

"Yes, sir. I understand. Should I report on my findings to you, or Venec?"

"Make a formal report, and have it on my desk before you leave tonight. Protocol, Bonnie. Everything gets documented."

"Yes, sir."

Ian nodded and went back to his discussion with Pietr.

"Sheesh, kiss his ass a little more, why don't you?"

Nifty had come into the hallway while I was being repri-manded, and was watching, his arms folded against his wide chest, looking like a block of supercilious ebony. He had changed for his interview, too, replacing the gray pullover with a blue dress shirt and striped tie.

"He's the boss," I said, my voice lower pitched than Nifty's had been. I tried to go around him, but he blocked the doorway. I didn't want to deal with this; my good mood slipping away like ice on a griddle. I was tired of the constant sniping and status-pulling that he and Sharon were engaging in, and I just wished they'd leave me out of it. I wasn't interested in being their chew toy, not about this. So I stared up— and up, because that boy was big—into Nifty's face, and bared my teeth in what might, to someone not paying attention, have looked like a smile. "You think I should challenge him? Or is that your job and you're warning me away? You gonna try to be lead dog, Nifty?"

"You ever hear the saying, if you ain't lead dog the view never changes?"

I was about to tell him he was an ass no matter what, when another voice joined the party.

"Lead dog doesn't just have the view, hotshot."

Oh hell. Despite our attempts to keep it low, Ian had decided to join us, and his grin wasn't a friendly smile at all. "You're not lead dog in this pack, Lawrence. *I'm* the goddamned lead dog. You're all a bunch of snot-nosed puppies still wet behind the ears and falling over your paws."

Nifty and Stosser glared at each other, me trying to shrink and disappear the way Pietr had once again managed. Bad current rising, hard and fast, and I really wanted to be anywhere but where I was. I seriously considered Translocating the hell out of there, but didn't want to even tap my current right then and there.

"Puppy, huh?" Nifty's voice was hard and hot, but the anger I'd been expecting wasn't there.

"Snot-nosed," Stosser agreed. "And not housebroken yet, either."

I braced myself for the smackdown, and then the two of them were laughing, and I wanted to slug them both myself, hard, for making my stress level skyrocket.

*Men.*

# fourteen

I don't know if it was my glaring, or the fact that they knew damn well they were getting punchy—and close to being punched—but the general hilarity died down pretty quick, thankfully. Stosser looked at Pietr, proving that he, at least, had no trouble finding our disappearing pup, and then at the rest of us. "All right," he said. "Since it looks like everyone's still in the office, why don't we do a debrief now. Find out if anything's come up or anybody's got any brilliant new developments to share." I wasn't sure if he was being sarcastic or not, but the three of us followed him to the main conference area, meeting Venec, with Sharon in tow, in the hallway. Nick was already in there, dumping sugar into his bright red, oversize coffee mug.

Venec looked at me, then away again. I stayed cool, but coming off my near-close encounter with Will Arcazy made me even more aware of my responses to Benjamin Venec. Not the casual fun sense of possibilities here, no. Just being in the same room as Venec made my rib cage feel smaller, as though it was harder to breathe, and my gut tightened, and yeah, I could practically feel my vagina contracting in anticipation. All without me even thinking anything remotely sexual. It was as if I couldn't *not* be aware of him. And not just physically, either, because my core was lighting up in tiny pinpricks of color, like miniature fireflies all excited for dusk.

I shushed them, and made myself breathe around the physical reactions, and made myself focus on the job stuff.

Right. Between yesterday and today, it was becoming clear that *nine to five* really didn't mean much when we had a job. I had no idea how long this was going to go on—I don't think anyone did—but we were going to need some serious downtime after, if it was all like this.

I made a mental note to stock up on vitamins, and make sure that there was a deli in the neighborhood that delivered, because while the coffee was more than decent, the fridge was too small to store more than milk and maybe a bottle or two of soda. If I was going to be here at midnight, I was going to need food, and I couldn't always count on someone inviting me out for munchies—although I was doing a pretty good job of it so far, wasn't I? A spark of smugness flashed and was quashed, all in one mental motion. Don't count on it, girl.

On second thought, I realized the boys had probably already thought of that, and would have taken care of the food-delivery situation. I made another mental note to check with Nifty, who likely never missed a meal.

"So," Stosser started, even as we walked in. "The first forty-eight are up. We've been attacked once, possibly twice, gotten yelled at by the client's kid, and cashed the retainer fee. So bark, puppies. What do we have to show for all that?"

Sharon and Nick looked confused at the "puppies" reference, while Nifty chuckled. Despite her knowing she'd missed a joke—or maybe because of that—Sharon took point, making an important-sounding noise so that we'd all know she was going first. Fine by me—I was still trying to figure out what I was going to say.

She walked to the far end of the table while we all grabbed seats, and mimicked Stosser, unintentionally or not, by standing in lecture pose. On her, it didn't work so well—now that my appreciation of her physical appearance had been modified by familiarity, I could see that she was too stiff, too aware of what she was doing. If being top dog required poise in front of groups, Nifty had her beat by a mile.

But she wasn't putting on a show for the nightly news, only reporting on what they had found poking around in my—our—trace.

Not that I was still annoyed about that, or anything. Okay, maybe a little. But I was starting to sniff out the method in their assignment-madness: nobody got to be possessive over the details.

Sharon paused, as if she was about to make some huge announcement, then said, "There wasn't, as expected, much that was useful in the current-debris that Bonnie collected."

I would have taken exception to that sidewise snipe, except I'd halfway expected it. The fact that I'd gotten anything at all had surprised me; for it to jump up and shout the name of the killer would've been damned unlikely. Sharon wouldn't have done any better, and might even have gotten less.

Sharon went on: "Because of the number of people who had gone over the vehicle, both Talent and Null, and the number of electrical instruments that had been used in and near it since the deaths, it was difficult to separate out distinct threads of current."

"Bet I could have done it," Nifty said, not quite softly enough. Without even looking, Venec reached over and hit him across the back of the neck with a rolled-up magazine. Nifty shut up.

Sharon, to give her credit, totally ignored their byplay. "We were, however, able to distinguish the victims' signatures, and bring them out of the tangle."

"It was like excavating a garbage dump," Nick said, breaking into Sharon's presentation. "You just keep peeling back one layer after another, until you get to the oldest. It's tricky, but we can do it."

"How did you know it was them?" Pietr asked, leaning forward in the chair he was sitting in—backward—and raising narrow, dark eyebrows in visual question. "None of us ever met them."

"I had," Stosser said quietly.

I had forgotten that. Not like me, to forget anything. I *was* tired, I guess.

Sharon took the reins back. "Yes. Ian gave me a comparative sample, and they matched. So we were able, starting from there, to peel each layer and assign it to a number of the items found in our physical search, as well. From the time the Reybeorns got into the car, every current-touched item has been accounted for."

"I smell a *however*," Venec said.

"Yes, indeed." Sharon managed not to look smug, but you could tell it was a stretch for her. Nick was actually grinning proudly. Oh, this was going to be good. "There was a signature layered *under* theirs, and mingled with it, indicating not only that this person had been in the car before them—was maybe the actual owner—but had shared the space with them for at least a brief period."

Ooooh. Nice work. I wondered how they'd managed to keep the signatures separate after the peel; had they managed to create a mounting slide that would keep the current intact?

While I was starting to geek out the details, Venec was picking up the *however* in their *however*. "Was any of the physical debris his? Was there a connection between the signature you found, and any of the physical evidence?"

Sharon had to admit failure, there. "We weren't able to connect anything with him, no."

Her partner went from euphoric to hangdog in an instant. "It's a major step—and a nonstarter all at once. Unless somehow we're going to walk all over Chicago sniffing out the signature of every person we run into? Lacking a database…" Nick sounded as though he wanted to kick something. "Yeah. We've got detail, and we're still nowhere."

"Except that we now know for certain the previous owner—" Nifty stopped, chose a different word "—the previous possessor of the car was in the car with them," he finished, surprisingly positive, considering it had been partly Sharon's work that he was referring to. Maybe he was geeking the details, too. Or maybe, just maybe, getting that moment of bonding with Stosser, then getting whapped in public, had settled him down a little? God, I hoped so.

Nick tapped the table, thinking out loud. "So maybe he sold it to them, or loaned it to them, a cash deal or under the table so there was no paperwork, and was showing them how to work the seat belts?"

"Damn." From Sharon, that relatively demure curse sounded a lot worse.

"All right," Stosser said. "Sharon, Nick, that was well done. The information may be incomplete, but it's more than we had before. Now we know that there was someone in the car with them, and that person had possession of the car previously."

"More than the cops managed to get," Venec added. "And we're not entirely without a place to go from here. Pietr? Did you find anything specific to the car?"

Pietr's expression was back to his usual deadpan, but I could still see the glimmer of self-satisfaction lingering around him. "The Chicago police had run a search on the VIN, but it was a dead end—the vehicle identification number was obscured so badly they couldn't be sure of it, and none of their tries turned up the right description. There were no plates on the car, and no registration papers, so the DMV wasn't able to kick back anything, either. The car itself was brand-new, barely on the dealers' lots yet, so the theory was it came straight from the factory. That implied an illegal car-trafficking ring, maybe, but without a VIN there was no way to confirm that hypothesis. Either way, it takes a pro to manage all that, not some garden-variety hoobah.

"If we were able to get another look at the car itself, I might be able to lift the original etching, or make a reproduction, but Ian nixed that idea."

"We managed to sneak in once, but I'm not willing to take the chance again, not after what happened the first time," Venec said, leaning back in his chair and stretching his legs in front of him, as though he were comfortably at home. Maybe he was, maybe to him this was home. Another few hours and I might just move in here myself, rather than trudge back to the hotel. "Someone clearly did not want us—or anyone—in there looking. You guys are too expensive to be used for target practice."

"And we appreciate that," Pietr assured him. "So. Dead end with the car. So I went and mucked around with the physical trace, since Sharon and her Boy Wonder were doing current. And that toenail clipping Bonnie found?"

I could feel my ears swivel forward, metaphorically, at that. We were coming to whatever had made him so pleased.

"Definitely human, and, based on the very faint remnants of polish, either female or seriously metrosexual male. Or a cross-dresser, but I don't think so. No drag queen I know would get a spa pedicure. Way too subtle." He pushed an envelope across the table. "More to the point, the impression we took off the door handle suggests that the clipping was caught under at least two sets of fingerprints, including one I determined belonged to the missus. So, we have someone, likely female, who is short-tempered enough to rip a toenail off rather than clipping it, and have it catch on her clothing, and then opened the door to the car...before the victims."

I'd taken a statistics class in college, and the one thing the professor had told us that stuck in my head even after the actual math fled, was that statistics can't convey how often impossible stuff actually happens.

"You're saying that the toenail belongs to the mystery person whose current-trace we have sort-of-not-really identified?" Nifty had pulled a small spiral-bound notepad out of his pocket and was making notes with a tiny pen that looked even smaller in his hands. The note-taking bug had caught everyone, looked like.

Pietr half rose from his seat to take a bow. "The very same, whoever she may be. Our Lady X. Lady, not gent. Please take note, and adjust your pronouns accordingly."

Oh, nice. Except... "I hate to be the bad guy here, but you realize that chain of connective logic won't hold up to a stiff breeze, much less a cross-examination?" It sounded good, though, and I was surprised to feel a warm glow of pride in Pietr. He might be the freak of our little group, but he was a *smart* freak. More, he was *our* smart freak.

"We are but 'umble techs in the infancy of our techiness," he said. "I have faith in our innate amazingness."

Geek-freak. But I was starting to think he had something there. Venec was right; in a little over forty-eight hours we'd gone from newbies with nothing, to far more information—

and more reasonable theories—than the police or Council snoops had managed in months. We had the advantage, though. We had magic on our side. And we didn't have an agenda to cloud the facts.

"All right, so we may be looking for a woman," Stosser started to say, when Nifty interrupted him.

"You really think a woman could kill two people like this?"

Six heads swiveled to look at the far end of the table as if a rock troll had just emerged from a wedding cake.

"Lawrence, how did you manage to survive this long saying stupid shit like that?"

For once, I couldn't find anything to object to in Sharon's words or her tone. I was wondering the same thing.

"I just meant…physical strength," he tried to explain, and then gave up. "Right. Never mind. I'm a sexist pig. And if she's Talent, physical strength doesn't mean squat."

"Especially if they're already dead. The cause of death was listed as asphyxiation from car fumes, rather than traumatic asphyxia, but did they have to be in the car when that happened?"

Nick pulled a sheet of paper—the autopsy report, I guessed—off the table and skimmed through it. "The guy had a skull fracture. It wouldn't be enough to kill him, and the ME thought that it happened during his death throes not as the cause of them, but if he'd been knocked out first, filling his lungs with carbon monoxide would be relatively easy, right?"

"Or a touch of gas could have knocked them out, and then the setup, and then the actual murder? You can kill rodents if you run a pipe from the exhaust into their hidey-holes," Pietr said. "Hypoxia would knock them out, and then the bodies could be dragged into the car. If you did it quickly enough, and set the scene right, the assumption, supported by the autopsy, would be suicide—and that's exactly what happened."

"Except that there was no indication of toxic gas being run anywhere except in the car, and yes, that was tested and listed in the notes," I said, a touch smugly. "So how did the killer get them to sit still and not struggle?"

"A Talent wouldn't even need to run a pipe to get at them," Nick said. He lifted his hand and made a gesture, as though he was choking someone. "I find your lack of faith…disturbing."

"Someone used current to choke both of them?" Sharon picked up the idea and ran with it. "Or one first and then the other, if they were in different rooms…"

Stosser slapped the table with the flat of his hand, making me jump. "And this, puppies, is why it's so important to be on the scene immediately. If we'd been able to see the bodies, before they were moved or pawed over, we would be able to determine if current was used offensively on the body, and pick up the aggressor's signature. But we weren't, we didn't, and we couldn't, and so we don't have that. So we need secondary support for this theory. We need to run some tests, see how much current is actually required to choke someone to death, and if it would leave physical trace."

Even Sharon looked taken aback at that, and Stosser did a double take at the looks. "What? Oh, no! Not on each other, no. We'll build a model. Do none of you watch *Myth-Busters?*"

Venec shook his head, clearly more used to the way his partner's brain worked than the rest of us. "I'm sure we can get an unemployed dummy that will do the job. No need to put temptation in Sharon's path."

There was a snicker from somewhere, quickly muffled before the source could be identified.

"Right." Venec kept us moving along. "What next?"

Nobody else seemed ready to say anything, so I figured it was my turn, get people away from the potentially pleasing thoughts of choking each other.

"I met with William Arcazy. Had a public spat with the vics about a month before they died. He's a lawyer, working in a very hot little boutique firm specializing in interesting problems."

"Interesting how?"

"They try not to talk too much about their clients, but I took a look at some of the papers that were left out on desks." I wasn't proud, but then, he should have put them away before letting me in, right? Ditto for his assistant, who walked away from his or her desk and left things out in full view of anyone with good eyesight and inquisitive intent. "Apparently Mr. Arcazy specializes in people who have long conversations with Federal Marshals, and then disappear, among other sidelines. That, by the way, means that they have access to a lot of privy information…and generally, for lawyers, are on the up-and-up. At least, the ones who aren't crooked, are." Some of that had been in the original file, complemented by the case they were working on now, via the paperwork I'd scoped. The last bit I'd gotten out of Will during dinner. He'd been pragmatic but disapproving of the level of corruption in his field. At least outwardly.

"And is Mr. Arcazy, Esquire, on the up-and-up?" Venec asked. It didn't sound as if he knew I'd gone above and beyond the order of business. Maybe. Maybe I wouldn't have to write up a report after all. Somehow, I suspected Stosser was still going to want a written report. As a physical reminder of the lesson, if nothing else.

"He admits to having been in business with the vics, and to having words with them when things started to go sour. But…I don't know. I got the vibe that he was telling me the truth."

Sharon's truth-scrying gift would have been useful to have, to confirm that vibe, and for the first time I wondered why the Guys hadn't sent her to interview anyone.

"You sure about that? That the vibe wasn't something else?"

Excuse me? There was an accusation in that question, oh yeah. I guess he did know, after all. I didn't want to look at Venec, not with those eyes looking my way, but I'd never been ashamed of my actions, and I wasn't going to start now. I lifted my head and gave as good as I got, glarewise.

"Yes, I'm sure. Nothing he said or did was the act of a man with any kind of grudge or—" I stopped, struck by something.

"Or what?"

I held up a forefinger, to indicate I was still processing. "Will said he did a lot of deals with the victims—their smarts and his money, investing in buildings and then reselling them once they were renovated. He was pleased with the return, but opted out because he wanted the money for something else, so if anything they'd be the ones to want to kill him, not the other way around."

"But they did have a loud, public argument?" Venec knew they did, damn him. It was in the dossier I'd read on the way to interview Will; that's how I had known to follow up on it.

"About his investing his money without them—I guess they weren't happy with him cutting them out of any deals, but again, isn't that more cause for them to do him harm, not the other way around? But what I was wondering was, are there other partners, people who gave them money and weren't happy with their returns? That car was expensive—maybe someone bought it with money they expected to get, and then didn't?"

I was starting to roll on that idea. "I don't know about the rest of you, but killing someone with the vehicle that symbolized everything that went wrong? That's the kind of thing that would appeal to anyone who would go to this kind of bother, including destroying all traces, rather than just shoot them. Plus, it would be a way to get rid of the car while they were at it."

"They had to have bought it first, though, so a dealer should've had records. And not file a police report?" Sharon said. "How would they get insurance money, which they'd probably want, after being out cash already?"

There's always a nitpicker. "Maybe they didn't insure it? If it was used in a murder scheme, I sure as hell wouldn't have. I don't know, I'm proposing theories here, not answers."

Venec seemed to think it was a reasonable theory. "This kind of deal, the whole setup, wasn't a spur-of-the-moment thing. There had to be a reason, and probably not a brand-new one. Going on Bonnie's idea, we should be looking at people with older grudges, not brand-new ones. Ian?"

Stosser nodded agreement at his partner. "Female, business deals, say two-year to two-month window, to start? I'll put in a call and see what I can get. The rest of you, it's late. Lawrence, your report is already on my desk?"

He nodded, looking a little smug.

"All right. Everyone go get some sleep, and we'll start fresh in the morning."

We stood, and started to file out. Stosser was right; everyone was dragging something fierce.

"Torres. A word with you?"

That? Was not the sound of anything good. Despite his approval of my theory, I had a sudden fear I was about to get canned.

I waited until the room had cleared out, and it was just me and Venec. The tension between us was well past simmering, but not in the good way.

"I don't care what you do on your own time. You're a smart

woman, and I'm not going to read you any lectures about inter-
personal relations or STDs because it's none of my damn
business. But I don't care how badly you need your itch
scratched, you do not, and I repeat *do not* ever screw a suspect,
no matter how many vibes you have or how ironclad his alibi
appears, or I will can your ass so fast you won't know what side
to sit down on. Are we understanding each other?"

We were.

Venec glared at me once for good measure, and walked out
of the room.

It took a few seconds, but my lungs unfroze and I could
breathe again. Contrary to recent events with J, I was not used
to screwing up, or being called on the carpet. It stung. Worse,
it stung because never mind how he found out, and never mind
what he might think of me, Venec was totally, completely
right. I'd let the itch overpower the brain.

Never again. As I'd said to J, this job was too important to
me, already. I wanted it. I might even *need* it.

Still, the fallout wasn't all bad. Sure, getting reamed by your
boss was decidedly un-nice, but I was still employed, my limbs
were all still attached, and he hadn't told me not to see Will
again ever, specifically....

Just not so long as he was still a suspect.

## fifteen

After pulling an all-nighter to get my report done and on the boss-Guy's desk as ordered, I still managed to get in at eight-fifty the next morning, and found the pot of coffee already half-gone and a buzz of voices flowing throughout the office. The rest of the day was pretty tense, everyone wound up tight with the waiting, and the coffeepot barely ran dry before another was made. Even so, Venec had to order us out around 8:00 p.m. before anyone would leave, and we were all back by 8:00 a.m. the next morning, looking sheepish but determined.

Something had to give, and it wasn't going to be us.

We needed another go at that car, but according to Venec's contact in the Chicago P.D., it was scheduled for auction this week, meaning that they were busy cleaning and prepping that sucker. Any evidence we might have missed was now hope-lessly compromised. We'd have to find another route.

Now, if someone could just come up with a brilliant idea what that route might be, we'd be all set. Until then, we were spinning our own wheels and fiddling thumbs, and generally getting on each other's nerves. We'd had a taste of what action would be like, and we wanted more of it.

Interestingly enough, other than a few blown fuses, we were all controlling our current pretty well, and the gremlins seemed to have taken a short break from pestering us.

On the nonwork side, Venec seemed to have dropped the entire question of how I spent my personal time, and I was avoiding the new voice mail on my hotel phone from Will, asking if he could see me again. It was easier to spend time at the office, helping Nick recraft the illumination spell so that it hit only the thing we were looking for, without giving the very retro disco flare. So far, no luck. How difficult could "find and illuminate" be?

"Careful!" Nick threw up his hands to protect his eyes, and I ducked and turned away a half second too late.

Apparently, really difficult.

After the last dose of neon-green sparkles left me with blurred vision and an oncoming headache, I left him to it, and went for more coffee.

"You know, if you're right—and I'm not saying you are, but if you are and the killer did choose the car for emotional reasons…he or she might want it back. You know, as a trophy."

Pietr was kicking on the sofa in the main room, talking out loud, while Sharon read the morning's *Times* and Stosser stared at the popcorn-treated ceiling as though he was contemplating putting in a skylight, and never mind the fact that we were only renting the place.

Interestingly enough, the entry/waiting room seemed to be becoming our main gathering spot, and not just because the coffee was there, or because the sofa was comfortable, although neither of those things hurt.

I finished doctoring my coffee—whatever beans Venec was

buying, they were too bitter to drink black—and sat on the chair opposite Pietr, knocking his feet off the edge. "That's nasty thinking," I told him.

"Doesn't mean it's not true," Sharon said without lifting her head from the paper.

"No, it actually means it probably *is* true. Human nature tends toward the nasty when nobody's looking. Good thought, Pietr."

From the gratified look on Pietr's face, I don't think he'd thought the boss was actually listening to him. He should have known better, by now. The Guys were always listening. Especially when you wished they weren't.

"So, let's follow up on that. Without any legal paper trail and no current-trail, we can't backtrack, so we'll have to go forward. I want you at that auction, to see who bids on it. Bonnie, you go with him. Get the auction details from Ben."

I didn't know why Stosser was sending me, considering my near-monumental screwup, but I wasn't going to argue. If this was another test, I wasn't going to fail. And if it wasn't—it got me out of the office, and away from that message on my answering machine.

I got up and checked in with Venec.

"What do you want, Bonnie?"

"A raise, for one," I said, and only after the words left my mouth realized that they could have been taken a number of different ways. Ooops. "Also world peace, a decent apartment for three hundred a month, and to be ten pounds lighter without giving up chocolate. What I've got is the day's orders, from Stosser."

"Humph."

"I'm supposed to get the information on the auction from you."

"You're going?"

"What, am I supposed to be grounded?"

We stared at each other for what felt like forever, and I could feel my core start to simmer again, little crackles of energy that were probably going to give me some kind of magical indigestion. Something moved under that iron control of his, and I'd swear I felt an answering surge from his core…and then it was gone, as if nothing had ever happened between us.

"Here you go." He handed me a slip of paper, and went back to whatever it was on the table that had his attention before I walked in.

I took the slip and left, shutting the door behind me as though it was made of spun sugar. *Men.* Maybe I'd start looking for a girlfriend; the drama was higher but the overall stress was usually a lot less.

I took the info to Pietr, and we made plans. The auction wasn't until the next afternoon, and since our budget wasn't exactly up to multiple airplane tickets cross-country, it looked like Translocation time again for us. Great. Translocation was a fabulous time-saver, and having someone else do it meant you didn't waste any of your own current. But the unavoidable seconds between looking and jumping meant that you always ran the risk of someone being there when you arrived, and that sometimes got sticky.

On the plus side, that allowed me time to go take a look at a couple of apartments before we left. I made a phone call, got grudging permission from Stosser to leave early, and hit the A train, heading even farther uptown with newspaper under my arm and a notepad in my bag.

Apartment-hunting in New York City isn't like finding a place to live anywhere else. Okay, first you have to know your neighborhoods; that's like anywhere. And you need your list of must-haves, and a budget, right. Only that list and that budget would probably put anyone outside of London, Tokyo, and San Francisco into a perpetual state of what-the-fuck? Because the three places I looked at, each in a semidecent but not fabulous neighborhood, were studios the size of a shoe box with kitchenettes the size of a postage stamp, and although the bathrooms were clean and functional, that was about all you could say for them.

On the plus side, two of the three were on the top floor, meaning I wouldn't have to worry about someone stomping overhead when I was trying to sleep, and one of those two actually had a reasonably pretty view out the largest window—a small park, complete with a dog-run. I didn't have a dog, and didn't want a dog, but they were fun to watch. It was a walk-up, but that also meant I never had to worry about the elevator breaking down, right? And the neighborhood, although not great, was trendy right now, which meant that there was an upside just waiting to happen.

J would be horrified, and demand that I look for somewhere in midtown with a doorman, never mind the extra cost. But there was something about the place, despite the flaws, that appealed to me. It was prewar, so the detailing was nice and the ceilings were high, meaning I could put in a loft bed, something that had always sounded like fun.

"Put a deposit down now," the broker told me, "and it's yours."

The rent would come near to killing me. I'd be stuck drinking office coffee, no more lattes from around the corner. On the other hand, the apartment was near the subway, only about twenty minutes from the office, and yeah the kitchen was sad, but the view was pretty….

"I need to think about it," I hedged.

The broker, an impatient-looking guy in his forties, with the body of a teddy bear and the face of a street brawler, sighed heavily. "Chicklet, there is no thinking. Either you take it, or the next person in will write a check and you're shit outa luck. Move fast or be homeless."

It might have been a sales pitch, but everyone else in the office already had a place...why was I waiting?

I walked around the one room, taking note of the paint, the worn tiles, the hum of the refrigerator in the otherwise-empty space, and thinking. It didn't take long, either the walking or the thinking. I was really, really tired of living out of a hotel room, even if that room was just about the same size as this entire apartment. And I could afford this place, if barely, and okay, the kitchen was sad, I could work with that because what other choice did I have? A place with a kitchen that met my standards would cost me another couple of hundred in rent, minimum, assuming I could even find one, and...

I was really tired of living out of J's pocket, no matter how comfortable that pocket might feel. And then there was that whole "mine and nobody else can come in" thing, too.

"All right," I said. "I'll take it."

That night in the hotel room, I almost erased the message from Will. Almost.

In the end, I went to bed with his voice still caught in electronic format, and I dreamed of a mastodon trying to take a shower in my new apartment.

I have no idea how the two were connected, but I was pretty sure they were.

Translocation the next morning went off without a problem, dropping me in the upper level of a parking garage near the location of the auction. Pietr appeared at the same time, a reassuring distance away. I'd never heard of a Translocation collision, but then again, who would be left to talk about it?

Chicago was pretty today, blue skies and a soft breeze. Perfect Autumn weather. The auction, though, was about as bare bones and depressing as such a thing could get. Forget about Sotheby's and think more closeout or lost-our-lease sale. For all that, though, there were a lot of people wandering around, some of them surprisingly well dressed, and the energy was pretty high with the anticipation of getting a deal, I guess. We sat in the back row, damped down and subdued, trying not to attract any attention while taking in as much detail as we could. I liked Pietr—he was good to work with—but I didn't really know him, not the way I'd gotten to know Nick. That made small talk difficult, even for me.

"You really think the—" I almost said killer, and changed it at the last moment to "—person we're looking for will try to buy the car, keep it like some kind of trophy?"

"It's possible," Pietr said, crossing his legs in front of him and flipping through the catalog idly. They were featuring cars today, but there was a lot of other stuff, too: a houseboat—not currently on the lot, but they had pictures—and a couple of speedboats. Vehicle seizure and resale was big business in Chicago, apparently.

"People are sick."

"People are not sick," he said, surprising me. "People are basic. The stuff that drives us is basic. Hunger. Hatred. Lust. Fear. Sometimes even love. Revenge is hatred and lust and fear all in one neat package, and packs three times the kick as any one of those things alone. That's why we crave it."

"Oh man, someone worked you over but good, didn't they?" I would never have said that in the group, or if we were alone, but surrounded by strangers, waiting to spy on strangers, the words just came out of my mouth.

"Nobody ever worked me over, good or bad." He flipped

a few more pages of the program. "Nobody ever noticed I was there long enough to do anything at all."

Pietr said it so quietly, so calmly, it took me a moment to process.

"You've always ...sorta disappeared under stress, huh?"

"Sometimes I didn't even need stress. When I was a kid—" he laughed, and it wasn't a ha-ha laugh "—my folks used to routinely leave without me, because they didn't remember I wasn't in the car with them. I thought it would get better, once we moved to the States, but... My junior prom, my date left with someone else, because she thought I'd skipped out on her."

"Oh...man." I really wanted to do something, or say something that would make, I don't know, all those crap memories go away, or never have happened. Wasn't a damn thing to do, though. The past isn't ever really gone. Everything we've been through, it makes us what we are now. For me, it was finding J, and losing Zaki. For Pietr...

I watched the people in the rows ahead of us, and determined that I would never, ever again make a comment about his disappearing on us. Not ever.

Most of the crap cars went first, sold for cheap enough I wondered if the local cops made back their costs, or if they got to take it as a tax deduction. A couple of them were in bad enough shape I wasn't sure they'd be drivable off the lot—I guess you could buy for scrap and parts, too.

"And here's lot 389, one a lot of people may have been waiting for. A beauty of a machine..."

We were on. The car was rolled out into the display area so everyone could get a good last look. It gleamed under the overhead fluorescents, practically begging for someone to take it for a mad spin down a deserted highway.

"Suicide scene," I heard someone say. "No bloodstains, though. Should go for a decent price."

The bidding started, and I tuned everything out, letting my eyes do all the work. Pan and scan, one end of the crowd to the other, looking at everything and not looking for anything in particular. I had no idea what Pietr was doing, although it was probably some variation of the same. There were a lot of people intent on the car, and even more who weren't paying a damn bit of attention. The auctioneer was hopping around and talking fast, and the numbers he was chanting kept going up.

Something caught my attention, and I slowed the pan down a bit, enough for that blur of color to come into focus.

Jack Reybeorn, and an older woman with him. Not the client, but maybe the other woman who had been part of the conference? Yes. An aunt or sister, some female relative, from the looks.

All right, they had a legitimate, if morbid reason to be here, I supposed. They were paying close attention, but didn't seem to be part of the bidding. Someone could be doing it for them, a broker or dealer, but…they might also just be here for some kind of closure. Maybe.

Make no assumptions, bring no bias. Just the evidence. Right.

So. The client's son, the victims' grandson, and a female relative, were here. That was fact. Move on. What else do we see?

The bidding seemed to be slowing a bit as the numbers climbed higher, and I followed the auctioneer's gaze to see who was still in the game. Two men, older, one distinguished looking, the other scruffier but still looking like the kind of guy who would drive this kind of car. Was there a type who would drive a high-end Mercedes-Benz? I mean, other than rich, and having a garage. I couldn't see this car being regularly parked out on the street, not even on the Upper East Side.

On the other side of the room there was an older woman who, despite her participation, might have been buying groceries for all the excitement she was showing. A broker, probably—she had a Bluetooth in her ear, so might have been taking direction from someone else. Or maybe she was just so Important that she couldn't be out of touch for five minutes....

Current twitched, and I patted it down. I had, maybe, been known to fry the occasional cell phone or PDA because the owner annoyed me, but that woman hadn't done anything, either to me or the investigation. This was no time to indulge in random pettiness.

My gaze slid past her, and stopped.

Will.

I could practically hear Stosser's unspoken "I told you so" in my ear. Damn it.

He didn't seem to be bidding. That was, I suppose, a good thing. Maybe. Maybe he, like Jack, was just here out of curiosity, to see the vehicle where his former business partners had died. Maybe he had a macabre streak. Maybe.

And maybe not.

The facts were: he was here, halfway across the country, same as me. Only I had a reason that didn't involve guilt. Did he?

The hammer slammed on the podium, and I almost jumped. The bidding was over. Someone had bought the car.

"Did you see who?" I asked Pietr without taking my sideways attention off Will.

"A woman in the back," he replied. "Two friends with her. Younger than most of the women here, giddy with the winning. I think this was their first auction. Don't recognize the faces."

"We've got two known—client's son, and the guy I interviewed."

"The lawyer?"

"Yeah."

"The one you thought was telling the truth about not having a reason to kill them?"

Damn it. "Yeah, him."

"The one you had dinner with?"

Ow. Note to self: secrets do not exist in the pack.

"Yeah, him."

"Uh-huh. You want to follow him, while I take the girls, or other way around?"

It would make sense to have Pietr follow Will, lessen the risk of being discovered, and a gaggle of girls would probably be less suspicious of a woman near them than a single lurking male, no matter how good-looking that male was. But the thought that Will had maybe pulled one over was starting to burn, and I needed to know, myself, and not rely on anyone else's notes.

We split up, Pietr to shadow the winner, and me to follow Will. That could have gotten tricky—we didn't have any transport, and contrary to old movies, saying "follow that car" works only in deserted streets where anyone would be able to spot you following them anyway, even assuming your driver understood what you were asking and was willing to do it. Fortunately for me, the auction facility—an old civic center of some kind—had a cab stand down the street for those of us not fortunate enough to make a winning bid, and I was able to hear the address Will gave the cabbie. It took me a few minutes, staying back enough in line to not be seen, to get my own car, and give the same address.

Hopefully, Pietr was managing, as well.

The cab drive didn't take long, despite my fears of a two-hour, two-hundred-dollar fare I'd have to explain to the Guys.

We pulled up in front of a pleasant-looking café, which was good, because it was almost dinnertime on the East Coast, and all I'd had to eat all day was a rushed breakfast in the office, and then a packet of roasted peanuts while we were waiting for the auction to start. Combining surveillance with food was an excellent idea.

I got out of the cab and paid the driver off, feeling suddenly absurdly surreal; neither a hardened detective following a dangerous suspect nor a spurned lover following her man to a rendezvous, but maybe somewhere in between and hopelessly foolish with it. It was an odd moment, realizing that I really would rather have been back in the office.

I guess Stosser knew what he was doing, sending me out. It wasn't a test, it was a damned punishment.

Will went in, and was seated at the patio outside, at a table where someone was already waiting. A woman. Slender, dark-haired, olive skin, dressed nicely in a skirt and top, a leather briefcase at her feet. It looked as though this was a business meeting of some sort, not a tryst. Not that I had any interest one way or the other, damn it. We'd had dinner—okay, we'd had a date—and I'd gotten a good vibe and obviously given off a good vibe, and I was just going to have to deal with the stupidity of that on my own. Feeling betrayed because he was sitting in public with another woman—a woman he seemed to be quite comfortable with, if that kiss on the cheek hello was any indication—wasn't going to do me a damn bit of good. Especially since I was the one who wasn't returning messages, not him.

Thankfully, I was dressed well enough in a blue, knee-length dress and sandals that could be either office wear or Ladies who Lunch Informally wear to blend with the late-afternoon crowd. I waved off the maître d' and took a seat at the bar. It was just out of direct line of sight, and a casual eavesdropper wouldn't have been able to hear anything.

I wasn't being casual, though.

It still didn't feel natural, tapping current like this for a premeditated offense, rather than a reactive defense, but it was getting easier. All those hours of practice in the lab did make a difference, allowing me to form and hold the spell in my head, order a glass of wine, and look totally casual chatting with the bartender without losing focus.

All the old stories, about magicians and wizards and all that, with magic blazing and spells thundering? Bullshit. You try that and I swear, thirty seconds later you'd be dead, because we're just not that coordinated. It would be like a Null trying to walk and chew gum and pat themselves on the head while rubbing their belly and oh yeah, whistling Dixie at the same time. On key.

I pulled a few threads of current from my core, my control braiding them together into a thicker cable until it *felt* right for what I wanted it to do. Slow and steady, that was the trick. Venec had warned us against trying to do anything too quick, because if someone was paying attention they might be able to sense the current being used. I'd never really thought about it; being sneaky took more work than I'd expected.

Once the cable felt ready, I directed it out, around the corner and, gently, slowly, indirectly, attached it to the bottom of the patio table where Will and his companion sat. I could have used a more direct route, maybe even attached it to them directly, but that would have raised a higher chance that they would notice something was up.

Attention was the last thing I wanted.

A tickle of current went along the cable, and then returned to my core. If I'd worked this properly, the spell would turn the cable into a 'scope, bringing me whatever they were saying without allowing any noise from my end to go back.

It was a damn big *if*, but short of trying to get a table next to theirs and straining to listen in without being noticed, it was the best we'd come up with.

I took a deep breath, and willed myself to be confident. Without control and confidence, no spell would ever work worth a damn.

"You saw that the vehicle sold?"

"At a surprisingly low price, yes." Will's voice was low, but clear. The woman with him was slightly more muffled, and I heard the clink of a glass. Maybe she'd had something near her mouth? "I would have thought a car like that...well."

"A sad ending, yes. But at least it is ending. Let the dead rest. A pity. Our deals with them were quite profitable."

"And profit is all you care about, isn't it, Katie?" Will didn't sound as though he was complimenting her.

She didn't seem to think he was, either. "I'm sorry that you think I am cold, Will. But if you recall, I didn't know them, I never met them, and I can't pretend any great personal loss, or mouth polite platitudes."

"All right, yes. But you could at least show a little human decency."

It didn't sound as if all was well in patio-land. It didn't sound as if Will had been there to claim a trophy, either. But maybe we'd been wrong about that. Maybe the killer just wanted to make sure the last bit of possible evidence got out of police custody?

The waiter came, and they gave their order. The woman, Katie, had a hanger steak, while Will ordered a chicken Caesar salad. I felt my mouth curl in disdain, almost instinctively. Neither choice showed any imagination or joy in food at all;

I had expected better of Will, somehow. I ordered another glass of wine to placate the bartender, and picked up the bar food menu in front of me to buy more time while I listened.

"I don't suppose I could talk you into reinvesting?"

Will laughed, the same sweet laugh he had used for my jokes. "Neither of us have the touch, Katie. That ship has sailed."

"Still. We have an opportunity, and it seems a shame to waste it."

He started to say something in response, then stopped. "Did you hear something?"

"What? Hear what?" She sounded puzzled, as though he'd asked her if she noticed the invisible elephant that had just sat down next to them. Shit. He had picked up on me, somehow. And she hadn't. Null, or just really low-res?

"Huh." He didn't clarify, so it was probably safe to assume she was not only Null, but didn't know that he was Talent. We don't advertise much, for obvious reasons. This may be a modern age, but the cry of "witch" still has unfortunate memories in some Talent families. So she was a Null's Null. That fact was possibly unimportant, but it was part of the investigation, and I filed it into my brain for reporting.

There was silence, and I felt a gentle wave of current rise through the café, not searching so much as filtering the air, trying to identify whatever it was that had triggered his awareness. I unraveled the cable, dropping the edge quickly, before it could be traced back to me. I hoped.

Paying for the wine I'd ordered and not tasted, I walked away from the bar, heading not toward the exit, where I might be spotted, but the back of the restaurant, where the ladies' room was probably located. Locking myself in the single-use lavatory, I ran the water cold, and splashed some on my face.

"Damn. Also, damn." My hands were shaking, and my skin

was paler than usual under the crappy lighting. I knew what Will's signature felt like…and that meant that, if he'd been paying attention at all, he probably knew mine, too. If he'd been a little bit faster, or if he were stronger than I thought, he could have gotten me back there. He might still, if he decided to push beyond a basic filter, if I'd left any trace hanging in the air. I didn't *think* I had, but…

Shit. Shit, shit, shit. The urge to Transloc rose, and was squashed. And I couldn't call for a Translocation, either. That would be like sending up a flare, now that he was aware, and even with someone else doing the work, he could maybe still find a trace of me….

I needed to be subtle, and tricky, and unobtrusive, things I generally wasn't really strong at. Whatever I did, it was definitely going to require more work than my usual blunt forward on all thrusters.

Or was it? I stared at myself in the mirror, and thought hard. Only one possible escape came to me: when subtle couldn't work, sometimes being obvious was the only answer. I was going to have to brazen it out; walk through the restaurant and out onto the street, praying that some of Pietr's disappearing skill rubbed off on me, enough to get me away unnoticed.

On the plus side, I realized as I stared into the mirror, Will had seen a curly-haired strawberry-tinged blonde. The woman looking back at me had blonder, straighter hair, in another city, in a totally unfamiliar context. All right, I could work that.

Taking another deep breath, I slicked back my hair so that I looked sleek and sexy, then I dried my face and hands, straightened my shoulders, and put my very best "bite me, yon inferior beings" swing into my stride as I walked out of the café and out into the street.

I had no idea where I was going, but it didn't matter. What

mattered was that I looked like I had a purpose and a destination, and that I just keep going, until I was far enough away that a current-surge wouldn't register. I walked right past the seating patio, and didn't let my gaze slide. Straight ahead, attention firmly on something else, and only when I was at the end of the block, swallowed in the crowd and out of sight, did I let myself breathe again.

Looking around to make sure nobody was paying undue attention, I sidestepped into an alcove, where a wrought-iron bench was placed under a leafy tree, and sent a ping back to the office.

*ticket home, please?*

## sixteen

The Guys kept me waiting for almost half an hour, pacing back and forth, worried that Will was going to appear and ask me what I was doing there, or a cop was going to cruise by and accuse me of loitering, or half a dozen other real and baseless worries.

My nerves weren't helped by a chittering of noise in the tree above me. It sounded too heavy for a bird, and too…intelligible for a squirrel. I really didn't want to look up, but eventually, of course, I did.

The ugliest mug God ever wrapped around a nose stared at me from a low-hanging branch, like the unholy love child of a bat and a Kewpie doll. Another damned piskie.

"Oh. What?" I really wasn't in the mood, but ignoring it would probably make things worse.

"You're new around here, buttercup," the mug chirped at me.

There was nothing wrong with piskies that a good hard sauté wouldn't cure. Winged pranksters, they were the most common, annoying, and irritating of all the fatae. Not even Nick could get excited about being accosted by one, and I didn't want to risk attracting attention by using current to make this one go away, the way I had back home.

"I'm not in the mood," I warned it. "Try pranking me and I'll singe your fur down to your bones."

"Ooooh. Cranky." It tsk-tsked like an old Irish granny, and I couldn't help myself; I laughed.

"Better," the piskie said, and leaped higher into the tree, its wings spreading just enough to help it rise—piskies could fly, but seemed to enjoy soaring, more. "Cranky no good, butter-cup," it said, and then it was gone.

Then the stirrings of current wrapped around me, fair warning, and the Translocation sucked me from Chi-town back to upper Manhattan.

"I hear lawyer-boy was among the attendees," greeted me before I'd even managed to take my first breath of East Coast air. Obviously, Pietr had gotten back before me.

"So was Jack Reybeorn," I growled, my crankiness in full force, and I had the satisfaction of seeing Nifty blink in surprise and shut up. I might look delicate-boned and feminine to the big bad football-player, but I could slap him down as good as any defensive lineman, if he got in my face. "Are you going to interrogate me here, or do we get to wait until everyone else arrives?"

"Sorry. I…" Nifty Lawrence was many things—arrogant, aggressive, etc.—but an asshole wasn't one of them, and he was smart enough to know by now that I wasn't competition, damn it. "I was jabbing, and I shouldn't have. I'm sorry."

"Yeah. Me, too." I let it go; we had other things to deal with. "Where's the huddle?"

"Main conference room. Ian ordered in pizzas, figured you guys hadn't had a chance to eat dinner."

"They're going to start docking our pay if they have to feed us, too." I reached down and took off my shoes, wiggling my newly freed toes against the rough carpeting. The sandals were adorable, and the heels made my legs look fabulous, but they were going-out-to-dinner shoes, not stomping-around-after-suspect shoes.

"We don't solve this, we may not have to worry about that anymore."

I stopped luxuriating in the feel of free toes, and looked at my coworker. More than one-upmanship had been in his voice. "What?"

"Somebody fried our electronics while you were gone. That's why we had to hold off on bringing you back—we wanted to make sure the building was current-stable."

My first thought was a sort of generalized so what—we'd had enough gremlins running in the office to be blasé about it, and anyway, power fries happened in major cities and it wasn't always the fault of a Talent. Then I heard the emphasis in his voice when he said "our" electronics, and stopped.

"Just our building? You think someone's trying to shut us down? I mean, it couldn't just have been some cadet making his mentor nuts?"

Nifty was shaking his head, and I noticed that his close-cropped hair had been allowed to grow out into tiny black ringlets. "Venec checked around. Not just our building—it only hit our offices. Not even anyone else on this floor. But every wire in the wall's been crisped. Going to cost a small fortune to replace."

"Damn."

"On the plus side," he said with forced cheerfulness, "we'll be able to customize it all now. And maybe open up a few walls, put in a larger kitchenette, maybe another bathroom…"

"Dreamer," I snorted, following him along the hallway, the lights dimmer than usual. Obviously, not everything was back up and running, underscoring what all his big talk didn't cover up: someone was gunning for us. Based on the evidence, someone Talented. Someone who seemed to have a really strong desire to not have PUPI succeed. All the gremlin incidents, which we'd been ascribing to our own twitches and coincidence, could have been someone trying out our defenses. Psi-bombs, current-strikes? They were all used for only one purpose: to crisp the short-hairs. The fact that neither attack—none of the three, if we counted the security guard shooting at us—were fatal could have meant that someone was only trying to scare us, or that they were bad shots. In either case, intentions could change, and aim could be improved.

The escalation happened when we went from "training" to "under contract." I didn't think that was a coincidence. I suspected the Guys didn't think so, either.

Enemies were bad. Unknown enemies were really bad. Unknown enemies and no allies was about as bad as it could get.

We needed allies.

But first, we needed to solve this damn case, and prove we were *worth* allies.

"Please tell me you got something," Pietr greeted me when we walked into the conference room. The windows still boarded up, and the lights on half power, the room felt smaller and strangely ominous, despite the comforting smell of sausage and cheese. "Please tell me two hours spent listening to spoiled rich girls giggle over a car not one of them is smart enough to drive was not suffered in vain."

I dropped my shoes by the door and glared at Nick until he got up and gave me his chair. To the on-site investigator went the padded seating, damn it.

The body language in the room was grim, but not hopeless. I hoped.

"So your girlies were a washout? Did you at least get their phone numbers?"

He shot me a pained look. "I'd sooner date a waxed ape. The conversation would be better."

Ouch.

"Torres." Stosser was in pacing mode. Looking at him made me dizzy, so I reached across the table and scored a greasy slice of pepperoni pizza instead. Sharon shoved a plate toward me and a couple of napkins. "Do you have anything to give us?" he asked, not waiting for me to put my dinner together.

"I don't know. Maybe. The suspect went to a café to meet with a woman. I managed to eavesdrop on some of their conversation. It sounded like they were business partners on at least one deal with the victims. They discussed the sale of the car, but only in passing, and Will didn't say why he had been there. It might have just been idle curiosity, if he was meeting this woman anyway. Oh, and she's Null, so that pretty much rules her out as a suspect, right?"

Venec looked at Stosser for a second opinion, then he nodded reluctantly. "It would be difficult, if not impossible, for a Null to subdue both victims without leaving any sign. However, we can't overlook the possibility that they worked together, since the toenail paring we found was most likely a woman's. I don't suppose you were able to get a look at her toes?"

Damn it, I hadn't even thought of that. Not that it would have been possible anyway, but…

"Her toes, no. Her hands…" I tried to remember, then shook my head. "I'm sorry. I remember that she was dark-skinned, Mediterranean, maybe, but I don't remember anything about her hands. Which might mean she wasn't wearing polish, or it just didn't stand out."

"Pity we can't just do an info-dump of everything you saw, share it out among all of us. Maybe we'd find something that way."

"There is a way to do that," Stosser said, "but it would not be helpful in this instance. We cannot afford to risk blurring the lines between observation and interpretation. Some of the evidence we have collected already has been compromised."

"What? How?" This was the first I'd heard about that.

"Not your fault, Bonnie," Nick said. "The retrieval procedure's flawed. I went into the locker to get something, and it was all…smudged, is the best way to describe it. We just need to find another way to keep it, I guess."

I deflated, my sole real contribution to the case now useless. "Man, the bad news just keeps on coming, doesn't it. Do you think it might have happened during the attack? Yeah, Nifty told me about it. Am I alone in thinking there's a pattern there, starting with the gremlins, and…"

The expressions around the table told me that my teammates, at least, were on the same page.

"Great. Any idea who's behind it?"

"Oh, that we know," Venec said grimly.

"What?"

"Why?"

"Who?"

The last question got the most volume, with me and Nick both asking at the same time. I don't know; that seemed more important than the why, since *knowing* who is a step closer to *stopping* it.

"And if you say 'it's not your concern,' we're going to stomp you, boss or not," Sharon warned Venec without the slightest hint of irony.

"Even if it's not?" Stosser asked, deflecting attention away from Venec in a smoothly timed interruption. "Because it has less than nothing to do with you all individually, than—"

"In this room, there is no us, individually," Nifty said. "Not anymore."

Stosser's pale blue eyes got really wide, and I think maybe his jaw dropped open a little. Venec just snorted, which from him might have been disgust, amusement, or approval. I'm pretty sure nobody expected Nifty to suddenly sprout up with that comment, all things considered.

"He's right." Sharon sounded sort of disgusted, too, although I couldn't tell if it was because of what Nifty said, or the fact that he was the one to say it. "You hired us as a team. Isn't that what you keep saying? Then in here, we are a team. So what involves one of us involves us all. Especially violence. Especially violence committed against the office, while we're all in it."

"Three strikes," I added. "The security guard, or cop, or whatever, who shot at us. The psi-bombing. The current-fry on our electronics, which could have been harassment, or it could have been a try at frying one of us, too. If anyone had been taking a hit off the tame current…" I wasn't sure what might have happened then, but at the very least, a few nose hairs would have gotten seriously real-time fried. "It all adds up to someone gunning for us as a team, and that means we have…" I almost said the right to know, but even I knew that wasn't going to fly with the Guys. "We have a need to know, so we can protect ourselves—and each other."

Stosser looked as though he was going to argue but, to my surprise, it was Venec who coughed up, earning him a really filthy look from his partner.

"This isn't about the case. Not directly, anyway," he said. "You already know that there are people who don't want us to succeed. For their own reasons, some of which I can, reluctantly, understand. We're going to be stirring up hornets going forward, and hornets aren't always particular about who they sting. That's why we're being careful, only taking assignments from direct clients, people involved in the incidents under question." The "for now" was silent but seriously implicit. "We have turned away several potential clients, under those guidelines."

Oh now, that was interesting....

"Hopefully," Venec went on, not letting anyone question him about that little bombshell, "our discretion will ease fears and reduce concerns. But there is…" He paused, trying to gather his words, which made me wildly curious. Stosser, the wordsmith, was silent, and Venec was trying to moderate himself? Oh boy.

"There are people who think that what we are doing is an abomination. That using current in this fashion is…wrong."

"What, to find out the truth?" Pietr shook his head, his forehead creasing in confusion. "We've had soothsayers and scryers since before anything else, how—"

"Not what we are doing, but how we are doing it. Turning current from a personal, individualized craft to a— how did she put it?" he asked his partner. "'A petrified work of noncreativity'?"

"Close enough," Ian said, looking like the words hurt like a mouthful of glass.

"She?" Sharon asked.

"Don't be so sexist," Nifty said. "Women can be the villains, too, right?"

"Bite me, Lawrence. She?"

Stosser was the one who answered this time, as though the words were getting dragged out with fishhooks. "She. My sister. Aden."

Oh. Well. This suddenly got all sorts of interesting....

★ ★ ★

That pretty much ended the meeting. Stosser went into the chat room and shut the door firmly; not that anyone had any desire to follow him. Venec looked at us for a minute, then shook his head and went off somewhere else.

"His sister is trying to kill him." Nick looked weirdly impressed. "Man, I'm suddenly glad I'm an only child."

"She's not trying to kill him. Just stop him."

"Right. By killing him. And maybe us, too."

"You scared?"

"Hell, yes. Ian Stosser is a Talent of significant ability, by all public and private accounts. Smart, savvy, sharp, and scary. His sister, if she's able to make him nervous, is at least at the same level."

"Talent isn't genetics. Just because one member of a family is strong…"

"You're not even remotely worried?"

"Of course I am. It would be stupid not to be worried that someone wants to shut us down. But I'm not *scared*."

"Potato, potahto."

Pietr and Sharon were going back and forth over the remains of dinner, and I wanted to slap both of them. I'd rather have someone scared of us than someone objecting on a more philosophical basis. Fear was a logical motivator. Theology? Not so much. And it was crazy, besides. Current might not be a science the way, say, chemistry was, but the days of superstition and ignorance about what we did were long gone—current was a verifiable, measurable source of power, shaped and manipulated by the force of your own will and skill. The only thing that tied it to the old magic was that not everyone could use it…but even back then, in the old days of hedge witches and alchemists, they still had set-spells and incantations….

"Don't even try," Nick said, glancing over at me.

"What?"

"I can practically see the water-wheel turning over your head. You're trying to make sense of Aden Stosser's reasons. Don't even try. There's no way to do it, not without walking the same path to crazytown. And we need you here, not there."

I rolled my eyes. "When did you suddenly get to be the wise old man around here?"

He laughed, and patted my arm in a way that was surprisingly reassuring. "Somebody has to be," was all he said, and then switched the subject. "Jack Reybeorn is in the clear, by the way. Turns out, through a very neat twist of rulings, the family is getting part of the proceeds from the auction. Don't ask me how or why. The legal system makes my head hurt. But that's why he was there, to watch, and to collect a check. I guess he didn't trust the City of Chicago to do direct deposit."

"Oh, I can't imagine why," I said, not quite as drily as he managed. "I don't suppose anyone's been able to get an identification of the woman our other suspect—" I couldn't call him Will, not now, not here, not anymore "—was talking to?"

"I'm going to be working on that. Tomorrow, because as tired as I am right now I'd be no good to anyone. And no, you may not ask how I am going to do it."

I hadn't been about to—all right, maybe I had. But his statement just made me even more curious, where before it had been just an idle question.

"Nicholas Merriweather Shune? What tricks do you have up your sleeve that you're not sharing with the rest of the pack?"

"Nothing." Not even the use of his full name—which he'd never told us—made him give.

"Uh-huh…"

"It's nothing I can share," he said, finally. "Really. Just let me do my job and you'll be the first to know as soon as I get something, okay?" His brown eyes met mine directly. "Even before I tell Ian or Benjamin. I'll tell you."

"Thanks," I said. I was not going to get choked up, damn it. It didn't mean anything. It didn't.

Nick just nodded, as if he could hear my thoughts and didn't believe them, and stood up. "I'm packing it in, people. Dump the leftovers and shut off the lights when you leave, we don't have Brownies here yet to clean up after you."

About half an hour later, the last of the garbage was tossed, the table was wiped, and I was more than ready to pack it in and go to the hotel. At least that was drawing to a close—the paperwork from the broker had been delivered and signed and sent back along with my first month's rent check to go with the godawful deposit check I'd had to write, and I could take possession of my new apartment as soon as the credit check cleared me.

Even that thought wasn't doing much to cheer me up. I felt…it took a minute for me to identify what I was feeling. I felt totally useless.

"Hey." Stosser was standing in the doorway. I guess I wasn't the last one out, after all. He was dressed for a long night in another granola-grungy outfit, his hair tied back, and an oversize mug of something that smelled like crap in his hand. Green tea, my brain finally identified the smell. Usually Pietr drank that stuff; I wondered if Stosser had lost a bet, or something.

"I feel totally useless," I told him, out of nowhere.

"I can understand that," Stosser said, nodding his head without surprise. "I mean, you haven't carried your weight once since you signed on. Haven't done a damn thing to add to the knowledge of the case, haven't figured out a single bit of evidence, or…"

I was amused despite myself, despite knowing that he was mocking me. "You know what I mean. I feel like we're standing still. Worse, like we're running in place."

"It always feels like that," he said, serious now. "No matter how much we gather, no matter how much we know that we didn't before, it always feels like nothing, not enough. The curse of giving a damn." He took a sip from his mug, and made a face. "This stuff is disgusting, but Pietr swears it will settle my guts better than Maalox. I should know better than to eat Chinese food. Anyway, yeah. From start to finish, mostly we're always going to be wading through muck, thinking we're not going anywhere—or worse, we'll think we're getting somewhere and then the hot lead becomes a cold dead end. All the way until we finally make the one connection that's needed to break it open and give us an answer. If you thought we were giving you an exciting, glamorous life of intuitive glory…sorry. No."

He looked at me, and I could feel the honey-ooze of his current stroking my skin. Normally that sort of thing would creep me out, but from him it was…okay. Soothing. Even knowing he was manipulating me somehow, I didn't mind, because he was doing it honestly, letting me see it in progress.

"We've only been on the case for a week, Bonita. A week, and we've already determined that they didn't commit suicide, and that a Talent, probably female, had a hand in their deaths. The client now knows that her parents didn't give up, that they didn't abandon her and the rest of her family. It's a sort of peace she didn't have, before."

It sounded good, and reasonable, and yet… "We're not here to give peace," I said. "We're here to get answers." I sounded, even to my own ears, sulky.

"And we will. But not tonight." He turned to leave, then stopped and, over his shoulder, threw back, "You've done nothing wrong, Bonnie. A little stupid, maybe, but nothing wrong, and nothing that can't be recovered from. Sleep on that, and I'll see you in the morning."

There really wasn't much to do after that except grab my coat and bag, and leave. The streets were oddly deserted, considering it wasn't that late, and I found myself walking a little faster toward the subway. I reached down and touched my core not to soothe, but to stir it up, to let a solid ribbon of dark red curl around my mental wrist, ready to use. It was an unfamiliar and unnerving instinct. Flickers of that neon thread wrapped tighter, reassuring me. If something came out of the still night air, I'd be prepared.

A siren rose and fell in the near distance, someone shouted at someone else through an open window, and the tension in the back of my neck eased a little.

"You shouldn't be out alone."

I swear to god, at first I thought it was that damn piskie returning to torment me. Then I remembered that it was back in Chicago, and the current-threads flared into thick cables, pulsing with the desire to wrap around someone's neck.

I'd never used current for violence. I didn't even think I was capable of it. But if I were...the power was there. Yeah. New thing to learn about myself, and one I wasn't sure I was liking.

I forced those cables to relax, and turned to look at the speaker.

"You're Bonita, yes?" He was short and broad, like a fireplug, and coated in brown fur that made my fingers ache to dig into it. The body could have belonged to half a dozen fatae breeds, but the face—flat, yet curiously mobile, with dark brown eyes that slanted at the edges—gave my brain the clues it needed. The fatae in front of me was Mesheadam, and the current-cables softened a little in response to that knowledge.

"Depends on who's asking, and why," I told him, flippant

now that I could place the breed and knew it was—generally—human-friendly.

"I'm Bobo, your escort."

It was nice to know that shit could still surprise me. "Beg pardon?"

He grinned, and the flat, plant-crunching teeth were a relief, even though I'd already identified the breed as being typically nonhostile. "Your escort. Hired for the evening to make sure you get back to your hotel in one piece. Tonight, and any night you leave after 10 p.m., although I promise that, if you're with someone, neither you nor they will see me unless I'm needed. I'd advise you not to argue, my employer seems like a stubborn kind of human."

J. Of course. Why I thought he'd back off and let me run my own life…

Still. Considering everything that had been going on recently, including Stosser's little surprise announcement about his sister, a little muscular company on the subway wasn't the worst thing in the world. The Guys might be training us to be proactive, but I still wasn't comfortable with the idea of using current to hurt someone. This guy looked as though he could just flex, and would-be assailants would pass out in fear.

"All right, Bobo." His name really was Bobo. There was no justice and much mockery in the Universe. "For now, I won't argue. But don't expect this to be a long-running gig." Until we knew that Aden Stosser had backed down, at least, I'd go along with it. But tomorrow, J and I were going to have a serious and possibly loud discussion about personal boundaries, letting fledglings leave the damn nest, and no-means-no, even for him.

Bobo offered me his fur-coated arm, and I took it. The urge to whistle "We're Off to See the Wizard" flickered through my head, and was quashed. I really needed to get a decent night's sleep....

But when I got back to the hotel room, the message light was blinking on the phone. The credit check had cleared, and the apartment was mine. J must have greased wheels. Or palms. I was too tired, and too relieved, to be upset about that, right now. The desire to be in my own place swamped everything else, but there was no way I was going to be able to move my stuff, much less hunt for furniture, while this case was hot.

It was late, but I picked up the phone and dialed the only number I knew from heart.

"All right," I said when my mentor picked up. "You win. I need your help."

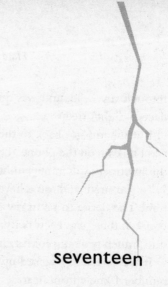

## seventeen

After rearranging my life, I finally fell into bed at oh-god-late and then got knocked out of bed at just after five in the morning by the phone ringing and an urgent ★ping★ in my head, all at once.

"Wha?" The phone got dealt with first, because my muscles worked better than my brain, when I first woke up.

"Office. Now."

Venec's voice. The ping tasted like Stosser, flavored with urgency and a bit of anxiety. Since I suspected he'd tell me the same thing, I batted it down with a sense of being awake and on my way, and it faded, satisfied.

Based on that wake-up call, I didn't bother to shower, but threw myself into jeans and a black mesh shirt, pulled on my stompy boots, and was out the door, remembering only halfway to work that I'd forgotten to brush my teeth. Gah. A pause at the bodega to pick up a pack of gum and an extra large, extra strong coffee—in case they hadn't gotten the coffee machine up and running after yesterday's fuse-out—and I felt almost ready to deal with whatever crisis was going down. Thankfully Bobo was nowhere in sight—I guess his shift ended with sunrise, or something. Explaining him to the pack would have been embarrassing— "Hi, my mentor thinks I'm still fourteen." Way to go establishing competence, yeah.

I ran into Sharon when I got on the subway, proving, I'm sure, something deep and profound about Fate, Karma, and the NYC mass transit system. She looked about as wrecked as I felt.

"If this doesn't involve blood, steel, or fire, I'm going to kill them and sleep on their pelts," Sharon said, taking a hard pull out of an expensive-looking chrome thermos. She took a good look at me, and offered a sip.

Expecting coffee, or maybe tea, I almost choked as the sharp scent of whiskey hit me, but I downed it anyway. Tea, yes, and honey, and the golden warmth of Kentucky's finest slid down my throat and made my eyes open a little wider. I assumed it was the finest, anyway. What I knew about whiskey could be fit in a shot glass, but Sharon didn't seem the sort to own rotgut, much less drink it, and nothing that hot-smooth could possibly be cheap or crap.

I returned the flask to her and had a chaser of coffee to settle my stomach. At our stop I pulled out the pack of gum and offered Sharon a piece. We ascended to the street, chewing spearmint in perfect, grumpy accord. The homeboys were sound asleep, the bodegas were just opening their doors, and the traffic was humming along at a pace you only ever saw before 6:00 a.m. on a Saturday.

"I am a god, and you will all bow down before me," Nick announced as we walked into the office. If he was a god I'd hate to see what his creations looked like, because he was a mess. He was still wearing the clothing he'd been in last night, and his hair, never exactly well-groomed, was tangled and matted, as if he'd fallen asleep leaning against a wall in a wind tunnel. But his nose was twitching. Something was up.

"I bow before no one who looks like you do," Sharon said, following my thoughts. "I assume from your 'tude that you know what's going on?"

"He's the cause." Venec came in from the inner office and went directly to the coffee counter, pouring more into the mug already in his hand. "And he may actually be half as good as he thinks he is."

"Praise from Caesar," Nick said. "I won't ask him to bow, though."

Ferret-boy definitely hadn't slept, because he was punchy as hell.

"Are you going to tell us, or just taunt us until we snap and dump your body off the GWB?" Sharon asked.

It took me a minute to remember she meant the George Washington Bridge. There was a slang locals used I hadn't quite gotten down yet, much as I had always loved the city.

"Patience, rose of the north, patience," Nick said. "Not until we're all here."

He crooked his finger at us, backing out into the main hallway as though luring us into his lair—or as though he was afraid to turn his back on anyone. Playing a hunch, I slipped into current-sight, and looked at him. Sure enough, his aura was static-filled and jagged, like he was running on fumes. However he'd been spending the night, it had required hard current, and a lot of it.

"You might want to give him a hit off that flask," I said to Sharon. "I think he needs it, just to sit."

Sharon looked doubtful, but offered him the thermos anyway. I was pretty sure the first hit made his hair uncurl, and the second, more cautious sip evened out the lines around his mouth.

"I love you both, and I mean that in a purely nonplatonic

fashion. Come, children. Come and grab a seat so that you won't be blown away by the sheer scope of my mad skills and Talent."

"You cracked the case?" That was the only reason he would be so manic, and the Guys so determined that we be here at oh-fuck-early.

"Like a crowbar, my dear dandelion, like a goddamned crowbar."

"Only problem is, inside we've got a tighter nut," Venec said, bringing up the rear in our sleep-deprived parade. Ah. And that would explain the level of frustration in the manic, yeah. Also why there was the urgency. If they were almost-there but still locked out, all brains were going to be needed, even half-asleep.

There were doughnuts on the conference room table; hot, glazed, disgusting-looking pastries that had clearly come right off the conveyer belt and been Translocated directly to us. Domino's delivery had nothing on a Talented friend in the right—or wrong—place. Nick fell on them like a ravening hound, and I waited until he'd filled a paper plate and retreated to his chair before risking my own hand to reach in.

"Those things are fried death," Stosser said. He had been sitting in the chair at the far end of the table, his hair pulled back and his eyes closed, and I'd almost thought he was asleep until he spoke.

"No Talent has ever died of coronary infarction," Venec said. "Relax and let the children gorge."

Sharon passed on the doughnuts. There was a reason why she was lean and elegant, and even with current-burn I needed to spend more time in the gym—as soon as I found a gym to join, anyway. By the time Pietr and Nifty showed up, the box held a few crumbs and a scattering of greasy sugar.

"Took you long enough," Stosser said, annoyed.

"I was in Pittsburgh," Pietr said. "It took some explaining why I had to leave."

"She still speaking to you?" Nifty asked, probably thinking that he was being funny.

"*They* promised to consider it, if I groveled prettily enough."

Nifty choked on his bagel, and Sharon rolled her eyes. Nick and Stosser seemed oblivious. Me, I just wondered what gender "they" were, and if they knew people in this town. I'd never done a threesome, interestingly enough. I wasn't sure it was something that actually appealed to me…but I wasn't going to rule it out, either, until the question came up.

Nick took the floor, as soon as everyone settled in. "So. Working my ass off, and flexing some extremely delicate and, dare I say it, elegant spellwork, I came up with the goods on the mystery woman Bonnie scoped, out in Chicago."

Whoa. "What kind of spell? Did you do a trace? How did you find something to lock onto?" My brain suddenly woke up in a way that even the sugar hadn't been able to effect, and I leaned forward, my fingers twitching even as my pad and pen appeared in my hands. What had I missed? How had he gotten that information?

"Trade secret." Coy did not look good on Nick.

"Calling bullshit! Tell!"

"Torres, heel. I appreciate your enthusiasm, but now is not the time."

Venec was right, damn him. I shot Nick a look that warned this wasn't over, and leaned back.

"Thank you. Yes, this woman is, as Bonnie suspected, a business partner—a *silent* business partner. She feeds Arcazy cash he doesn't have, and he uses his contacts she can't access, and everyone's happy, far as I could tell. Certainly their bank accounts were benefiting."

"What contacts couldn't she get?" Sharon for the practical questions. "Was there some reason the Reybeorns wouldn't or couldn't know about her?"

"They wouldn't do a deal with a Null," I said, as sure of that fact as I was of the sugar crash I was going to have by mid-morning. "They were high-end Council, and she was a Null from another territory. They might have mingled in the same social circles, and they wouldn't have blinked about working for or with her indirectly, but they weren't going to cut her in on a business deal. Not one that they cared about the way they did these real estate things."

"You're sure of that?" Venec asked, even as Stosser was nodding agreement. It was one of those things, I guess, that you knew or didn't, just growing up around it. A lonejack wouldn't understand, not really. From what I remembered about my dad, admittedly not the best judge of things, lone-jacks could be particular about who they were friends with, but business was business. You held your nose and you did the deal. "Yeah, I'm sure." It made sense, and all the things I'd over-heard at the café fell into place with a satisfying click. Damn. But...

"Then she's not a suspect," Pietr said, matching my own thoughts. "A Null couldn't have killed them that way, not without leaving a physical trace. And if she was going to kill anyone, wouldn't she kill her partner? I mean, he's the one who backed out and won't play with the Reybeorns any longer, costing her money. Same problem we started with—means and motive."

Nifty drummed his fingers on the table, thinking out loud. Unlike the rest of us, he wasn't sucking down caffeine, and looked disgustingly alert. "Could she have killed them in order to set him up? I mean, we looked at him right away, and so did the cops. She had to know their public spat would make him a nice-looking suspect."

"But, again, how?" Venec got up to pace the length of the room. As usual, watching him made me dizzy, so I looked at the table instead. "The cops couldn't find any trace of physical evidence. We found evidence of current being used by a third person who was in the car before, and during the murders. We also have evidence that suggests that person was female. If this woman was a Talent, we'd have her. If the evidence pointed toward a male, we'd have him. Is there any way they worked together, intentionally clouding the issue?"

"There's always a possibility," Stosser said. "How do we rule it in or out?"

"I could… Someone could go back and ask him." He was still a suspect. I was still in the doghouse for letting my interview with him become more. Someone else would be better at talking to him…but he would answer my questions without suspicion, if I phrased them right.

But if I had been wrong about him to begin with, how could I trust my evaluation now?

"Sharon," Venec started to say, "could you…?"

"Already on it," she replied. "Bonnie, there's a way, maybe, to determine if our guy was full of shit or not. But it's going to require that you trust me."

"All right."

"No. I mean…trust me. Really trust me."

There were only three things that required that kind of trust, and I was pretty sure she didn't have anything kinky in mind, so that ruled out two of them.

★ ★ ★

An hour later, I was thinking that maybe I was going to have to redefine my idea of kinky. Tying someone up and covering them with butterscotch and strawberries was totally normal. This? This was a little weird. And uncomfortable. And I really wasn't sure I did trust Sharon enough to let it happen.

Not that she would hurt me; I trusted all my coworkers with my back. I even trusted them with my front. It was the insides I was still sorta protective about.

"Are you comfortable?"

"No."

We were in the smallest of the meeting rooms, the one where Venec had held his current-conference. The table was pushed to one side, and someone had scrounged a folding massage table thing, like the kind they used for blood drives, and set it up against the far wall. That was for me. Sharon got a club chair, a padded leather one I don't know where they found, but I was so damn stealing it when this was done. Maybe Nifty would lug it to the apartment for me. Translocation would be too traceable.

Putting aside my thoughts of larceny, I hopped onto the indicated surface, letting my feet dangle a few inches off the floor. I'd taken off my boots, and my socks suddenly looked dingy.

"Lie back. You need to be relaxed for this to work." Sharon seemed to think that just telling me that was going to do the trick. Not exactly.

"Tell me again what you're going to be doing." This was twice now people had worked current on me, with my permission. The others didn't seem to have any trouble with what we were learning to do; just me. My entire life, current had been a thing I used, not the definition of who I was—not because I didn't have much, or because I didn't appreciate it, but just because it didn't really connect with who I was or what I was doing. J trained me to think like a person, not specifically a Talent. I guess that's why I'd never really felt part of either world, Null or *Cosa.* I didn't, as the psych books say, Identify. Now, suddenly, everything I did revolved around what I was, what I could do, around being a *Talent,* and it was scaring me. But it was also fascinating, and like everything else that ever caught my fancy, I wanted to know everything possible about how it worked.

"It's like the trace-dump Ian worked out, a little," Sharon said, but she was clearly hedging, meaning that it wasn't like that at all. "Except that I'll be looking at your memories of the event."

"In my head."

"In your memory of the event. It's not like I'll be able to read your thoughts or anything. Just focus on that event, and so will I, and I'll be in and out before you know it."

Sharon was a damn good tactician, and was probably great out in the field, but she had a lousy bedside manner. I could feel my anxiety actually spike, rather than decrease.

"I don't like doing this, either," she said, I guess picking up from my expression that her reassurances hadn't helped. "I don't want to know what people are thinking. It's not comfortable for me, either—everyone's got just enough room in their head for themselves, and anyone more makes for crazy. So believe me, I've got no interest in poking anywhere else but what we're after."

"And you're just going to look? No touching?" I didn't mean it in the physical sense. She understood.

"No touching, no taking. Imagine it…like having a painting you think is an undiscovered Master's work. You can hang it on your wall, and tell everyone it's real, but the insurance company wants to be certain. So you bring in an expert, who can tell just by studying the brushstrokes if the work is real, or if it was done by the Master's apprentice, or some hack ten years ago. The painting stays on the wall, in your possession, and the expert walks away with a memory of having seen something that, like all memories, will fade over time, or be pushed out by new memories."

All right. That…made sense. I could visualize what she was talking about, make it work for me.

Lying back, my head and shoulders elevated slightly, I took a deep breath, held it in, and then let it out, counting the way she'd told me to:

"Ten. Nine. Eight."

At seven, Sharon's voice joined mine in the count-back. At four, I stopped counting out loud and just did it in my head, Sharon's voice still accompanying. At two, I realized that Sharon's voice was in my head, too.

That easily, I was back in Will's office, looking at him across the desk, listening to him answer my questions, but it wasn't exactly the same as the moment, and it wasn't exactly the same as a memory. It was like…watching through a one-way mirror, the kind they use in cop shops when questioning a witness. You can see them but they can't see you. Although anyone who has ever seen one of those shows knows there are people staring at them behind that huge-ass mirror, don't they?

*Focus on the memory,* Sharon chided me, inside my head. *You're blurring it, sending me elsewhere.*

Ooops.

I concentrated on the memory, on the words Will said, the way he said them, the way his body moved…okay maybe not so much on that.

*All of it.*

All right, then.

Some other stuff leaked through; the way he'd looked at the bar that evening, his gaze intent on mine, the way he'd taken my hand, thumb sliding under my palm, the tilt of his head when he listened to what I was saying rather than thinking about what he was going to say next…the touch of his lips on my skin and okay, not going there.

*Thank you for that.* Sharon's mental voice was distracted, dry…but not totally disapproving. I guess I'd been more worried about that than I thought.

Worrying about what someone not-J thought about me was a new thing. I wasn't sure I liked it.

*All right. Going to back out now. Will leave you here, all you have to do to come back is let go of the memory, and count forward to ten.*

There was something in her voice that made me think it wasn't as easy as all that, but worrying wasn't going to make it happen any easier. She'd have to explain to Venec if she left me trapped in my own brain, after all, and I didn't think she'd want to do that.

I waited what seemed like only a few seconds after I "felt" Sharon leave. The sense of that mirrored wall disappeared, and I was back in the room with Will again. He was still handsome. Still charming. Still intense. I still wouldn't mind getting horizontal with him, yeah. And yet there was a distance there that hadn't been before, not at the time, and not in my memories. I wanted to blame Sharon for it, but knew, even then, it wasn't her fault.

I was looking at him as a possible suspect, now. Things could never go back. Forward, maybe. But not back.

One. Two. Three. Four.

"Five. Six. Seven. Ow. Eight. Nine." My back was killing me, but I finished the count-back the way Sharon had told me, just in case breaking it off had dire consequences. "Ten."

"Sit up slowly. If you feel dizzy, let me know right away."

I'd been expecting Sharon, or maybe Stosser. Not Venec, and certainly not with that gentle touch on my arm, and soft voice in my ear.

"We get what we needed?" I asked, even before I could open my eyes. They felt gummed shut, and might take some working open to avoid tearing the lashes.

"We did." Sharon's voice, a little farther away. Someone— Venec?—held a damp pad to my eyes, and the gunk softened enough that I could open them.

"Thanks."

"No problem." His voice was cooler now, or maybe I'd hallucinated that softer, warmer tone.

There was a glass of water in his other hand, held up in offering, and I took it thankfully. My throat was dry, but not sore, and nothing else hurt, so I guess I came through the experience okay. Wasn't sure I ever wanted to do it again, though. Being a stranger in your own memories is *weird* shit.

"So what's the judgment call?" Venec asked, leaving the glass in my hand and moving away.

"He wasn't lying to her."

Before I could even think about being relieved, she added, "But he wasn't telling the truth, either."

"Well, we already knew that," I said. "I mean, that he had a silent partner he wasn't telling us about."

"No, it was more than that, like there was something else entirely on his mind, something he was trying to keep from you but couldn't stop thinking about, and it was distracting him. Something that had nothing to do with what you were asking him."

Sharon sounded so puzzled and annoyed about not being able to figure it out, that I tried really hard not to laugh. Venec had no such hesitation.

"He was on the make," he said bluntly.

Sharon's expression was worth getting up at oh-fuck-early for—a combination of dawning comprehension, horror, and an embarrassment I didn't quite get until I realized that she was embarrassed for *me*.

Then, I admit it, I did laugh. "Well, that made two of us then. Oh, stop glaring at me, Venec. I admit I was an idiot, and it won't happen again. But scoping someone out doesn't make you a criminal. Especially if it's mutual."

"Hmm." He sounded so noncommittally disapproving, it just made me laugh harder. Inappropriate stress-responses 101.

Sharon took refuge in clinical pissiness. "I don't think that was all he was avoiding," she said. "There was something on his mind that he didn't want you to know about, something he didn't want anyone to know about, but it kept coming into his mind anyway."

Venec paid attention, then. "The kind of thing he didn't want anyone else to know about? Or the kind of thing he didn't want to know about, either? Something he was trying to not-know?"

Wow. I would never have thought of that. Venec was a *tricky* bastard.

"Maybe…" Sharon sounded as if she was trying the idea on for size, too. "It fits, yes. How he was sliding around, telling the truth but not, as he was aware of the truth, letting himself not-know, yes."

"Would you recognize it again, if you encountered that?"

"I…I'd like to say yes. I don't know. But I'd be looking for it, as a possibility, now."

"Good enough." Venec nodded once to me, then to Sharon, and left the room, leaving the two of us staring at each other.

Oh hell. Might as well deal with the elephant in the room, before it crapped all over everything. "The initial interview.

They should have sent you to talk to him, not me. He would have opened up to any female, and you would have known right away something wasn't on the up-and-up."

"Damn straight," Sharon muttered. Then she shook her head, sighing, and sat back down in the club chair and looked at me, as direct a gaze as I'd gotten from her since day one. "Do you get any of this? I mean, not what we're doing, but how we're being handled? The big dogs knew about my truth-sensing, the same way they knew about Pietr's invisibility thing, and your ability to see and remember details—and by the way? You are absolutely awesome. I've never dipped into anyone with that much recall. I couldn't have gotten such a good reading if you hadn't seen and stored it all."

I'm pretty good at accepting compliments, but Sharon's sort of floored me. "Um, thanks."

"Earn praise, get praise. Earn ass-kicking, get ass-kicking. I just resent like hell that my one seriously useful skill is being overlooked, especially since it cost us time. It's stupid, and I don't like working for people who are stupid."

"How about forethoughtful?"

We both jumped. Damn it, Stosser had just ghosted in like he was taking lessons from Pietr, and I was going to bell everyone in this damn office before I had a heart attack.

"Do you expect to speak to every suspect, every time?" he asked Sharon.

"No. Of course not. But—"

"Do you think that you will be the only one out in the field?"

"No. Of course not. But—"

"Then you allow that your coworkers, not blessed with your natural skill set, will need to learn how to ask the right questions and listen for responses? To determine on their own, through experience and training, if someone is lying or not? Even though they might not be as immediately accurate as you?"

Sharon clenched her jaw, but I could see that what he was saying was clicking inside.

"And what happens if you run into someone who can block you? If we all come to depend on your skills, and don't develop any of our own in that range?"

"All right." She didn't sound angry, just tired. "All right. I get it. I don't like it, but I get it. Point made."

"But where does that leave us now?" I had to ask. "Having used Sharon's skill in conjunction with mine—and I think we deserve an attagirl for that, by the way—we're now left with the fact that Wi—that the suspect was not—truthful about something beyond being a hound and that he had a silent partner, something that he didn't even want to let himself think about. So what is it, and how do we find it? And is it even relevant or just another goose chase? That's our uncracked nut, right there."

I guess maybe I should have been more upset about Will, about getting my brain searched, about, I don't know, all the stuff I was being stuck with. But all I could see was the puzzle, shiny and bright in front of me. The prize was inside, but the puzzle was what fascinated me.

*It's what makes you good at this.*

"Get out of there," I said out loud, without thinking, and had the other two stare at me with confused expressions.

"Sorry. Thinking out loud." Damn it, did Venec do that to everyone, or just me? And if just me, how come I was so blessed?

The little voice in my head had disappeared. Of course.

Meanwhile, Stosser took the nut—and us—to our resident nutcracker.

"Can you do it?"

Nick looked up at the ceiling, as though he was calculating his chances in the tiles. Sharon and I, not knowing what it was Stosser wanted him to do or why he needed to calculate it, held our breath, waiting for a response.

"It'll be tricky. And maybe ugly. But…yeah. I think I can do it. You going to foot the bill?"

"So long as you're on the clock, we're covering the costs. You know that."

"Yah."

Whatever it was that he was going to do, Nick didn't seem too happy about it.

"All right, later—"

"Now."

Nick looked like he was going to balk. Funny, he was still the skinny geek I'd met that first day, but something was different. Something I couldn't quite see, but knew was there. We were all changing, I guess. I wondered what they saw in me now.

"Come on, Shune. You're going to have to trust them with it sooner or later. Might as well be now."

Nick swallowed, then nodded. "They might be useful at that, anyway. Bonny Bonnie, you've got some solid grounding in you. Would you be willing to loan me some of that?"

"Sure." I didn't even have to think about it. "But what for?"

"I'm going to go surfing."

"You weren't shitting me. Wow." The computer system wasn't brand-new or, as far as I could tell, particularly powerful. But it was a computer, and that meant it was to be treated with caution. A computer, kept in an office filled with Talent under significant stress? I was amazed it hadn't been reduced to a plastic shell of smoking and melted metals by now, especially considering the bad case of gremlins we'd had.

"It's grounded and warded. There are ways to make it reasonably safe to use."

The pile of cables behind the desk were thicker than normal, and plugged into a surge protector strip that looked as though it came straight from NASA. "Reasonably safe can still cost you significantly in repairs. That's something Old Ben and the Founders never foresaw."

"Old Ben was a genius diplomat and inventor, not a genius prognosticator." Nick got down on his hands and knees and fiddled with the cables, making sure everything was set to his satisfaction. He was muttering something under his breath; I assume to reinforce whatever protections he'd put on them in the first place. Stosser had deposited us in this room and muttered something about getting everyone out of the office for lunch. Part of me wanted to be with them. The other part was totally fascinated about what I thought we were about to do.

He paused in his fiddling, and I took the opportunity. "You're a hacker, aren't you?"

He nodded, not looking up at me.

Rare. Oh my god rare, like flawless-diamond rare. No wonder he was quiet about it. No wonder why the Guys wanted him. Most Talent could, carefully, use technology. Some could even use spell-tech, a specific cantrip designed to interact with tech, not conflict. A Talent-hacker? That was someone who could slip inside that most delicate of technology, the computer, and use free-form current to make it…do things. A Talent-hacker could ferret his or her way into the virtual world and make it dance to their tune, not crash….

The most famous Talent in the *Cosa Nostradamus* was McCunney, who had used current to siphon seven million dollars from a military contractor's account, and then disappear so well that even ten years later nobody knew where he was. He was alive, though, because every year on the date of the heist, that company got a postcard, mailed from a different location, addressed to the current CEO. Sort of our version of D. B. Cooper, I guess, except that we knew McCunney was alive and well and having a blast.

Ferret-boy hadn't been kidding, back in Chicago, about having his choice of job offers.

"What do you need me to do?"

"How are you set for current?"

I reached inside to check my core. It was cool and settled, surprisingly—I guess whatever Sharon had done hadn't touched it. Good to know. The threads coiled neatly, shading from dark to light and then back again, pulsing gently, like the purring of a sleeping cat. "I don't actually run full-up...."

"You should start. We all should. The building's still screwed from the hit we took, but—"

"I'm fine."

"You're sure?"

"Yeah." No, but I could fake it. J taught me never to be un-prepared, no matter what the situation. I always had cash, condoms, and a backup source of current, if needed. My core might not be overflowing, but I had enough to get by. Reaching out, I felt the shimmery charge of the subway, rumbling under the street, ready and waiting like a patient dog, if I called it.

"Yeah. I'm set. You?"

Nick nodded. "Never unprepared. Talent Scouts motto."

"No such thing." There should be, though. Maybe it was us. The thought—and the resulting image of Nick in a Scout's outfit, knobby knees and all—made me laugh.

"Just sit there, and sink yourself down as much as you can.

If I need you, I'll need you fast and probably won't have time to ask nice first. Okay?"

"Gotcha. Lightning Rod Torres, that's me."

Current ran with electricity, in most things. It also grounded like electricity. One of the first things you learn in mentorship is how to ground so that current can pass right through you. Useful if you get caught up in shit you can't handle, psi-bombed, or just pull too much down. Or someone near you overrushes, and grabs at you in their panic.

Grounding's easy, for the most part. You just let your awareness sink down, through your core and past it, down through your soles, making yourself heavy and solid until you come to something that's even more heavy and solid. On the East Coast it doesn't take too long—the geologic history that gave us the Appalachian Mountains also left a solid rock mass with lots of toeholds for twitchy Talent. I connected with the bedrock, settled myself to match its gravitas, and went from anticipatory to stone-calm in the breadth of a breath. Wired and ready, but calm.

Nick sat in front of the computer, and started typing. It looked as though he was hitting the keys randomly, and the screen remained blank, so I looked down—and the surge protector was unplugged.

Um. Okay.

Even as I thought that, a bolt of dark red current jumped from the plug to the socket, and the screen lit up with a pale green glow.

I think my eyebrows actually hit my hairline. Wow. Demon in the box, for sure.

I'm not a total e-loser. I have a computer, stored in J's apartment, and an e-mail address, and when I was in school I even had an instant-message account, to keep in touch with everyone. I just never got into tech, because what was the point? A cell phone, carried next to a Talent's body, would crackle and die within three months, just by sheer proximity to the core. I once managed to keep a really simple portable CD player working an entire year, using it every day, but I killed a professor's PDA dead just by sitting in the front row during a stressful semester.

I still felt bad about that.

Nick probably didn't have any more luck with casual electronics than any of us. But when he focused…

"Come on, let me in, let me in, let me in."

As spells go, it was pretty stripped down. Seemed to work, though, because the screen went from a dizzying shade of swirly pale green to darker blue, and then suddenly it resolved into a vortex that made me want to throw up.

I looked away, focusing on the reassuring solidity of the earth beneath my physical and metaphorical feet. Okay. Right.

Normally, you could tell when someone was working current nearby. Even if you weren't paying attention there was a thickness to the air, like a storm front was moving in. As open and waiting as I was, the sense of whatever Nick was doing should have been practically visible. Instead, it was as if I was in the room all by my lonesome. I couldn't even get a vibe off the computer, unless I looked at it, and I really didn't want to do that again. He was totally locked down, tight like a tick.

Then a sudden spike hit the room, a jolt of clear current that hit me dead center in the chest. Normally, it would have raced down into my core, sparking my own current into action and causing some potentially nasty chaos. Because I was grounded and prepared, instead it slid through my bones, leaving me a quivering, sweaty mess but otherwise untouched when it exited out and dispersed along the tendrils of my grounding.

"Whoa."

Nick cackled like a mad scientist. "Sorry about that. Did warn ya."

"Yeah. Right." I checked my grounding, reformed my calm, and only then went into my core to make sure everything was working okay. I felt a little scorched around the edges, but intact.

Nick was already moving on. I could hear the computer whir and hum, and then he was clicking keys again. "Gotcha. Hello, Unca. What do you have for me today?"

Unca? Oh, he hadn't. Had he?

I risked looking long enough to confirm that Nick had, yeah, current-hacked his way into the IRS database, and was pulling up our suspect's files.

"That's like, how many years in prison?"

"Only if they catch us."

"Us? What us, ferret-boy? I'm throwing you totally to the wolves, anyone comes knocking."

"Shhh. I'm trying to figure this stuff out." He waved his left hand—the right busy moving over the keyboard—and a printer I hadn't noticed before hummed to life and started printing out pages.

Curious, I got up and, carefully, approached the printer. When it didn't implode or otherwise melt down, I swiped the top sheets and started to read. The forms were unfamiliar, but I had worked with J on his investments enough to be able to pick up the basics.

"He was still doing business with them, when they died."

"Mmm-hmm."

"He said he—" I stopped and thought. "He said he wasn't going into any more deals, that he wanted them to buy him out. He never said they had. He never said he didn't still have money with them when they died." A distinction and a difference, that. Question was, had he meant to obscure the answer, or was it just an accident, him not thinking his words all the way through?

Nick finished whatever he was doing, and started backing out of the system. Now that I'd been tagged by his current, I could feel something happening, but it was so tightly focused, it felt farther away and less impressive than I knew it was.

"So if the suspect and his silent partner were still in business with the Reybeorns when they died, and were on good terms, despite their argument... Why didn't they just sell his real estate, and give him his money?"

There was a click and a thump and the sense of something flattening in the air pressure, and Nick pushed away from the computer with the air of a man who'd just tightrope walked, successfully, between mountaintops.

"Because it was still unrenovated," he said. "The location was in a prime area for urban renewal, though—the estimated value had gone up more than forty percent even before they started anything. Looks like they had a buyer ready to take it off their hands immediately. But from what your report said, the Reybeorns wanted to finish the job, and the way the deal was structured, nobody could pull out without losing their initial investment. Smart, to keep everyone honest."

I shook my head. "Not so smart, to give them a motive for murder."

## eighteen

My words echoed between the two of us. In trying to narrow the field, we'd opened it back up again. Damn.

I handed Nick his printouts, then excused myself and took five minutes to hit the bathroom. I had to pee, yeah, but I also had sweat running down my back and arms, and I wanted a few quality minutes with cold water and paper towels. We so had to get a shower installed in here. Seriously. The way things were going, cold sweat was probably going to be much in my future, and I'd lay cash money that I wasn't going to be the only one.

It wasn't the current that made you sweat. It was the holy-shit-what-am-I-doing rush you got, after. We were making this shit up as we went along, and the odds were high that someday something was not only not going to work, but it would make a kaboom in our faces. And every day, the odds on that got higher and higher.

The thought probably should have unnerved me more than it did. God knows J would be having the proverbial cow, and then some, if he knew the details. It wasn't that I didn't have a healthy sense of self-preservation. My brain was just chewing over something else, instead.

Will might be guilty.

Splashing water on my face, I bent forward and sucked up some water to rinse my mouth. The water tasted metallic and flat, but that pretty much fit my mood. If everything we'd learned was right, and I had no reason to believe otherwise, then I'd been played for a fool. It wasn't the first time, and it probably wouldn't be the last, but it was the first in a professional capacity, and even though there was no way I could have known, I was still pissed. And I still felt stupid.

I was not used to feeling stupid. I didn't like it. At all.

By the time I forced myself out of the bathroom, Nick had already gone to the guys with what we'd discovered. I followed the sound of voices.

"If this guy needed money to buy property, he would have wanted to get his investment back. All of his investments. If they wouldn't sell…"

"That would be motive for him, I agree." They were in the small conference room, Stosser leaning against the edge of the desk, Venec seated behind it. The Guys. By now the sight was not only familiar, but comforting. Our Guys.

Stosser had the floor, as usual. "But Arcazy has an alibi, and his signature's nowhere in the car. Plus, the physical evidence suggests that a woman was in the car with them, and we have Torres's personal testimony that he is indeed male."

Bastard. At some point someone else was going to screw up, and they were going to have to leave me alone already, or I was going to shave his head some night while he slept. If he ever did sleep.

Since my name had already been abused, I felt no hesitation walking in without knocking. "And his silent partner, being Null, couldn't manage the killing the way it went down…so who did?"

"That's the question, isn't it?" Venec sounded tired and wound up all at once. "I think we need another look at our sole piece of evidence."

While Stosser was off doing whatever schmoozing he had to do in order to get us access to the car from its new owners, Venec herded us all into the secondary workroom and sealed it from the inside. Whatever it was that he wanted us to try, he thought it was going to get messy. Or at least noisy.

He stood facing us, and once again I was struck by how tired he looked, around the eyes and mouth. The urge to smooth those lines away came over me, mingling with the usual desire to tangle my fingers in his hair, in no way, shape, or form the way I petted Pietr's softer strands. "All right, puppies. We've already gleaned this car as well as can be expected, and the new owner will have contaminated it thoroughly by now. So what can we hope to pick up?"

There was silence.

"Come on, people. Use the brains I know are in there somewhere."

"Emotions." Pietr sounded tentative at first, but when Venec didn't growl at him, he went on, gaining confidence as he sounded out the idea. "We've been looking for the physical stuff, even with current. Trace evidence. Stuff. But we're forgetting that people *died* in that car, and that someone killed them. That's got to be a lot of emotion built up, right?"

He didn't wait for anyone's response, but plowed on. "We've been focusing on the controlled side of current. That's how we're trained—control, control, and always control. That's what creates the signature in the first place, that control, imprinting on fresh current, personalizing it. But when someone dies, or is driven enough to murder…there has to be a lot of emotion in that, enough to overpower control. If current was used to commit the murder, then that emotion's got to leave its own kind of imprint in it, even if the killer used totally fresh, wild-sourced current. Right? And even if the new owners are totally giddy over their new toy, that's not going to be strong enough to wipe out that kind of signature. So maybe we can use that, to…I don't know, trace it back? Or something."

He ran out of steam, and almost collapsed in on himself, slumping in his chair and looking around for a response.

"Good idea, but how the hell do you pick up something like that? We know how to identify current-signature, or pick up bits of physical debris. Emotions?" Sharon wasn't tearing him down, though; she was asking.

Pietr shrugged. He'd done his bit, now it was someone else's turn to step up.

"Same thing we do every night," Nifty said matter-of-factly, his eyes wide with an inner glee that really, really disturbed me. "We make it up, and we make it work."

Oh man. More improvised current. J was *definitely* going to have a cow if he ever heard about the risks we were taking….

"First to find, then to tap, and then to follow back," I said, sorting through what I knew. "The finding's going to be the hardest part. Emotions are slippery, they're changeable. Current is a science. Emotions…emotions are slippery," I said again, uselessly.

"What's the base spell?" Nick asked, leaning forward and putting his elbows on the table. "We don't have any empathy-based spells that I know of. Anyone?"

Heads shook, and even Venec looked blank. Current was a hard science, not like old magic. Emotions weren't supposed to get involved. Except Pietr was right: this was murder. Emotions *were* involved. We had to get down and dirty with that. Standing back and being analytical about it wasn't going to get the job done.

"Maybe a basic healing pattern?" Nick looked as though he almost had something in mind, but couldn't quite get it. "When we're sick, or hurting, we're really all about the emotion. So…maybe a pain-management spell?"

"That might do it," Sharon said. She was our de facto medic, which meant that she was the only one with real first-aid training beyond CPR and how to apply a Band-Aid. There really weren't many true healing spells. Healing with current was tricky, because the entire body runs on electricity and too much could—and had, in some spectacular cases that still get told—blow out the very thing the Talent was trying to repair. Mostly we kept spellwork to superficial damages: broken bones, scarring, sinus congestion, that sort of thing, and hoped nothing major went wrong. A Talent in an emergency room, if he was awake and in pain, could melt down an entire hospital.

J said that a lot of paramedics, Talent or Null, learned to recognize current in victims, and knocked us out with the good stuff en route, to keep us from going all overrush and making a bad situation worse—or deadly.

"Pain management. Maybe. There's a spell I learned for that, a long time ago." Nifty saw the look Venec shot him, and shrugged, grinning ruefully. "Okay, when I was in high school. My coach was Talent, and he saw no reason for me to risk getting hooked on painkillers when a little current could do the trick and get me through the game."

Sharon's sharp glare made it clear what she thought of that—probably equated it with taking steroids or something. Me, I just wanted to know if it would work on menstrual cramps.

"Anyway," Nifty said, ignoring Sharon, "it's not really what we're looking for, but it might be a place to start. First, you have to know where the pain is coming from...."

As usual, the basics were simple. Adapting it to the particulars we needed it to do; that was where it got tricky.

Because Nick and I had been at the impound center, and the auction, it was decided that we should sit this one out. Nick made like he was going to protest, but I kicked his shins and he subsided.

"You and I need a break," was all I said to him. Let the Guys explain their theory of a multipurpose, multidisciplinary team, if folk hadn't figured it out yet. I was just as happy to let someone else do the heavy lifting for a change.

Not that we were getting left out entirely. The only way we'd been able to cobble together an emotion-finding-and-tracking-and-catching spell required the current to be spread around among multiple players, so we'd be working remotely once Sharon and Stosser made contact.

Until then, we were stuck in the office, recharging and getting antsy.

The spell itself wasn't so difficult, really. It's just what we were doing, and what we were going to have to do, that really didn't stand up to thinking about. We had created a spell that would use control to take down lack-of-control, spreading it out among seven people, and using it on the fly, without any trial runs. When the Guys promised us on-the-job training, I don't think this was what we'd envisioned.

Less thinking, Bonnie. More preparing.

I staked out the sofa in the main lounge before anyone else could get to it, and draped myself over the full length, my feet propped up on the arm, my head on a cushion. Closing my eyes, I dived down inside, the same way I had to ground, only this time instead of looking for an external security, I was spreading my awareness throughout my entire system, checking to make sure that everything was flowing. Sort of like balancing your chi, I guess; making sure all the nodes were unblocked and happy. All right, happy might have been pushing it—I'd been asking a lot, and not giving much back—but it was all well enough. Admitting that Venec might have had something to his "fill-up" orders after all, I let a few tendrils drift off, looking for an open source of current I could siphon a bit from. Taking from our own building, except in emergency, was probably tacky, and I wasn't sure how well we'd recovered from that attack, anyway.

That led me off to wonder what Stosser was doing about his oh so uncivil sibling. I did note that we hadn't been bothered by any more gremlins since the psi-bomb, which could mean she'd left off the low-level attacks—or it had been our own current and we were shielding better now.

As to Aden, Stosser had assured us that she was being dealt with, and he said it in such a way that you didn't ask again. I didn't doubt it was going to be the same sort of putting-down that got him asked to leave Chicago. Hopefully, it would be more final this time.

That thought set me back on my mental heels, a bit. Had I just, even to myself, advocated fratricide? I looked long and hard at the thought, and realized that yeah, I had. Okay, take a step back, Bloodthirsty Bonita, and get some perspective. She hadn't killed anyone. Hadn't even really tried.

Yet.

Innocent until proven an asshole, as J used to say. And right now, not my problem. Venec was holding the wards around the office, I didn't need to tense up. Relax, relax, and look for a quick hit....

There was a spare generator in a building a few blocks over. Probably hitched up to one of the bodegas' refrigeration units, in case ConEd flaked again and left us in a blackout. The generator was turned on and humming along quietly, so I felt no guilt about slipping in and skimming current off the top. There would be a slight fluctuation in the energy consumption, but since I was taking current, which they couldn't use, and not Null power, it wasn't a crime. Really. You just had to be careful....

"Hey."

I opened my eyes, and saw Pietr standing over me.

"We're a go."

I nodded and sat up, maybe a little too quickly. The current I'd lifted ran shimmering through my body, pooling in my core and being absorbed into the threads already there. In a few hours, the new current would be almost indistinguishable from the pre-existing core, all imbued with my own signature. I'd always thought of that as comforting—it was *mine*—but now I was starting to wonder. Not that I ever thought I'd be driven to commit a crime, but if we learned how to track Talent... who was to say the bad guys couldn't, too?

Bad guys, and maybe even just people who wanted to shut us down. Like Stosser's sister. My throat felt weirdly tight, and I reached for my iced coffee, trying to ease it.

We didn't have to be physically gathered for this, but somehow we all ended up in the lounge, Nifty and me on the sofa, Nick taking over the armchair, and Pietr leaning against the wall like usual. Venec sat on the arm of the sofa, next to me.

*ready?*

As usual with Stosser's pings, it was less words and more a sensation. Funny, considering he was so good with spoken words. By contrast, Venec could come through with an actual *sound,* when he pinged.

*we're all here* Venec sent back.

Just like that, the connection opened, and it was as if we were standing in the garage with Ian and Sharon and another male—older, well-dressed, impatient-looking. The father of the new owner, I guessed. He looked as though he regretted ever giving Darling Daughter the checkbook.

The origin spell had been used to clean up bruising and torn muscles just under the skin of another person. We'd dumped that part, and focused on the way the bruises and tears had been found, by following the awareness of pain in the patient. Strong emotions and current would, we hoped, create a sort of mini-record, intense enough for us to pick it up even months later.

It was a little more difficult here, natch, because there wasn't a conscious—or even unconscious—entity to touch. That was why all of us were needed. Like when I collected the trace, we were going to create a net, only this time it was going to be a tighter-woven one, sticky on all the strands, and we were going to cast it not over empty space, but Stosser's own memory of the victims. That was why he was there, to hold that memory, while Sharon directed us over the actual physical space.

*give* It was less a command than a plea, and the surprise of that let the current flow out of me in a smoother pattern than I'd anticipated, threads weaving and unweaving as they went. My threads were dark green, and I saw them merging with darker blue cables—Nifty, my brain identified—winding around and disappearing, then adding themselves to red snakes—Pietr—snapping and hissing until they became part of the whole as well, weaving docilely into a golden-brown wave of silky water that *felt* like Venec.

*nick?*

A loop of bright yellow came down with a flicker, giggling an apology. He'd gotten lost.

Nicky had just gotten himself a new nickname, we all agreed without speaking a word. He protested, but the image of a swooping, blushing yellow butterfly was already set.

*attention* Stosser told us, then we were in his hands, our current, still attached to ourselves, being woven into a spell by the sheer force of his will.

To say that it was a weird sensation was an understatement. My usually mellow temper got a splash of ire, and then cool sadness, sweet intelligence, and a warmly burning flame of affection, and then all the emotions of the entire group merged, even as I was trying to sort them out. There was a moment of panic, and then a sense of calm imposed from within. It was all right. This was what I/We intended to do.

I/We made a sweep over the car, a flowing wave of intermingled current, each point distinct, but linked. One pass, then another, looking for any surface emotions, anything that might connect to the scrap of physical evidence in Stosser's hand, the nail clipping the "injury" I/We were working from.

Nothing. Nothing but a faint cool minty-stale sensation, like canned air.

*all right. move on.*

If I/We couldn't find the killer, we would work backward from the victims. The emotional image formed in our awareness, not the physical aspects of what they had looked like, but the sense of them, the affection they'd had for each other, the joy they had taken in their work.

From that, it seemed as though outlines rose up from the car in front of Me/Us, shadowed bodies, half translucent, half filled with an intensity, a bright sharp flare of—

*Oh god. Oh god oh god please make it stop make it stop!*

## nineteen

"Mother of freaking God!"

If the words hadn't hurt my head so much, I'd have echoed them. Maybe I did, but there was too much pounding and thudding inside my skull for me to hear it.

A much quieter voice asked: "Is everyone still with us?"

It was a valid question. I'd had overrush described to me, the way current burned you up from the inside, and this didn't feel like it, but the memory of that flaring pain had to have been something dire....

"We felt them die."

My eyes cracked open, expecting to be blinded by nasty bright lights, but it was blessedly dark. Someone had thought to turn off the lights. Or, possibly, we'd blown the fuses again.

"We *were* them dying."

Nobody contradicted Venec's correction. The memory— the *experience*—was still too much with me, and probably the others, too, to quibble.

A cold sort of clammy hand slid into mine, grasping it firmly. My fingers were probably just as cold, from the way the rest of me felt. I couldn't tell whose hand it was, holding mine, but it didn't really matter. They were living hands. Clammy, but living.

"Lawrence? Shune?"

"Here, boss," came a low voice, and I lifted my head enough to see two bodies sitting on the floor, leaning against each other like the rubble of a bombed-out building. If that was them, then the hand in mine was probably Pietr's. I managed to move my head slowly enough that the pounding and thudding didn't up the intensity, and looked across my body to the form curled up alongside me. Yeah, that sleeve was connected to the shirt that was on Pietr. He hadn't disappeared.

"Hi," I said. Lame, but it was all I could think of. The head burrowed into my rib cage lifted, and his gray eyes looked into mine, and any thought I ever had of Pietr as just good-looking was pretty much gone. He was still a fine piece of flesh, don't get me wrong. But I didn't see the physical there, then. I saw Pietr.

And he saw me. I don't know what it was, exactly, he saw…but it was *me*.

"Sharon and Ian?" I asked, not looking away from that shadowed gaze.

*okay* came back the ping, not okay by a long shot but the awareness of them both breathing and recovering, and coming home soon.

"Everyone's okay." Venec, recovering faster, turned on one of the lamps, shading the light away from us, moving around and touching us on the shoulder or arm, making physical contact with a gentleness that I should have been surprised to encounter in him, but wasn't. "We made it out. Next time, we'll know better."

"What went wrong?" I needed to know. The spell had been

working perfectly, we had been totally on the track of the actual moment of the murder, and…

"Nothing went wrong. It went too right."

That made sense, I guess. "But if the spell worked, and it had to, for us to get that much from the echoes of dead people, then why didn't we feel anything from the killer?"

"I don't know," Venec admitted, sitting down on the floor next to the sofa, his left shoulder about even with my rib cage. I felt the urge again to pet his hair in reassurance, the same way I would Pietr, and before I could stop myself, that's what my hand was doing.

Amazingly, he let me. His hair was coarse, not soft, and thicker than I'd thought it would be. It didn't feel anything like touching Pietr, at all.

"We need to try again."

"Agreed."

"And go through that again?" But Nifty sounded more annoyed than protesting.

"Not a chance in hell." Ian, standing in the doorway, Sharon half-hidden behind him. He was paler than I thought a human being could get, and his suit was rumpled, but his expression was determined.

"We have to. We were so close…."

"We were so close to dying!"

Ian seemed taken aback by his own shout, and he shuddered once, a faint full-body ripple. "That much emotion, it almost pulled us all in. We meddled with a form of blood-magic there, not even realizing, siphoning off the power of their death. Necromancy is a nasty word for a reason. Not moral, but practical. Death only begets death."

Even falling-over wiped, Ian could still make pretty with the words. I'd have been impressed, if I had the energy. We. Not you, not I, not us: we. Pack was right; and not just any pack, but *his* pack.

"We won't go there," Nick said. "We know now that's a dead end."

Someone groaned at the unintentional pun.

"Sorry. I mean…we still need to find the killer. Now that we know the spell does work, we just have to look harder, more carefully, for the trace that leads back to him. Or her. Everything leaves a trace."

"I don't…"

Venec interrupted his partner, his voice still and calm, but firm. "If we stop now, if we come this close and the killer still gets away…what have we accomplished, Ian? What have we done, other than prove the naysayers right, that current is not meant to be used for anything other than personal gain? Is that what you want?"

"You know it isn't. But the cost—"

"The cost is what it always was. You and I knew that. Now, so do they. And they want to go on. They *believe,* Ian. You can't give with one hand and take away with the other."

I wasn't quite sure what was going on between those two, but something was about to simmer over, and as wasted as my body was, I could feel every inch of me leaning toward Venec, willing Ian to hear, to understand. I didn't know what it was that I believed, exactly, but it meant we couldn't stop now. We had to *know.*

Ian looked over his shoulder at Sharon, who gave a small but firm nod. He looked at us, sprawled on the floor and furniture. We looked back at him, all of us looking like hell and probably shaking in our metaphorical boots, but we didn't even have to check with each other. We were a team. We were in.

"All right." He sounded resigned, but his shoulders were straighter than they'd been just a minute ago, and there was a little tinge of color back in his skin. Boss was proud of us.

It turned out that we hadn't actually blown the fuses; Venec had shut out the lights as an immediate reaction, when he came to. Good thing, that, since our eyes were all sparkle-dazed from the not-memory of flames up around us, when we were trapped inside the Reybeorns' last minutes. It took a while for the headache to subside and a while longer for our eyes to adjust again to normal lighting. Once we did, Nifty was the first one to point out what was wrong with the whole experience.

"There wasn't any fire."

Sharon stopped with her forkful of pizza halfway to her mouth. "You noticed that too, huh?"

We had expected the spell to take a chunk out of us, current-wise. Interestingly, though, we were less drawn-down than expected. We were ravenous, though. Ian had taken one hard look at us, and placed an order for our now-usual pizzas and caffeine that arrived with impressive speed. At some point we had apparently established an account at the pizza place on the corner, because no money changed hands when the delivery guy appeared at the door.

Yeah, I could see myself getting really tired of pizza, fast. There was a Thai place a couple of blocks over, maybe I'd stage a take-out coup.

If we made it to next week. If we didn't get killed, or fired. If I wasn't standing on the unemployment line, trying to make rent on a place I suddenly couldn't afford…

"It could just have been a visual representation of the pain, their brains trying to translate suffocation into something they could see, and try to fight?"

"Maybe it was hell," Pietr said.

"You think they went to hell?" Nifty asked, surprised.

"I have no idea. I just said maybe it was."

"I don't believe in hell." Of course Sharon didn't.

"Ah," Nifty said, waggling his finger in her face. "But does hell believe in you?"

I shoved the crust of my slice into my mouth, to keep from laughing.

"My head hurts," Sharon grumbled. "Now is not the time to start any pseudo rational theistic conversations that will result in you getting your face bashed with a pillow."

Our wannabe lead dogs were doing their usual dominance squabble, turning every possible conversation into a can-you-top-this, and Pietr was just egging them on for a distraction. Finished with my dinner, I tuned the three of them out, and tried to focus on the graph paper Nick had just put down on the table in front of me.

"If we arrange ourselves that way, we should be able to disperse the emotional energy evenly, keep it moving at a steady rate and not let it pool in any one of us." He wasn't trying to ignore the others, he had totally shut them out. Yay for geek focus.

I looked carefully at the sheet, then back up at him. "You know that's a pentagram, right?"

He made that spastic shrug movement thing. "There was a reason it was traditional?"

Made as much sense as anything else. Venec came over, a slice of pizza in his hand, and leaned over my shoulder to see what Nick had drawn. The smell of pepperoni battled with his own scent and made me dizzy. I grabbed a garlic knot from the container in front of me, and told myself it smelled just as good.

"Interesting. That should work. But we only have five points?"

"That leaves someone to be the grounding wire," Nick said. "Like I used Bonnie, before. If we're going to do this again, or any other kind of spellwork, we really should have a grounder outside the activity. Just in case. One less person in the wave, before, and I don't know if we all would have made it out."

I wasn't sure what made Nick the expert, but Venec nodded in agreement. "Solid strategy. I don't suppose you play chess?"

"Not against you, I don't," Nick said.

I played chess, and well, too. I decided to keep that fact to myself, for now, and ate another garlic knot.

So, we'd be playing chess this time. Going in not like a healer, the way we'd approached it the first time, but as a strategic…not an attack, but an opening move. Invite the other player—the ghost of the killer's emotions, to step onto the board. I was probably mangling metaphors, but I knew what I meant.

"I'll ground," Ian said. He had changed out of his suit, and was back in his usual grungies. There was even a faint shadow of beard growth that I'd swear hadn't been there an hour ago. Could current hold back hair growth? I was so going to look into that, once shorts season came around again. I hate waxing.

"You're planning on going back there?"

"I made an excuse rather swiftly to the Johbs family, and left my briefcase there. It would make perfect sense for me to swing by and pick it up again, once my companion had recovered. From her dizzy spell."

"Yeah, because you didn't look like you were about to toss cookies yourself," Sharon said. "Tell them it was bad tuna salad at lunch. Anyone who's ever been to a conference will understand that."

Ian scanned all of our faces, as if he was looking for something, some sign that we shouldn't go through with it. Whatever he saw, it seemed to satisfy him, because he just gave a nod and was gone. Poof. No shimmer, no flicker, not even the crack of electricity you sometimes got when you Transloc'd yourself.

"Day-um." Nifty said it for everyone.

"I'd tell you to take notes on how it should be done," Venec said, "but we have other things to do right now. Everyone pick a point on the graph, and hold it."

The sense of connection was fading, and Ian hadn't been hard in it to begin with, but we still knew the moment he was back in place. It was like hearing a door open down the hallway; unless you knew the slight squeak it made halfway on the hinges, you'd miss noticing it entirely, but once you knew, it was impossible to miss.

The pizza sat heavy in my gut, and I could feel the indigestion building up, along with the tension.

"Hang in there, people. A little more, and we're done. Just a little more."

"Please would be nice," Nifty said, and got a glare from everyone. But that focused us, and the count from ten to five got us into sync, and *here*

Ian's pointer, bringing us around from the outside, rather than the internal approach we took the last time. The wave flowed around the car, surrounding it, avoiding the front seat and the hotspots that caught us last time, just in case.

*down and out* someone suggested, and we flowed along the sides of the car, touching every inch, over paint and under chrome, into keyholes and around the handles....

The sense of stale mint returned.

*catch that?*

We caught it. Cool, stale, flat. Definitely minty, like mouth-wash. Distantly, a sense of flames; not the agonizing burn of before, but a cool crackling, like an artificial log in a gas-powered fireplace.

Cool. Practical. Distanced. Uninvolved. Smooth and slick like fresh Plexiglas, and absolutely nothing we could use.

It took Ian a little longer to get back than it did for him to go out. I guess he had to make actual goodbyes this time. We spent the time waiting coming up with—and shooting down—theories.

"Fatae? A fatae could have killed them, easy, and even if someone saw something they'd never admit to it." Nick was, I guessed, reacting to the one fatae he'd seen, rather than going home and reading up on the fairy tales the way I told him to. Not all of them were big and scary. In fact, a lot of them were small and scary, and, according to J, you never saw them until they'd already drowned you in the bog.

J had laughed when he said that. I never really thought it was funny.

"Fatae don't use current," Pietr pointed out. "We've established that current was used, was in fact essential to them dying that way."

"Have we? There are a lot of different breeds, and we don't know all that much about all of them," Sharon said. "One of them might be able to kill, and not leave a trace, and the rest is all just our conjecture and could be wrong."

It was an interesting theory. I hadn't met enough fatae per-sonally to say yes or no, but Venec, it seemed, had. "We're for-getting one thing, in that otherwise plausible theory. Fatae aren't much for secrecy or keeping quiet after the fact. There would be a lot fewer fairy tales if they could—you think that *we* started all those myths?"

Oh. I hadn't thought of that. From the looks on everyone else's faces, neither had they.

"Anyway," Venec went on, "Midwest Council isn't totally incompetent. They checked for that, thoroughly. Pinning it on a breed would have been easier all around."

"Council would rather it be a fatae killer than a human," I agreed. "Just makes their life easier." Lonejack and Council both were human organizations; the nonhuman members of the *Cosa Nostradamus* tended to stay within their own enclaves, associating mostly with their own kind. That made me think of Bobo, and wonder if maybe he'd take me somewhere fatae tended to hang out, in the city. Maybe we could take Nick, really make his weekend. Except I was going to tell J to can it with the bodyguard. Wasn't I?

"Well, are we absolutely sure that the killer's female?" Nifty asked. "Could the toenail shred be a plant, to distract us?"

Nick made a rude noise. "If the killer was going to plant something, why the hell would it be a toenail? And where would he get it? Okay, please don't answer that. I'm really not up for the *Cosa* to have their very own foot fetishist killer."

Without thinking, I sent out a thread of current, rocking him back in his chair. "Oh, thank you so much for that image, Shune."

He recovered and pushed back, just enough to let me know he knew it was me, and made a mocking half bow for the comment.

"Hey, Torres, did your guy have a foot thing?"

"It's not Will," I shot back, still kind of distracted by what I'd just done. I mean, not that it was a big deal, but I'd never done that even to J, and it happened so casually, as natural a reaction as reaching out a hand—and it was that natural, I guess. But…

"Are you sure?"

"Yes, I'm sure, damn it!" I got up and started pacing through the office, wishing that we had a single room large enough to really get some good stomping going. I wanted to stomp. Hard.

Ian took that moment to walk in through the door, and I veered to avoid crashing into him. I kept talking, though.

"What we felt—that was the killer. We didn't miss anything. There just wasn't anything to get. We were wrong, our killer didn't feel anything, no strong emotions at all, and Will's not a sociopath, okay? I'd recognize that. And even if I didn't, Sharon would have picked it up when she scanned my memories."

Ian, managing to pick up what we were talking about, looked over at Sharon, waiting patiently in one of the chairs. She nodded. "I've met one or two, in my last job. Not killers, but definitely at least borderline socios, and there's no mistaking that total and utter ick. Even secondhand. Her Will's not our guy."

He wasn't my Will, not my guy. Not yet, and after I'd blown his messages off, maybe not anytime soon. But maybe we had a chance, if we could just close this damn case.

"So we're looking for a female sociopath who also happens to be a Talent?" Pietr summed it up pretty well, and with an expression of doubt. "Man, I don't know much about killers, crazies, or odds-making, but that seems, um, damned unlikely?"

"Our killer's not a sociopath," Venec said, after doing some sort of subdued, nonverbal exchange with his partner that we could see but not follow.

"How can you be so sure about that?" Nifty was all puffed up and aggressive, and I could see Sharon bristling in response, even though he wasn't challenging her, directly. I guess he'd invested in the whole crazy killer idea. It was easier to think of a deviant doing this sort of thing, but…

"A sociopath may not think of others as being human, or equal, but he—or she—still has emotions. Only a paid killer is that distanced."

"A what?" That got Pietr's attention, enough that I think he almost faded a bit, even as I was looking right at him.

"A professional," Ian clarified.

"Impossible." Nifty sounded so final, so confident in his dismissal of the idea. I didn't think it was just because he liked the whole crazy thing, either. The thought was unthinkable, impossible. Of all the scenarios we had created and considered, the thought of a hired hit man—hit woman—had never occurred, not to me, and not to the others, based on their reaction to that bombshell. Talent might kill, in passion or fear, but to do it for pay? Thinking about it made me feel queasy, as though I'd been dunked by a wave, and swallowed too much seawater.

"There's never been—"

"There's never been a lot of things," Ian said calmly, pouring himself a cup of coffee. "Never been an us before, either. May not be coincidence they both appear about the same time."

"Cause and effect?" I guess I hadn't shaken college off my heels as much as I'd hoped, because my first thought was what an awesome paper that would make for my sociology class. Maybe I'd write it anyway. If we were going to have deviants, we'd need paperwork on them eventually, right? And here I was, ground floor on an exciting new field: not even J could find fault with an academic aside, right?

"Maybe." Ian actually looked worn down, showing how damn tired we all were by this point. "May be just that the world is changing. It does that every now and again. That's why we're needed."

"To hunt Talent who take money to kill other Talent."

"Among other things, yes."

Ian looked tired, but he didn't sound as taken aback by the idea as the rest of us, even Venec. I guess because he was the one who thought of it. Also, I was starting to suspect, that smooth slick-talking guy facade of his covered up a significantly hard core. A guy who could face down an entire Council, and his own family, to do what he felt was right.

And I wondered, for the first time, what had made him so hard, and so determined.

"All this is just great," Nifty said in disgust, not sounding as if any of it was great at all, "but if you're right, we have no way at all to track this guy. Woman. Whatever."

"We don't have to," Venec said. "We just have to figure out who hired her."

I walked out of the office, blinking against the setting sun. After the bombshell of who our killer might be, and the mental reshuffling demanded, Venec had decided that we needed to switch gears and shove all of the case stuff to the background before we got stuck in a rut. His words, not mine. So we'd spent all afternoon working on identifying spell residue, which meant focusing on such a tight detail that, after a while, your eyes crossed and your brain felt condensed into the size of a walnut, but we'd made real progress in establishing a spell that not only worked, but we could pull up at need. Having to let go of the case even for a few hours was really frustrating, but, damn him, he had been right. Ending the day on a positive note was a much better thing.

After all that, though, seeing the outside world was a shock to the system, and a painful one at that. All these people, these buildings, this huge, noisy, busy world going on around us, without a clue… My brain wasn't used to jumping around between perspectives like this. It hurt.

"*New experiences are good for you, Bonita.*" J's voice, from way back when I was, what, eleven? The first time I'd ever eaten roasted pigeon, and had to deal with the fact that this bird was both the same and very different from the winged rats that infested Boston. Not quite the same thing, but I understood why I'd remembered it now.

I started to walk toward the subway station, and realized I was going to the wrong line. No more hotel. I got to go home. The thought, despite the exhaustion of the day, made me smile, as did the fact that, although Bobo had said he was only supposed to be on-duty when I left after 10:00 p.m., I could swear I'd seen him when I left the office. I didn't need a body-guard, or a nursemaid, or whatever he was. Still, the idea that someone was keeping an eye out was…nice. Especially when that eye was attached to a near ton of furry muscle.

I was still smiling when I made it all the way up the stairs of my building, closed the door behind me, and was confronted by the reality.

My apartment. I said it out loud a few times, just because I could. "My apartment. Mine."

All right, so it was my very empty apartment, at the moment. During our late-night confab, J had offered to send my bedroom furniture, but I'd—as nicely as I could—said no.

"It's…it's nice furniture, J. Really." It was fucking fabulous furniture, actually. Way better than anything I could afford on my own. "But…"

"But it was what you used when you were a teenager, and you're not a teenager now, and you need your own stuff and I need to start accepting that?"

"Um. Yeah?"

He'd hired workmen to build my sleeping loft, in between the crazy work-stuff, so he'd be able to sleep knowing it wasn't going to collapse some night with me in it. For now, a mattress and box spring rested on the bare floor underneath, waiting to get carried up into the loft area. A beat-up but amazingly comfortable chaise lounge in paisley velvet was shoved against the far wall next to a floor lamp and a bookcase—boxes of books still on the floor next to it. On the other side of the space, under the window, there was an old table and two chairs that had been taken out of storage and polished until the chestnut inlay gleamed. I didn't know much about furniture, but I had a strong suspicion that I could sell that table to an antique dealer and pay the rent for half a year. Using it as a dinner table/desk seemed almost sacrilegious, but it was so pretty I couldn't say no when it arrived. All my clothing, except the dirty laundry, was still in a huge wardrobe box.

The kitchenette was the only thing that was fully unpacked and stocked, from the cabinets to the fridge. I guess it was pretty obvious where J's priorities were.

There was a sharp *bzzzt* in the air, and I jumped half a foot before realizing that it was the doorbell.

I walked over and pressed the door switch without thinking, then shook my head. This wasn't the hotel, where everyone got vetted. I had to remember to hit the talk button first, and ask who was there, not just let anyone in!

Fortunately, I hadn't let any serial killers into the building. Just a lot of crazy people.

"Greetings, salutations, happy housewarming, where's the booze?"

I wasn't sure how I felt about this invasion, but I wasn't given any time to think about it. A parade of coworkers streamed into my studio, making what had just seemed like a reasonable space into something the size of a closet. They must have gathered and left right after I did, based on the objects they brought with them.

"Jesus, woman, this place is so small, you're going to have to go next door to change your mind!" Nifty stood in the middle of the main room and looked horrified.

"That's just because you're a moose," Pietr said. "People who are normal-size find this perfectly—Ai! Oh my god, look at this floor! Real hardwood parquet! Do you know how much money you could get for this, from someone redoing their place?"

Sharon thwapped Pietr on the back of the head. "She's renting, you idiot. Pulling up the floor is probably cause to break the lease."

"Or at least raise the rent," I agreed, taking the handoff of a bunch of daisies, two bottles of wine, and a bakery box wrapped in red string and juggling them until I could get them safely onto the counter. "Do I want to know how you guys found me?"

Sharon looked at me in disbelief. "We're investigators, Torres."

"Also, Stosser told us," Nick said, sitting on the mattress and bouncing slightly. "Hey, nice bed. Wanna…?"

"Forget about it, Shune." But his attempt at lechery was so puppy-dog cute, I couldn't help laugh. "Not even if you were the second-to-last hetero boy in town."

Nifty was in my kitchen, rummaging through the drawers. "Bonnnnnita, where the hell do you keep the corkscrew?"

"Left drawer. Glasses are in the left-hand cabinet." I ducked around him to get to the fridge, where there was a chunk of cheese and a bag of ripe pears and…yep, some crackers and fresh figs. J had taught me to always be prepared in case unexpected company arrived. I just hadn't thought they'd show up the same day I officially moved in!

"Wow! Check that view! Torres, you have one seriously smokin' hot neighbor!" Nick, of course.

"Her name is Jennie," I said. "She's twenty-nine, five-ten, never married, not seeing anyone, works at Saint Vincent's." I'd already gotten the details, when the workmen were building my bed.

"She's a nurse?" His grin almost ate his face. "Oooo, mama!"

"She's a doctor," I said, cutting off his fantasies at the knees. "And you're not her type."

"Figures. That's the story of my luck. If you're her type, can I watch?"

I wasn't her type, either—she liked them big and Italian. "No."

Then Nifty got the first bottle open, and things started to get a little hazy. I woke up the next morning with a serious headache, half a dozen wine bottles—all empty—in the sink, and the feeling that my little apartment had just been dubbed PUPI party central.

It was… A pretty good feeling, actually.

I lay in bed, stared at the ceiling, and, for the first time since all this started, I let myself believe that it was going to last.

But first, I had to get through today.

## twenty

"Bonita Torres and Sharon Mendelssohn here to see Will Arcazy."

The receptionist behind the chrome-to-impress desk—an older man this time instead of the young woman who was there my first visit—gave us both a once-over that should have been insulting but instead felt coolly, impersonally professional. He was either a security guard or a slaver, in his other job. I was glad I'd opted for a crème-colored linen blouse and dark green knee-length skirt out of my "look adult and responsible" wardrobe. The shoes were crème-colored, too, and cost more than the rest of the outfit combined.

"Is he expecting you?"

Yeah. That was the question, wasn't it?

"We don't have an appointment. But I think he'll see us," I said, trying to channel Sharon's natural cool. Curiosity, if nothing else, should motivate him. That was what we were betting on, and why Venec had—reluctantly, I thought—sent us out, rather than the guys. Even the least chauvinistic male was going to see a female as less of a threat, at least if he liked women, and we knew that Will did. So two women—even if the attention wasn't flattering—wouldn't be seen as threatening or off-putting.

I was beginning to understand the way they thought, our tricky guys. It gave me a headache, but I figured I'd get better with practice.

The receptionist picked up his phone and spoke quietly into it. I didn't try to listen in. Sharon might have—I didn't look at her to see. The trick was to ignore her so much that everyone else would, too.

The phone went down, and the receptionist's expression changed from politely noncommittal to an impersonal sort of friendliness they must teach at receptionist school. "He is with a client right now, but if you'd like to take a seat, he will be with you as soon as possible."

"Thank you."

"Nice place," Sharon said as we made our way over to the cream leather love seats in a square around the glass-and-chrome coffee table. "If we ever need a lawyer, you think they'd take us on?"

Same thought I'd had, the first time I was here. That made me smile. "I don't think we can afford them," I said.

"Mmm. Yeah." Sharon stared over my shoulder, I guess at the wall, then suddenly said, "Speaking of money, you think the client's going to pay us? Honestly? Because if she's not, I'm going to have to put my résumé out there again. This job is…it's crazy and it's great, but I need some stability in the paycheck, you know? Walking in some day to find the office empty 'cause the furniture got repossessed is not my idea of fun times."

Wow. Not that the thought itself was a surprise, just that of all of us, I'd figured Sharon for the last-woman-out, not first rat overboard. "She'll pay. It would be a matter of respect—all the Guys would have to do would be to let it out that she failed to pay a legitimate bill, even if it was to a disreputable-by-her-standards firm, and the embarrassment alone would destroy her standing in the Council."

"And that's important?" Sharon was looking directly at me now, really needing to know the answer.

Again I felt that gulf between us, the divide in our upbringings, that something so obvious to me eluded her. "Yes." No hesitation in that response. "To someone like our client? It's that important. More to the point, she knows that the boss knows it's that important, and won't hesitate to use it as a stick, if he has to."

It struck me then that we had all fallen into the habit of not using names outside the office. Interesting.

Sharon looked as though she was digesting what I'd said. "That's…a whole level of politics I'm not used to considering."

"It's Council."

"Yes, I understand that. In a sort of don't-understand-it way." She crossed her legs, adjusted her dark blue skirt to lie neatly across her knees, and double-checked the attaché case that rested at her feet. It was empty—just a prop—but it looked as expensive as my shoes.

"You see people differently than I do," she said finally. "I look at someone and see an individual, whole unto themselves. You…you see how they're connected, don't you? Not just one person, but this endless web of ties and obligations around them. I guess that's Council, too."

Did I? Now it was my turn to digest her words. So we sat there, two well-dressed women in the waiting area of a very expensive legal office, indistinguishable from any other client-in-waiting, mulling over our thoughts, deep and shallow. When Will came out through the frosted glass doors, it was a relief to be shaken out of them, and back into the game.

His gaze took me in first, and then slid sideways to include Sharon. There was a moment of understandable appreciation before he recalled his manners, or something, and turned his attention back to me. "I take it that this isn't entirely a social visit," he said.

"I wish it were." I really did.

Give him credit, despite Will's confusion he was a gracious host, escorting us to his office, offering us coffee, the whole deal, like we really might be potential clients for the firm. Maybe he was just putting on a good show for the partners.

"All right," he said, after we'd refused refreshments and gotten settled in the guest chairs. "What's going on?"

The plan wasn't so much good cop/bad cop as talky cop/silent cop. Sharon was here to observe while I, hopefully, prodded him into revealing more than he meant to. More of Ian's on-the-job-training, since I was the demonstrably better observer. Not that I didn't trust Sharon to see things, but I was on overdrive, trying to make sure every twitch and flicker registered, just in case she missed something. And, yes, because I felt that I had something to prove, now.

"You didn't play fair with me, Will."

I could see it in his eyes. He was genuinely confused; he didn't know what I was talking about. I didn't need Sharon's confirmation to know that was real.

"Your association with the Reybeorns. You concealed details."

"Ah." He leaned back in his chair, like every television show lawyer I'd ever seen, confronted with something tricky. "I answered every question you asked."

"You didn't lie, and you didn't evade," I agreed. "But you didn't play fair. You didn't tell me about your silent partner—or the deal that was still in play when the Reybeorns died."

"What does Katie have to do with any of this?" He blinked,

and again I could see in his eyes when the penny dropped. He leaned forward, all pretense at relaxation gone. Interesting, that he focused in on that part. "You weren't investigating their deaths, before. You were investigating me?"

"Only incidentally," I said, hoping to hell that Sharon was picking *something* up, because I had to pay attention to the words, both his and mine, and not the deeds. "Because of your connections to the victims. Your possible connections to the killer."

Even half-distracted, I could tell when he went from hurt and confusion to anger.

"I told you, I would never do anything to hurt them! I liked them! And you...you've been investigating me. All this time, even when...even at dinner? You used me."

I hadn't, damn it. I had done everything I could short of quitting to not use him. So why did his words make me feel guilty? I could feel my current stir, cool but awake, and I had to take a second to quiet it. That never used to happen, damn it. I didn't want to constantly be on the offensive. It took too much out of you. Was it because of Will? Or the fact that I was using so much current lately, it assumed every flicker meant that it was time to play? I needed to ask J about that. Later.

"If I'd been using you, Will, I would have returned your calls. I would have asked questions over dinner, after a bottle of wine—" or in bed, I thought but didn't say "—not sober in your office with a desk between us.

"So tell me now. Tell me everything, Will. Tell me why you didn't mention Katie, or the deal. Because it might be important. It might be really important to finding out who killed them."

"I can't help you." His gaze flicked from my face to Sharon's. I guess he didn't like what he saw there, because he flicked back to me, as though I was the better hope. "I really can't. Even if I wanted to, which I'm not sure I do right now, I told you everything useful."

"Why don't you let us decide if it's useful or not?"

He looked again to Sharon, who stared at him with that unreadable can't-shock-me expression I was starting to understand was a total put-on, and he crumbled. "Katie…we were friends-of-friends. I met her at a party in Chicago—that's where she's from. We got to talking one day about investments, and I told her about the deals I'd done with the Reybeorns, and she was interested, but I knew they wouldn't be interested. They were, um—"

"They ran a closed shop," Sharon said, more polite than I would have been, and he nodded.

"Katie knew, a little, about…what we are. So I just told her it was like that, that they weren't going to trust anyone who wasn't Talent, that it wasn't personal, and she suggested that we partner up, her money supplementing mine. That way we had a larger slice of the pie, and more say about what was done."

"And you were okay with deceiving your friends like that?" I asked.

"I…I thought it was tacky, to keep someone out because of what they could or couldn't do, something they had no control over, in a situation where Talent was not an issue. Whatever you may think of me, discrimination's discrimination, okay?"

I slid my gaze toward Sharon, whose fingers were still on her lap. That meant she thought he was telling the truth.

"I figured, if they never knew, and Katie and I made money, who could it hurt? All the paperwork was in my name, and I had a side agreement with Kate, so it was all up-and-up."

Legally, yeah. Morally… I didn't know. I didn't support Talent-only any more than I'd not hang with Nifty because he was black, or Sharon because she was WASPy…but something about the way Will wiggled around honesty made me uncomfortable. He had his reasons, and they sounded like good ones, but…

"And that last deal? The one you said you got out of?"

"I had gotten out. I asked them to sell to the developer who was sniffing around. We'd already made enough profit, even without the renovations. But they wanted to hold the course. So Katie bought me out. That way I had the cash I needed, and she got to ride the full term of the deal, and make even more money. It was a done deal, nothing in my agreement with the Reybeorns said I couldn't sell my shares, and they'd have no choice but to accept it.

"Honestly, I figured that they would dump the property when Katie showed up, rather than work with a Null."

Sharon's fingers twitched, then went still.

"Only it didn't work that way," I said. "They still owned the property when they died."

"They refused to honor the paper Katie and I signed. They just…they refused to accept it. Said it was worthless, that without me there was no deal." He sounded like a little kid who had been knocked off his bicycle. I didn't have to look at Sharon to know that this, at least partially, was what he hadn't wanted to think about. He'd taken a hit to his ego—he'd been *wrong*—and wasn't dealing with it. Did he also suspect, somehow, that that chain of events might have been what led to the Reybeorns' deaths?

"And you didn't think it was important to mention this, when we talked the first time?"

"I didn't know. I didn't know until…"

"Until you had lunch with her in Chicago."

I shriveled a little even as Sharon's words fell into the air. Will looked at me like I had just told him there was no more chocolate in the world: disbelieving, hurt, and a little panicked.

"You were following me."

Damn it, Sharon… "You showed up at the auction, Will. You made yourself a person of interest. As a lawyer, you know what that means."

"I can't believe you followed me."

I was starting to get a little pissed off. He was the one who had screwed up, not me!

"When did you sign the papers over to this woman?"

He thought a bit, then shook his head. "About three months ago, I think. I can't remember the exact date."

Sharon's fingers flicked up and down, once.

"Do you have copies of the papers?"

"Do you have a warrant?" he asked in return.

Current coiled, cool and slow, deep in my gut. This time, I didn't hush it. "You know we don't. If you want us to, we can go to the Council and ask them to push you on it."

A Council push wasn't binding, but it had a lot of weight. Like shunning, among the Amish. I didn't know if Ian had enough influence to swing one…but I was betting that J did.

We played stare-me-down, and I was the first one to blink…but Will backed down. "I have copies here." He stood up and walked over to a small filing cabinet. A double tap on the door, and a current-lock was released, the drawer smoothly rolling out.

He ruffled through the files, more for show than anything else, I thought, and pulled out a slim folder.

"Here."

I took a quick skim, and the name "Kate Walker" jumped out at me. So far, so good.

"If you could make us copies?"

"These are copies. I keep everything in triplicate. Take them and go."

I took the folder. "Will…"

"Just go, Bonnie."

The subway back uptown was packed with everyone fleeing their offices for the day, so we didn't have a chance to talk. I'm not sure what I would have said, anyway. The papers were in Sharon's attaché case, and I'd swear they were magnetized, the way I couldn't stop glancing over, like there would suddenly be glowing letters floating midair, proclaiming his innocence….

Please, let him be innocent. Even as I was whispering a prayer, though, I didn't believe it. I wanted to…but I didn't. It wasn't cynicism, just pragmatism. There were too many omissions in his story. A layperson might do that without realizing it. A lawyer? He might not be guilty, but he wasn't innocent.

"Hey." Sharon had gotten out of her seat and tapped me on the shoulder. We were coming up on our stop.

"He's hot."

"What?"

"Your Will. He's hot. And he couldn't take his eyes off you, even when he was pissed off."

"And he lied to us."

Sharon couldn't deny that, since she was the one who had identified it. "I can only tell when they're lying, not why. It may be he had a reason…one that's not related to the case. Maybe he really didn't know, or was defending a friend he thought got a raw deal?"

"Yeah. Maybe."

I wanted to go home, crawl into my new bed, pull my old

quilt over my head, and not come out for a month. Instead, we buzzed our way into the lobby, and back to the office where the Guys were waiting.

Sharon handed over the papers, and Venec stalked back to the main workroom with them. I left Sharon getting debriefed by Ian and followed Venec, drawn by some masochistic impulse I hadn't known I had, until then. He spread the papers over the table, then without even looking at me said, "Close and seal the door."

Current lashed out to establish a sealing block almost before I could formalize the thought. I wasn't sure if that was impressive control on my part, or an impressive *lack* of control, and didn't really care, right then.

"Are they—"

"If you're going to stay, sit down and shut up."

I sat.

Sometimes, current is a tidal wave, knocking everything else out of your awareness. Sometimes, it's just a single thread, stitching up a hem you didn't realize had fallen. Inside that sealed room, without any other distractions, I couldn't sense Venec's current, even sitting a foot away from him. Even more than Nick's focus while hacking, that took depth, and training, and control that, honestly, scared me a little. Because it meant that when I did feel him, it was because he meant me to.

His hands hovered over the papers. Since I couldn't sense anything magically, I looked with my physical eyes. He had rolled his sleeves up, exposing his forearms. They were muscled, but not overly so, and tapered to thick wrists and those surprisingly long fingers. Nice hands. I had no idea what he was doing, and without a tail end of current to track, I couldn't extrapolate, either.

"Well?"

"Only one ink was used. Here. Follow this."

I took a deep breath, set myself into a calm, receptive mode, and waited. A crack in the wall appeared, and an invitation was issued. I accepted it, and followed the stream of energy that was now visible. I hadn't done this since I was fourteen, but this was one of the basic teaching tools every mentor used. You couldn't actually interfere or influence the spell, but you could see it, exactly the same way the caster did.

The papers were black, in mage-sight, the computer-generated letters thin glowing lines of silver—traces of the energy used to create them? Maybe. The signatures and addendums on the side where someone had inked their initials were what drew my attention: they were all the same dark orange, pulsing against the black paper.

I couldn't stay mad, or distanced. I was too fascinated. "That is totally awesome. Are you tracing it through the metallic elements in the ink, or something else? Is there a way to judge the depth of the impression, see if the same person was doing all the writing, or if there was more than one?"

Venec laughed, and I double-heard it through the current like warm butterscotch. "You're a geek," he said, and there was nothing I could do but agree. Who knew?

"Let's take a look, shall we?" The orange flared, and turned three-dimensional, making me dizzy as hell. It paused until I adjusted, and then dipped again.

"Two signatures, repeated twice each. The pen looks like it went into the paper the same depth, each time. Same with the initials."

I saw what he was pointing at. "Looks like we have two people, each signing their names with the same pen, in the same period of time."

The stream of energy let me out, more abruptly than I was

expecting, and I was back in my own body, seeing with my own normal eyes again. "So. It's legit?"

"Assuming both those signatures belong to the right people, yes."

"So…" My brain was processing everything, and starting to hurt. "If the Reybeorns refused to honor the paper, that meant that Kate Walker, the silent partner, was out in the cold—no legal claim on the property, and already out the cash she paid to Will. He might have paid her back—and he might not have had the money to do so, anymore, if he'd already bought that new property."

"He had," Venec murmured.

"So she could have brought them to court, sued them for damages?"

"She might have, and it might have gone either way, especially with them not being able to say why they had refused to honor the papers, not without sounding like crazy people, since they couldn't guarantee they'd get a Talent judge."

Well, maybe they could; Venec and I both knew it was possible to buy anything, if you had enough money—but it still wasn't a sure thing, and could expose them to a lot of publicity they seemed to have spent their lives avoiding.

"Whatever they might have done, the Reybeorns died two days after this paper was signed. Leaving Arcazy, since the Reybeorns refused the paper, the only living participant of the deal, legally. He gets the money from his partner…*and* the property."

Venec looked at me with something that might have been pity. "Which means that we have means and motive for him, too."

"But not the right gender," I said. Even if Will had been involved up to his elbows, he hadn't done the actual killing. I had to hold on to that, and Venec let me.

For now.

## twenty-one

The whole butterfly-and-hurricane theory, boiled down, means nothing stands alone. You make one move, even a small one, even in reaction to another move, and something else happens, maybe nearby, maybe far away. It's one of the reasons why we don't play with the weather, even though a powerful thunderstorm is one of the best ways to source wild current. You increase the force of a thunderstorm in one place, and halfway around the world, someone gets hit with a drought. Or a tsunami.

We pushed Will. Will pushed back. Someone else got hit with a tsunami.

When the phone in her office rang, Kate Walker didn't even glance at the caller ID before picking it up, so the panicked voice at the other end of the line took her by surprise. "Katie. What the hell have you been doing?"

Her breath hitched in her throat. "What do you mean?"

"Katie, please. Don't do this. We were friends for a long time."

"Were? That sounds like past tense, William." She tried for

surprised and casually mocking, but a tick started just over her right eye, clicking faster and faster until it was like a moth beating at her face. The four gargoyles placed one in each corner of her office suddenly seemed less protective and more mocking, as though laughing at her.

"You killed them. Didn't you? Somehow. And then sat there and offered condolences on my loss. You idiot. Why didn't you come to me? Did you really think that the Council would allow this to go unpunished? Did you think that nobody would find out?"

"Will, you're talking crazy, and I'm not going to have this conversation with you. Calm down, sober up, and then we'll talk, okay?"

She had barely hung up the phone when she felt the shiver of air behind her. By now, it was a familiar sensation, even if she didn't understand quite how the other woman did it. Magic. Always and forever that damned magic. It was a tool, she knew that. A tool, and occasionally a weapon, but nothing more than a thing to be used. It didn't make them any better, any more high-and-mighty, those damned freaks…. They died just as easily as regular humans did.

"Something's gone wrong," she said to the newcomer. "Will knows. How the hell does he know?"

"It doesn't matter." The familiar, soothing voice reassured her, just long enough for the loop of rope to drop over her neck, and yank violently upward. Her neck broke instantly, leaving her body to flop in the air, even as the end of the clothesline knotted itself to the stair railing.

The killer stared at the results, judging, then shrugged in acceptance. It wasn't perfect, but it would have to do. The job had suddenly gotten more complicated, and needed cleaning up. Quickly, and all the way down the line.

★ ★ ★

*incoming!*

"You have got to be shitting me," Venec said, even as the warning ping slammed into our brains. The room was warded, so we only got the sense of something slamming into us, rather than the actual impact. Even so, the hangover I'd been fighting all day intensified, until my brain felt as though it was being squeezed into my nasal passages.

"Who the hell…"

But I knew, even my own current rose up in an involuntary and somewhat disturbing response. Sister Stosser. It had to be. So much for "taking care of things."

"We need to—"

"We need to stay here," Venec said. "We have no idea what's going on out there, and undoing the seal might make it worse, not better."

"You think it's Ian's sister again?"

He nodded, a tight little nod.

"Why does she hate him so much?"

That almost got a laugh out of him. A bitter laugh, but a laugh. "Oh, she doesn't. In fact, they used to adore each other. Totally devoted siblings, them against the world."

"What happened?"

"I don't know. I wish I did. He won't tell me."

"It had to do with what went down in Chicago?"

He didn't look at me, staring instead at the door, as though he could somehow see what was happening out there, beyond my seal. "You know about that?"

"A little. My mentor told me some. He went up against the Council, and won, and walked. That took guts. And a lot of…"

"Stupidity?"

"Integrity."

There was Council, and then there was Council. If you bucked the sitting members, you had two choices. Lose, or win. And if you won, you usually weren't left to float around as a reminder of that win—you became a sitting member by default, because Council wasn't going to let someone with that reputation be a free-floater.

Ian Stosser had left, rather than join a Council he disagreed with. Had given up an amazing amount of influence and power, for a principle. Never mind I didn't know what the fight had been about, or what that point of principle was, it still impressed me.

It didn't seem to have that same effect on Venec, though.

"He was an idiot. We could have done all this so much easier, if he'd stayed. No scrambling, no scurrying for a client…"

"And no sibling trying to blow us out of the water?"

"If Aden wanted us dead, we'd already be dead. She's trying to teach him a lesson."

"About what?" But I thought I already knew, and from the look Venec shot me, he knew I already knew.

You might walk away from a Council seat, if you had some crazy reason for it. That could be forgiven—J had done the same thing, although more diplomatically and without severing all his ties. You could even walk away from Council entirely—it was called Crossing the River, when you jumped affiliations, Council to lonejack, or vice versa. The one thing you never, ever did was take Council issues outside.

Whatever the fight had been, back in Chicago, PUPI was the result. Ian had gone Outside.

I was about to say something—I have no idea what—when another blast hit the building, cutting right through my seal and slamming into us.

\*bonnie?\* J, distant through the layers of protection around us, but clearly worried. He'd felt that, too, all the way in Boston, through some remnant connection.

\*not now\* I sent back, and shut him out. I opened my eyes expecting to feel my body mashed into slime against the far wall. I was still intact, barely—and Venec was up and at the door. "Open it!" he roared back at me, a trickle of blood coming from his nose. "Now!"

I dropped the seal instinctively. He could have broken it himself, but even in his fury, Venec had manners. The door opened, and he was out into the maelstrom, disappearing down the hallway.

I raised a hand to my own face, and found a matching stream of blood coming from my left nostril. This wasn't gremlins, or an ego-driven slapfight. The second attack had been different. The second attack had meant to kill.

Part of me wanted to pull myself under the table and cower until it was all over. Instead, I got up, wobbling a little, and followed Venec.

This was my office, too, goddamn it.

Ian was standing in the hallway, his long red hair loose and flying around his head with the amount of current he was handling, like some primer in static electricity. He was yelling, directing the others in the office, plugging problems as soon as they developed. Venec reached his side and, without touching him or saying a word, slipped into that weird mirroring stance I'd noticed the first time I saw them standing together, each a bookend of the other. Current jumped from Ian to Venec, bright to dark, and my breath hitched in awe. Tandem spellcasting. So rare, so very rare, not because it was difficult but because it required an absolute trust, a willingness to let another into your core, to *use* your core, without limitation or restriction....

Everything we had done until then, everything we had achieved together, faded into insignificance.

★don't be an idiot, torres★

Venec, scornful and sarcastic in my head, and that made me feel better, long enough to get my shit back together and add my current to the battle.

Council training was to throw your current toward the clear-cut leader, and let him or her do all the directing. Lone-jacks tended to do their own thing, a massed attack rather than a directed one. This…wasn't either of those things. Almost naturally, we fell into the same formation as the healing-adapted spell, our core-icons familiar to each other. The scream of a hawk stooping for the kill was new, but easily identifiable: Ian. And yet, there was no single leader, no one mind directing the action. We saw a weakness and attacked it; felt a break and re-inforced it; thought of a new plan, and implemented it. Not a perfect hive mind—we were all still distinct, still pushing and pulling for the decision, but…

★a sled team★ An image came to us. ★one direction, many legs★

★many baying voices★ another thought agreed, only a little sarcastic.

I was tempted to respond, but could feel the wiring shivering in the building, overwhelmed with the current, and couldn't spare the energy. As fast as we could suck it out, our assailant shoved more in.

"This isn't Aden," Ian said, his voice almost lost in the static filling the hallway. "This isn't her."

Another blast hit the building, making the lights flicker.

"That was," Venec said grimly, his face set in hard lines, his eyes narrowed in concentration. "At this point, I know her signature as well as I know yours. I put up with this because you were certain she was just having a temper tantrum. I even overlooked her shooting at our people because you were certain she wouldn't harm anyone, and I thought you were right. But enough is enough. If you won't spank her, I will."

Another surge went through the building before Ian could respond, and the hairs on my arms and the nape of my neck went up, because that felt different. It felt like a killing strike. It felt like the taste of murder in an empty car.

Our killer was here.

"What the hell…"

Something broke in the building, and my stomach plummeted with it. "The elevator!" I was already down the hallway as the words left my mouth, even as I heard the scream I'd been dreading. Oh hell no, no…

The front door opened without a hand on it, even as I was dropping everything else and mobbing current from my core into as strong a net as I could, then casting it out and down. Another current-net went under mine, and something coated on top, making it stronger, more elastic, and I thought maybe that we had it, maybe…

Until the impact slammed me to the ground, face into the carpet, and I could *feel* the shock of a metric ton of elevator cage crashing into the basement.

And one small light, caught in our tsunami, flickering out of existence.

"No…" It was less a word than a moan, and less a moan than a purely physical reaction, gut-to-skin.

I'd never tried to save someone before. I'd never failed like that before, never felt anything like the gut-wrenching agony of feeling that life slip through my awareness and dissipate. Even the awareness of others around me, of the psi-blasts slamming into the building and making the electrical systems hiss and flare in protest, couldn't move me one inch farther.

Then a wave came along, green-black like the deepest ocean, cold and furious and implacable, tasting of brine and tears and ancient magics, and washed it all out of me. There was no awareness save the foremost wave, the directing intelligence that gathered us, focused us, and let us fly.

I knew that current. It was Ben taking lead, moving us out along a single line, curled and yellowing-white, like the edge of a toenail. Magical DNA, a dowsing stick; useful now that our killer had come within reach, within range. Her mistake: thinking that we would not be ready and waiting.

We slammed down hard, the wave crashing at her knees. All along the avenue lamppost lights burst, neon signs shattered, wiring sparked and died, and the tiny howls of a million elementals evicted from their cozy homes echoed in my core.

I could also see her, almost taste her signature, but the cool lack of emotion that had shielded her before extended to the current she used. Slick, smooth, and polished, the current attacking us came from everywhere and nowhere, totally impersonal, totally unidentifiable.

*hold!* It was a command, thundering through the wave like fucking Neptune throwing his trident. We tried. We really did. But there wasn't enough, we didn't know enough, and she squirmed free, slick and smooth, and was gone.

The wave collapsed, and we were left, sweaty and disoriented, in our own bodies, our own cores diminished and dizzy. I was on my knees in front of a silent elevator shaft, and in the distance I could hear a siren—an ambulance coming, too late.

"Damn," a voice murmured over my head. Ian, sounding as wiped out as I felt.

"Sorry, boss," I said.

"No." And his hand rested on my shoulder. "You kids did good. You did better than good. I just—"

Another psi-bomb exploded, our weakened defenses allowing it access inside the office, and I heard the yelp of someone who'd been too close to whatever piece of electronics exploded.

"Oh for…" Ian said, and I could feel him draw in a deep breath, preparing to raise our shields again.

"Stupid stubborn bitch, this is *over*," Venec muttered, and reached out a hand, closing it abruptly, as though grabbing something out of thin air.

A woman appeared, shocked out of thin air. She was tall, pale, and thin, and had dark red hair like a fox's tail over her shoulders.

Snatching someone—Translocating them without their consent—was rude at best. I didn't think Venec was much caring. She whirled around and stared at us.

"Benjamin. How dare you!"

"I dare because you've gone a mile too far, Aden. Your idiotic attack distracted us, left us unable to properly defend ourselves, and others in this building, when someone with a nastier agenda than yours came calling. Because of that, an innocent just died."

"I didn't—" She looked to her brother, who looked away. Sharon and Nick appeared in the doorway, holding Pietr up between them. His face was bleeding from cuts, and Sharon's left arm hung awkwardly at her side, but otherwise they seemed okay. Nifty came up out of the stairwell, a length of pipe in his hand as if he knew how to use it and a look in his eyes like desolation.

"The kid was twelve, if he was that," he said, and his voice was like broken glass.

Venec took the news, and spun it into venom. "Do you hear that, Aden? A boy is dead. Because you had a temper tantrum about your beloved brother disagreeing with you. Because you thought that he had humiliated you, disgraced your oh so proud and useless family name, and so you were set on making sure that he failed, you distracted us when a real killer needed to be taken down."

"I didn't— I would never—!"

"You might not have killed that boy directly," Venec said, biting off the words as though he'd rather have been biting off her head, "but his blood is on your hands, you stupid, thoughtless brat. It will be there for the rest of your worthless life."

When Benjamin Venec spanked someone, they didn't sit down for a month. I felt no sympathy for her at all.

"Ian, I…"

Ian turned and looked at her. "Go away, Aden." He stood straight and tall and anyone else might have thought he was unmarked. I knew better. Our Alpha was weak, and tired, and even a few days ago one of us might have tried to find the advantage.

Not now. Not in front of outsiders.

She walked out past Nifty, who held the door wide-open for her. We could hear the soft sound of her feet on the stairs, and the shouting of the paramedics and firefighters rising from the lobby.

And then there was silence, and the endless stink of burned-out wiring, and the bitter singe of blood.

## twenty-two

Nobody went home that night, despite the advice of the fire-fighters who came through to check the damages. The smell was nasty, but after a while I didn't even notice it through the bitterness in my mouth, and the comfort of the others was…comforting.

I slept a little, and I know Nick did, too, because I woke up with him sacked out against my shoulder, a now-melted cold pack pressed against his face. There was fresh coffee in the pot, and a sack of egg-and-bacon sandwiches on the counter that smelled disgusting and irresistible all at once.

I got up carefully, but Nick, other than a midsnore snort, didn't react. My stomach warned me that coffee might be a bad idea, but food was probably necessary. I pulled a sandwich out of the sack, wrapped it in a napkin, and went in search of a phone that might still work. My first call didn't go so well, and my hand trembled as I dialed the second. I could have just pinged J and let him know that I was okay, but I…

I wanted to hear his voice.

"Bonnie?"

"Hi."

There was a long silence, then a heavy sigh. "You're all right."

I started to reassure him, then stopped. "I'm okay. I'm not sure 'all right' is all that, though. And no, I'm not going—" I almost said home, and switched midway "—back to Boston. Not yet, anyway."

"I understand." He didn't. But he was trying. "You will come and visit the old man? Soon?"

I tucked the phone between ear and shoulder, and unwrapped the sandwich. My mouth watered. "The old man can come down and see me this weekend."

He chuckled, a warm and comforting sound. "He could. He could even bring a bottle of wine."

"That would be nice."

A chime sounded, deep in the office.

"J, I gotta go."

"All right. Bonita…"

My eyes watered. "I love you, too."

Hanging up the phone, I crammed the greasy biscuit into my mouth, and went in search of the meeting.


Almost instinctively, I went to the lounge, meeting Nifty in the hallway as he came out of the bathroom, his hands still wet and his shirt untucked, but the worst of that look faded from his eyes. Nick was now awake and pouring out coffee. Everyone scrunched together, Nick, Pietr and I on the sofa, Nifty on the loveseat, Sharon perched on the arm. Venec pulled a chair in from somewhere and turned it backward, sitting with his arms crossed over the frame. Ian, wearing a pinstripe go-to-Council suit, with his hair slicked and neatly queued, paced while he talked.

"Kate Walker, Arcazy's silent partner, is dead." He let that float a moment, then went on. "It looks like suicide. Again."

"Our killer?" Nick's voice was bleak, and my hand found his, squeezing once.

"Probably no way to know. Phone records show that a call came in to her from Arcazy's office just before time of death, a little while after Bonnie and Sharon visited him. Either he let her know we were onto her, and she killed herself rather than be found out, or..."

"Or her hired killer killed her, to clean up the scene."

"It's a theory."

It was a good theory. If Will had been telling us the truth about not being involved, he had nothing to fear. If he did know...then the killer might be after him next. I hoped he had been truthful.

"Other than that," Ian said, "we had it nailed, more or less. Despite the situation with the silent partner, Null or not, the Reybeorns decided not to sell, waiting for property values to rise even more.

"And Walker, pissed off and dissed by both the Reybeorns and her former partner—in her mind, anyway—set out to get what she felt was rightfully hers."

"How?" That was what I couldn't figure out. "I mean, if the Reybeorns' agreement was only with Will, and she had reason to believe he had screwed her over..."

"The only thing I can figure," Nifty said, slowly, "is our original scenario—she assumed that she would then be able to force the legally remaining partner, through blackmail or guilt, to either sell it to her, so she could make a deal with the developers, or sell directly and cut her in for her share—presumably more than the original agreement, since the Reybeorns were now out of the picture. So everyone wins."

"Except the dead people," Pietr said.

"A valid point. I'm thinking maybe she wasn't all that worried about them."

Sharon cupped her mug of coffee in both hands, as though she was suffering hypothermia and that was the only source of warmth in the room. "It might have worked," she said. "It would have worked, except that our client wasn't happy with the cause of death findings, and got too many people involved, making everything drag out even longer and delaying her ability to confront Arcazy, because the estate wasn't settled yet."

"Do you think she hired a Talent to do the job for the irony?" Pietr asked. "I mean, since the Reybeorns wouldn't let her play, she hired one of their own to do the job on them? Or was she trying to frame her ex-partner for the job?"

"No way to know, short of a miraculous confessional paper turning up in her belongings, and I'm not going to hold my breath for that." Ian reached up and took his hair out of the thong, shaking it loose a little. I've never had any objections to my hair, really, but when I was a kid I would have done anything for hair like his.

I thought about that thought for a second, and amended it. Almost anything.

"What's going to happen now?"

"This morning I attended a session of the Midwest Council." That explained the suit and hair. God, they must have met at the crack of dawn, out there! I suppose it was an extraordinary session....

"I gave all of our information to the client, and then to the Council itself. It has taken full accountability, since it was their locale and their people, and they have announced their solemn intent to track down the killer."

"And insist she get a license and pay tithe in order to continue working in their region?" Pietr was cynical. I couldn't really say as I blamed him, because that did sound like Council rationale.

"Maybe. Who knows. I don't think even the Council knows, right now." Venec seemed honestly vexed, especially in the face of Ian's cool, calm collectedness. "We're not enforcement, just investigation, and nobody's ever had to deal with a case like this, a hired killer within the community."

"They're still working out the details," Ian said, still calm. "But the proceeds of the property sale, when it sells, will go to the rightful heirs, not either partner involved in the original deception. We made sure that they won't profit. And word will get out that we made sure they didn't profit."

On the surface it seemed unfair to poor Will, who hadn't—far as we could determine—been involved in the murders at all. But by Council standards, it was fair and just, and Will was Council; he had to have known that, from the very beginning, whatever his motives. It sucked, but there it was.

"And we were paid our full fee, for a job accomplished. For a Council member, no less." Nifty tried to smile. "Guess we're gonna be around for another few months, huh?"

"At least. I've already renewed the lease."

You could almost hear the sighs of relief coming from all the pups, me included.

"I also…" There was a pause. "I also made a contribution to the funeral expenses of the boy who died. And the Council has matched it."

I closed my eyes against the prickling sensation, and tried to force away the guilt that hit me again. This time, it was Nick's hand in mine that squeezed comfort.

"Is your sister…" Nick started to ask, and then trailed off, I guess not really knowing what to say. None of us did.

"I don't think she's going to be a…physical problem again," Ian said wryly, finally folding his long legs under him to sit on the floor next to the sofa. He still sat upright, though, not collapsed against the nearest support like the rest of us. "The Council might have turned a blind and approving eye to her harassing us, but her timing and the resulting death of the boy has embarrassed them greatly."

Someone snorted in disgust, and I had to agree. They should be a hell of a lot more than embarrassed. The boy had just been getting his damn braces checked at the orthodontist's office on the 5th floor. Twelve—a child. A baby.

"I know," he said to us all. "I know. But they are what they are, and part of what they are is distanced. And you need to learn to do the same. What happened here was in no way your fault. Aden bears some responsibility, as do I for not stopping her firmly the moment the attacks started, rather than waiting for her to wear herself out. But the weight of that death needs to be placed squarely on the shoulders of our killer. Rest assured, when she is caught—and she will be caught—that is one of the things that will be considered in her punishment."

I had the weird, unformed thought that Ian wasn't, entirely, talking about the Council's judgment. No sooner had that thought half surfaced, though, than it dug itself back in. I didn't want to know. Not right now. I couldn't handle any more responsibility. Not right now. Not until I'd dealt with my own guilt, my own responsibility. My own failure.

I guess I zoned out a bit, because when I came back to the conversation, the team had moved on to their plans for what Stosser had apparently declared "Downtime Days."

"How about you, Bonnie?" Nick asked. "Gonna go find lawyer-boy and kick off a little steam?"

I tried not to let it sting, but I guess something escaped. Pietr's hand touched my shoulder, briefly, and only the fact that I knew his touch let me identify it because, as usual, I didn't see him.

"Oh hell." For the first time in the months I'd known her, Sharon's voice actually sounded…not warm, exactly, but empathetic. "Bonnie…I'm sorry."

I let myself shrug, even knowing that somehow J would hear about it and read me a lecture about posture and appearances, later. "He didn't take kindly to being suspected. By us, but especially by me. You'd think a lawyer would understand, but…" The vibe I'd gotten in the office was pretty clear. The brush-off I'd gotten when I tried to call his office just now had been even clearer. I didn't even reach his assistant—the receptionist told me, in a professionally flat tone that my call wasn't being picked up. No, he couldn't leave a message.

Whatever Will and I might have had was dead before it even got started.

There was a bar down the street from my apartment that I kept passing, and never having a chance to check out. It turned out to be a nice, quiet kind of bar: not a pickup palace, just a place where you could go in and grab a drink and have a quiet conversation with friends or maybe a new date. Comfortable chairs, sturdy wooden tables, and efficient bartenders: It was a good place for a first date, clean and well-lit and the booze was solid but not froufrou. And they poured a damn good vodka martini.

*bonnie?*

It was the third ping of the evening. I treated it the same way I treated the first two. I ignored it. The pack meant well, and eventually I knew I'd be more in the mood for a group hug, for sympathy and understanding, but…not right now.

Eventually I'd have to sit down and really talk to J, too. Confirm our much-delayed dinner date. Catch him up on everything—everything I thought he needed to know, anyway.

Deal with his occasionally fussy, nitpicking worry, because that was how he showed he cared.

Caring was important.

I'd gotten what I wanted—a job that meant something, that could actually make changes in the world. Be careful what you ask for, as the saying goes. Now that I had it, I didn't know who—or what—this job was making me. But I had to keep caring. Otherwise…what was the point?

It was just hard, some nights. To know that there was a killer out there, still, despite our best efforts. That a young boy had died because I wasn't fast enough or strong enough to save him. That a man I liked thought I had somehow betrayed him, because I was doing my job…

"Another?"

The bartender's name was Stacy, and she was a middle-aged woman with a long black braid and watchful gray eyes, like Pietr's. She had the habit of appearing in front of you without a sound, like Pietr, too. I thought about asking her if she had any kids.

"Yes, please." Always be polite to your bartender. Especially your local neighborhood bartender.

When I reached the bottom of my glass, the warning tightness in my forehead told me that it was probably time to call it a night, or risk the consequences. A small stubborn ghoul on my shoulder urged me to ignore that warning, and order another. Or maybe tequila, this time. Tequila would be good. Tequila would punish me properly, for not being fast enough. For not having enough current ready to make the net stronger. For not knowing who was innocent, and who was not-guilty. For not being perfect, right off the bat.

A hand came down on my shoulder. I'd known someone was standing there, and still the contact surprised me. I restrained the urge to yelp, or throw my drink. Nick. Had to be. Unlike Pietr, the boy could not take a hint.

"Come on, Torres." The voice was familiar, but not the one I'd been expecting. It was warm, and rough, and totally devoid of pity. "Time to pour you into bed. Tomorrow it's back to work."

I closed my eyes, and let my fingers unclench from my glass. Venec. I must be out of it, if he was able to slip up on me.

"Torres?" he said, and waited for me to make my decision.

An instant passed, where I told him to get lost, invited him to join me for a drink, quit.

I slipped Stacy a folded tenner under my glass, and let him take me home.

★ ★ ★ ★ ★

*Regency London—a whirl of balls and young ladies pursued by charming men. But the Woodmore sisters are hunted by a more sinister breed: Lucifer's own.*

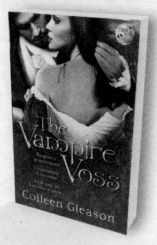

Voss, also known as Viscount Dewhurst, is a member of the Dracule—a cabal of powerful, secretive noblemen marked with a talisman that reveals their bartered souls. The mercenary Voss has remained carefully neutral…until Angelica.

Angelica Woodmore possesses the Sight, an ability invaluable to both sides of a looming war among the Dracule. Her very scent envelops Voss in a scarlet fog of hunger—for her body and her blood.

## Available 15th April 2011

www.mirabooks.co.uk

*Regency London loves a society*
*wedding—even if there are vampires*
*on the guest list...*

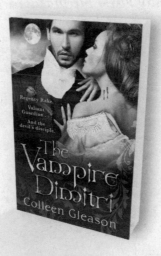

Dimitri, also known as the Earl of Corvindale, should
be delighted that Maia Woodmore is getting married.
His mortal ward and houseguest has annoyed—and
bewitched—the Dracule nobleman too long, and
denying his animal cravings grows more
excruciating by the day.

But in the looming battle between Dracule factions,
all pretences will shatter as Maia and Dimitri come
together in an unholy union of danger, desperation
and fiercest desire.

## Available 20th May 2011

www.mirabooks.co.uk